TEST PATTERNS:
CREATURE FEATURES

A PLANET X PUBLICATIONS BOOK

TEST PATTERNS: CREATURE FEATURES

A Planet X Publications book
Second in the "Test Patterns" anthology series

(https://www.facebook.com/planetxpubs)
(https://www.facebook.com/tpcreaturefeatures)

Copyright © 2018 by the individual authors
All rights reserved

This is a work of fiction.

No part of this book may be reproduced in any form or by any electronic or mechanical means, including information storage and retrieval systems, without written permission from the author, except for the use of brief quotations in a book review.

Cover Art "TV Sets" by Yves Tourigny
Cover Art "Monsters" by: Alan Sessler, Ashley Dioses, Brendan O'Connell, Duane Pesice, Farah Rose Smith, Jb Lee, Judson Hand, K.A. Opperman, Lucy Alvarado, Rachel Sklaney, S.M. Wright, Steve Orlando, & Thom Davidson

Book Design by Michael Adams with
Special Thanks to AW Baader
Edited by Duane Pesice

ISBN 13: 978-1-7326839-1-4
ISBN 10: 1-7326839-1-3

TABLE OF CONTENTS

YOU'RE THE STAR NOW	5
Michael Adams	
FRANKENSTEIN'S MONSTER'S MONSTER	7
Danger Slater	
THE GREEDY GRAVE	19
Cody Goodfellow	
PRETTY IN THE DARK	31
Erica Ruppert	
THE EYE DOCTOR	43
Robert Guffey	
APHANTASIA	61
Robert S. Wilson	
IN THE ROOM OF RED NIGHT	77
Farah Rose Smith	
LITTLE HOUSE IN THE SUBURBS	87
James Fallweather	
AMADIS THE ENCHANTRESS	95
Ashley Dioses	
SPIRIT OF PLACE	105
James Russell	
SIGNALS	119
John Paul Fitch	
FROM LITTLE ACORNS GROW	137
Brenda Kezar	
WITH ALL HER TROUBLES BEHIND HER	145
S.L. Edwards	
CHAOS AND VOID	159
Debra Robinson	
THE RIVER RAN RED	173
Calvin Demmer	

EXTINCTION IN GREEN	185
Kurt Fawver	
CHOSEN	201
Aaron J. French	
BONE SEQUENCE	211
Duane Pesice	
THE BRIDE OF THE ASTOUNDING GIGANTIC MONSTER	223
Buzz Dixon	
UNDERGROUND ROSE	231
Natasha Bennett	
THE PEPYS LAKE MONSTER	241
Orrin Grey	
THE BRIDE OF CASTLE FRANKENSTEIN	249
Jill Hand	
NO MORE IRON CROSS	261
Jayaprakash Satyamurthy	
ADMITTED INHABITANTS	269
Dominique Lamssies	
BITTER WATERS	279
Daniel Brock	
MRS. DOOGAN	291
Lana Cooper	
FOR WHOM THERE IS NO JOURNEY	307
John Linwood Grant	
NORMAL	319
John Claude Smith	
SOMETHING HUNGRIER THAN LOVE	327
Aksel Dadswell	
E	345
Jeffrey Thomas	
FADE OUT	357
Duane Pesice	

YOU'RE THE STAR NOW
MICHAEL ADAMS

You wake as the first dull gray rays of dawn pierce your window – you made it through another night. The dreams the test pattern told you begin to fade from memory. You painfully stretch the stiffness from your limbs as you rise from your easy chair – how can you keep doing this to yourself? These journeys through unimaginable mindscapes take their toll. Dreams become nightmares and you wake in a cold sweat more often than you care to admit.

You start a pot of coffee and prepare to shamble through your morning routine, feeling like a zombie out of some midnight movie. Body heavy, eyes bloodshot, ears ringing. No, not ringing, what is that sound? Familiar, constant, something halfway between a hiss and growl. Ah! The television. In your stupor you never turned it off, and the station has now gone off the air? Strange. The broadcast day should just be beginning...

Crossing back to the living room you stop dead in your tracks when you see the set is already off, but the noise persists.

A radio? No, your music listening is mostly limited to your commute these days. Someone next door with the volume up painfully loud? You pull the curtain back, and feel your insides go cold. The sky is a color out of a William Gibson novel. Your mind refuses to accept what it's seeing, and so you clamber out the door to confirm what you know can't be true, but there it persists. The firmament spanning the horizon
is now the static of a broadcast tuned to a dead channel. Last night's trip never ended.

In a panic you hurry next door to beg for help, but what answers isn't your neighbor. Tendrils writhe like worms and there are more eyes than you would have thought possible, but it's the hideous grin that truly warns you off. You begin running.

The woman on the sidewalk is an insect, an angel, an alien... the thing in the baby carriage a giant eye trailing nerves and tendons.

You find yourself downtown, the transformations continue. Toys in shop windows turn sinister, and trees glare at you with muted malevolence.

Shopkeepers wear jackal grins and things you can't even describe lurk in the shadows.

Time dilates as the realization washes over you. The world has become a TV. You're no longer watching, you're the star now... and you've found yourself trapped in a monster movie.

FRANKENSTEIN'S MONSTER'S MONSTER
DANGER SLATER

"Frankie, Frankie, Frankie," Mr. Butterton growled through his teeth, streaked yellow like the storm windows on an abandoned seaside home. His malevolent smile looked like the aftermath of a hurricane, like the foam in a monsoon's tide. "What are we going to do with you, Frankie?"

The manager sat across from Frankenstein, his tiny office cluttered up by piles of empty fast food boxes and cigar ash. From the ceiling dangled a few strips of flesh-colored flypaper. The carcasses of dead flies stuck to them like pimples. Frankenstein shifted uncomfortably in his chair.

"But Mr. Butterton," Frankenstein said, "I don't think it's fair that I have to sell the townspeople the very same pitchforks and 2x4s they're gonna use to chase me down with later. Isn't there something else around here I can do? I'm pretty tall and strong. You sure you don't want me stocking shelves?"

Mr. Butterton took off his glasses and rubbed the bridge of his nose. His swollen belly, corralled only the equatorial hug of his ever-shrinking belt, pressed up against the desk as he leaned in towards the nervous monster.

"Look Frankie, those townspeople out there are the only ones keeping us afloat. How do you expect us to keep up with the Home Depots and Lowe's of the world if you keep refusing to sell our customers merchandise?"

Mr. Butterton stood up and walked over to the window. Outside, the townspeople were already lined up around the block. Waiting patiently to buy their makeshift weaponry. Waiting patiently for Frankenstein to get off his shift, so they could chase him home and try to kill him.

Mr. Butterton said:

"As I'm sure you're well aware, my father opened Ingolstadt Hardware over 50 YEARS AGO. Shit, Frankie, you weren't even reanimated yet. Back then you were probably still normal, living flesh on a dozen different, disparate people. This place has certainly been around much longer than you have. We're a goddamn *institution* in this town. But, alas, look around you. It's a different world than it was a half-century ago, and those big box home improvement stores, with their huge inventories and competitive prices, they're eating us alive. So I ask it to you, how do you think we've managed to stay in business after all this time?"

He spun around on the heels of his off-brand oxfords and faced the monster now, placing his knuckles on his desk as he leaned in. Frankenstein cowered into the fold-up chair.

"I - uhm - I don't know," Frankenstein said.

"It's because at Ingolstadt Hardware we are KNOWN for our excellent customer service!" he shouted. "It's because of employees like you, Frankie Boy. Do you think the Home Depot over on Route 10 has any terrifying, aberrant half-rotten monster freaks working there?"

"Probably not."

"Of course they don't! They've only got a bunch of snot-nosed teenagers who don't know the FIRST THING about which tools are most effective when assaulting an ungodly fiend such as yourself. You think your average high-schooler can properly raise and burn an effigy of your likeness? It takes FINESSE. That's the Ingolstadt Hardware difference! Do you get what I'm saying to you, Frankie?"

"But sir..." Frankenstein said.

"Listen," the store manager cut him off as he sat back down behind the desk. "I'm not going to take any disciplinary action, *this time*. But believe me, Frankie, I don't care how big and ugly you are, I'm not gonna put up with your insubordinate shit a second time. Do we understand each other?"

Frankenstein nodded yes.

"Good," Mr. Butterton said. "Then get back out on the sales floor and go to work."

It was past dusk when Frankenstein's shift ended.

He closed up the store, locking the door and quietly exit through the backdoor. The townspeople were still mobbed up in the parking lot. Milling about. Sharing stories. Sharpening their blades. Laughing.

It was the same damn thing, day-after-day. The townspeople would buy their weapons from Ingolstadt Hardware, wait for Frankenstein to get off work, and then chase him home.

This was his routine. His job. What he was paid to do.

Most nights Frankenstein just accepted this. He had a wife to take care of and a mortgage to pay. One can't concern themselves too much with the *why* of it all. But every once in a while, he would find himself wondering if he was built for something more...important...than this. It wasn't his fault he was a reanimated corpse. He knew in a more perfect world he would be disemboweling these people. Ripping their heads off their slouching shoulders. Cracking femurs like pretzel sticks. Splattering brain meat across blacktops like art from the tip of Jackson Pollack's brush.

But instead, he was just a friggin' wage slave, a register jockey, a retail employee. Living paycheck-to-paycheck. Like every other shmuck in this stupid village.

"OH SHIT, THERE HE IS!" someone in the crowd shouted as he tried to scuttle by. Just a few more feet and Frankenstein would've made it into the shadows, undisturbed. After the day he had, he could've used a nice, leisurely skulk home.

"GET HIM!" someone else cried out.

Oh well, thought the monster. And he started running.

The townspeople ran after him, of course, weapons held high in the air. Pitchforks, hatchets, board-and-nails, torches. All the junk he had sold them throughout the day, now turned back on him. It was darkly poetic.

He hobbled down the road, his gait somewhere between a drunken stagger and an equine trot. Frankenstein was not very limber. His left leg used to belong to a dude with osteoarthritis. And his right leg was about a half-inch too short.

Frankenstein thought back to when he was first reanimated -- when he was first brought back to life -- those brief fuzzy moments after the electricity woke him up, but before he could compose a conscious thought. His brain seemed to flicker on, like the reel of a projector. Lights and colors suddenly sprung up, but it was a mess in his head. Disjointed scenes playing backwards on the movie screens behind his eyes. Just little bits and pieces of an all-encompassing whole. Bits and pieces of the quickly-fading memories of all the people whose dead bodies made up his. He saw a caregiver, an alcoholic, a scientist, an artist, a businessman, a soldier, an idiot, a friend. He was all those things, if only briefly. And then it went out. The screen went dark. They disappeared. And Frankenstein began.

He supposed all those people were a part of him now, even if it was just anatomically. This was his ancestry. His lineage. The dirt that came before him; the dirt from which he was born. And although he can no longer feel them inside him, he sometimes wondered if they could hear him. Hear his thoughts. He wondered if they truly got to live on through him, or if the present in which he was trapped was just a water-down version of the past, perverted by time, perverted by his own mind…

And then, he was hit in the head by a rock thrown by one of the townspeople. He forgot what he was just thinking about. And he ran.

He just keep running.

💀💀💀

He made it home, barely in front of the angry mob, slamming the front door behind him. Outside, he could hear the crowd let out a collective groan. Disappointed he got away. For today, at least. They all know he'll be back at work tomorrow.

They were always there tomorrow.

"Hey, honey," Bride-of greeted Frankenstein with a kiss on the cheek.

"Hello, dear," he said, swooping her up in an embrace. He held her. Let the palm of his hand run down the back of her black-and-white striped beehive hairdo to the pale-green skin on the nape of her neck.

"How was work?" she said.

"Terrible, as usual," he replied.

He plopped down into his easy chair. She climbed into his lap and wrapped her arms around his wide shoulders.

"Mr. Butterton was being a real boner today, because I didn't want to sell some hick the pitchfork he was gonna try to stab me with later," Frankenstein said. "This job is such bullshit. Butterton's never been chased by a bloodthirsty mob before, what does he know about what it's like down in the trenches? Fuckin' management. I should be the manager! I know more about these townspeople than he does. I'm the one who constantly has to deal with them."

"Don't let him get you down, honey," Bride-of said. "There's always brighter things on the horizon."

She leaned in and kissed him on the neck and whispered seductively in his ear:

"You know, I know of one thing that can take your mind off of work..."

He looked at her. She smiled, her black lips curling up at the corners like Salvador Dali's moustache.

He picked her up and carried her into the bedroom.

💀💀💀

Candles lit. Tongues of fire dripped their sepia saliva all over the bedroom walls. Shades of brown and orange. Autumnal and sinister. The room glowing like the two of them were in the belly of a jack-o-lantern.

Bride-of laid down on the bed. Her green skin freckled by goosebumps; braille letters on her body. Frankenstein ran his hands over her thighs; his hands that used to be someone else's hands over her thighs that used to be someone else's thighs - and yet, here they both were, sharing this beautiful moment together, using all of these other people's parts to feel brand-new things.

Bride-of and Frankenstein had been planning to have a baby for quite some time. It seemed like the next natural step in their relationship. To stitch their lives together in much the manner their skins were stitched together. Create a life of their own, the way Victor created them. But there had been a problem. When Victor was making Bride-of, he neglected to give her a functioning vagina. Sure, there was a hole there. It looked like it was supposed to. Felt like it was supposed to. But inside, the parts didn't work quite right. It was empty. Barren So Frankenstein and his bride were forced to improvise:

A few days back, Frankenstein had caught an opossum that had been rooting around in their trashcans. It was an ugly little fucker, all dirty and gray. For their part, Frankenstein and Bride-of would've preferred it be a dog or a deer or something a little less...feral. But they were in no position to be picky.

He scooped the opossum up in his massive hand, gave it a quick pet, then ripped it in half. He slid off its skin. Peeled away its muscle. Picked apart its entrails like the petals from a flower. *She loves me, she loves me not, she loves me, she loves me not.* He tore that tiny opossum apart until he found what he was looking for, deep inside its abdomen:

The uterus….

Now, Frankenstein was no great surgeon. He was not Victor - no, he was not his father. But he managed to insert that bloody possum pussy inside of her, stapling it in place and hot gluing all the flaps and tubes and assorted loose ends where they were supposed to go. He managed to give his wife a working womb. And now, he was on top of her, in bed, sticking his rotten dick in her rotten hole. Pumping away, over and over and over and over again. And it felt so goddamn good. And she bit his lip and tore part of it off, chewing it up, swallowing it. And he pulled her high-rise of hair. And she clawed his back.

And he gouged her eyes with his thumbs. And he could feel the pressure building inside of him. Building like a symphony towards a crescendo. The Nutsack Philharmonic. Violins screeching, timpani rolling, organ blaring, cymbals clapping:

CLIMAX!

And as he came, his dick broke off inside of her, and from the putrid, dusty stump between his legs came spiders. Thousands and thousands of tiny spiders, marching out of his body and into hers. She moaned in ecstasy, her hair pressed up against the wall now like a cigarette being squashed against the concrete, her eyes falling backwards into her skull - she moaned and came and was filled with Frankenstein's spiders. And when she was done and he rolled off of her, he could see her belly had already ballooned up like a beach ball.

"Oh wow. I guess I failed to take into account that the gestation period of a North American opossum is only 14 days long," he said.

"Frank," she said. "I think we're pregnant."

Two weeks later and he was in the employee restroom at work.

The sink hissed. Steady. As steady as the heart trying to beat in his chest. *Ka-thunk*, went his heart. *Hssssssss*, went the sink. The two sounds talking over one another until they're blended, blurred, into a singular din.

He splashed his face with a handful of water and looked at himself in the mirror: His gray eyes carrying weary, discolored bags beneath them. The scars across his face like the tracks in a train yard. Haphazard and vile. He ran a cold finger across the most egregious scar, the one on his forehead, the one Victor sewed up after he inserted his brain.

Maybe the townspeople were right, he thought. Maybe I am a freak.

There was a knock.

"Frankie, you in there?"

It was Mr. Butterton, talking through the bathroom door. And from his tone, Frankenstein could tell he was already upset.

"Um...hold on," Frankenstein said, turning the sink off. He opened the door. Mr. Butterton stood there, an unlit cigar clutched between his scowling banana-colored teeth, his eyebrows arched and angry, like electric caterpillars. And even though the monster stood a good two feet taller than the frumpy man, Mr. Butterton seemed to engulf his timid employee.

"Yes, Mr. Butterton?" said Frankenstein.

"Frankie," Mr. Butterton said, his voice all venom. "What did we talk about the other week?"

"What are you..."

"I just talked to a gentleman who said you ABSOLUTELY REFUSED to sell him a bow rake. Care to explain?"

"Sir," Frankenstein stammered. "That man…he wanted me to get on my knees so he could measure the end of the rake up against the size my head. He told me he was planning on using it to split my skull open later…"

"Goddamn it, Frank!" Mr. Butterton shouted. "I tried to be patient with you, tried to stress how important customer service is, but this is the last fucking straw! I'm sorry, but I just don't see a future for you here at Ingolstadt Hardware. I'm afraid we're going to have to let you go, effective immediately."

"Mr. Butterton, please! You can't fire me! I *need* this job! Mr. Butterton, my wife...she's pregnant. She's actually due today. We're gonna have a baby."

"I don't give a fuck if your wife was the goddamn Queen of England," he said. "When I pay you to do a job I don't think it's unreasonable for you to *do your fucking job*! Now quit sniveling, you pathetic freak. Have some goddamn dignity. Collect yourself, clean out the shit from your locker, and go the hell home."

"Mr. Butterton..."

But the manager had turned his back. Refusing to listen. Refusing to care. He started waddling back towards his office.

And in that moment, all Frankenstein could think of was his future. Of his wife and his unborn child. He could only think of all the ways he had failed them.

At first, Frankenstein thought:

How did I allow my entire fate to be held in the hands of a piece of shit like Butterton? What was wrong with me? And the worst part is, Butterton was right. This is all my fault. I let it happen. But why? Why have I accepted this life for so long? Why must I continue to accept it? What is holding me back?

And then, something broke. It imploded inward and turned red. His helplessness, his hopelessness, his disappointment, his inadequacy, all his disappointment – in an instant, he felt it all invert. Violence filled his brain.

Took him over. A tidal wave of blood. Sadness became furor. Like fire it flowed through his body. Through the tips of his fingers and the ends of his toes. Through his head and his chest and his bones and his heart. This was not simple anger. No, anger felt like a child's toy compared to the fury that was erupting inside him.

And now, Frankenstein thought:

I AM RAGE! I AM VENGEANCE! I AM A MIRROR OF ALL THE WORLD'S FOLLY PERSONIFIED AND TURNED BACK AROUND ON ITSELF! I AM FRANKENSTEIN! I'M A MONSTER!

He stomped forward and grabbed Mr. Butterton by the shoulders and spun him around so that they were face-to-face.

"Get your disgusting hands off me, you motherfu--" Mr. Butterton started to say, but before he could finish his sentence, Frankenstein pulled his head off his shoulders. The stupid manager's dead dumb face still grimaced at the monster, like it was judging him, even in death. Frankenstein threw it against the wall as hard as he could and it exploded like a watermelon. Chunks of fatty flesh splattered against the stockroom floor. Pink meat. Former man.

Mr. Butterton's decapitated body fell to its knees, almost as if it were begging for mercy just a few moments too late, and a geyser of crimson slime squirted out of his neck wound like a fountain in a park.

Frankenstein's chest heaved in and out as he made his way onto the sales floor.

"Hey, excuse me," a customer said upon seeing him, "Could you tell me what kind of hammer would be best for bashing your brains in? I know the sledge seems like an obvious choice, but I was thinking I might *enjoy* it more if I used something smaller, like ballpeen or something."

Frankenstein picked up the man and threw him into a display. The customer was impaled a pair of hedge clippers. They poked out through the center of his chest. He screamed, then seized, then shit himself while shaking violently. Then he died, stolen away by jet black oblivion. Gone forever.

The other customers froze. Looked up at the panting monster. Frankenstein froze and looked back at them. He slowly reached down. Grabbed the name tag that read FRANK off the lapel of his jacket and tossed it aside. He cleared his throat, smiled malevolently and said:

"GGGGGGRRRRRRAAAAAAAGGGGGGRRRRROOOAAAARRRR!"

Everyone in the hardware store screamed. Trampled each other to escape the building as Frankenstein swung his arms wildly about, striking whatever, whoever, he could. Shelves were knocked over. Windows were smashed. The monster punched a hole through some poor guy's clavicle. Customers poured out of the emergency exits like water from a fire hydrant. They spilled into the parking lot where a larger mob of townspeople were already waiting for Frankenstein to get off work.

"What's going on?" one of them said, and then the creature appeared in the doorway to the store. Frankenstein unleashed, in all his horrid glory. He growled and brayed. He let out an inhuman, guttural moan in a cyclone of freedom and agony, terror and release.

Frankenstein charged into the crowd, spinning around in furious circles, taking out as many of them as he could. Limbs were torn off. Chunks of flesh clawed out.

The townspeople gave him a wide breadth. They backed off. His own circumference, his own little orbit.

No one was sure what to do next. In truth, not even Frankenstein was sure of what to do either.

Then everyone sobered up. Realized what was happening. Someone held up a pitchfork and let out the rallying cry:

"LET'S GET HIM!"

And so, once again, he ran. But this time he ran not because of duty, not because it was his job, but because of genuine fear. He was running for his life. And it felt liberating.

😱💀😱

Frankenstein made it to his house. Slammed the front door behind him and locked the deadbolt. The townspeople normally kept their distance, never actually trespassing on his private property, but now they were pushing up against the door. Against the house. Screaming. Pounding. Demanding retribution. Demanding his head.

"Honey? Honey?" Frankenstein called out, searching frantically for his wife. "You need to get your bags packed. And quick. We need to get out of here. It's not safe. I killed Mr. Butterton and then I went on a rampage and took out a half-dozen townspeople. You shoulda seen it. I punched this one guy so hard his ribcage shot out of his back! He had a hole in him like he was a cartoon character that got struck by a cannonball! It was actually kinda awesome, to be honest with you. But now they're after us. If they catch me, they're not going to let me go. We need to go."

"Frank!" Bride-of yelped from the other room. "Frank, help!"

Frankenstein ran down the hall and popped into the doorway of their bedroom.

Bride-of was lying on the bed, totally nude, her legs spread apart wide, her opossum-swollen vagina dilated, staring up at him like a Cyclops eye. She was clammy. Pained. Breathing heavy.

"It's happening," she said through the labor pangs. "Frank, I'm having this baby RIGHT NOW!"

From inside of her, a plume of black smoke started to rise, forming into a swirling cloud against the ceiling. Drizzle fell from the nebulous veil as thunder rolled and lightning flashed. A furious storm. This microclimatological anomaly was localized only to the bedroom though, and except for the windows townspeople had busted in and were reaching through, the rest of the house remained exactly the same.

She threw her head back and screamed out, gargling through the black bile that she was puking up like pen ink. It ran down her cheeks and chin and in between her stitched-on breasts. Now that same black ink-like substance started pouring out of her vagina too, pooling up on the bed like an oil puddle under a beat-up old car. The thunder growled more intensely. She screamed even louder. The front door splintered apart as a townsperson shattered it with an axe. The mob forced their way into Frankenstein's humble suburban home. And there the monster stood, in the doorframe to the bedroom, watching his wife give birth, unsure of what to do next.

And then, there it was. An arm. Breaching. A tiny, little infant arm poking out of Bride-of's womb. She screamed again. Pushed. The arm shot out across the room and hit Frankenstein in the chest. I caught it and looked at the severed limb quizzically. She screams again and another arm shot out. Then a leg. Another leg. A torso. And finally a head. The thunder lulled as the last piece of the child was ejected, but the clouds in the bedroom remained. Rain continued to pour down on the both of them.

The townspeople were in the house now. Trashing the living room. Overturning tables. Smashing TVs. Setting fire to the kitchen.

Someone spotted Frankenstein standing in the doorway at the end of the hall and alerted the rest of the throng.

"There!" they said.

The angry mob pushed their way towards him, taking up every inch of the hall, tighter than the air itself, but Frankenstein paid them no heed. Bride-of sat up. Disheveled. Exasperated. Expectant.

"Is everything okay?" his wife asked.

Frankenstein looked down at the cluttered pile of baby parts cradled up in his arms like a bunch of broken and mixed-up dolls. Inert. Stillborn. Useless, dead garbage.

Frankenstein thought:

Is this it? Is this all we are? Just a bunch of puzzle pieces that we're constantly struggling to keep together? Am I the sum of my parts or am I the sum of my actions? What is the point of even going on?

And then, in the jumble of junk he held in his hands - the jumble of junk that he would've called his son – he could see a finger on one of the hands twitch. Ever so slightly. The eyes on the baby's severed head blinked a few times, turned to the side, look towards his father. The lips moved. Gurgled. Then smiled.

Tears of joy and pride filled the monster's eyes at the exact same moment the razor-sharp end of a townsperson's hatchet found its way into the back of his skull.

Time was running out. Time had always been running out.

And he had so much love to give.

[the end]

THE GREEDY GRAVE
CODY GOODFELLOW

The sun brought only a deeper chill when it rose above the lavender peaks enclosing the Great Basin, drawing traces of damp from sour soil, stirring a bitter winter wind and shedding its pale pink light on sights better left unseen.

Inigo Hull returned to camp at dawn to find Ed Schaffroth, Elmer Braden, and Buck Marriot already awake and in a high state of excitement with the discovery that the fifth member of their expedition had their throat cut and scalp taken sometime in the night.

"I told you and I told you," Braden was shouting, "the damned curse ain't even waiting for us to dig it up."

"Ain't no curse," Marriot snapped, spitting a brown gob of tobacco juice into the ashes. "This here's still Shoshone country..."

Schaffroth saw the half-Comanche tracker riding up, and lifted his rifle to coax him off his mount. "Here comes a simpler explanation," he said, his dour mouth pinched so severely that it could be seen out from under the drooping wings of his mustache.

Hull climbed down from his red and white palomino and approached the body of Bob Resley where it slouched over the dying embers of the campfire. Resley, a backslider Mormon prospector out of Utah, had taken the last watch of the night and had plainly been murdered near the end of it, while making coffee. Person or persons unknown had cut his throat and taken his scalp, indeed his whole face, leaving only the red memento mori of bare, crimson bone to greet his comrades.

"If the Shoshone set upon you," Hull said, "they wouldn't creep in and take one man. They would take every horse and mule and all your guns without disturbing your sleep. None of you would've woken up at all.

"As for myself... I can't figure why I'd want to whittle down your numbers, when I could've just taken off after the gold myself. Why don't you paint the picture for me?"

"Maybe you don't hear so good," Schaffroth said, cocking an eyebrow at the scarry concavity where someone once chopped off one of the tracker's ears. "It's all there in plain red." Schaffroth pointed at Resley's naked skull. "You went out to scout up the spot, you found it, and figured you'd take a bigger share for yourself, maybe scare the rest of us off and take the whole lode for yourself."

Hull was a man ill-inclined toward moments of levity, but the grave accusation almost brought a smile to his grim, scarred face. "And maybe I did away with your other friend, Watt, when you weren't watching me cut a trail out from Fort Ruby. Maybe there's two of me."

The men had been on edge from the start, like any party of strangers bound only by the lust for gold. They set out from Fort Ruby only three days ago. The mountains had proved slow going, as trails went dead in tortuous box canyons, off sheer bluffs, or into brush as thick as the hair on an Indian's head. Hull knew the land well enough, and had scouted the landmarks that led to what these men sought, but he also knew the Shoshone legends about this stretch of the Ruby Mountains, where the terrain was said to change like a blanket thrown over a restless sleeper.

"Maybe there *are* two of you," Schaffroth said impatiently. "You're here for a share of the gold, same as any of us. Maybe you already have it. Maybe you just kept us alive to dig it up for you."

"And maybe *I'm* only alive because I haven't led you to it yet," Hull said. He leaned over Resley and took the fine brass telescope the dead prospector kept in the breast pocket of his potato-sack coat. He looked through it, tapped it and looked again, puzzled that it conveyed no wondrous powers of magnification at all.

Marriot took the coffee off its cradle of charred sticks, shook it to hear the slosh of a half-full pot, and grumbled, "Hope the poor bastard left us a decent pot of coffee, for once."

Hull knew he could trust none of them any more than they trusted him. Ed Schaffroth was a foreman at the Bar S Ranch. Braden and Marriot were two of his hired hands. Schaffroth was the one who heard the legend from Resley, who'd panned for gold from California to Texas and come up with only tall tales. It was enough to set their minds on fire with dreams of hidden gold in these godforsaken mountains.

Schaffroth and Resley approached Hull with Lionel Watt, a quiet, dapper type with a pianist's hands and gunslinger's dead gray eyes, who acted like another hired hand, but Hull reckoned he represented the money that backed this misadventure. Watt let Schaffroth bark all he liked while gently holding the leash. The Bar S was more of a plantation than a ranch, the owner famous for tying up his hands in debt-bondage and beating them like slaves when they came up short.

Hull's suspicion became certainty when Watt was the first to die.

In his years with the Comanche, the Union Cavalry and as a bounty hunter and tracker, Inigo Hull had seen more than his share of scalped men, women and children, but the violence visited upon Watt's remains went beyond the cruel but practical collection of a trophy or proof of a bounty. Whoever killed Watt and Resley took each man's scalp and skin down to the chin while he sat watch over the sleeping camp. Hull, who had ridden ahead to search the hills for landmarks by moonlight for reasons he refused to explain, was charged with the foul deeds, but their entirely justified fear of Hull had prevailed where their faith in reason had not. That, and their lust for gold.

No Indians under the sun, or even the most depraved white men, took such trophies. But the gold they were after came with a curse that hearkened to a race of Indians who were long gone when the sun itself was young.

According to the legend, the Spaniards who came to Ruby Valley in the late 1500's were desperate, seizing upon every tribe they encountered for rumors of Cibola, of El Dorado, of another Machu Pichu or Tenochtitlan. Canny Indians fed them enough lies to send them over the next mountain range, where the legend was added to and spiked with whatever fabulous details they could concoct to keep the gold-mad conquistadors searching somewhere else.

So it was inevitable that when they finally met a Shoshone chief who foolishly showed them a medallion of pure, flawless gold the size of his palm, they took him captive and tortured him for the secret of its source.

He told them that an ancestor many generations past had taken it in trade from the men of the Shadow Cities. They placed little value on gold, for they knew the secret of making it—but no one had seen them since the world was young. But more than that, on his life, he could not tell, for their splendid cities lay far beneath the surface of the earth, and all their secret roads had long since been swallowed up.

Mad with greed and bedeviled by years of fruitless questing after phantoms, the Spaniards buried the chief up to his neck and starved him, and when he was delirious with hunger, they began to feed him raw meat and deluge him with icy mountain water, which made him sick.

After weeks of torment, the chief surrendered and agreed to draw a map to the cavern where the unclaimed gold of the Shadow Cities lay buried, not a day's journey from their encampment. With a sharp rock, he inscribed the location on the gold medallion itself, and asked to be reunited with his family.

At this, his cruel captors laughed, and explained to him at what he had been eating during his captivity. The chief submitted to add a crucial detail to the map, but then he spoke a curse upon the gold and any who sought it, and swallowed it.

Vexed beyond reason, the Spaniards beat the chief to death and cut open his belly, but were somehow unable to find the gold coin. They threw his broken body into a shallow grave and resolved to quit their doomed quest; but their leader, an ambitious disinherited noble facing ruin at home, returned to the grave to dig up the Shoshone chief and recover the gold coin.

Not even his compatriots knew what became of the desecrator, but their tale ended with the unedifying observation that the grave simply ate him, and his demoralized henchmen faded away into history's shameful backwaters.

It was the longest of long shots, a hope resting on a shadowy legend that promised only doom and misfortune, but there was already little else left to chase in this prematurely domesticated state more enclosed by rancher's fences every day, whose booming silver mines offered only the chance to make another man rich.

Hull turned from these confusing eddies of morbid fancy to the question of the telescope. The prospector had precious little to show for his years of treasure-hunting, but why would anyone just take the glass out of it?

"You'd better find it before sundown today," Schaffroth said, "or we won't wait to see who gets scalped next."

Hull studied the landmark against which they'd made camp—an outcropping of yellow-white boulders that jutted out of the mouth of a narrow ravine. Utterly unlike the surrounding stones, the postpile culminated in a wall of fluted spires like chimneys or minarets, almost a hundred feet above the gentle slope where they camped.

He'd had to ride in ever-widening circles for most of the night before he found the next landmark about half a mile away, beside which he'd bedded down without incident for the few hours of rest he needed. He had sketched in these peculiar landscape features on a recent but worse-than-useless survey map, and he had a fair notion of where their final destination lay, despite the terrain's best efforts to defy him. It would be best if he got them there before dark for all kinds of reasons, before any more of them went missing.

"I know this land better than any of you," Hull said, "and better than most Shoshone. If I wanted the gold for myself, I'd never have brought you along. I don't expect you to believe me, but if you want to make something of it, you're welcome to try."

"I don't see why we shouldn't," Schaffroth said. "He's probably got them redskins all lined up to bushwhack us, soon as we've dug up the gold."

"All I'll tell you," Hull said, "is that I'm not a greedy man."

"Damn, this coffee's bitter," Marriot said, but he bolted it down and went to pour another cup. Just then, Hull dropped the telescope and barked, "Don't drink it!" He went to knock the pot out of his hands, but the ranchhand dropped it all on his own.

Marriot reached out for Hull, to choke him or to plead for help. The next words from his lips were drowned in a gusher of blood.

Schaffroth and Braden recoiled in horror, but Hull took hold of Marriot and smelled his dying breath. It had no odor, but Hull deduced, correctly, if too late, that the crystal lenses in the prospector's telescope had been ground up and added to the morning coffee.

"I told you!" Braden shouted, "told you and told you…"

"Braden's right," Hull said. "Sure as shit there's a curse on us, but Indians got nothing to do with it."

😀😵💀

The depleted expedition led its string of riderless horses and pack mules up the ravine beyond the odd outcropping, Braden regaling them all the way with Indian ghost stories. With his own two eyes, he'd seen a redskin woman glowing like the moon, standing by night on the top of one of those mysterious mounds in Kansas, waving and beckoning though she had no head, and the tales he told of the Shadow Cities were more far-fetched still, but the Indians who told them to him feared those bygone people as much as white men loved gold.

The undulating land took its toll on them, eating up the day. They followed the steep, treacherous ravine up to a false peak that gave out in a snarl of canyons. Hull chose their path after some hesitation, wishing he had Resley's telescope.

"Maybe he don't know the way, after all," Braden sneered.

"I'm waiting on our other man," Hull said.

"Now hold on," Schaffroth said. "Don't try to complicate things. Right now, only one man had the motive and the means to do what you did to Resley and Watt."

"And put on a pot of ground-glass coffee to do for the rest of you," Braden put in.

"Maybe so," Schaffroth said.

"Maybe a simpler explanation," Hull said. "Maybe this party trailed us from Fort Ruby and came into camp night before last, and Mr. Watt didn't raise the alarm, because he was expected."

Schaffroth vividly disapproved of where this was going, but he didn't interrupt again.

"Maybe this other one answered to you, and maybe he answered to the same fellow who pays Watt's wages, which I reckon would be the owner of the Bar S. You didn't seem all that busted up when Watt turned up dead."

"I won't go broke buying flowers if either of you cayuses turn up dead tomorrow," Schaffroth said, "but it don't add up to nothing."

"Not by itself, I freely allow," Hull answered. "You didn't even concern yourself with burying him under those rocks and brush, but Elmer here did."

"Don't drag me into this," Braden said.

"You notice his hands?" Hull asked.

"I noticed his head, and how it had no damned face."

"His fingers were short and hairy," Hull said. "Watt had long, fine fingers, and he kept his nails short and clean. Man we buried was wearing Watt's fine broadcloth suit, but he had hands like an ape."

Schaffroth scowled, but his eyes were wide and suddenly searching the broken land around them with barely suppressed panic.

"So you see, it's pretty simple. There was an outside man in our camp that night, and he and Mr. Watt were reading from the same book. But not from the same page."

The trail forked again. Hull stopped, looking up at the sun. "Next landmark is just ahead."

"What about the coffee?" Braden demanded.

Hull shook his head. He didn't come out this far from people to have to talk so damn much. "Maybe Resley figured he didn't much care who was killing who over what, and thought he'd put all of you down, and split the take with me when I came back, as the sole survivor."

"All I know is, I'd think twice before I let a Mormon make my coffee."

It was nearly noon when they came into sight of the next landmark, a badly weathered hoodoo rearing up out of a jumble of shattered granite on the opposite face of the canyon. It was of the same pitted, yellow-white stone and similar even in formation, with a row of crooked columns scraping at the ruthlessly blue sky, like the pipes of an organ atop a base of tightly packed boulders.

Braden uneasily stared at it as they rode closer and seemed to shy away from crossing its shadow, but Schaffroth watched the rising ridgetops with his rifle braced across the horn of his saddle. "Is this it?" he demanded.

"No, but it's close by." He pointed at a depression in the soft sand above the hoodoo, where a small campfire had been kicked in and thoroughly buried. "Where I camped last night," he said.

"That's no alibi," Schaffroth shot back.

Hull rode up a winding draw that broke out of the enclosing ridges, so the setting sun fell full upon his profile. Schaffroth wached him, hesitating, then rode up alongside him.

"What makes you believe this story is even true, let alone worth killing for?" Hull asked.

Schaffroth was just surprised enough by the question to answer it. "It just feels true. You look out on these mountains and you can just feel that vitality, that power, that wealth, locked up in it, waiting for you to rip it out and strike it rich. Those dumb redskins been sitting on it all this time, doing not a damned thing with it. Be better off when they're all gone."

"Conquistadors couldn't find gold in this country… they couldn't even find gold in one dead indian."

Schaffroth snapped his fingers. "And there's the rub, damn it. That old Shoshone chief pulled a fast one on those idiots, like a riverboat magician. All I know is, them Spaniards went away empty-handed, and the Shoshone sure as hell don't have it, but whether it's somewhere in his guts or tucked away in the highest goddamn tree on this here mountain, I aim to find it."

The mountaintop was a cracked dome of the same uncanny white rock, eroded and hollowed out so the trail ended in a roofless grotto with only a few stunted pines and knots of scrub. The dirt underfoot was hard as baked adobe in all but one patch dead center in the eerie canyon. The rock walls curled over them in jaggied, serried formations that reminded even the stolid Schaffroth of gigantic teeth. The ranch foreman stood behind Hull when he dished out the shovels. The tracker didn't need to be told he had a rifle aimed at his back.

"Unless there really are two of you," Schaffroth said, "you best take up a shovel and commence to digging."

Hull shook his head, but joined Elmer Braden in turning over the soft dirt that was the only sensible place hereabouts, to dig a grave.

"Damn conniving half-breed," Schaffroth grated. "Think you're two steps ahead of everybody."

Hull put his back into shoveling, into a rhythm that complemented the slower, less deliberate labor of the older, heavier ranchhand at his side.

"No more smart talk, Mr. Consulting Detective? Got our brains all stirred with that talk about some other fella on our trail, working the outside, when it's been you all along."

"I was just wondering when Mr. Watt would come to collect for his boss. There's still a lot of work to do yet, even if that gold coin does turn up in the grave, even if there is a map, even if any of that legend is true…"

"And what would you know about it?"

"I'd know it was a lie, if I was the one who spread it around…"

Schaffroth jumped to his feet and raised his rifle. "What the hell're you talking about? You better hope this ain't some wild goose chase—"

The next thing to come out of Schaffroth's mouth was the back of his skull. The poleaxed foreman stumbled for a moment, transfixed by the echoing thunderclap of the shot that killed him.

"Oh, you snake-blooded, two-faced, half-breed sonofabitch," Braden said.

"Bite your tongue," Hull said. "You got no idea how many faces I wear." He looked up to spot the wisp of smoke from among the jagged overhanging rocks. "Just keep digging."

By and by, a slim, soiled but still dapper figure, even in homespun secondhand clothes, came down out of the rocks with a rifle and a pistol trained on them.

"Evening, Mr. Watt," Hull said. "Care to take up a shovel?"

"I'm better suited to this kind of iron," Watt said, casually weighing the Winchester in one hand and the bone-handled Colt revolver in the other. "You all seem to have the job well in hand, I wouldn't dream of interrupting with my inexpert contributions."

Hull nodded and resumed digging. They were knee-deep in a wide hole, and the shovelfuls of earth came easier and faster all the time. Braden was ruddy and gleaming with sweat. He finally threw down his shovel. "You may as well know," he shouted, "this-here snake made up the whole thing!"

"What's this, now?" Watt asked. He'd set the rifle down and was rolling a cigarette one-handed while dangling the revolver by its trigger-guard. "Why would you get these boys' hopes up with a tall tale? If we don't find no Indian in yonder grave, we just gonna have to leave one…"

Hull kept digging. "There's a Shoshone chief buried right here. That much is true. His name was Woshiute of the Mahaguaduka Seed Eater band of the Western Shoshone nation. But he wasn't killed three hundred years ago by Spaniards over gold. He was killed twenty years ago, by Union cavalry officers trying to take the only gold he possessed."

"The coin?" Braden wheezed. "Well, it was still a fair hunk of gold…"

"The land," Hull said, "was all the gold he had, and they wanted it all."

Watt cocked his pistol and lit his cigarette. "Both of you, keep digging. And you… half-breed. Keep talking."

Hull obeyed, talking as he dug. "They took Woshiute prisoner, beat him, broke his limbs and buried him up to his neck, starved him to make him sign a treaty surrendering the whole Ruby Valley. Woshiute could no more give away the land than he could give away the stars, but he was willing to give it his body. When he wouldn't do it even as he neared death by hunger, they began to feed him meat. At first, it made him sick, but then he began to crave it, to cry out for it in a voice that they found amusing at first, but then came to hate and fear.

"For the cavalry officers had raided Woshiute's village and slaughtered his whole band—babies with brains dashed out on rocks, women raped and gutted like fish, children scalped and impaled on blazing stakes… and they had been feeding them to Woshiute.

"They had all but forgotten what they came for, so lost were they in their own evil, in the evil they'd created. Woshiute only laughed when they told him what he'd been eating, because he'd known all along, and by this time, the Shoshone chief was no longer the man he was. For one thing, he'd been growing. He kept threatening to break out, so they piled the dirt on top of him until only his face looked up from the bottom of a wide grave, but every time they filled it, somehow, he emptied it."

"I don't want to hear it," Braden said.

"I do," Watt said. "I'll get paid the same, whatever you boys find or don't. For that matter, so will you. So how much did this ol' Shoshone chief eat, anyway?"

"In the end, they fed every last corpse, forty-seven men, women and children, into the hole, but the chief wasn't satisfied. He'd sign the treaty, he said, if they only set him free. A few of them filled in the hole and went away to try to forget what they'd seen, what they'd fed and created."

"And what was that, boy?" Watt asked.

Hull stopped digging and fixed the hired killer with his flinty eyes. "A Wendigo," he said.

Braden stopped digging, shifting his feet uneasily in the hole, which had begun to fill in with mud. "Judas get home, that's strange…" he observed, but no one took notice.

Hull pointed at his saddlebag on the flank of his red-white palomino. Watt went over and dug out the map. Hull stepped out of the hole as he came over, tapping on the marked-up survey. "So that pile of rocks back there—"

"Where you killed Resley…"

"Yes, indeed. What was it?"

"One of his feet."

Watt twisted his lips into a smile. "Do tell. And that other one over yonder, about half a mile away as the crow files…"

"His left hand. They decayed pretty fast once they were exposed."

Chuckling in disbelief, the gunslinger traced the outline sketched over a map, the stick figure delineated by the exposed hand and foot, leading to the craggy, rudimentary mouth drawn over the mountaintop. "He sure did grow awful big in, what, twenty years? Eating all those Indians…"

"He's been fed a lot more than forty-seven people," Hull admitted. "In the years since he's been down there, not even I know how many treasure hunters have come to dig up his grave, but he welcomes them. He's become what the Algonqian call *wendigo*, and he knows only hunger."

This was finally too much for Watt's indulgent character. "You sayin' he's still *alive* down there?"

"I am saying only that he is still hungry."

So engrossed had Watt been in the map's fanciful embellishments that he didn't notice until now that Braden was gone, leaving his shovel standing upright in the mud.

Watt took up the shovel, noticing how the hole tapered but never terminated, the blackness at its bottom gobbling up the clods and pebbles knocked loose by his boots. "Where the hell did that no-account get off to?"

Hull looked up at the moon rising up above the jagged walls of the canyon. "You know what happened to him."

"Horseshit," Watt said, probing the edge of the hole with the shovel, gun poised, mesmerised by the illusion of a great, gray wave down in the blackness, softly lapping at the earth from a vast space beneath his feet. "You're a bigger damn liar than that chiseling foreman, that poisoning prospector or the other chowder-head who got himself lost right under my nose."

"I have not lied to you," Hull said. "And I only lied to them once."

The walls of the canyon shuddered, shedding rocks. The walls of the grave shivered, the hole widening on its own. Watt took a clumsy step backwards, still staring down into it as if it contained treasure, after all. "When was that? When you told them about the gold?"

"I didn't have to do that," Hull said. "I lied when I told them I wasn't a greedy man." He struck Watt over the head with the shovel and pushed the gunslinger into the greedy grave.

"I sorely wish," Hull said, "that I had more of you to feed him."

PRETTY IN THE DARK
ERICA RUPPERT

Their first night in camp the wind was up, and Syl heard the old dinner bell ring. It sounded as far away as Mars.

No one had rung it on purpose in years.

But for the wind and the muffled tolling, the night was quiet. Mike dozed restlessly beside her in cabin 9's deep bed. As soon as he saw the cabin he had complained about the lack of modern amenities, but Syl didn't care. Syl's family had come here for decades. Tucked into her wallet was a picture of her at five months old, in her grandfather's arms, in front of cabin 6. Over the years she had slept in every cabin on the property, and knew the rise and fall of the land within the camp well enough to run it at night.

She looked up at the wood plank ceiling. She couldn't see it in the dark, but she knew the knots and grain and the faces they hid. It was good to be back at the lodge after so many years away, and to find so much unchanged.

Long Lake Lodge was how Syl thought of Canada. The camp endured in genteel decline on the northeastern shore of Lake Kashwakamak, a deep gouge in the rock of the Ontario highlands, one of the thousands of water-filled scars left behind by the glaciers. Trapped, the Mississippi River fed the lake, the remains of its currents pushing cold water eastward to the dam.

☻☻☻

The dam was a destination, every year.

Syl had rented one of the old metal motorboats when she booked the cabin, and talked Mike into putting on a stained life vest before they set off. Her father had always insisted on the life vests – the lake might be familiar, but that did not make it safe.

Mike volunteered to man the motor, and Syl sat in the prow and pointed the way he should steer. In the final sweep around a shaggy island Syl leaned forward, waiting to see the low line of the dam with its blue metal framework and yellow warning chain.

"Slow, now," Syl said to him. "Aim for the tree on the left."

Mike cut the engine and used the oars to push them into the undercut shore. Syl clambered out to tie the boat to the birch that leaned over the water, half its roots tangled in air.

While Mike climbed onto land Syl ran up the metal steps of the dam and onto the platform. From there she could peer through the grate at the point where the lake became a river again.

She called Mike up beside her to look down the path of the stream here, how the water had jostled and carved the great slabs of rock, rolled them and hollowed them and worn them away.

"The water is down," she said. "We can walk the stream bed."

Syl led him down the sharp slope beside the dam and under the heavy cedar branches, and then splashed her way shin-deep into the cold flowing stream. She waded to a dry outcropping and climbed up. He stayed on the bank.

"Come on," she said. "Follow me. We can go most of the way on the big ones."

Trusting that Mike was behind her, she picked her way downstream. She heard him curse as he stepped into the water. After a minute he caught up.

At points they navigated the shallow water, careful of their footing. Where the stream's path bent, a long slab of pitted granite rose like an island and forced the water into a deep channel against the opposite shore. They climbed up. Sapling birch, cardinal flowers, and yellow grasses found rootholds in the island's water-carved rock. The afternoon sun threw shards of light up from the rushing water. Mike stood still, taking pictures of the trees and the sky. Syl squinted as she looked downstream, then kept moving.

She scrambled over the island, easy as a goat. Every few feet she bent to peer at a loose stone, pocketing the ones banded with quartz. The ones she did not take went back exactly as she had found them.

Then she picked up something different from the litter of sticks and dry crayfish claws that filled the hollows. Not a rock. Not a bleached twig. "Mike," she called out. "Come look at this." She held out the slender bone to him as he bent near.

"Is it a fossil?"

"Hardly," Syl said, turning it between her fingers. It was thin as a drinking straw, dry and grey from exposure. "Probably from a raccoon or a beaver. Maybe a rabbit."

The sound of a branch snapping echoed from the wooded shore. Syl's attention turned.

"There are bears, sometimes," she said. "Be loud."

She sang a few lines from a show tune, but Mike did not join her.

"I think I'd like to go now," he said.

"The pond isn't much farther."

"I don't want to go to the pond. Come on. I'm tired," he said.

"We'll take the trail back, then," she said.

They climbed away from the stream through the ancient cedars to the portage trail. It was rougher than she had thought it would be, unused, untended, and cluttered with fallen trees, broken by steps made of twisted roots and jutting, lichened rocks. Even where it was relatively level, the trail was littered with pine needles and slippery underfoot.

Over their heads the wind caught high in the trees, rushing through without touching the ground. Clouds turned daylight to shadow.

Syl realized she was moving fast, leaving Mike too far behind. As she turned to wait for him she caught a shape at the corner of her eye, small and slender and dirty pale. It moved, and she looked straight at it to see a girl in a long, yellowed white dress. The girl looked like a toddler but her face was so old, so drawn and jaundiced. The girl opened her mouth without making a sound, brown lips stretching around a red, red tongue.

Syl screamed and fell backward down the slope off the trail. Boulders and scrub kept her from sliding too far on the slick pine needles.

Mike ran to her as quickly as he could on the rough ground. He skidded down off the trail to where Syl had stopped and helped her climb the short distance back up.

"I thought I saw something," Syl said thinly, her breath still catching. She pointed to a rotten birch stump beside the trail. "I thought that was a person,"

"Jeez, Syl," Mike said. "You're lucky you didn't fall where there's a real drop."

Syl brushed brown needles and rotten leaves from her hair and clothes. Her palms were scraped and tattooed with black dirt. She felt a knot growing behind her right ear where she'd clipped a rock.

Syl looked down the trail, back the way they'd come. Wind whistled above them.

"Let's go," she said. "I think it's going to rain."

When rain came at Long Lake Lodge, the cabins became claustrophobic. Syl talked Mike into going up to the common room in the lodge.

Here, the relentless changes of time could not be glossed over. The stone fireplace had been scrubbed clean and filled with a bank of electric logs, the old varnished wood bin removed to make room for a magazine table. A flat screen television stood in one corner, its satellite connection offering some link to the wider world. Mike picked up the remote and scrolled through the channels, but he soon turned the set off.

Syl remembered how it had been when she was younger, building fires here on rainy days, and reading and working on whatever jigsaw puzzle had been started. She remembered the old jukebox, and the soda machine that vended bottles. She had never missed watching TV, then.

At least the bearskin still hung on the wall, and a faded map of the lake drawn in 1973, and the deer antlers, and a taxidermized marten. The wall lamps were still made of birch logs, and there was still a random assortment of puzzles and left-behind books stacked on a narrow set of shelves.

Here is where Syl first read To Kill a Mockingbird, on a rainy day like this one, curled up on the wood-framed sofa beneath the windows. She'd finished it in one sitting.

Mike looked around at the room, picked up a fishing magazine, put it down again.

"Could we get out of here for a while? Go into town?"

Syl kept her eyes on the books, searching for something she knew was gone.

"The nearest real town is Northbrook. It's about half an hour. There's a Foodland that's open 24 hours, but not a whole lot else. Well, a beer store," she said.

She remembered when the lodge had been busy enough to supply the guests with beer, with cases stacked behind the garage to be delivered as requested. But the lodge was winding down, with no children in the family to continue it, no advertising to draw in new business, no improvements to the buildings and services. No more lunches served, no more daily housekeeping. All the sinks had been removed from the cabins because it was no longer acceptable to pump in untreated lake water for washing up, even though everyone who came here knew not to drink it.

Syl spotted a slender red book tucked in among the throwaway novels, and reached up to pull it down. Away Back in Clarendon and Miller was the only local history book she had ever seen on the area. Her mother had once had a copy of it, a gift from Catherine MacHugh.

🎭💀🎭

Catherine MacHugh had been born Catherine Mueller, the middle daughter from the first, fertile wife of the lodge's founder. Catherine and her husband, Tom MacHugh, took over the lodge after Howard Mueller's death in 1972. Their children, Arnold and Grace, both unmarried and childless, took over the lodge in their own turn.

The lodge family history Syl learned had been Howard and Margie, then Catherine and Tom, then Arnold and Grace. Syl never knew Catherine's mother's name. Howard's first wife was like a ghost, not spoken of among the guests.

But his second was, and vividly. Margie MacDonald was a party girl from a comfortable Toronto family, bright and vivacious and athletic. Howard Mueller met her on a business trip, and convinced her to marry him and move to the wilds of Ontario's highlands.

Margie used to swim out to the point, every morning from late spring until autumn. Margie liked the privacy of her morning swim, away from the clamor of the kitchen and the demands of the men. In the water, Margie was free of her earthly weight and too far out to answer if anyone called her. She was not afraid of the lake, or its weeds.

🎭💀🎭

The rain ended during dinner, but Syl wanted to stay in the common room for a while. She paged through an old Reader's Digest, passing time as the daylight faded. Mike went back to the cabin to watch videos on his phone, bored in the silence. With him gone Syl realized the lodge was empty, even the kitchen cleaned and dark. But Syl wasn't ready to settle, yet.

She made her way down to the big dock and sat in one of the wet, weathered Adirondack chairs at its end, the lights of the lodge at her back, aware of the black water that stretched away around her. The sky above was enormous, dark and deep and dusted with stars. Looking up, she reminded herself that she was seeing the Milky Way, that it was always there. She tilted her head back against the chair's back and waited for a shooting star.

A light wind ruffled the water and brushed like a spiderweb against her cheek. Watching the stars was not enough of a distraction. She felt isolated, laid bare under such a wide sky. She wished there were more people in camp this week. The quiet was enough to drown in. She was certain that something watched her, waiting for its chance.

Syl turned to look down the path of the moonlight on the water. A dark shape bobbed along on the white-lit ripples, drifting toward the dock. It looked like a small, round head held above the water. She broke out in an icy sweat, rose and walked as quickly and softly as she could back to land.

And then she ran, her gait flat-footed and strange to accommodate the uneven ground, her knees loose to absorb the impact. She was sure of the terrain, but the slippery grass beneath her feet slowed her down. She would not look behind her.

She couldn't help but think of a lodge story she had always heard told as a joke, of the night back in '62 that Charlie Kormutter ran his boat full-speed into the big dock while coming back from Bingo Bay. They always said he was drunk. They never said why he was in such a hurry.

It was years later, long after he'd given up night fishing, that he said he'd seen the baby.

The baby. There were oblique references to the baby in a few of the camp stories, but as the older guests died off the references were less often repeated. The stories still got told, worn down to jokes now with no hint of warnings.

Except for one, that Syl overheard accidentally when she was seven or eight. The adults didn't know she was still awake, didn't realize how clearly their low voices carried in the quiet night as they sat on the cabin's porch, drinking whiskey and retelling themselves the camp's darker rumors.

They said that Margie was so used to her morning solitude she did not notice her small daughter follow her to the lake's edge and into the water. At least, they said, that's what must have happened. The baby was in her cot in the house when Margie left for her swim, and gone when Margie waded back onto shore.

One of the kitchen girls thought she had seen a white shape in the water while she set the dining room for breakfast, but she couldn't be sure. It might have been light striking off the water. The baby was never found, although Howard and the neighbors crossed and recrossed the lake for any sign of her, and combed the woods with their hunting dogs without any hope.

They said Maggie stopped swimming to the Point for a long time. They said she told Catherine she was afraid of finding the baby there in the weeds. Catherine was still a teenager, then, and had filled in the blank mystery with wild imagination. Catherine had said she pictured the baby's face swollen with water, her eyes open and her fat young fingers wrapped around the weeds.

And everyone knew that was why Catherine would not swim at all.

😀💀😜

Syl had only tried to swim to the Point once, when she was fifteen. No one warned her not to.

Syl grew up knowing that you did not go near the dump at dusk, and you did not go to the sandpit alone. But, the weeds--she didn't learn that until she was in them.

She and a girl up from Ohio who's name was lost to memory had set out from the big dock with Syl's brother in a rowboat beside them. At first it seemed fun, an adventure, but when the girls reached the weed bed they both began screaming at the slimy fronds stroking their legs, and scrambled panicking into the boat to be rowed back to shore.

After that, Syl refused to swim outside the small bathing area, with its clean sand bottom and clear water. She claimed she was afraid of the big pike in the lake, and the snapping turtles, but that wasn't the truth. She was afraid of what she couldn't see.

😀💀😜

She didn't like being out in a boat, either, especially at dusk. The lake was inscrutable, then, between reflection and darkness, and the boat such a small thing to float upon it. But sometimes her father insisted she and her brothers come out with him, for company.

As a child Syl preferred to fish off the short dock across from the boathouse, casting into the shallow weed bed there for perch and sunnies, a step from the shore. Once, she had caught a pike, lithe and slimy and too small to keep. More often, she caught only weeds.

Her father always sought out the pike and the large-mouth bass, the weedy spots and the monsters that lurked in them. He was not deterred by the fronds that tangled his lures and stripped off his bait, or his daughter's nervous complaints.

This was, after all, the Land O' Lakes, and he was here to fish. When nothing was biting on Kashwakamak, her father would leave camp to fish at Marble Lake, or Skootamatta, or Little Mink, but then he went with other fishermen and the kids stayed behind with their mother. Rarely, he would bring his children on the rough mile-long hike into Mannerheim, which he stubbornly called Monahan's.

Syl hated that hike. The path cut up and over a steep ridge, to a swampy lake surrounded by rock walls. The mosquitoes were always thick, and if the water was high there was no shoreline. Syl remembered being trapped on a muddy patch at the edge of the lake, waiting until her father would declare defeat and bring them back to the lodge.

Like every cabin at Long Lake Lodge, cabin 9 faced the water. Syl latched the screen door as soon as it shut behind her and slid the wide porch windows closed, but the glass seemed an inadequate shield against what might be in the dark.

The moon had followed her, and made a fresh path to the short dock in front of her cabin.

She turned away before she could see a round shape floating there, if it had followed her, too. The baby must be there in the mud beneath the tangled logs above the dam, Syl thought, drifted to a stopping place on the slow lake currents.

Mike snored from the darkness of the bedroom. Syl climbed quietly into the depths of the narrow second bed and pulled the red wool blanket over her head.

The bell rang again that night, long after the camp was quiet, swaying in the inconstant wind.

"Mike," Syl said over breakfast, "Let's leave camp for a while today. I want to head over toward Plevna."

Mike sipped his coffee. "Why? What's there?"

"I want to go to the cemetery where Grace and Arnold's family is buried. It's not far."

Mike looked out over the lake. In the bright morning sun it reflected the wide blue sky.

"Sounds fun," he said.

Syl followed his gaze toward the water.

There was only one other family here this week, and they had already finished eating and left the dining room. They didn't seem to stay in camp during the day. Syl missed the years when the dining room was full, and the conversations stretched across multiple tables.

Voices drifted out from the kitchen, punctuated by the clink of dishes. She heard Grace call out to one of the other women, teasing, and then a burst of laughter.

"I'll drive," Syl said.

💀💀💀

St. Killian's cemetery was a narrow swath along Road 509 marked by a faded sign, laid plain under the wide sky with no trees among the graves to offer shade. A waist-high chain link fence set back about twenty feet from the road marked its boundary.

There was no parking lot, no paved path snaking through a crowd of grave markers, no benches for visitors. Here it was only a field, and scattered stones. Syl parked in front of the gate, where the scrubby grass had been worn away.

"I'll wait here," Mike said, not looking at her.

Syl looked at her hands, still holding the wheel.

"I won't be long," Syl said after a moment, and climbed out of the car.

Syl had been here once, years ago, when Tom had died. It took her a minute to find his grave again. She remembered it being closer to the road than it was. Now, she saw, Catherine's name had been added beside her husband's.

Catherine had been dead for five years already. Syl didn't think that much time had passed.

Syl bent down to read the dates again. Tom had died twelve years ago. She could remember him so clearly, more clearly than she remembered Catherine.

Visitors had left pebbles on the headstones. Syl thought it was only a Jewish tradition, but it seemed important here as well. She found a chip of granite and placed it on the ledge made by the stone's base, careful to set it midway between the names. She offered no prayers.

When she stood again she glanced back at the car. Mike's head was tilted down, either asleep or engrossed in his phone.

She cast about for Howard and Margie's grave. It wasn't far from Catherine's, in a cluster of headstones all engraved with Mueller.

There were no stones on this one.

Syl stared at the headstone, at the graven names, at the dates so far in the past she hadn't been born yet. She glanced at the surrounding markers, looking for a child's grave. There was nothing that fit the story, no buried child close-by that could have been Margie's.

She walked quickly up and down the long cemetery, looking for any small headstone that might be the one. Maybe, she thought, there was no body to bury.

Before she went back to the car she scratched a rock out of the dirt and laid it on Howard and Margie's headstone. It looked strange, all by itself.

She wondered if anyone would visit, and notice.

😁😌😈

Syl went into the kitchen after breakfast was done, circling the lodge to use the back door. She hoped to catch Grace alone, but there was an old woman still with her, peeling potatoes for dinner.

"Sylvia, hello!" Grace said, coming toward her. "I'm so glad you made it up this year, with your friend. How are you?"

"I'm good, Grace. It's been hard since Dad died, but I'm really glad to be up here."

Grace smiled. Syl shifted her weight.

"Look, Grace, I need to ask you something." Syl glanced around the familiar kitchen, hoping the woman inside couldn't hear.

"Sure," Grace said, a small frown creasing her forehead.

"I went to the cemetery yesterday. I found your grandparents' graves, but I didn't find any marker for the baby."

Grace looked at her, the frown deepening. "What baby?"

Syl realized that she didn't know Grace well at all after so many years, not well enough for this question. Syl reached out for Grace's hand so she wouldn't pull away. "The one who drowned. The one who followed Margie out into the lake and drowned."

"There was no baby," Grace said quickly. "There never was a baby."

Syl blinked.

"But...I saw something, in the water, off the big dock. What about Charlie Kormutter? What about the stories Margie told your mother? Please, Grace," Syl begged. She heard her own voice rising with frustration.

Grace tugged her hand loose. "Sylvia, stop it."

The woman peeling potatoes had stopped her task to watch them. Syl felt her cheeks flare red.

"That's an old yarn some of the men used to spin just to scare the kids. There never was a baby. Margie never had a baby. I didn't know anyone believed that."

Syl slumped, and turned away.

"I'm sorry," she said. "I saw something in the water. I remembered the story."

Grace smiled at her, tight and cool. "Probably a beaver," she said. "No one has drowned here since the lodge has been here. No ghosts."

"I'm sorry," Syl said again, and fled.

😀💀😀

When she got back to the cabin she saw that the car was gone. Mike had left a note on the porch table--Gone to find Northbrook, don't wait up.

She crumpled up the paper and put it in the recycling can. It was barely noon.

Syl was too restless to stay in the cabin, or pass the day in the lodge. She went back out into the sunlight. The sky was so bright, and the wind so warm. The air smelled clean. It was a beautiful day. She closed her eyes and forced herself to bask in it, to prove that this was why she had come back. The camp was quiet around her, yet she did not feel alone. She felt as if something was just behind her, ready to reach out and touch her arm. She opened her eyes.

It was only the camp, and the trees, and the lake before her.

She wandered down to the lake, trailing along the line of logs protecting the grassy edge, past cabins set deep in shade. As she reached the far side of the camp she climbed up to the overgrown road behind the MacHugh's house, thinking of ticks when the grass brushed her legs. Birch leaves rustled like paper in the high wind, turning to show their silver.

The trees were thin through here. She could see the yellow cabins scattered along the curve of the lake, and the soft green banks of moss growing on the shingled roofs.

If she followed the road to its end she would reach the swamp, a pocket in the lake shore where the currents never reached.

Sweat stung her eyes, and she wiped it away. She wished Mike were here with her. She wished Mike were interested in being here with her.

She kept going, the sense of another presence growing as she got closer to the end of the road. The grass gave way to a stand of horsetail reeds and listing cedars and birch. She used to catch bullfrogs here, years ago. She had expected to hear their croaks and heavy splashes. But the small cove was only full of rotten logs and cattails, and utterly quiet except for the wind. She looked around slowly.

From the corner of her eye, she saw something move. She turned, trying to track it. Wind ruffled the curling shreds of bark that clung to a broken birch stump. Her stomach knotted, knowing what was here.

Syl stumbled back as the bark of the splintered birch peeled away with a sudden gust, unfurling as a tattered dress around the wasted form of a small child. A child whose mouth was wide, and red, and empty. The child raised its arms to her, begging to be lifted. It stepped toward her.

"No!" Syl cried, her voice echoing off the trees. She shut her eyes and struck out at the small figure, scraping her hands on rough bark. She felt it break and crumble beneath her flailing hands. She heard herself screaming, her voice jagged in terror.

She thrashed at the air until she lost her balance and fell to the muddy ground, then wrapped her arms around her head and cried, waiting to feel a cold small hand on her cheek. She heard startled voices, far off but coming closer. She heard the hard thud of running feet.

She opened her eyes.

There in the mud and tangled roots before her, tiny teeth like chips of ivory grinned up in a scattered smile.

THE EYE DOCTOR
ROBERT GUFFEY

1. Once

Once upon a time, a few weeks after her seventh birthday, Isabella learned about the existence of a malignant creature called The Eye Doctor. She didn't like doctors. She'd seen too many of their offices during her short lifespan. Every time she visited one, she'd get a pointy. It always hurt. Isabella hated pointies and hated the doctors who relished giving them to her. The Eye Doctor sounded even worse. Mommy once used him to threaten her.

This is how it happened:

Isabella was quite clumsy and kept bumping into things. This particular afternoon she was darting through the house and ran into Mommy. Unfortunately, it just so happened that Mommy was carrying one of her little sculptures, which she'd been working on all day; the sculpture slipped out of Mommy's hand and crashed into the kitchen linoleum, shattering into a million sharp pieces.

A million little pointies.

"*Oh, Isabella!*" Mommy shouted. "Why don't you watch where you're going?"

"What happened?" Daddy asked, emerging from his office.

Isabella stared down at the dark green carpet, ashamed.

"Bella was running through the house, which I've told her a *million times* not to do, and she crashed right into me and *now* look." Mommy sighed.

"I'm sorry," Daddy said, seeing the ruins scattered across the kitchen floor. "Don't give up. You'll just have to start over again, that's all."

"That's not the point. Why can't you just watch where you're going for once?" Mommy put her fingers under Isabella's chin and lifted the girl's head gently. Mommy looked like a giant staring down at her from some sort of vast mountain of judgment, like something out of a crazy cartoon or the Bible. "Is there something wrong with your eyes? Do you need to see *The Eye Doctor*?"

"The Eye Doctor?" asked Isabella.

"Do we need to take you to him, *hm*?"

Isabella pushed back her tears. She couldn't believe Mommy was threatening to give her away forever to some horrible monster.

The Eye Doctor.

She knew instantly what he looked like: a giant man dressed in a dirty white coat with frayed cuffs and a constricting tie and wrinkled slacks and dull black shoes, and bulging out above the man's soiled white collar is a most unusual head: nothing but an immense eyeball the size of Isabella's entire body, a searching pupil the color of night, bloodshot veins spread out across that eye like a vast spider web. Adorning the top of the eyeball is a gray elastic strap, and connected to this strap is a circular mirror that reflects the harsh fluorescent lights hovering above Isabella as *The Eye Doctor* conducts his unorthodox examination. He rubs his nonexistent chin as he peers down at her, staring deeply into the very center of her being, and says, "*Hm*." Then adds, "I think, my dear, you have something wrong with your *eyes*. I think we'll need to give you a *pointy*." His hands lower slowly towards the thick belt strapped to his waist, the kind of belt worn by the little man who fixes the plumbing in the apartment building. But instead of wrenches and screwdrivers, this belt contains nothing but deadly pointies of various sizes. "I think," says *The Eye Doctor*, "we need to give you a shot in your *eyes*. Let's do the left one first." He removes the longest needle from his belt, squirts some noxious black liquid from the top of the syringe, then bends down towards Isabella. The closer he gets, the more she can see how dry his eye-head is becoming. "I'll need a drink of water soon," he whispers, and Isabella wonders how he can drink with no mouth. She squeezes her eyes shut, waiting for the needle to penetrate her tear duct….

Now Isabella began to cry, seeing the whole scenario so clearly in her mind. "*Please*," she said, "*please* don't take me to *The Eye Doctor*! I'll be good!"

She heard her Daddy laughing behind her. "*The Eye Doctor's* not a punishment," he explained. "You only go to him if you need to, if there's something wrong with your vision. Do you think there's something wrong with your eyes?"

Isabella opened them and could barely see Daddy through her tears. "*I can't see you*!" she screamed.

She heard Mommy sigh with frustration. "Then maybe we need to make an appointment." Mommy bent down and began picking up the shattered pieces of her sculpture.

Isabella ran to Daddy and wrapped her arms around his long legs. She looked up at him through a haze of tears. "Please don't take me to *The Eye Doctor*!"

"You won't have to go if you can see, and you won't be able to see if you don't wipe your tears. So let's go into the bathroom and wipe those tears away, okay?"

Isabella nodded, took Daddy's hand, and followed him into the bathroom where he lowered himself to one knee, grabbed some Kleenex from a bright pink box, and began wiping away the tears. She liked it when Daddy comforted her.

"I think you're all fixed up now," Daddy said. "Can you see better?"

The haze was gone. Isabella nodded.

"Good. Listen, Mommy didn't mean to yell at you. It's just that it takes a very long time to make something like that, so when it gets destroyed for no reason, it can be very frustrating. Mommy loves you, even when she's mad at you. She just wants you to be more careful. Think how upset you would be if Mommy wasn't being careful and accidentally broke your favorite doll. That'd probably make you angry, right?"

Isabella nodded. She understood so well when Daddy explained things.

"Well… that's why Mommy's angry. And, you know, this isn't the first time you've done something like this. You do seem to keep bumping into things." He reached out and stroked Isabella's long brown hair. "I think you inherited your Mommy's clumsiness and your Daddy's eyes." He reached up and adjusted his black, rectangular glasses. "You sure you don't need to see *The Eye Doctor*?"

Isabella felt herself going pale again. She wanted to make sure that never happened. "I'm sure, Daddy," she said, trying to remain calm. Mommy and Daddy seemed to get upset when she didn't remain calm. And she wanted to give them no reason to send her away forever to the glaring, dull-white offices of the dreaded *Eye Doctor*. "I never want to see him. Ever."

"Well, we'll see," he said, patting her on the back. "Let's go help Mommy clean up that mess out there, okay?"

Isabella nodded and followed him back into the kitchen.

2. Lost

There was no more talk of *The Eye Doctor* for some time. Several months passed without any further images of the monster impinging upon her thoughts.

Everything seemed wonderful. One day she and her parents were laughing and having fun at Disneyland. She loved Pirates of the Caribbean and The Haunted Mansion and The Tiki Room and Space Mountain and that crazy Roger Rabbit ride and… and then, the next day, her parents were sitting her down in the living room to tell her something "very serious."

"Oh, no," said Isabella, staring with wonder at her mommy's flat belly. "Am I… am I gonna have a *baby sister*?"

Daddy laughed briefly. "No, no. Mommy's not pregnant, nothing like that."

Mommy and Daddy, he explained slowly, were "splitting up." Isabella would be living in the apartment with Mommy, but Daddy would be living somewhere else.

Daddy was going away? Why was Daddy going away? She turned toward Mommy. "Why're you sending Daddy away?"

"No, honey, *I'm* not sending him away."

"Then why is he going?"

"Because…." Mommy began to choke up. She shoved her fist into her teeth and tried to stop the tears from coming. But they came anyway. "Oh, this is so complicated. I don't know how to make you understand this. It's nothing you did, it's nothing I did, it's nothing Daddy did. It's just… Daddy and I need some time apart to think things through… we… we've just grown… I…." She fumbled over her own words, faltered, then lapsed into confused silence.

Daddy broke in: "Mommy didn't do anything wrong. Me and Mommy… we just have disagreements that can't be worked out right away. So we need to separate to think it all through."

"You mean… like when me and Lianne got into a fight at school and the teacher separated us until the next day when we made up and became friends again?"

"Sort of like that."

"So… is that how long it's gonna take for you to come back? A day?"

Daddy shook his head. "Longer than that."

"Then *how* long?"

Daddy patted her knee. "That's the point. We don't know. We can't give you a specific answer. It could be a couple of weeks—"

"Richard," Mommy said with a harsh tone in her voice.

Daddy glanced at Mommy with nervous eyes. "—or it could be several months… or maybe never."

"Never?" Isabella shot to her feet. "You're never coming back?" Tears began to well up in her eyes.

Daddy laughed, but it wasn't a pleasant laugh. Not like he usually laughs. "No, no, I'll always be here for you. I'm going to see you every weekend. You're going to come to my apartment and spend some time with me. We decided you should stay with Mommy because you need to be close to school and your friends, and I'm just not equipped to do what needs to be done to take you to school everyday on my own. I need to be at work, you see."

"But I don't want to live with Mommy. I want to live with *you*."

The look on Daddy's face grew even more serious than before. His eyes were dark clouds. He looked kind of like how he did the day he attended Grandpa's dreary old funeral. That seemed so long ago. Isabella was only six then.

Daddy sighed. "You're going to live with both of us. Just… separately. Neither of us are leaving you. You'll see both of us all the time."

Now the tears began to pour out of Isabella's eyes. "Why is this happening? What did I do wrong?"

"Oh, honey, you didn't do anything wrong," Mommy said and reached out for her daughter. Isabella repelled her hands with a furious slap. "I *hate* you!" And Isabella went running toward her room.

"Wait!" Mommy shouted.

She heard Daddy say gently, "Just let her go for now."

She slammed the bedroom door behind her and buried her face into the pillow and cried and cried and cried. She hated her parents for turning her life upside down. Why couldn't her life have ended yesterday, right when they walked through the gates of Disneyland at the end of the night? That would have been the perfect conclusion to a perfect life. This… this was the beginning of something else altogether. Something she wanted no part of. Hers would be an *ugly* life from here on out, she knew that, knew it as well as she knew her own bones.

Out in the hall she heard her parents whispering to each other.

Mommy: "Should we go in there?"

Daddy: "No… just let her be by herself for now. If we try to explain it any further, we'll just make it even more confusing. Let's take it slowly. The worst part's over. It could've been even more devastating for her. I think we got off lucky."

"Maybe you're right."

And they wandered away… where? To do what? To plot new ways to ruin her life? The tears kept coming, but at some point she closed her eyes and fell into darkness.

3. Blind

When she woke up, she was surprised to discover that the darkness had not gone away.

She was blind.

She panicked. She reached up to her face to see if something was obstructing her vision. A blindfold? A pillowcase? A blanket? No. Nothing was wrapped around her head except air. She could feel her hands pressing against her own face.

She lashed out. Her hand hit something hard. The lamp next to her bed? It went crashing to the floor. She climbed out of bed and staggered for the door. "Mommy!" she shrieked. "Daddy!"

Was this a nightmare? Was she dreaming? Her hand hit something hard. The door? The closet? Her bookshelf? Where were Mommy and Daddy? Why weren't they here to help her? Suddenly, she remembered last night's conversation. Had they both decided to leave her? Was she alone forever in this darkness?

Then she heard feet running down the hall outside, the sound of a knob being turned frantically, her parents' voices overlapping one another….

Daddy: "Isabella?"

Mommy: "Bella? You okay? What's wrong, honey?"

She reached out, hoping to feel them, to make sure both of them were really there. Not just their voices. Their bodies too. Her hands rammed into the silky smoothness of Mommy's pajama bottoms. Isabella had seen them a million times. They were bright blue and had little pictures of Garfield all over them. They felt like they were made of clouds. She clutched at the cotton material and held on tight, as if at any moment the two of them and Daddy and the whole apartment building might get swept up in a mighty wind.

"I can't *see*," Isabella whispered, trying to breathe. "I can't see…." She felt tears streaming down her cheeks.

"*What*?" Mommy said. "What do you mean?"

"*I can't see!*" Isabella wasn't whispering anymore. She held on tight to Mommy's waist.

"Just calm down for a second," Daddy said. "How many fingers am I holding up?"

Isabella shrieked her next words: *"I can't see! I can't see anything! Everything's black. Everything's just black."*

She heard Mommy gasp and begin to cry. "Oh my God."

"I'll call 911," Daddy said and ran out of the room.

Her Mommy sank to her knees and held Isabella close and patted her hair and whispered, "Shh, baby, everything'll be all right… everything'll be all right." But Mommy couldn't stop crying herself.

So how could she expect Isabella to somehow hold back her tears?

Isabella didn't even try. What was the point? What was happening to her?

Why was she being punished?

What had she done *wrong*?

4. Hospital

In the ambulance on the way to the hospital, she realized she was on her way to *The Eye Doctor*. Of course. Who else could help her with her eyes but *The Eye Doctor*? She clutched at Mommy's hand and tried to block out the sounds of the sirens outside and asked, "Will The Doctor give me a pointy?"

"I don't know," Mommy said. "I don't think so. I don't know."

Mommy's hand was trembling. Mommy was now sobbing more than Isabella.

This didn't make Isabella feel any better.

This made her extremely scared.

But she decided to remain silent because the more she spoke, the more upset her mother became.

She remained silent as they rolled her into the hospital, as a cacophony of grownup voices and unpleasant, mechanical noises assaulted her ears. She could only imagine what *The Doctor* would look like. She didn't want to imagine him at all, but she couldn't help it. And then something happened. She was so scared, and so tired of bottling in her terror, that she once again escaped into unconsciousness. Is that what happened? Perhaps not. Whether awake or asleep, the darkness seemed happy to take her.

5. Chase

When she awoke, she could see again. She was no longer in the hospital. Or rather, it was like no hospital she had ever seen before. It looked exactly like her apartment. But there was no furniture in the apartment, except for a sterile white bed in the corner of what used to be her bedroom. All of her possessions had been moved out… and destroyed?

What was happening? Why could she see again?

Where were Mommy and Daddy?

She sat up in bed. A pair of thin needles and clear plastic tubes trailed off behind her into the white plaster walls. The tubes were attached directly to her temples. But where did these tubes lead? As far as she could tell, nothing at all appeared to be coming through the tubes. Nothing except air. And she didn't need air because she didn't have any problems breathing. Why would her temples need to breathe? She decided to pull the tubes out of her head. This wasn't painful. They slipped away easily. She allowed the tubes to fall to the carpet, then allowed her bare legs to dangle off the edge of the bed. Her feet didn't touch the floor. Someone had changed her into her favorite pajamas: tops and bottoms covered in pictures of little rocket-powered unicorns against a hot pink background. Isabella allowed her feet to touch the carpet, which was unusually soft, as if newly cleaned. Why, the only time she'd seen a carpet as clean as this was when they had moved into this place about a year before.

And now it was almost empty again, looking very much like it had when she and Mommy and Daddy had checked out the place, trying to decide if they wanted to live here permanently.

Where was Mommy and Daddy? She called for them. No one answered.

She crept over to the door and pushed it open. Those creaking hinges seemed to echo in the apartment. She called out into the hallway, which was obscured by darkness. If her friends ever told her they were afraid of the dark again, she would explain to them what that phrase really meant. *This* was dark.

But would she ever see her friends again?

How long had she been in the hospital? Had her parents separated and moved on without her? Maybe they'd forgotten her and left her behind by accident. both of her parents were very busy. Was that possible? Maybe. How else to explain the fact that neither of them were here?

She couldn't see the end of the hallway in either direction. To the right, to the left—everything just stretched off into limbo. From memory, she knew that the living room lay toward the left, her parents' bedroom toward the right. She started toward this bedroom when she heard a voice behind her.

It was a fey male voice that attempted to sound chummy and calm but failed—not too dissimilar from the voices of so many doctors she'd encountered during her seven years on the planet. The voice said, "And just where do you think *you're* going, missy?"

She turned her head toward the left. At the end of the endless hallway, outlined in an intense silver glow that would have seemed heavenly under different circumstances, stood a nightmare. At first she thought the bulbous shape atop the doctor's head was a massive tumor pregnant with blood and bulging veins, like the thing the hospital had removed from Grandpa's neck the year before. But no. The bulbous shape was the man's head. It was an eye. This physician looked like the creature she'd seen in her imagination.

The Eye Doctor's hands, covered in white surgical gloves, pressed against the silver outline that surrounded him, as if struggling to make the outline just a little bigger to accommodate his size. When he'd stretched the silvery substance enough, he lifted up one leg and stepped over the glowing outline, as if he were stepping through a rip in space itself. Once he'd stepped out of it, the silver outline snapped into place and became nothing more than a little irregular glowing line hovering in the air just behind The Eye Doctor. The line shrank into a dot, and then into nothing at all.

The Eye Doctor pulled his left glove on tighter, repeated the same action with the right glove, then squared his shoulders and said, "You're not following The Doctor's orders… are you." This was not a question.

How was the man speaking? He had no mouth. Just that humongous, bloodshot eye erupting from his collar like a deformed white rose that was so ugly it refused to bloom.

On various parts of The Doctor's lanky body, including his clothes, more eyeballs grew. Their pupils were all different colors, and they seemed to have a life of their own. They rolled about in their tight sockets, looking sad and tired, as if wanting nothing more than to be free of the prison that was The Doctor's body. It was disturbing to stare at them too long. It was as if there were dozens of little people buried in The Doctor's torso, only their freakishly bulging, bloodshot eyes visible, each one of them holding onto a thin strand of hope that independence could be theirs if they strained *just a little bit more* against the walking, talking flesh-cage that surrounded them… the flesh-cage that now chastised Isabella so fervently.

"How do you respond?" said The Doctor. "You *must* answer when spoken to, girl."

For some reason Isabella imagined that if she listened to The Doctor's strident words, she too would end up trapped within his horrid body.

"How… how should I know if I'm following your orders?" Isabella said. "What *are* your orders?"

The Eye Doctor smiled despite the fact that he had no lips. "You're a *sassy* one, aren't you? Did your parents teach you to talk back to your betters?"

"I wasn't talking back. I was just asking a question. Anyway… who says you're my better?"

That grating laugh again. "I love *spirit*, particularly in the smaller ones. It tastes better when I draw it out of you with my little pointies here." He reached down toward the thick, brown leather belt strapped around his slender waist. A panoply of multicolored needles of various sizes wrapped around his stomach. His long fingers wiggled above his belt, like a gunfighter preparing to fire. "Which one should I use on you now? The purple one? The red one? How about the *pink* one? I know how you so love pink."

Isabella stomped her foot on the ground. "You don't know *anything* about me!"

"No? Ask me a question then. Go ahead, anything, before I put you back to bed. This isn't the first time you've disobeyed The Doctor's orders, you know. You do it often. And then you forget, and I have to do this all over again. It's getting tiresome. I may have to put you out permanently this time, if you keep trying my patience."

Tears began to form in Isabella's eyes. How long had she been here? "Why don't you *do* that then if you're so scary-mean?" Her voice cracked and the tears began to stream down her cheeks.

"Because I took an oath: The Eye Doctor oath. Would you like to hear it? I know you do. I had to memorize it in order to receive my degree. I worked hard for that degree. Worked hour after hour to memorize every line. Why waste all that effort? Here it goes. You ready?" He didn't wait for a response. Instead he launched into the Oath:

"I swear to ignore the wisdom of the past; to make the sick even sicker; to favor the knife and the needle over sympathy and understanding; to never admit ignorance (even when said ignorance is transparent to all); to reveal at the first opportunity the most embarrassing secrets of my patients if offered enough compliments and coinage; to not only play the role of God, but to aspire to be *greater* than God in every way; to deny the individuality of my patients and all their simpering loved ones; to encourage disease and overcrowding and malnutrition in the most blighted cities of Earth and its tangential satellites; to abdicate responsibility for that befuddled mass of diseased flesh known as the human race, with the important exception of fomenting among them the inherent evil that makes their otherwise empty lives meaningful; to reap forever the benefits of my perfectly beautiful malignancy until the day of my extinction, an event that will never occur as long as my utter infallibility is forever worshipped by the frightened patients who sacrifice their unsouls to my holy whims.

"You see?" continued The Doctor. "I can't eliminate your problem outright. How much genuine evil would be created by such an act? No, no... that can only be a final resort. First I need to drag your suffering out as much as possible by isolating the root of your problem and *exacerbating* it. Otherwise, my dear, I might lose my license."

"But what's my problem?" asked Isabella. "Not being able to see? I *can* see again. The problem's gone."

"Oh, not being able to see wasn't your problem, missy." The Eye Doctor began to walk toward her down the hall. "Not being able to see was simply a *symptom* of your problem."

She backed away from him as he neared her. "So... what's my problem then?"

He leaned his "head" forward. She could just barely see a faint trace of a stubby, pale neck beneath that roving ball of unblinking vision. Blue veins popped out of that neck. "You're problem is that you don't *listen*! And you're annoying! And your parents are tired of saying the same thing to you over and over and over again and you not listening to a single word, as if nothing they say matters. Why should they even bother with a brat like you? They decided you were more trouble than you were worth. And then when you lost your sight—a feeble attempt at attention grabbing, if I've ever seen one—they decided to call in the experts. I'm the last desperate measure, you see. Parents call me in when there's no other choice. When all other options have failed. When girls can't quite learn to be little adults who listen politely to their Mommy and Daddy and say 'No, sir,' and 'Yes, ma'am,' like all good girls should. The blindness from which you suffer, you see, is a *spiritual* blindness. It's not entirely your fault. You're the product of a certain age, a certain time, when core values are not taught by teachers or parents or ministers or Girl Scout leaders or anybody. That's when it's time to call in The Doctor and make sure these lessons are instilled in your brain in the *proper* way. I inject the core values into you, you see, straight through your eyes, with all these beautiful little pointies strapped to my hip. I've tried so many of them, but for some reason they have a problem taking a hold of you. Why is that, do you think? Is there something *extra*-wrong with you?"

Isabella continued backing away. She glanced over her shoulder. The hallway just continued stretching off into the shadows despite the fact that she should have reached her parents' bedroom by now. "My daddy always taught me to think for myself, not to just do what other people tell me to do."

"And look where that got him," said The Doctor. "Look where it got *you*. It got you here. With me. Such thinking, you see, is very dangerous in these times. And your daddy's had a change of heart. I know. I've spoken to him. Your disobedience has built a wedge between your mommy and your daddy. You're the reason they're getting a divorce. If you could just behave, perhaps they would stay together. But you're too much for them to handle now, at this time in their lives, when they're both working very important jobs. They don't have time for work and each other and holding your miserable, ungrateful little hand every second of the day. Something had to go. And it was you. So they went their separate ways and left you with The Doctor. And if The Doctor could successfully alter your warped perception of reality, perhaps there's a chance for all three of you to be a happy family again. But you have to sit still and allow me to inject a new vision through your pupils and into the withered, sick, stupid little brain that lies behind them."

"You're a liar," Isabella whispered.

"You can say whatever you wish… for now." His fingers danced lovingly along the numerous plastic syringes strapped to his belt. "This is the last measure. I don't like performing this procedure, you understand. But all else has failed. Your body has refused to cooperate with my prior, less invasive measures: the Air of Emptiness, for example, which you removed from your dumb little skull *without your doctor's permission*. And so it comes to this then. Which pointy shall we start with first?" He gestured toward one syringe filled with a black, tar-like substance marked OBEDIENCE. "Or perhaps this one?" His bony index finger alighted upon a rust-colored syringe marked REVERENCE. "Or maybe this one would hit the spot instead?" A brackish, gray substance marked SHAME. "Or perhaps all three, one after the other after the other." He withdrew OBEDIENCE and REVERENCE out of his belt at the same time. With one needle gripped in either fist, The Doctor took off down the corridor toward her like a sprinter in a mad marathon of death. Isabella didn't waste her energy screaming. Instead she screamed inside her head and ran as fast as she could toward the bedroom she knew lay somewhere before her… if only she could find it.

"Looking for your parents, kid?" The Doctor laughed. "They can't see you. Not now." Could The Doctor see into her mind? Was his vision that good? But how could that be? It seemed to Isabella that the smaller your eye, the better your vision would be. If your eye is so big, like The Doctor's, how could you ever focus on the small details… small details like Isabella herself? Who really had the advantage here?

A second later Isabella's shoulder was pressing against her parents' bedroom door. Sometimes, when they had private time, they told her not to come in and locked it. She hoped they hadn't locked it this time. Her little fist wrapped around the golden knob and turned it, thrusting the door open. On the other side Isabella expected to see her parents' familiar bedroom. What she saw was something quite different.

She stood in the doorway of a hospital room. Mommy and Daddy sat next to each other beside a sterile white hospital bed. Mommy was crying and Daddy was trying to comfort her, but apparently not succeeding. Who lay in the hospital bed? Isabella was surprised to see a sickly, pale version of herself. How could that be? How could she be in two places at once?

Isabella ran to Mommy and Daddy and said, "Please help me! There's this *man* after me! He… he's not really a man at all. He's a *monster*!" They weren't paying any attention to her. Why? Were they still mad at her? Was everything The Doctor said… true? She reached out toward Mommy's elbow, but Isabella's hand went right through it, as if Mommy and Daddy were both ghosts.

"They can't see you."

Isabella spun around and saw The Doctor filling up the doorway. He had to duck his massive head in order to slink into the room.

"They can't see you because I removed you from their world. The world I live in, the world where sick little children go to die and be reborn, exists in the peripheral vision of grownups. They can't see or hear or touch or smell us. They can't even taste this precious little world of ours. It was constructed by me, by my own hands." Here he held out his gloved hands, the syringes held firmly between his spidery fingers. He wiggled his fingers in the air. They didn't seem to move like normal fingers. They seemed double-jointed, and danced instead like upside down spiders with minds of their own. "These hands built this world and its rules and everything in it, and only these hands can tear it down and let you leave it. And I'll never do that. Never. Not until you're fixed for good. You have my word on that. That's the sacred oath I took so many years ago, and I intend to stick to my word. Doctors do that, you see. They don't ever lie. Not ever. Come here, little girl. Let me fix you."

"No," Isabella said. She didn't know what to do. She wasn't as smart or as old as her parents. All she could do was make stuff up as she went along. So she backed up against her own bed, her parents still sitting on either side of her, her mother still crying, her father still patting her on the back and whispering encouraging sayings that he'd stored away in his brain, telling her jokes to try to lighten her mood. At one point Mommy even laughed a little bit, just a little. Daddy told good jokes. He was always like that. Always silly and horsing around. Isabella remembered one joke he told her once. The joke went like this

Isabella crawled up onto the bed, over her own sleeping body. She pressed her back against the wall.

A man is sitting in a hospital waiting for his son to be born. The doctor walks into the lobby and says, "Sir, I've got some good news and some bad news." He holds out the man's newborn baby: a grotesque giant eyeball, with big pudgy feet, wrapped in a blue blanket. "This is the good news," the doctor says.

"*That's* the good news?" the man says. "What the heck is the *bad* news?"

The doctor shakes his head sadly and says: "The kid's blind."

The Eye Doctor moved toward her, the heels of his black leather shoes clicking against the shiny white floor. "Where are you going to run?" The Doctor asked. "Into your body? You can't. I evicted you from it. Into your parent's arms? You can't, because they can't even see you. What's left? The moon? Are you going to run to the moon, little girl? Even if you could do that, I would find you there. In this world, I own the moon and everything on it. The moon is just a giant white eyeball with my pupil in it, roving and watching and roving and watching all the sick little children on Earth and making sure that none of them get out of line. Including you. Most especially you. So, you see, you *must* stop running."

The Eye Doctor's hazel pupil was now only inches from the foot of the hospital bed.

"You're right," Isabella whispered, not moving a single muscle.

"Eh? What did you say?" The Eye Doctor stood up straight and craned his eye forward, as if to hear her better.

"There's nowhere left to run," she said with a small, soft voice. The voice of someone who's giving up all hope. No doubt, it was a sound The Doctor was used to hearing. A sound The Doctor lived to hear.

The Doctor seemed to grow ten inches taller as he preened. He rubbed his palms together, completely satisfied with this development. "I'm so glad you've come around and have decided to see things my way—which, of course, is really the *only* way. Despite what you might think, I much prefer my patients to relent to their treatments *willingly*. That's far more satisfying than forcing them to cooperate. The treatments are always much more effective when they're agreed to by the patients. Come, my dear child." The Doctor pulled up an orange vinyl swivel chair and sat down. "Come sit on my lap."

Isabella nodded. Her eyes fixed on the floor, she climbed down off the bed and walked toward him with her pouty face, the one that always worked so well with Daddy.

"Now, now, my child," said The Doctor, patting his lap. "No need to be sad. This is the beginning of a whole new life for you—a life devoid of sickness. Are you ready to accept the treatment you so richly deserve?"

Isabella nodded, being careful to say nothing. She mumbled something under her breath as she climbed up onto his lap.

"What was that, my child?" asked The Doctor.

She mumbled something again, and as she did so The Doctor didn't seem to notice her little hand removing the empty hypodermic syringe from his belt...

"Say it a little louder," said The Doctor as he leaned forward even further.

...the needle that she now plunged into the center of the hazel bullseye he called his pupil. The Doctor screamed, dropped the syringes from his fist, and shot to his feet. His hands reached for the needle, trying to pull the weapon out of his head. As he did so, Isabella bent down and grabbed the black needle marked OBEDIENCE. She climbed up onto the chair, which put her within arm's reach of the wound, and rammed the needle into The Doctor's bleeding head, right below the first gash. He shrieked in pain and pulled away, but not before she squirted the dark liquid into his head. Was there an actual brain inside there, or just the normal squishy parts you'd find in any old eye? Who knew? Who cared? All Isabella cared about was seeing The Doctor's massive eye go blank and misty. He stood there rigidly, patiently, like a soldier waiting for his commands. She reached up and pulled the needle out again with a slight ripping sound, not caring if she harmed The Doctor even further in the process. She watched as the needle refilled instantly with more black liquid.

Isabella snapped the fingers of her left hand, something Daddy had taught her to do. "You need to learn to listen more," Isabella said, repeating something Mommy often told her. "First you're going to take me back to my parents, and then you know what you're going to do?"

The Doctor said in a robotic tone, "I... am... listening."

"I want you... *to not be around anymore*. You got that? Just disappear and never come back."

"How... do... you... suggest... that... I... disappear...miss?"

Isabella shrugged, as if the answer was obvious. She shouldn't have to explain it. "Just do what you do. Use your hands. Dig into that head of yours with your *hands* and start pulling everything out. Just keep pulling and pulling and pulling until there's nothing left in there or until you can't think or move anymore. Understand?"

"I... understand."

"Good. Take me to my parents."

The Doctor reached into his belt and pulled out a shiny silver scalpel. He held the scalpel out before him and cut a thin line in space, as if he were performing surgery on the air itself. And in a way he was. What appeared in the air was very similar to the silver outline Isabella had seen wavering around The Doctor when he first appeared to her. Isabella knew it was like a tear in one's flesh, except that the flesh was invisible, and what lay on the other side was far more than just the messy insides of someone's body. What lay on the other side was a world radically different from the one in which The Doctor lived. Isabella was eager to return to her own home. She mimicked The Doctor's method of travelling between these worlds by sticking her left leg in, stepping through the air, and into limbo. As she felt herself being sucked through the wound, she glanced over her shoulder and saw The Doctor beginning to fulfill her final command. He was using the scalpel to perform invasive surgery on his *head*.

The last surgery The Doctor would ever perform.

6. After

After the journey through silver-tinged space, there was a moment of blackness. Then Isabella opened her eyes to find her parents staring down at her, smiling.

"Oh my God, Isabella, can you see us?" asked Mommy. "Can you *hear* us?"

"Are you all right?" asked Daddy.

Isabella blinked a few times to remove the residual traces of silver mist from her eyes.

"Yeah," she said. "I think so." She glanced down and saw that the two of them were now holding hands. "Are you two… is everything *okay* again?"

Mommy and Daddy glanced at each other, as if in shame.

"I can't lie to you," Mommy said as she began to cry. "I just can't fib and make it all better. I *can't*."

"What?" Isabella said. "No. I want you to be together. you *have* to be together. You're grownups. You can do whatever you want, whenever you want. everything can just go back to the way it was… if you want it to."

Daddy patted her on the back of her hand. "Please, honey, let's talk about this later. You're too weak—"

"I'm *strong*!" Isabella screamed. "*You* two are weak!"

Daddy said, "Honey—"

"You're both killing me! Can't you see that? Can't you *hear* me?"

They seemed to stare at her in shock, as if they didn't know what to say. It was like they were paralyzed.

Isabella realized that they really didn't know what they were doing. They were just making up stuff as they went along. They were confused and doing the best they could. Pretty much like her.

"I can hear you," Daddy said. "Believe me, the whole hospital can hear you. Now why don't *you* try listening for a bit, okay? No matter what happens, we'll always love you. Do... do you understand?"

"I guess so," Isabella said.

Her mother held her hand and told her everything was going to work out in the end.

"Believe me," Mommy said, "everything works out the way it's supposed to."

Isabella knew that probably wasn't true, but she also knew her mother meant well and so cut her some slack. These were her parents after all. Neither of them were perfect, but they were all she had. And they were worth listening to.

Most of the time.

"Sometimes grownups don't listen," Isabella whispered.

"I suppose that's true," Mommy said sadly.

"But sometimes they *do*," Isabella added, grinning, thinking about The Doctor removing the viscera from his own head.

Beneath the clean white sheets, in her hidden fist, she gripped The Eye Doctor's black hypodermic needle tightly. For the most part parents could be trusted to do the right thing, but at other times they just needed a little nudge in the proper direction.

Isabella hoped that accepting the many weaknesses of these flawed creatures, and coming to terms with the fact that from time to time a little parenting would have to be done *for* them, would allow her to live (more or less) happily ever after.

The End

APHANTASIA
ROBERT S. WILSON

Sharon tries not to look at the huge swelling mound on Robert's forehead as he lies there in the dark bedroom, trembling and moaning. "Here, sit up. This should help." He scoots into a sitting position, eyes scrunched shut as he swallows the pills.

"It hurts so fucking bad." Tears run from his eyes as he turns to lay back down, pulling the blanket up to his shoulder.

"Robert, I really think you should let me take you to the hospital."

"No." His response is a barking whine more than a word.

Twenty years on the force and a lifetime of strength training reminds her that she could pick him up and take him herself if she has to. But she doesn't want to *make* him go if she can avoid it.

"All right then, how about this? You still feel like this in the morning, I'm taking you to Regional North, okay?"

His tight flushed face nods as he pulls the blanket over his head.

Sharon knows when to take a cue, and slips quietly from the room. Whatever happened to his head — *No fucking way he woke up like that* — has him super-sensitive to light, sound, and touch. He wouldn't even let her kiss him when she got to his apartment. She fights the urge to grab his cell phone and search through his messages for an explanation. A tight fury coils in her belly when the thought of someone hurting Robert fully registers. Her hand grips the handle of her service revolver. *Keep your cool, Share.*

The last thing she needs is to do something stupid. She opens the fridge, stands there holding the door open. A moment in time flashes; she's walking into the station the first day after *coming out*. Everybody's watching her. A sea of stunned faces. A handful of the fuckers struggling to keep from lurching with disgust. She hates them. All of them. The moment passes. Five years ago feels like yesterday and yet it's like a lifetime came and went. She sighs. Closes the fridge. Her rage cools. But a slight noise registers from the bedroom. Like heavy breathing. *Not Robert's.*

Instinct sends her sprinting through the kitchen and down the hall. She shoves open the door and yellow light shines into the room. A large pale man stands over Robert's bed, looking down at him. The black pinstripe suit is neatly pressed upon his body and the fedora hiding the top of his face blends in with the remaining shadow.

"What the —"

Robert stirs, moans. The man in the suit looks in Sharon's direction but his face is still hidden. That's when she notices the knife in his hand. An ancient ceremonial blade, the gold hilt decorative and scripted. Her revolver goes up before she has a chance to think. As the man's head lifts fully into the light, his blood-red irises stare into hers, face a sneer of hatred. His mouth draws open and an ear-splitting trill reaches into Sharon's brain, stretches out every tendril of gray matter inside. Her eyes scrunch shut and her finger squeezes the trigger. In the split second between the gunshot and Sharon opening her eyes, there is a loud crash. No man, no blood. Nothing.

She rushes into the room, opening the door the rest of the way, and sees the window, a gaping mouth letting in the wind and the rain. No sound of footsteps. No black-speckled crimson eyes watching from the darkness. And Robert lies there sleeping through it all.

The next morning, Sharon checks on Robert. He lies in bed awake, staring up at the ceiling. A small crusted layer of yellow-purple slime glistens along the mound on his forehead. She glances at the dime-sized hole in the drywall where she fired her weapon the night before. If it weren't for the neighbor's loud ass bass-rumbling stereo, she would've been in deep shit. Even if there had been some kind of evidence to corroborate her story.

"What the fuck is going on, Rob?"

He blinks, finally stops staring at the hanging plaster long enough to look in her direction. He looks exhausted even though he's slept for nearly seventeen hours. "I told you, I woke up with the biggest fucking headache. Got up to get some Ibuprofen and saw my head in the mirror. Nobody jumped me, I swear, okay?" He seems more focused now.

"Nobody jumped you? So, motherfucker who showed up last night, probably tripped out on god-fucking-knows-what wearing devil-red fucking contacts about to *cut* you was just a figment of my imagination then?"

Robert sits up, eyes wide. "What?"

"Dude took a flying leap out your window before I could do anything more than fire a warning shot."

"Warning shot?!"

Sharon nods in the direction of the hole in the wall and Robert turns to look, rises slowly to his feet and plugs his finger into the opening, snuffing out the sunbeam that previously stretched into the room from it.

"Well?" Sharon says, nails scraping the door jam.

She waits, takes a deep breath. He turns, wipes off the stuff that had collected on his forehead. Flaps his hand to try and fling it away. Sharon's stomach turns. She grabs a towel she'd brought in the night before and hands it to him then takes a step back and looks away. She's seen bodies ripped asunder that looked better than that slop.

"I said, *well?*"

"I'm telling you the truth. You ever seen anything like this stuff?" He tries to hand her the towel back but she motions it away.

He has a point. "I've seen a lot of fucked up shit come out of bodies, but no, now that you mention it, I don't think I've seen anything quite like that."

He throws the towel into a trash can in the corner of the room. "My head doesn't hurt so much now. So maybe whatever this is will go away. But... what the fuck, Share? Why didn't you call the..."

"Police? Seriously?"

"I... Sorry. I just answered my own question. I just... some meth-head was in my place, in my room."

"Yup. Big dude, dressed to the nines. Mean-looking as fuck."

Robert's eyebrows scrunch together and he sits on the bed. If he's lying to her, he deserves a goddamn Emmy. And besides. He's not the most creative of human beings, having been afflicted with Aphantasia since the day he was born. Sharon tries to imagine what it would be like to never visualize anything in her mind's eye. To never be able to bring up the visage of her mother's thin pale face or the shuddering of a tree in mid October, its leaves hemorrhaging out from pale branches like dozens of outreached arms. She's reminded again that to imagine such a state destroys its reality in and of itself.

She walks over, brushes the hair from his forehead. The bulging thing there looks bigger now. Purple. But at least he doesn't cringe at her touch anymore. "All right, then. We're getting the fuck out of here. Yogi wasn't your average methhead. I don't know what he wanted, but I don't think we should stay here and find out."

The Walker Motel on the East side of town is a bottom-of-the-barrel shithole but it has style and a greasy kind of charm. A giant man-statue with a top hat on his head and a cane tapping at his heel holds the blue and red-bulbed sign like some life-sized Monopoly diorama. By the time they settle in, Robert is worn down and in severe pain again. Sharon turns out all the lights in the room as Robert curls up on the bed, covering himself with all the blankets.

The night is quiet as Sharon sits by the window, listening to some nearby neighbors ramble on about the giant sinkhole that devastated some remote hole-in-the-ground Tennessee town with a name like Beagles Hollow or Beetles Boro or something. From what Sharon gathered, the hole grew nearly a quarter of a mile in diameter and the locals went nutzoid in the interim of it all, blockading themselves inside the town. "Fucking crazies," she whispers.

Eventually, the dudebros next door go to bed and silence hangs like a fog throughout the motel's property save for the occasional rustling from Robert's bed accompanied by his short, soft groans. Sharon's head begins to droop, her chin gently meeting with her collarbone. A small trace of drool runs down from her mouth and a sense of nothingness fills her brain as she slips into a dreamless sleep. And just as colors begin to dance like sashaying ceremonial dresses within her mind's eye, a presence wrenches her from slumber.

The man in the pinstripe suit—the *same* goddamn suit—stands over Robert, staring down at him, knife gently tracing across Robert's face. The dim light from the motel parking lot casts an eerie glow on his muscular form. Half asleep, Sharon lunges over the bed, slams into Robert in the process, and grabs hold of the man's arm. Their eyes lock as they struggle for the blade.

Robert screams, backs up against the headboard. Even as Sharon fights to tear the knife away, she notices the mound has almost doubled in size, nearly taking up the entire middle of Robert's forehead.

Without warning, Pinstripe head-butts Sharon—knocking her off balance—and lunges for Robert who rolls off the bed in a twirling heap of blankets and hits his head on the wall, falling silent on the floor. The knife plunges into the ugly tan-finished headboard with a *thwack*. He tries frantically to pull it free but the knife won't give. Sharon finally manages to shake off the dizziness long enough to grab Robert like a sack of potatoes and, with a grunting heave, pull him into a fireman's carry, blankets and all and dashes for the door.

A solid blow reels into her back sending her forward and vacating the air from her lungs, but she doesn't stop, doesn't turn around. The momentum sends her closer to the door, but it's closed, locked. She turns, Robert hanging limp from her shoulders like an enormous towel, and the two of them are trapped.

The man stands there, a sneering grin stretching with his jawline. "Give me the eye and I will let you go." His thick accent—Hispanic maybe?—discords with the soft, almost pink paleness of his skin.

Sharon struggles to make sense of his words, notices the flushed bald skin atop his head where the fedora had been. There's a small dark quarter-sized hole there and she wonders if she's losing her mind.

The man moves closer. *"Give me the eye and I will let you live."*

Something in his voice is soothing, like some faraway waterfall, its gentle static landscape stretching out below for her to lie upon. Giving in seems like it would be effortless. The man hovers over her now, looks down into her eyes. That's a hole on top of his head, all right. She can see the flesh within the rim of it. Like it's *supposed* to be there. But now his eyes are gentle; a soft handsome blue.

A series of grunts and squeaks and a long throaty creak erupt from his mouth. Sharon backs against the door, hand feeling its way behind her until it comes to the deadbolt and she turns the latch without taking her eyes off of him. No longer enthralled by his voice, she puts on her best poker face. His grin doesn't falter.

A trilling high pitch tapers off into a series of clicks and pops from deep within his chest, covering the sound of her fingers blindly fidgeting with the door knob as she unlocks it.

Elbow turned almost beyond its limit, she slowly turns the knob until the door comes free. She spins, slamming the door into the man's face, and the vocal cacophony explodes into a screeching whistle. She sprints into the parking lot and stuffs Robert's unconscious body into the backseat of the black Crown Victoria. Plopping into the driver seat, she starts the car. The headlights cast a yellow figure-eight on the man as he walks toward them, clicking and grunting, his disheveled fedora back on his head. Sharon jerks the shifter into reverse and leans into the gas. The man and the motel room shrink away as the car spins with shrieks and roars and then charges onto the road.

The white lines on the highway strobe into one continuous blurry boundary between each second and the next as the Crown Vic trudges along I-70, rain beating down on the windshield faster than the wipers can clear it. Black clouds hang over a line of semi trucks stretching on as far as Sharon can see. She's been lucky if she can keep the red line at fifty for a good half-hour now. If that fucker is behind them, it's only a matter of time before he catches up.

Unsure where to go from the motel, she went straight for the freeway, pointed east, and hit the gas. Left Indy behind. Now they're somewhere between Cloverdale and Terre Haute and she couldn't give one dirty fuck exactly where so long as that motherfucker isn't anywhere near Robert.

She reaches back to check his pulse every few minutes, unable to stop worrying that he suffered some kind of concussion when his head smacked against that wall. It's been an hour now and he still hasn't woken.

"Robby? *Rob?* You're fucking worrying me here."

No response, and it's too dark to see in the mirror if he stirred. She sucks in a deep breath, reminds herself that whatever's going on with his head has him in a lot of pain and extremely weak. This doesn't make her feel any better. Worse actually. Because now she has a whole other thing she forgot to worry about bouncing around in her skull.

She wonders if maybe it's safe now to take an exit and find a place to hide. But she can't get it out of her head that the man had found them at the Walker. She doesn't even know how he managed to get inside the room without waking her.

She hesitates for just a second when she comes to the exit and then whips over into the turn lane then onto the ramp. *Fuck it. Gonna have to stop somewhere sooner or later.* She keeps a watch on the mirror as she rolls past the yield sign and picks up speed.

She checks the mirror again out of reflex. No other cars. She tries to chase away the image of the man in the pinstripe suit walking casually up to the back of the car, red eyes lighting that hateful grin under his black fedora. *Get a grip, Share.* Houses swing by in tandem, cookie cutter white two-story jobs, big porches draped by thick round pillars, lights out in every home. She's somewhere outside the shitty little town of Brazil if she's guessing correctly. Two-lane road, yellow-dotted lines, bland trees everywhere. And not a soul out but them as far as she can tell. *Great. At least maybe there's a chance I'll see him coming.*

A yellow glowing haze approaches ahead, the lights of the town one big stretching entity waiting to swallow them into itself. One last arrival into the end of everything. One by one, street lamps pop up overhead and up a mile or so, a gas station sign blinks on and off like somebody forgot to change a bulb or something. It's as good a place as any to stop and get her bearings, grab something to eat and drink. It's not like she had time to raid the fridge on the way out the door. And hunger growls in her stomach at just the passing thought of a crappy gas station hot dog.

She eases into the small lot of the Sunoco and parks her car under the metal umbrella of the gas pumps. Once she's killed the engine and taken her keys from the ignition, she's struck by the realization that going in means abandoning Robert to the backseat alone and unable to defend himself. But they need gas to stay on the road. So, she gets out, leans against the car, starts pumping and tries not to jump at every tiny noise she hears amid the dull throbbing drone of faraway traffic.

Movement up the road catches her eye. Two men—almost dots from this distance—come walking along the sidewalk. They move fast, nearly jogging in her direction. Probably nothing to worry about, just twenty-something kids out for a late night pack of Camels or something. But she turns, looks the other way and three more men jog toward her.

They each wear hats. One plain red ball cap, one brimmed straw hat, and a black Under Armour cap turned backward and just slightly to one side. And they're looking at her. She scrambles to twist the gas cap back on the car and put away the fuel pump, fucking up both at least two times before she can fumble open the car door. As she gets in, the other two men start running. One of them wears a pinstripe suit.

She turns the key and the car revs to life. And as her hand grips the gearshift, something crashes hard into the back of the vehicle and the Crown Vic jiggles forward and back. In the rearview, the three men climb onto the back of the car and one of them lifts a crowbar. She slams into reverse and taps the gas but the man doesn't lose his balance, doesn't even wobble as she swerves backward toward the street.

She stops the car and his hat flies off. The uncovered head reveals a neat, round hole as he leans forward and raises both arms.

He brings down the crowbar swift and strong. The crash from the back window is thick and dull. The glass dents inward above Robert, who lies there, none the ware of anything. Sharon faces forward to drive but the man in the pinstripe suit and another guy in a gray hood pulled over his head are crawling up the hood toward the windshield. Eyes blazing scarlet.

Sharon punches her foot down on the gas and the two men grab onto the edge of the hood, pink-white knuckles clenching to hold on for dear life. The car shoots backwards as Sharon turns into the cross road. She slams on the brakes and the three assholes on the back of the car go flying. Robert groans, the relieving sound of it conflicting with the flood of adrenaline in Sharon's system. But Pinstripe and Gray Hood are on their feet now, shoes loudly denting in the hood. Pinstripe reaches down, grabs on to the driver side mirror.

Sharon shifts into drive, her hand moving like slow motion, and the car springs forward sending Pinstripe swinging around the side of the car, but he doesn't fall. Instead his fist crashes in through the window and latches onto Sharon's throat. Oxygen takes its leave and Sharon croaks and wheezes. The Crown Vic barrels forward and the creature clutching her throat seems to float alongside the car, grasping desperately on to the mirror which now starts bending downward.

Spots form in Sharon's vision and she wonders why Robert still hasn't gotten up to try and help her. With a sharp crack the mirror snaps off and Pinstripe goes tumbling away from the car, pulling Sharon by the throat and slamming her head into the window frame. And then his hand rips away from her with a searing, ripping pain. Both hands free of the steering wheel, the car veers right and crashes into something unseen. The airbag explodes open and swallows her into darkness.

The crash of shattering glass and Robert's blood-curdling scream pry Sharon from the void. Wedged against her seat by the airbag and her seatbelt, she scrambles to unlatch herself. She glances in the rearview mirror but doesn't see Robert. "Rob, you okay?"

An oozing chorus of clicks and grunts and squeaks surrounds the car, echoing off of dirt-encrusted once-white houses littering both sides of the road. Broken glass clinks and rattles from the back seat driver-side window and the vehicle jars violently side to side. An inhuman voice creeps in through the car. The man in the pinstripe suit is reaching into the car and trying to get to Robert.

She can't bend her right hand to release the seat belt so Sharon continues to squish her left hand toward it beneath the pressing fabric of the airbag. Robert's screams punctuate the struggle from the backseat.

"Rob, are you okay?"

Robert screams again.

"Rob, answer me. Are you fucking okay?"

Still nothing but streaking movement against interior leather and the rattling of glass and steel and plastic. A long string of vocal clicks jitter in a rising rhythm like the locking of teeth in some massive closing zipper of flesh. Sharon squirms and struggles to reach the latch.

There's a sudden crinkle of breaking glass and several glints of light bounce off of small jagged pieces as they skitter inward from the passenger side window. Robert grunts, low and deep Sharon is gripped with a certainty that his life is about to end as her hand finally touches the cold steel of the seat belt latch. She unlatches it and squeezes her way toward the middle of the seat and reaches her arms toward Robert's flailing body. The man in the gray hoodie, his hood now ruffled up behind his bare bald head, pink and adorned with that same single hole in the middle of his crown.

Robert's eyes are squeezed shut and the mound upon his head has grown, the swollen stretching flesh there covered in purple goo. Something rips at the rough scabbed wound, splitting it along a central, horizontal line. Sharon's stomach turns from both disgust and fear as she struggles to free herself from the weight of the airbag. Her right leg loosens and scoots over enough to wrest one of Gray Hood's hands from around Robert's neck. Robert pulls free and lunges forward but not quick enough to escape the diving blade from behind him. The gold-handled dagger puncture his shoulder, its jagged steel blade lodging beneath his collar. Robert screams and Gray Hood's hand slips from the handle of the knife as Robert scoots away, but the other man has managed to squeeze in through the driver side window, arms first. Sharon twists, pulling her ankle in a sharp painful turn and takes a swing at Pinstripe but she misses his face by about an inch.

Pinstripe's hands clamp down on Robert's knees and tug desperately at his body. Robert's eyes never open and the blade in his shoulder protrudes there like some new alien body part stretching out from the front and back of his shoulder. Sharon screams, trying to block out the jagged pain in her ankle as she breaks loose completely then lunges over the seat and slams her shoulder into Pinstrip's reaching arms.

He lets go of Robert and grabs hold of her. She sends her elbow into his face and her head into his chest. Robert feels around with his hands like he's trying to find his way out of the backseat and still never opens his eyes. The man in the gray hoodie jumps forward and reaches into the car, sending stray hanging bits of shattered glass into his face and arms as he grabs hold of

Robert. Sharon remembers her service revolver then and reaches for it but it's still on the other side of the seat.

She thrashes her head at the man as he pulls her toward a large shard of glass reaching up from the broken window. Her head makes contact with his and he emits an inhuman screech and falls back from the window. Sharon dives over the seat and awkwardly manages to free her gun from its holster and points it directly at gray hood's face. His grin falters and he quickly pulls Robert in front of him, ruffling the blade still sticking in Robert's body and causing him to cry out.

Blood soaks Robert's shirt in a big round circle growing out from the wound. A switch flips in Sharon's head and she brings the butt of the revolver down on the man's hand and both him and Robert let out a deep loud bellow as the man's hands loosen and Robert pulls away. Without hesitation, Sharon fires a bullet into the gray man's throat sending him away from the car and reaching for his neck, blood bubbling up from behind his hands.

A loud high-pitched screech erupts from each of the creatures and the piercing tension of it creates a brutal brain-splitting dissonance in her head. She grabs Robert around his chest, careful to avoid the blade stuck in his shoulder, and scoots him toward the passenger door.

They burst from the car to find gray hood writhing on the sidewalk. The others hang back in a half moon circling around the back of the car. Robert just stands there, pale, limp and moaning, eyes shut. He's lost an awful lot of blood. Sharon looks at the obstacle of *things* surrounding them and raises her gun. Each pair of red glowing eyes glares from below scrunched up brows but they neither flee nor approach. She's got five shots left and four stationary targets. "We're leaving now and you're not going to follow us, do you hear me?"

The man in the pinstripe suit—its fabric torn and bloodied—smiles and shakes his head. She was hoping one of them bleeding out on the ground would give her a little bit of leverage. Without warning, she shoots one of the other four men in the face. Each of the others, including pinstripe, flinch but their eyes don't waver as the man with the hole where his right eye and cheekbone used to be falls down onto a bloody broken face and lies still.

Sharon raises her pistol up to the sky. "Who's next?"

Pinstripe isn't smiling anymore. He nods at the other two and all three men begin to back away and in a single blink they flee in pink streaks of alien motion. The gurgling sound from the man on the pavement finally stops and Sharon and Robert stand there in silence.

😀😵😈

Sharon sits in the waiting room, repeating the night's events to the local redneck Sheriff for the third time without mentioning the flesh holes atop each man's head and, like each time before, he grunts and nods and raises an eyebrow skeptically. There's a hint of revulsion in his every expression as he looks her body up and down like she's some creature unfit to exist. And she knows exactly why.

It's not the first time and it won't be the last. The timbre of her voice, the build of her body. These things don't conform to the structure of society's expectations and it unsettles those who confine themselves to a tiny pristine *utopia* where men and women stand divided by some solid unseen border in which anything that dares to encroach becomes ugly and unclean. An abomination. A thing that should not be.

The old huge dizzy hurt wraps itself around her. It means to smother, but she long ago learned to keep it at bay until it shrinks down to the ground. To stamp her foot down and crush the little nothing it becomes. When her statement is fully transcribed and the Sheriff finally leaves, she waits there uneasy. The nurses wouldn't let her into Robert's room but from time to time one of them slips in to give her an update on his progress. He's stable, the bleeding has stopped but there's likely some permanent muscle damage.

After asking a flurry of questions about his head, the doctor decides to give him an MRI. He simply refuses to elaborate on what he thinks is going on. So with nothing else to do, Sharon sits and waits for Robert's scan. The TV drones on in the background as she stares at the wall. She can't stop the throbbing panic within her. She gets up and peeks out the long curtained window. The town below is dimly lit and hollow in a way only the twilight morning hours in a small shitty town can be. There's an almost fuzzy glow of warmth contrasted by a cold inhuman emptiness there.

She lets the curtain fall back in to place and sits down.

😀😵😈

Sharon wakes to the sound of a female voice. She looks up from dreary crusty eyes and a nurse she hasn't seen before crouches down in front of her, sunlight draping the gaunt features of her face. "Ma'am, Doctor Hudson says you can see Mr. Davis now." Sharon nods, and follows as the nurse leads her down a hallway and into a small room. Robert lies there, eyes closed and forehead bandaged.

"Did they do the MRI?"

The nurse looks over his chart. "Yes, there seems to be some kind of growth in Robert's head." She bites her lip as she reads. "He'll be going in for surgery this afternoon. Doctor Davis wants to do a biopsy."

Sharon sits down in a chair backed against the wall. "Is it cancer?"

"Honey, I can't say. We won't know until the doctor can take a look *inside*."

Sharon nods, watches Robert gently sleeping.

The time comes for Robert's biopsy and several nurses and an anesthesiologist come to prep him. Sharon's sent from the room, protest weighing on her tongue and in her heart. She doesn't want to complicate such a delicate procedure. She tries not to let the question at the root of all this crumble her. She swallows her fear and the hurt of worry down.

Walking the hall quickly becomes a demonstration in redundancy and Sharon finds her way into the cafeteria on the first floor. Only the generic after-hours options remain, the hot food line long since closed. She's not hungry anyway, she only wants to fill the empty space between now and the end of Robert's surgery. She gets herself a cup of coffee and walks over to a booth along the outer wall. Sits there letting the steam rise from her cup. It fills her face with moisture and the aroma of cheap shitty coffee. She glances out the window for a moment and when she sees them, she drops the coffee and it splashes hot against her hand but she doesn't so much as flinch.

Outside in the parking lot, walking casually toward the hospital, the man in the pinstripe suit and several dozen other men in hats of all shapes, colors, and sizes make their way toward the main entrance of the hospital. If they can see her, they show no sign of it, and Sharon takes the opportunity to slip away from the windows and make for the elevator.

When the electric double doors open behind her, she takes one quick glance back and locks eyes with the man in the suit and there's no mistaking that he sees her. The thought of those slow elevator doors trapping her inside, unwilling to close in time to protect her sends her heading for the stairs. The clutter of dozens of footsteps scrambling behind her quickens her pace as she nears the stairwell entrance. It slows her down to have to stop and open the door, but as soon as she's inside, she runs up the stairs toward the fourth floor. Shoes tapping on concrete from below begin to echo together into a growing reverberated frenzy of noise as Sharon passes the door for the second floor.

The clicks and grunts of her pursuers begin to intermingle with the dull cloudy thudding of their footsteps and the heavy humid air, giving the stairwell a dreamy atmosphere like some stuffy aquarium nightmare. The echoes close around her as Sharon passes the third level entryway. She can feel the heat from the creatures behind her coming closer.

A hand grabs Sharon's ankle as she plants her other foot on the floor. She kicks at her attacker, but his grip is tight. She loses her balance for just a second but it's all they need to overtake her. She turns and falls on her back and they're scrambling over her. Tens of men, eyes as fire, an awkward variety of hats on their heads and clothes on their bodies rushing through the fourth level door, Sharon all but forgotten. She struggles to make it through the doorway amid the crowd that nearly crushes her in the process.

She struggles to keep up as they flood into the large open hallway, the sound of far off screams and gurgles barely registering in the distance. Some surgery gone wrong, some patient overdue on their pain meds, but it's more than just one voice and the sound, even as faint and distant as it is, chills Sharon to the bone. And still the dolphin men run as one like they know exactly where to find their prize.

She runs with everything she has to try and get ahead, but they push and grunt and trill and it's all she can do to keep from being trampled. The distant screams taper off as they turn a corner. The doors marked "Operating Room" stand before them, watching, waiting, inviting the men to enter and retrieve the bounty they have sought.

Sharon dives into a glob of them toward the front and a domino effect sends some of them rolling into others until only the man in the pinstripe suit remains ahead of her. She slips back into a run before she can lose her balance and struggles to go faster. Within reach now, she grabs hold of the man's shoulder and pulls, slowing him as he's about to reach the door. He turns and sends a fist toward her stomach but she shifts, grabs his arm and sends him hurdling into the rest of the men.

She rushes through the doors.

Inside the operating theater, a rising panic fills Sharon's every pore as she slips on thick fluid and tattered blue and white uniforms and random cosmetic accessories. The place is dark save for the dim glow of a broken flashing computer screen sitting on top of a white, wheeled cart. She scrambles around the room for every piece of furniture she can find and begins to barricade the doors.

The room is void of people save for herself and Robert who lies on the hospital bed, a ruffled bloody gown wrapped around his forehead. His eyes remain closed as his head jerks blindly to and fro. *Sharon, is that you? I'm so afraid.* Staring at the amber-lit blanket of pale gel that covers the floor, it takes her a moment to realize that the voice she hears is not emitting from his mouth. A scream catches in the back of her throat at the carnage she's currently stepping in everywhere she sets her feet. She wants to ask what happened but the things outside are quickly shifting the furniture blocking the doors.

It's all right, Sharon. Everything will be just fine. Let them come. I have something to show them. Something they've wanted to see for so very long. But you mustn't look, Sharon. When the doors give way and they come inside, you must go. You cannot see what I have saved for them.

Sharon is speechless. She wants to scream for Robert to come with her. To get away from this place before they can hurt him. But somehow she knows the men behind the door are no longer what she's afraid of. No longer what she *should* be afraid of. But even though, she cannot bear the thought of leaving. Cannot imagine running away. She must be sure that he'll be safe.

The carts and chairs and footstools blocking the door shimmy forward as the doors break through the barricade, and twenty bald men with holes atop their heads stand just inside the door, eyes narrowed and watching. Robert sits up in his bed and begins to unravel the thin blue gown from around his head. *If you won't go then please, Sharon, turn away so you cannot see. Turn away!*

Sharon does as Robert says as the nurse's gown splashes in goo by her feet, the sound of it setting off a chain of events of unfathomable horror. The men staring in Robert's direction begin to glisten, each of their bodies seeming to melt and transform. Their heads shrink down into their torsos and their legs curve out behind them as their noses stretch and their bodies elongate and flop to the floor in a pile of greasy pink dolphin bodies folding and flapping against the linoleum. The sounds of their screams are like whistles at the highest sonic frequency, shrieking into Sharon's brain and ripping every nerve asunder.

The slick rubbery skin of their bodies begins to soften and then runs and slides and pools until the soft pale gel covering the floor swirls with pink and white and gray and nothing but the thick viscous liquid remains. The scream clawing from Sharon's lungs is a jagged broken chord of thorny rigid tendrils wrapping together in putrid harmony. Robert's attempts to comfort her inside her head only further unhinge her sanity at the thing in which she sees.

And now the need to see compels her. Beyond any previous desire. She waits for her sobs and screams to falter and when she's left there quiet and shaking, the outpour contained for now, she closes her eyes and turns herself around. She had expected Robert's voice to fill with warning, to show some sign of fear at the inevitability of what she has chosen. But instead, when he speaks, his voice is calm, soothing. Pleased even.

When you open your eyes all will be laid bare before you and you will see as I see now. Every atom, every quark, every galaxy and hidden shadow will be exposed including the most terrifying truths within. I love you, Sharon. I always have.

Tears streaming down her face, fists clenched together in red trembling balls, Sharon opens her eyes.

And *sees*.

Upon Robert's forehead, the flesh has fully opened along that horizontal line and the thing within has broken through. Rolling and gleaming and sliding from side to side, the eye stretches from one side of his head to the other. The pupil is black as onyx surrounded by a dull gray iris the color of bloated flesh. The white of the eye is more yellow and purple hued than pale and the veins that branch and encircle it are black and pulsating. In the reflection of that pupil, Sharon sees it all. The Universe, the world, and all the things that lurk just behind the mundane veil of reality.

And beyond it all, one devastatingly beautiful vision engulfs everything.

In that eye she sees herself, her true self, unbridled and unchained.

For one glimmer of a second before the end, the woman staring back at her —not the complex carbon body of her exterior, but the intangible essence within—is who she's always truly been regardless of how the world masked and distorted the light bending off of her for everyone to see.

And then everything around her begins to wax and run and slip away forever.

IN THE ROOM OF RED NIGHT
FARAH ROSE SMITH

Bodies. Delicate, with a dying breath, caught in the stillness of the world.

Bodies. Bloodless and betrayed. Art as death, death as desire under the northern flame.

Bodies. Lovers entangled by bones. The womb of the mother—infected, dribbling. A gentle sway without reason other than to welcome us through --our procession.

There were too many good days before this—and now, there is a price to pay for them, in the room of red night.

☻☻☻

We come over the dune like cattle—a long dried-out species in these plains. Forms are muddled in the fog, appearing as bundles of blackness beneath tattered passage coats. Fur drapes over the body entire, most notably at the crown of the head. Long scarves of black mesh cover our mouths to keep the bitter sting at bay. One would not look upon a sky so red and think of winter. In this way, our souls hold some seed of exception in the universe.

Colton, on the leash, is like the Hyena. Dragged in his derangement alongside us because he cannot bear the chamber that calls him back. Dalton, the bear among men, taking the front. Busiris and Bostro, the brutes, and the quiet woman Gelia, walking ten paces to the left, without speech. All here have had an excess of good days.

We set out broken on the path of death and dust – human life. Here we wait and wade. Wait and wade. Into oblivion. Into the accursed hue. The birds are lost. The memory of them is vague, like the madness I imagine waits for me. I've lost my love for this scarlet world.

Swinging on frail threads, floating over us. One thousand bodies, perhaps two. Skin that would be green is white, soaked with the water we know as sacred. It keeps them. It calls us to them from the farthest reaches of the dunes.

I look to one man, the closest hanging above me. Dried vomit clings to his extremities. Castrated, colorless-- two gaping voids where once his eyes were.

The bodies drip white paint. Busiris has taken to a woman's corpse, with child. A mass of larvae erupts from her pregnant stomach with one faint poke to the skin.

Dalton spits into his palm and rubs the phlegm on the soles of the Eromaeon's feet. We know this blessing.

"Once tormented, life is distilled to an abbreviated grievance."

"Is there not some way around this, some detour?" I ask. Dalton looks to me with rage and I fall silent. I would not annoy him for the least of conveniences. Even this, they would remember from on high.

"The sky is as red as the old years," they say. "The Meiser can sense everything!"

Great mountains bleed into the valley below. The skies turn to blood. Red rivers bleed out to a forgotten sea. No one has ever seen it, but they say it washes clean the wounds of men.

Might the Meiser be flesh and blood? Or a gnome of rancor, built for no human eye? A rumor rode from other villages, far from Hule, that a horrid thing fell from the sky and spoke to them without sound, and then disappeared into the sand. At times of aggravation, it becomes a giant, pulling itself out of the den of the swarm with great gaunt hands. Up from the sand, into the sky…

And the swarm! To pursue the memory is to pursue that familiar delirium of a forgotten world. Savage beasts that would not hide their wings, living as men until the moon shattered. With one long parting look to logic in a secreted haze, the villages fell to them. Their nest, a subterranean slime pit, hides far beneath us. There they wait. There they writhe.

Meteors scar the night sky, bleeding clouds of fire behind them. A broken moon quivers behind the fury. Scattered rocks, as omens, pull closer from the point of birth to our world. A tarnished globe, plummeting under the black protean gloom. Space- and all kings it cradles in our senses. Lungs, tongues, trash, and terror. All things familiar in this monstrous array. There is no juice so bitter as that of the dying body. The resurgence, thick with bleakness of the brine.

Thoughts drift to a dream of flowers, enchanted winds, words spoken, only to be heard in the strangest of places. The imagination haunts, as it perhaps should, after deep study and hours of bereavement. I require a degree of rest.

A sound; faint whistling from the strange mist, gathering ever-thicker around my bloody collar bones. Without internal motion, save for the dribbling of bodily muck into the green abyss, I hang, suspended over the mythic eternal--indefinable nothingness. This is my condition, within a dream.

I think the end must be coming. I've lifted the shards of myself in search of the way out. Curse this place of enchanted despair, and the years of measured days! God is gone, and I am on the road again. We march on.

😀😵😜

The structure speaks to the otherness below. One could count thousands of the strange, crooked boxes that form the basis of its structure. It is enormous – a damaged pupil in a bleeding eye. The building of the deepest hue—black designed to absorb all light, in rigid blocks piled askew. No windows, and no doors, save for the secret entrance beneath the piled stones.

The mountains encroach, painting jagged horizons of black against burnished skies. Thoughts of hellfire plague every step. Red fog rolls in from the valley, blurring every man from knee to toe.

The vaulted halls, splendid in ornament, wretched in deceit. It has the look of an earnest pleasure garden – or the entry parlor of one. I would remember, as I frequented them in youth, if only for gentle observation. A purveyor of life, married to avoidance, sipping the pleasures of the body through the mind alone. I could only betray myself as lightly as this, after the coming of the swarm. She. She. She.

Margaerta, deep in the mud.

Her copper hair soaked in blood. The girl of no earth. Her face mutilated by the passing tendrils of the swarm. Her heart ripped from her chest, for what? I dare not imagine. Corpses strewn about the village shared this dismal fate. An open chest, freed of the heart.

I know of eternal despair. Of mourning. How it teases the mind. Can man cradle madness in memory alone? I grow weary of false men in quiet places. Even myself. There is too much time to think in these conditions.

Gelia's long fingers reach up to untie the sheath from her mouth. Scores of red dust fall from the black fabric as she lowers it from her face. I will avert my eyes before she sees me so unnerved. I fear the strength in her would take it as insult. And why shouldn't she? She crossed the land with as much fervor as any. And she did so, having been here before.

She has the look of the girl of no earth—there, in the enormous grey eyes. But none of this would matter, if not for memory of Margaerta. I lurch, and she raises her brow. Everything around us is madness. Two bodies wonder why they are separate and anguish over time. I imagine her-- the spirit, returned to me, and feign a cosmic kiss to the air. I seal myself a river in this kiss. Without faith or feeling. Only the tenderness of a hurting heart as the others pass through the door and into the depths of the accursed underground.

We descend into the bitter depths with little light, save for the glow of lichen looming overhead. Black rock intermingling with organic tubes. The farther down we travel, the more it breathes, this horrid place. There is no sign of life yet. At the point of exhaustion, hissing rolls into the atmosphere. Fetid mist brings on deep delirium. We are on our knees. On our knees…

A long wooden table, stained black, is large enough to seat hundreds. Our eyes, caked in phlegm, struggle to open. We are tied into strange, mangled chairs.

"Our villages send their candidates in the off-season," Dalton says, seeing me look around for other unfortunates. "To be sure we receive the fullest attention."

Gelia takes the seat across from me. Our eyes meet in a singular daze. I pull away. She continues to stare before our eyes turn to the cloaked servers lurching into the hall. Colt lets out a whimper at the sight of the silver plates.

Gelia whispers something unintelligible, leaning close to me across the table. She leans back again.

"Enough of your ancient drivel!" Dalton bangs his fist on the table. The men are nervous. The servers stand to the right as they place their hands over the plate covers, ready to reveal our dinner.

I wonder now what the chamber will do to him. I wonder what it has in store for me. They say that when you leave (if you do), the only memory you have is of those horrible hours.

The covers lift. On each plate sits a mass of charred meat – pure black, powdered in ash—we are expected to eat.

"He will pull the pink," Gelia says to me.

Busiris and Bostro have already made way with the cutting of the hocks. The smell is peutrid. I look up from my plate to see Gelia laughing.

"Is this the first of their torture?"

"Overcooked dinner? My, have you seen so little of pain?"

I look away again, not bothering to answer. I have seen pains to rival the room of red night. There is no doubt of it. But I have bore them in such a way as to live. This she will not understand, and so it is perhaps best that we meet in such a way. We would not find ourselves at ease outside these walls.

She chews with expectation. Her fingers reach to the back of her throat. The sound is slimy – the mechanical wetness of experience. She pulls. The lanterns bearing down on us illuminate a single strand of white. A hair, dangling between her fingers. She watches it with knowing eyes.

"What?" I ask. She motions to my plate. I look down on the black hock of meat. Fingers jammed down throats proceed with pulling. From the depths, strands of every kind emerge. Black, gray, purple, green…

He will pull the pink.

And I do. From the soreness of my throat, I pull a long, pink strand-- a color that makes no sense to my eyes. Glistening, garish. My stomach turns. The servers come around to gather the remnants of the meal. I give them the plate and goblet, satiated by disgust.

"You would not drink? Gelia adds, downing the brown liquid. A loathsome concoction of desert herbs, no doubt.

"I would not drink their hell juice, no."

"Then there will be a price to pay for it."

"What price is any worse than what will already become of me?" I ask, the weight of fatigue pulling me down into a half-slump.

"The juice was a numbing agent. Given with mercy."

I swallow hard.

💀💀💀

We are escorted to sleeping chambers for one night of rest. My limbs grow weak in this labyrinth of gloom. One might dream of random things, and find some undercurrent of truth; a strain of allegory in an otherwise ceaseless cacophony of mental anguish.

Must the devil get into my head tonight? Where blood is equal currency with thought? From the depths of the mountain. Like the harvested swarm, learning best to be men. Murky sea, milky sea, the multitude calls, and I am deeper--still in the ache of dreams…

It begins with the plummeting of my body through a damp tunnel, down from some impossible door. A void of black rock—the path growing smaller with each step. I've curled from full height to a guided crouch, unnerved by the noiseless path ahead. I trip and smash my face on a hard slate. The end of the passageway. Searching hands fall only upon skeletons—others lost in the attempt to flee, perhaps downed by their wounds from above.

At the point of giving up, I move aside the mortal remains and find a hole in the wall big enough for me to crawl through. Burrowing down into the rock, I feel less of a worm than above. There is something of a peaceful honor to dying in one's own way, rather than by hands held against the world.

A sliver of light illuminates my filthy arms, reaching out to the next swath of black rock. The narrow path has turned upward. There is a question of remaining strength in my upper body—if there is any left, or if I am destined to die with the light on my arms only. I pull and pull. Up up up to the light. It is a light I have not seen. Not scarlet, or red in any way—but a gentle yellow.

As I pull myself out, leaving the burrow of the mountain, I find myself in a cave. A gentle sound stirs outside. Limping forward, blood continues to seep from my gut, caked in the black dirt of the mountain depths.

With my hand on my stomach, I walk to the edge and see what very few have ever seen in this world. A vast ocean of milk white, as far as my eyes will take me. If I were to have wings to soar over the distance, I believe that I would find nothing but these waters from here to the ever after.

I look down and note that the water is shallow. No deeper than two meters, perhaps. The gentle ebb shifts in stages, revealing the ocean floor—populated by what may be millions of shards of pearlescent glass.

There is no land, or so says my wandering eyes. With the sea floor being so shallow, I could walk to some forgotten distance. As I think this, numbness cascades through my insides. Blood continues to ooze. I know in this moment that there is little chance of life for me beyond this precipice.

As my flesh commits to the surface, I am not within myself. I feel, rather, that I have become a wondrous multitude. My body breaks into ten thousand pieces. I have no eyes of flesh to look upon the wall, though I can still see. In these depths, the art of my existence will not cease. Frightened awake by the rocks above, echoes and delusions possessed my mind. I am now one of fractured millions, and the haunt of missing limbs is far from my mind.

I promise my pieces magic in these depths. I promise to succeed in the fullness of my flesh over the waves. To think that time might wait for me to reassemble – to emerge again from waters without birth – sets the roots of deeper vision in my hardened gut than any earthly thing. I will watch the mountainside from this place, in wait for those who seek this painless rest. To this liquid life, I now surrender. I can hear her there.

He will pull the pink.

🎭💀🎭

I choose not to shame my companions by looking at them now, but I know what I would see. Dalton's ocular veil, dissolved. A quiet apprehension in both Busiris and Bostro, seen only in their sloped shoulders and downcast eyes. Colton sipping up the remnants of his drool, the last of his twitches slowing to a mild turn of the head. Gelia is another matter. She stands in honor before the door, with more scars and haunts than the best of men.

My worry is not of life after death. I have come to a silent worship of an undying light; an everlasting current of energy connecting all life. This is all I can commit myself to as it comes to belief in my earthly incarnation. But my concerns do not lie with it. Rather, they lie with the fate of the universe itself.

Are spirit worlds bound together by some cosmic strain, or are they planet-bound, doomed to the inevitable annihilation that will devour their worlds entire? It is during these gloomy wanderings of the mind that the organic door, caked in rust, creaks open.

🎭💀🎭

I am surrounded by enormity—a decadent fracture in the subterranean hall. A cavern fit for giants. The ceiling is so high that it is drowned in shadow. The walls are sinking in, bordered by sculptured beasts with horns over every orifice, bulging in obscenity. Deep, deep red consumes my mind. Even my ill-clotting blood. Winding, velvet carpets beneath breaking toes. The ceiling tilts overhead--paned glass set into stone. Everything is peculiar. Every dressing, every chair, every surface wails with the infernal blessing of the Meiser. Every reliquary bursting with the dormant pride of slain giants. This decadent décor, we have all seen it in the forbidden books. Couches with carved ornament on gilded handles, curved desks with marble tops of black and blood, chairs of the finest fibers from the last slaughter of beasts. A bed, even. Fit for the erotic horrors of a star-fallen Emperor who would revel in this mud. Red sheets showering down-- shimmering black rods. The rot of ages covered with the glistening fall of eyes on embers. These are the things that come with first glances. Second glances reveal the anguish of our predicament.

Horrid metal—twisting, turning, gutting instruments. Ropes. Bottles of strange liquid. What looks like a strange, ambling device in the far corner. So many things that I have not the time to examine them before the turn of fortune. The door is closing behind us.

I see her, set into the wall. As though she herself were part of the ornament, carved into the rocks. A crown of death hovers over her. A pile of skulls, as a monument, breathing in and out of the visible plane, a heated mess of gutted flesh dribbling over. One single eyelid admits the burden. It shuts halfway. The other is wide. A drip of ghoulish blood berates her. Perfumed with the syrup of dead angels. Deep pink hair twists upward, intermingling with auburn wire atop her head. Her eyes are quite large for her triangular face. Red robes of rare cloth flow down to the floor. The deep v-neck of the garment leaves much of her cleavage and stomach exposed. The most horrid feature of all is her inhumanly long neck- green and luminous in a sea of glowing shards, cascading down between her breasts. Sharp teeth, long fingers. A cast of gold to the swamp-like skin, the marriage of beauty and horror. A dark doll, fit with a position beyond her capacity to reconcile. I can see myself forgiving her abuse of me in one of my delicate dreams, but that is before I have stepped myself entirely within the chamber. I am in shock, knowing death is coming.

With a greater swiftness than that of our approach, we are whisked to the center of the cavern by the beasts of the swarm. Our tormentors remove their sheaths to the sound of the screeching door—their long, humanoid locks fall down over bodies cloaked in shadow. The faint glow of mutant lichen reveals them to be extraordinarily deformed. Man or insect, one could never discern.

The woman from the wall descends. On the approach, I come to realize her enormity. Gelia throws me a fearsome look, as if to say *don't speak*. This is where the terror begins.

The giant slides her fingers along her scalp, lifting the crown of her head off to reveal a gaping emptiness-- her skull. Insect limbs reach and pull the pulsing, grey masses from the ceiling of the cavern. They appear to be hearts. Each is held close to the enormous stalactite in the center of the chamber. Warming them. Warming them….

The swarm bows to the woman from the wall, handing her the organs. She lifts the squirming masses one by one and places them in the bloody depression, closing her head again and sealing the shaft with her pink saliva. We have no time to think after this moment. It has begun.

I feel the vomit rise up, and it is black, black blood. I have known no pain like this in living. Since my birth into the broken world. Toxic bubbles burst out of tiny holes in the wall. They pop and drop down on the skin, acid. I want to spit out my soul and be done with it. I want to be cast in the white water, frozen in time above the perilous dune. Bewitched, groping for pink hair and green flesh.

The tormentors signal to each other with their strange limbs. I know such language of war. It is the way of speaking during the swarm's ascent. Our hands rush to our ears to block the wheezing screams.

Before my mind can comprehend the turn of fate, my comrades are a mess of flesh all around me. Dalton is thrown on a wall of spikes, impaled at the face and gut. Busiris is made to swallow the black poison. His body turns green and expires before my eyes. Colt's head is submerged in the festering lagoon. Bostro's jaw is ripped off to make room for the burrowing snake, which slithers down his throat and bursts out of his gut.

Gelia's face. I can see her, in my mind.

I search for her wildly in the clash—searching, *searching*.

She turns her head to me—the slowness, the grace- all familiar. I know the way bodies moves at the end of time. A phantom limb drags a giant blade across her neck. Her head, nearly decapitated but for a still spine, tilts backwards. Blood gushes to the floor, trailing down her limp arms. A lifeless finger points stiffly towards… a hidden door. Jutting out from beneath a puddle of blood. I watch until her eyes forfeit the soul to the great unspoken night.

I am ruined. Ruined! The agony! The motions left and right away from swords and poison! As I look down to see I have been gutted in some way, with blood pouring from the stomach, the woman from the wall locks her hands around my neck, digging in her talons. She means to strangle the life from me with the strength of ten men, but this is not my ending day. I bend my knees and throw her overhead. The mess continues as she wavers in and out of consciousness.

Looking at her now, I don't see what I thought I would. Her face holds a compelling, human hardness. Her eyes are glassy, revealing her for what she was – something wanting, something lost. I wonder what she may have been before all of this? Was she someone like I was, once?

I drag myself out from underneath her. The latch is pulled, and I descend into the black depths of the mountain.

I can only remember the essence of myself. My face. These hands and limbs. I drag my mangled body through rocks without clothes, or light, or direction. Only the memory of the room of red night.

THE END

LITTLE HOUSE IN THE SUBURBS
James Fallweather

The year is 1945 and the War has been won. With a bomb and a bullet, the greatest conflict of a lifetime came to a close. The world mourned the enormous loss of life, and many families were forced to lock bedroom doors for good, the pain of accepting death too great a burden to bear. Having sacrificed blood for economic success, many families ran to small homes within driving distance of the city. These homes, cookie-cutter on the outside, walls painted with garish colors to distract from the inside, layers of wallpaper to cover the rot.

Night falls over one of these very suburbs, 10 miles outside of Detroit. The wind is picking up, carrying the pollution away from the city, west, toward the farmland. A stream of cars leaving the city, each one headed to a similar house, to have dinner with a similar family. A somber happiness rests over these communities, a happiness born of security and sameness. Meal rituals performed and perfected since the dawn of time. Each member of the family filling their roles and responsibilities to a tee.

Violence was a thing of war, a thing of the past. It stayed behind that locked bedroom door. Something to be thought about in passing, never consciously pondered. Those men that survived would mourn in small groups, speaking with hushed tones, a bottle of scotch empty a couple of hours after dinner. The mothers would act on their pain, creating a safer space for their other children and neighbors. A stifling safety that promoted procrastination and stagnation.

The Smith family was no different than many who had lost much during the war. The Father would arise every morning to leave his station as the head of his house, to drive an hour or more to shoulder the eight hours of manufacturing that put food on his family's table and a roof over their heads. The mother would cook and clean and keep the house in order, creating a safe space for their remaining child, Alice.

Alice was but a small child when her older brother Michael went off to war. Pearl Harbor shook the nation and Michael's heart as he swore vengeance on America's enemies, joining the Navy. His parents begged him not to go, saying it was not his fight, not his burden to bear, but the groundswell of patriotism gripped his heart. The smell of gunpowder and the sea beckoned, and he left before the sun broke, a small note begging forgiveness left on his pillow.

Michael would write as often as he could. The days his letters arrived were always a momentous occasion. The Father would solemnly listen while the Mother read, seemingly indifferent to his son's adventures and struggles, but Alice would catch him sometimes in his study, staring at the letter as if imagining that Michael was with him once more.

Propaganda filled the streets of the small community. Young men continued to line up in front of the recruitment office to take part in a great adventure overseas, not realizing the horrors that awaited them. To Alice, it seemed exciting. The movies were filled with the stirring exploits of soldiers overseas. Alice would imagine Michael flying one of the fighter planes, performing advanced aerial maneuvers, being on the ground pushing the enemy out of frightened island villages, rescuing damsels in distress, and being a shining light to native savages. These imaginative dreams would continue until one day, the letters stopped coming. Then, the letter came. Mother wouldn't stop crying. Father immediately went to his study, closing the door behind him. Michael was missing, presumed dead.

The daily rituals are all that keep the Mother and Father together. That, and their unflinching refusal to open Michael's room. Alice understands that he isn't coming back. At first the very thought filled her with anger. Anger toward the evil enemies that took her brother from her. Anger at her parents for letting him go. Anger at Michael for not coming back. Many afternoons are spent lost in her books. Treasure Island isn't a story about a boy leaving his home on an adventure but of Michael escaping the war, lost at sea fighting a one-legged pirate. She becomes so absorbed in these fantasy worlds that her parents' pain goes unnoticed until a plate crashes next to her head at the table. Startled, she ducks as a glass flies out of nowhere to land somewhere in the living room. Parents are fighting again. Time to hide.

Night falls over the suburbs. A full moon illuminates empty roads. Stray cats rummage through trash cans put out for the morning. Where once you could find many houses unlocked, it was now a rare occurrence. The fighting might be over, but trust is a fickle virtue. The sound of crickets can be heard from the Smith home. A small creek runs nearby separating two sections of the neighborhood. At one time you could find Michael hauling scrap wood he had found down toward a treehouse he swore would be the greatest treehouse ever built in the history of the whole entire world. He never did finish that treehouse, though large pieces of scrap wood nailed to a tree would beg to differ. A small collection of drawings Alice did of Michael, decomposing due to moisture, create a delicate shrine in honor of his many aspirations. Things he would never be able to accomplish.

The Smith family is restless. While the community sleeps, the Sandman missed them. Tossing and turning, Mother sits up rubbing her eyes, reaching over to her nightstand, fishing for large gaudy glasses that her husband hated. Once her vision has cleared, her gaze rests on the form of her sleeping husband. With a murderous pause and defeated sigh, she pushes the covers away and gets out of bed. Leaving her room to stop and check on Alice, her child, her… only child. Clutching her breast, the ache in her heart stops her in her tracks. The pain had become almost bearable with the constant fighting between her and her husband. Anger fills the void and adrenaline is a rush that keeps her from remembering.

If only she could forget, if only the whole family could forget, then they could continue forward with their lives. A forlorn glance at her daughter's door and she finds the strength to keep going. Averting her gaze from her son's room as she passes, something grabs her attention. Out of the corner of her eye, a shadow-like figure seems to pass her and enter her sons room. Goosebumps spread up and down her arm as a feeling of anxiety fills her. Stomach dropping, she puts her ear against the cool wood of the door to Michael's room.

A few seconds pass and relief spreads through her body. It must have been a trick of the eye, she thinks to herself. She gathers her wits, turning around to put the door behind her. Suddenly, fear courses through her veins. In front of her, a dark figure stands seven feet tall with no discernible features or appendages. A dark mass that fills her vision. A loud noise, like radio static, blares in her ears. A scream erupts from her lips and blinding, unwavering light appears in the center of the black emptiness, drawing her in. She can see her son, Michael, playing catch with her husband. A scraping sensation and the memory is gone. The same memory plays again, this time with her husband now playing ball with some local kids. One by one, memories of Michael are replaced with a stranger. The boy carrying some scrap wood toward the creek… Mike? Was that his name? Memories of a young boy…must be the neighbors' kid. For what seems an eternity, she watches the life of a boy she no longer recognizes. The door to the room behind her flies open and with a large pull of air like a vacuum depressurizing, she's ripped away from the entity and into the room. The door slams with a resounding thunk and the mother finds herself in a dark and wet chamber with the only light stemming from a small barred window that opens to an unfamiliar landscape. Without time to process what had just happened, the sound of chains and a soft voice whispers from the corner,

"Mom?"

With a small shriek, she sees a young man, emaciated and dirty, chained to a small bed in the corner. With a small chuckle and a sigh, relief washes over her -- this is just a dream.

"Hello, young man, I am so very sorry you had to be a part of this terrible nightmare," she replies to the dumbstruck man still seated in his bed, knuckles white from gripping the metal bedframe.

"Mom? it's Michael!" he states, a hopeful expression spreads across his face. "This can't be real, this can't be happening," he mutters, pulling his legs up close to his chest, dirty chains clinking once more against the metal bedframe.

Tears appear in his eyes. "I'm sorry. I should've never left. I'm so scared."

The mother, moving closer, sits at the foot of the bed, "It's okay dear. Don't cry, this will all be over, once I wake. Now, you wouldn't happen to know where the door is?" Calmly taking his right hand away from his face, she is startled to see deep bloody grooves where the shackles have eaten their way into his wrists.

The feeling of her hand in his shakes Michael from his stupor. He pulls her close, to whisper in her ear, knowing that even in his dreams, this would be the last time he sees her.

"I love you, mom. Tell Alice and Father that I love them too. I am gonna try to escape. I am to be tortured tomorrow. Seventeen. Seventeen deaths, seventeen prisoners, seventeen regrets."

The sound of a door pulls the mothers attention away, the portal to her hallway opens wide, and without another thought, she leaves the young boy to his fate and steps back into her home.

What was I doing again? She asks herself. That's right, I was checking on Alice. Alice, my only child.

A quick glance into her daughter's room fills her with unending joy. The love of a mother is unfathomable. With an endearing smile and a small tear welling up in her eye she returns to her bed. Sleep comes easily now, knowing her family is safe and sound.

War never ended for the Father. Having served in the trenches himself, he knew firsthand the living hell that his son had endured until his untimely death. The nightmares that had plagued him in his early years had come back with a vengeance with the news of his son. Over and over, he watched his brothers die serving with him- not from bullets. That would have been lucky. One had taken the short straw and on a routine check was in the wrong trench at the wrong time. Mustard gas melting his skin as he crawled his way back, screaming for his mother.

Sleep was a distant memory and tonight is no exception. A door slam woke him up with a start, and swinging his legs out of bed, he fumbles for his revolver, making sure its loaded before venturing out into the hallway. He begins to count to himself to stay focused: one, two, three, four. Revolver in front of him he steps out into the hallway, pausing for a moment to let his eyes adjust. It seemed… darker than normal. The loud bang seems to come from the right where Michael's door stands, tall and imposing, in contrast to the Father, cowering before a dark hallway. Taking a deep breath, he continues to count: five, six, seven, eight, nine, ten, eleven. The hallway continues to darken. His steps slow as if caught in mud, static fills his mind. Twelve, Thirteen, Fourteen, Sixteen, Seventeen… looking down at his feet he sees them sunk in dark black mud. Another loud bang pushes him forward face first in the sludge. Screams, explosions and gunfire rage about him as the father lifts himself from the mud to find himself in the trenches of his past. Adrenaline surges through his body as he narrowly dodges two medics carrying half a person. Looking above him, the grey clouds and slight drizzle welcome him home.

Looking to his right and left, the trench he found himself in stretched as far as the eye could see. No use standing around. Noticing that he still has the revolver, he pushes himself away from the wall and starts heading to the right, in the direction of the medics. Hours pass with no end or turn in sight. Every time he tries to climb up the trench to gain a peek at the landscape, bullets whiz by, narrowly missing his head. Tired, wet and exhausted, the Father pauses to catch his breath. An annoyed expression crosses his face, patience wearing thin for an end to this tedious nightmare. A bullet to the head seems like an easy way to wake up. Lost in thought over the chance that a death in a dream would constitute a death in real life, a cold wind whips through the trench, almost knocking him over. After catching himself, he notices a left turn he must have missed. This must be it, the way out.

Making his way into the other trench, he feels a familiar presence.

"Michael?" He asks the wind; his voice being swallowed in the sounds of war. His vision begins to blur as his feet sink into the mud, stopping him in his tracks. The loud sound of fabric tearing draws his attention away from his slowly sinking self. Fear forces its way into his heart. About thirty feet in front of him, a large black mass stretches almost taking up the entire width of the trench. Wind sweeps over his body, pulling the trench towards the entity. The force pulling the trench in was barely matched by the cemented grip the mud had on his legs. Inside the void before him, blacker then the darkest room, an outline of a person appeared. It walks out of the void with its arm outstretched.

Feeling the urge to scream, he resists as static fills his head once more, pressure building up in his mind, and the unpleasant feeling of a nail on a chalk board permeating him to his very core. Memories of Michael are jerked to the forefront of his mind and peeled off, layer by layer. Seeing his wife hold out his son, his baby boy. Alice, his baby girl. How happy he was in that moment, helping Alice with her homework, was Michael there? The war, a boy leaving a note, anger and sadness. Sadness he felt for his neighbors losing their son to the violent machine of war. Thankfully Alice was too young to fully understand. Thankfully, he had no children he could lose like his friends and brothers.

The pressure in his head becoming too great to stand his legs buckle and he feels his body thrown past a door and slammed into the wall of a cramped room. Light streams through a small barred window above him illuminating a pile of dark rags in the corner and savage scratches etched into the wall by rabid prisoners.

"Father?" a weak voice cries out from the corner. The Father gets up quickly, finger on the trigger as he squints to make out a young man chained to a piss-soaked bed.

"Father, I am so glad it's you. You see, you can end the pain, please father, I can't last much longer." The skeleton of a man reaches out, beckoning. The chain keeps him from stretching his right arm too far, but it would not have made much difference. Both of Michael's legs had been cut off at the knee, resulting in two black stumps of pus and dried blood. It was only a matter of time before the infection took the boy to the great beyond.

Speechless, the Father keeps his revolver trained directly at the unknown person before him.

"Please Dad, put me out of my misery." Michael begins to sob, "even if it is all a dream. Please God, take me now, spare me this torment."

The father remembers a similar conversation he had with God when he was stuck in the trenches of France.

"I will help you, boy." And like the angel of death enacting judgement on the Egyptians, the father places his revolver between the boy's eyes. Steeling himself for the noise and recoil, he takes one shot. The boy's lifeless body slumps back down onto the mat. An alarm goes off in the distance. The sound of footsteps is the last thing he hears as he finds himself on the floor of his hallway.

Must have tripped and scared myself again, he says to himself. The furniture in the hallway, lit by the moon, casts shadows that send shivers down the father's spine as he picks himself up from the floor. His revolver is missing a bullet. I must have dropped it last time I loaded it, he reflects, eyes squinting in confusion. Cursing himself for his lack of care, he heads back to his warm bed and loving wife. The memory of his past means nothing, compared to the joy of not having any of his children go through the pain and torment he went through as a young soldier. With a satisfied sigh, he looks at the sleeping form of his wife. What a catch, he thinks to himself as he pulls the covers close to his face and falls into a deep and dreamless sleep.

Once more, silence falls over the Smith home. Papers scattered by the wind rushing through an open window settle. Alice's door opens with a familiar creak. The ambient noise of a house sleeping fades to silence. The small, shadowy form of a young man steps into the room and pauses for a moment at the foot of Alice's bed before squatting down to shuffle closer. As the creature nears Alice, it starts to gain more detailed features. On a nightstand, a small family photo reflects the light into its eyes. Entranced, it stands up sharply, picking up the photo with its right hand, left hand pressing hard against its face.

"Michael?" a small voice whispers. Half covered by the bedspread, two small eyes peer out, trying to focus on the figure in front of her.

"Hello, Alice," it responds stepping away from the light streaming through the window. "I escaped the war. I came back as a surprise."

"I knew it!" Alice shouts. The bedspread gets flung away from her as she prepares to slingshot from the bed toward her missing brother. "I never gave up hope! You were just on an adventure. Mom and Dad are gonna be so excited!"

"Stop." The creature points its hand toward Alice, with the light hitting the arm. Alice notices how the hand, black as night, didn't seem to be there but it was as if she could see an outline of something *not* there. The soft sound of static enters her mind, growing louder by the second. As the volume increases, the static becomes decipherable… voices. Screaming, people gripped in eternal anguish, women crying out in anger, men sobbing, filled in with the soft hiss of air rushing past blown out vocal chords.

For what seems like an eternity, she gazes upon the dark abysmal clay in the shape of her brother as it fills itself with memories. Going to the park after sundown. Playing Peter Pan where she got to be Peter. The stories Michael would tell her when she was sad. All of them being eaten, eaten by this thing.

And with the rush of air coming back into a room it was done. An unfamiliar young man stood before her bed.

"Is this a dream?" Alice asks. It must be a dream. Daddy wouldn't let strange men inside the house.

"Of course, this is a dream, young one. Now Sleep."

Alice hesitates for a moment before letting her eyes close, the night's natural rhythm taking over. The creature picks up the photograph. A happy family in front of a newly purchased home. Mother, Father and Alice. The door to Alice's room once again closes, and with the three of them lost in the land of dreams, the creature makes its way downstairs. A large mirror, in the hallway, reflecting the full moon's light through large windows above the front door, catches its attention. It takes a moment to run its hand through its hair as it gazes into the mirror image. Michael smiles, adjusts his coat, and steps out into the bright moonlight.

AMADIS THE ENCHANTRESS
ASHLEY DIOSES

Sasha, a Vexterian, furrowed her violet-hued brow as she sought the source of a strange humming in her Vixen gliders, but, having found nothing, she assumed it was from another area of the mother ship. It was not loud, never unpleasant, but persistent.

Ove, another Vexterian of tough green skin and black eyes, hurried to inform her of some unusual activity happening on Vexteria. The sand dwellers, toad-like creatures, had become more active and emerged from beneath the sands. They had started to build temples composed of bones, malformed skulls, scales, and wings all for…something. But the Vexterians and the human scientists on the ship had no idea what or who they were for.

The people of Vexteria did not believe in higher beings or deities. The enchanters, sorcerers, wizards, witches, magicians, and any holder of magick were the only respected people and the closest to being worshiped.

"They are building shrines and temples, Sasha," Ove said, in his thick voice.

"That's impossible. They aren't an intelligent species," Sasha said, looking through a high powered telescope at Vexteria below them.

Sasha always knew Vexteria as a desolate planet. It was covered in ruined cities once thriving and grand, dried up bodies of water, and jagged, protruding monoliths. It had been like that for around a thousand years and the few oases that inhabited it now, were made from the generations of Vexterians that lived in the spaceship, Vex, above the planet, in order to provide food and water. The planet had not seen rain since Amadis left.

As Sasha looked though the telescope, she could see the great structures of sun bleached bones of all sizes and other various body parts, fresh and old alike, converted roughly into towering arches and window frames. Giant leathery wings, some black, others crimson wine, were draped across doorways and bright putrid yellow scales created strange hieroglyphs and images that looked like lightning bolts on many windows.

"Does Amadis mention anything like this in her diary?" Ove asked. Sasha tore away from the telescope and ruffled through her desk to find the diary.

"I don't know, I don't think so," she muttered as she started to read from the beginning.

I. Book of Amadis

We have not always lived in the ship above our beloved Vexteria. We were once a great people of the Valda, the City of the Light, a lush and peaceful place where all were welcome. The palace was constructed out of glowing blue and green crystals and stretched toward the skies. It was a welcoming beacon and could be seen for many miles and from many cities. I, Amadis, am an enchantress and therefore, became leader of the city. I kept the land thriving and created peace with all the nearest cities, except for one.

Scevola, the City of the Flame, was ruled by my sister, Severina. She was known as a sorceress but necromancy was why our father exiled her from Valda and that was the undoing of our friendship and love.

Years went by as I ruled and my powers grew to great strengths. At a young age I could create orbs of light, yet as I grew, I could light up the whole city and later, summon lightning from the very skies.

Many people from all over Vexteria came and offered me gifts. Most wished for peace and others sought help my powers could provide. One day, however, I received visitors not of Vexteria. They said they were scientists and that they came in peace to learn of us and our ways. I allowed some to stay and, in return, they taught us how to build spaceships and taught us of the cosmos beyond the skies. I became very interested in the different planets and stars and what beings could possibly live on them. It was amazing to hear of such things!

If it was not for the scientists, all of Vexteria's population would have become extinct.

Severina grew jealous of my lush land and her hatred of me strengthened knowing that I was loved by all. So one day a thunder, not of my own doing, was heard in the distance. Steadily, it grew louder until the horizon turned black.

Severina could manifest heat and eventually could summon an inferno from her fingertips. Yet she also controlled another flame. She found out at a young age that she could rekindle the very spark of life itself and brought dead creatures, at first, back to life. Later on, she delighted in killing beasts and then people, to only watch them return to life, deranged and twisted. I found out later, when our father discovered it, that she had written many experiments and various executions in a diary.

It was a dark and terrible gift for the dead awoke with a hunger for the beating heart, the hot rivers of blood, and the steaming vapors of breath that the living possessed. They hungered for the things they lacked and that Severina could not provide them.

They were the ones who approached my city. Their feet thundered and shook the land. Blackened burned corpses, some still smoking, few red and raw, and still others were on fire. Out of pure jealousy, she had destroyed her own people to defeat me.

I was a ruler of peace but that did not mean I was naïve or weak. I summoned the water dwellers of the marshes that surrounded my city. Most were grayish green creatures with tough skin, webbed appendages with sharp black claws, and yellow eyes yet some resembled giant dragonflies with elongated teeth and still others were like great sea serpents. I always had a way with creatures and they emerged from murky waters to defend my city at my command.

Fire followed in the wake of Severina's army as she sought to, not only destroy me, but my land and my people. The trees lit up like matches and the crops turned to ash as she set my world on fire.

My rains did little for if I had brought on a tempest, I would have equally destroyed my land. All I could do was keep the fire at bay yet I could not bring the land back to life. I rained bolts of lightning down upon the corpses yet it did little, for they seemed to thrive on its heat and rose again. I had to tear their limbs from their torso to stop them.

Her army grew in number as the creatures they killed were brought back to life and turned against me. Our army dwindled and soon my people began to fight in place of the marshland beasts yet to no avail. There was no hope of winning.

I ushered what was left of the people of Valda into the spaceships the scientists taught us to build and we left Valda and our beautiful Vexteria.

Severina was furious at my departure and continued her warpath. She immediately marched toward all my allies and destroyed them. One by one, her army grew with burnt corpses from every city. But she did not stop there. With a seeming unending rage, she continued on and eventually conquered every city on Vexteria and laid it all to waste. All the cities became graveyards and the raging oceans became seas of sand. She was the only one left with her army of the dead.

She returned to her city, Scevola, and after decades had gone by, life slowly began to return to Vexteria. Sand dwellers, creatures of darkness, lived in deep caverns under the sand and rarely surfaced. Severina left them alone and instead, had often focused her attention to the skies and seemed to wait for something. Time passed and finally Severina closed the city and sealed herself up inside. Perhaps she still waited in sleep. Perhaps she thought I would return and take revenge for all the destruction and ruin she had caused. But I would never return, not alone.

😀😵😈

Sasha slowly shut the diary and looked up at Ove. "Amadis said that she thought Severina looked like she was waiting for something. Amadis thought that it was probably her but what if it wasn't?" Sasha said.

"What do you mean?" Ove asked.

"Amadis said Severina often looked up to the skies so what if she was waiting for something else? What if they are the same thing these creatures are worshipping?"

"But what could she have possibly been waiting for? It says in Amadis's diary that they knew nothing of the cosmos and anything beyond the skies," Ove said.

"Maybe she heard from one of the scientists somehow. I don't know! I wondered if Severina wrote it in her diary. If only I could have her diary!"

"Ha, good luck with finding that," Ove said laughing.

She sighed. "I just don't understand why Amadis would just leave her home, her whole planet. I'm sure she had a good reason though. Where is that humming come from?" Sasha exclaimed, jumping up from her desk, as suddenly the humming grew increasingly louder.

She heard distant startled outcries from the nearby compartments as it echoed throughout the ship. The humming reverberated through her very bones and the force of the vibration caused her insides to shake. It did not sound like any spacecraft she knew of, for she designed all the gliders on the ship, for quick trips to the planet, and helped in the continuous maintenance of Vex. They were all modified to be quieter. She could not imagine any machine or generator creating such a noise as to echo throughout the entire ship.

"It's not from the Vixens?" Ove asked.

"My gliders don't make that sound and neither does this ship."

They entered the metal walkway in the hallway and saw the others, human scientists, and robots alike, had come out of their various rooms as well.

Machinery continued to click, clank, grind, and steam throughout the ship as usual. Even with the construction work, which could be seen through the holes in the walkway levels below them, they used no tool that could mimic such a sound as the humming.

"What's going on?" Ove asked Dr. Alvar, a human scientist, who was the nearest person.

"I don't know, they say it's not coming from the ship," he said nervously.

"What do you mean it's not coming from the ship? Where else would it be coming from?" Sasha snapped. Alvar shrugged as he exchanged a look with Ove.

"They say it's coming from space, they say it just came into our atmosphere," he said quietly.

"What just came into our atmosphere?" Sasha asked. The ship suddenly jolted and many things and people, crashed into walls and fell. More jolts proceeded at different magnitudes, though none seemed to deal great damage to the ship yet. Sasha raced to her telescope again and pointed it skyward.

Sasha's eyes widened as realization seeped into her expression. Her body became rigid as she turned to look at Ove. Ove gently took her by the arms and looked into her eyes.

"Sasha, what is it?" he asked, gently.

"I was wrong. They were waiting for *her* and she has finally returned," Sasha said softly.

A portal to what could only be described as another dimension tore through the atmosphere above them and as the gateway opened wider, the humming escalated and its force strengthened the jolts of the ship. The skies then opened up and the first rain in a thousand years poured along with great peals of thunder. Lightning streaked from the black clouds and above them a ship of foreign design emerged, emitting bright blue and green light. More ships followed the first and they slowly headed toward the ancient city of Scevola.

"That's an old ship, Ove. That style is described in her entries on ship design. That has to be the ship she left with," Sasha said in shock.

"That's impossible, how can she be alive after a thousand years?" Ove said, shaking her slightly by her shoulders.

"She's an enchantress, Ove!"

"So what?" Ove said, looking at her as if she were mad.

"So, let's find out how she did it." Sasha escaped Ove's grip and raced to one of her gliders.

"Wait!" he yelled as he raced after her. He said something inaudible and Sasha could hear another set of feet fall behind his. When she entered her glider, Ove and Alvar followed her inside. "What are you doing?"

"She said she would never return alone. You read her diary, she became obsessed with the cosmos and what could be out there. She found something, Ove. She found another civilization and she brought an army with her," Sasha said, starting the glider and taking off toward Vexteria.

"Listen to yourself, Sasha! You are talking about a thousand year old leader coming back with an army to defeat her thousand year sister," Ove said.

"Dr. Alvar, is it possible for someone to create portals or dimensions through space?" Sasha asked, not looking at him.

"Well you know of the liquid formulas we've developed that allow us to transport to different planets, which is how we originally came to Vexteria, so I suppose it is possible that another race of beings could have found another variation of space travel, like the creation of portals or gateways of some kind," he pondered.

"See?" Sasha said.

"Those formulas are dangerous, you can never be sure where you'll turn up." Ove turned to Sasha. "That does not prove that it's her or if it is, how she's still alive." Sasha sped toward the small fleet of ships but kept her distance. Her glider was beige in color and blended in well with the terrain and rock formations that jutted toward the sky.

She curved around the side of a mountain and stopped. The ruins of Scevola lay before them. Like Amadis's palace mentioned in her diary, Severina's palace was made out of crystals as well but were red and orange in color and appeared in the sun light like a blazing flame above the city. It was the only building intact. The city surrounding it was in complete ruin. Some houses and buildings were black from, no doubt, Severina's rage while others were crumpled and deteriorated to dust over time.

Many scientists and explorers, including Sasha, visited Scevola and many of the other cities on Vexteria many times, but no one had ever been able to enter Severina's palace. Every crystalline window and every doorway had been sealed tight with ancient magick that burned anyone or anything that tried to open them. Nothing could penetrate through the thick crystal and its sealing magick.

Sasha held back awhile to see where they landed their ships and then circled around the cliffs before finding a hidden spot on a nearby cliff. After she landed, she raced outside with high powered binoculars in her hand. Ove and Alvar followed and joined her at the ledge.

The fleet had landed in front of Scevola's fallen wall that surrounded the city and just emerging from the first ship, was Amadis. The Vexterians had pieced together what Amadis would have looked like when she lived by brief descriptions of her throughout many of her entries. She had long wavy sky blue hair, pale green skin, and electric blue eyes that pulsed with electricity. Her feet never touched the ground and instead, she hovered, gliding through the air. Amadis was the last to leave her ship for Sasha did not see anyone exit the rest of the ships. They must have gone ahead of her.

The humming abruptly burst through her ear drums and she let out a piercing scream but it was drowned out. Sasha looked toward the sky and saw that the dimension's gateway had encompassed nearly all the sky above them.

The border of the gateway pulsed and radiated with electric light and beyond the opening was a perpetual blackness that appeared almost liquid. As she watched it widen, she saw that Vex was being pulled into it. Many Vixens were speeding away from their mother ship, trying to escape, but it was harder for them to resist the pull and the ones she saw were quickly swallowed up by the blackness.

Sasha looked back at Amadis and saw her simply gaze at Vex without concern. Then she turned her gaze and looked directly at Sasha. Sasha dropped her binoculars and laid as flat as she could on the cliff edge and motioned Ove and Alvar to do the same. After a few minutes, Sasha dared to look through the binoculars again but Amadis had vanished.

Sasha looked back to the sky and saw that Vex was closer to the portal. "What are we going to do?" Alvar muttered barely above a whisper. Sasha looked at him and realized that he wasn't used to dealing with such things as enchantresses, sorceresses, ship swallowing dimensions, and dangerous ancient magick on Earth. She felt a surge of pity for him but there was nothing to do or say to comfort him.

"We'll have to talk to Amadis," Sasha said, trying to keep her voice steady.

"What? That's insane!" Ove said, staring at her.

"Amadis came from that dimension so she would be the only one who can tell us where that leads and how to get back to our ship. We have to go to Scevola's palace," Sasha said as calmly as she could. Ove looked as if he was going to argue but said nothing. Sasha nodded.

Sasha's heart slammed against her chest and panic began to seize her. Ove gripped her shoulders and looked at her. He took a deep breath and she immediately mimicked him. They both took a few more deep breaths to calm down before Sasha flew the glider down the cliff and landed behind a rock formation, a little ways behind the last ship of the fleet. They waited and scouted it out first.

Amadis's ship was the only ship Sasha recognized from the diary. The rest were made by a design she had never seen described anywhere before. They were gliders but the entryways were huge. The Vixens were designed to be compact, light, and designed to hold a few people. These gliders were clunky and massive. They were built and designed to hold something huge and tall.

"Sasha," Ove whispered. Sasha turned to him and saw that he was holding up what looked like a piece of shed reptilian skin. It was transparent and thin. "It was stuck in the door." Sasha paled at the sight of it. Dr. Alvar gaped at it and looked at Sasha.

"Amadis found another race and she brought them here," Sasha said.

"Amadis is an enchantress of peace, right? So we wouldn't have to be afraid to confront her, right?" Dr. Alvar asked, looking from Sasha to Ove. Sasha said nothing and instead headed for the palace.

The sand dwelling creatures slowly began to emerge from beneath the sands and looked curiously at them, but they kept their distance. Sasha knew that they only cared about the return of Amadis, though she did not know why.

The palace doors were cracked open and shards of crystal lay scattered on the ground. A musky stale scent overwhelmed them as they cautiously entered the palace. They walked through a dark narrow hallway with the only light shining behind them.

They kept walking, daring not to make the slightest sound, and soon saw bright light ahead that resembled sun light. Sasha relaxed a little, but as they neared the archway of the entrance, they saw that it was not sun light that illuminated the room but a throne of red glowing crystal. But it was what was in front of it that petrified them.

Gently bobbing as she hovered above the ground was Amadis, drenched in still bubbling blood. It streamed down her pale blue gown and dripped from her matching slippers. She hung in the air with her neck broken and twisted to one side and her hair was matted in sticky red tendrils. It was her eyes, however, that made Sasha's blood run frigid. Amadis's eyes were wide open and were no longer blue and pulsing. They were completely crimson and stared straight through Sasha.

A soft noise caused them to notice, for the first time, someone else in the room. Sasha tore her eyes away from Amadis and looked for the source. Standing by the throne and off to the side, was Severina.

Her hair was fiery orange and her skin was a pale red, yet her eyes could penetrate the darkest of abysses for they were searing orbs of scarlet flames. More soft noises erupted from the silence and emerging from the darkness behind her were monstrosities unfound in this world and Earth.

A handful of giant reptilian-like monsters that were part of Amadis's army, stepped into the light of the throne and instantly, their claws shined like black obsidian and their gray scales shimmered like knight's armor. They towered above their new mistress and stared, in death, blankly through Sasha and her crew.

Sasha stood petrified, unable to scream, to even breathe, and before she could even comprehend what was happening, a sudden warmth overcame her. A pale green arm flew passed her face and drenched her torso before it hit the opposite wall. Pieces of Ove flew through the chamber while the monsters hungrily devoured him and before they even neared Alvar, he crashed to the floor, dead.

Sasha regained her senses and turned to run back through the hallway, but ran straight into Amadis. Amadis shot her hand around Sasha's neck, her cold fingers strong around her throat, and sent shards of ice through Sasha's veins.

Amadis's crimson eyes bored into Sasha's and she slowly twisted her neck upward, cracking her bones back into place to stare at Sasha at eye level. Laughter as smooth and cold as ice echoed through the chamber but was silenced as quickly as it came. The sound of dozens of scurrying feet rushed through the corridor and dry rough skin bumped into Sasha as the sand dwellers rushed toward Severina in a fury.

As Sasha struggled with Amadis's grip, the room lit up as sand dwellers everywhere caught on fire from Severina's defense. Sasha could only see Amadis and the on coming sand dwellers, for Severina and the monsters were behind her, but the shadows revealed that Severina was losing the fight by being overcome by the creatures.

Flaming sand dwellers flew all around her from being hurled by the massive reptilian monsters, yet the dwellers kept coming into the palace. Ground shaking thuds resounded from the fallen monsters and the shrieks from Severina's rage became louder.

Sasha grew weaker as Amadis still tightened her grip and continued to stare with dead red eyes. A flaming sand dweller was thrown near them and crashed into Dr. Alvar's body. A glass vial slowly rolled out of one of his pockets and Sasha assumed it was one of the portal jumping formulas.

Movement in Amadis's expression abruptly brought back Sasha's attention. Amadis's eyes began to pulse again, showing hints of blue and her mouth began to open in an expression of terror. Sasha saw Amadis on fire, yet Amadis's fear was not in being burnt, on the contrary it was bringing her back to life, but her fear was directed at something behind Sasha.

Amadis loosened her grip on Sasha's throat and Sasha used this opportunity to break free. She grabbed the vial and bolted through the hallway, not daring to look back to see what Amadis saw. But something rushed after her. Sasha knew she wasn't going to make it to her glider, so she shakily uncapped the vial as she ran and drank just as she felt four sharp nails slice through her shirt and brush her back.

The pull through space nauseated her yet she arrived at Dr. Alvar's laboratory on Earth in no time. The human scientists regarded her curiously, yet none seemed surprised at her presence. Earth must get traffic all the time from people using the vials. She wheezed and trembled as her adrenaline still pumped from the touch on the unknown pursuer, which still felt real on her skin. She clutched her chest but the panic remained, for she feared what might have happened to her people and what would now become of her.

SPIRIT OF PLACE
James Russell

The *thing* loomed above Joel Ashton as he stood out front of his house, rising to what must have been a height of a hundred feet and stretching to a width of what must have been about five times that. How far it receded into the distance was something he could not begin to estimate. It lay like… whatever the hell it was across Wakefield Road, the rear end of it stretching over into the park across the road from Ashton's house and the front of it flopping down on the pavement before him. Traffic continued to come streaming along both sides of the road, past the shopping centre in one direction and past the school on the far side in the other, driving through the *thing* as if it weren't there.

Which, after all, it technically wasn't.

Frankly, Ashton was starting to really get the shits with it.

Not least of his problems with it, of course, was the very fact that it wasn't actually there. He had accepted it pretty much straight away as a hallucination the first time he saw it, after all, and had no trouble dealing with the idea that only he could see it (well, him and *one* other person). He just wished he could stop seeing it.

Then there was the fact that he couldn't describe what it was like. He lacked the words to define it, or perhaps language itself was deficient in the face of it; if there were no words in English, there were also none in French or German or Arabic or Mongolian or Basque or any other language you might name. The nearest he could come was to call it a mass, though a mass of what he didn't know, a mass of a colour he was fairly sure did not exist within the visible light spectrum, a mass that seemed to be highly variable and move through multiple other dimensions, vague tentacles of something not entirely material erupting forth and separating from the mass to be reabsorbed. Within the space of a second it might shift from something approximately cube-shaped, with vaguely distinct lines, to something completely amorphous that might've resembled a cloud of vomit if vomit came in *that* disturbingly obtuse shade of violet.

Also he didn't like the way it was getting bigger every time it manifested.

Nor the feeling of malevolence it increasingly radiated towards him.

Ashton looked at it one more time, then down at the somewhat scrappy garden in front of his house, and went back indoors without engaging the *thing*.

Ashton's house had been owned by his late parents, which was the sole reason he now lived in it. He used to have a nice place in West Stettin, a share house whose residents all kept to themselves and lived in remarkable harmony; unfortunately it was also a place whose owner was prone to jacking up the rent regularly until it was unaffordable. The availability of the house on Wakefield Road in the South East district came perfectly timed, and the fact that there was no rent to cough up every week made it very attractive. Goodbye West 48 and hello SE 36, therefore.

He had no other fondness for South East 36. The place at West 48 had been fairly conveniently located near a train station wherefrom it was a trip of less than ten minutes into the city centre. SE 36 had no train station and a wholly inadequate bus service that took markedly longer to reach the city. It was almost the end of the line, just a short distance from Port Magra which was about as far as the line went in this part of Stettin, i.e. just to the edge of the ocean. All the *fun* things that happened in the city and immediately surrounding eastern and western suburbs did not happen in SE 36 (the returned soldiers' club and the pub down the bottom end of the suburb could only be called "happening" insofar as the occasional drunken fight broke out). It was a boring residential suburb with boring residents, the sort of place that people had to make a particular effort to visit and they needed a particular reason, and no easy way to get out of it and go anywhere interesting if you didn't have a car, which Ashton did not.

After a few weeks living there, Ashton had started to actively hate the place after just finding it an inconvenience and annoyance. The thing that irritated him in the most irrational way, though, was how expensive it was to move there (if you weren't dropped there by the Department of Housing, anyway). One day Ashton had gone idly browsing the online news services, and had actually found a story in the real estate section about someone buying a house in SE 36 for nearly two million dollars. This stunned him, not least because the photo accompanying the article didn't exactly make the property look like it was worth that much. Ashton had scrolled through the article, mystified by it. The new owner was an apparently world-renowned DJ of whom he'd never heard, and apparently they were also a local, too, having grown up nearby in SE 35. He still didn't understand it; even if you were from the area, if you had an exciting career and two million dollars to casually drop on a new house, why wouldn't you buy one in a more exciting place? A nice three-floor terrace in East 22 or something. Or another country altogether. Mystifying and ludicrous.

Ashton had first sighted the *thing* not long after reading this story. He'd been out visiting the old gang at their new, more sensibly priced place in West 42; a few drinks were had and certain other substances consumed, until around midnight he realised he'd better get going if he didn't want to have to pay for a taxi all the way home. As such, he hastily went for the last bus back to Central Station and from there took the last bus back to SE 36. This was, unfortunately, not the one that took him past his house, being the route that instead went past Port Magra from the south, so he had a fairly lengthy walk back to it. And then, just as he got home, he saw the *thing* over in Wakefield Park.

The park was the one thing Ashton actually did like about SE 36. It was pretty much right across the road from the house and it made for an appealing view when you could see it through the traffic along the main road. Some nights when it got cold and he was having trouble sleeping, he would sit and look out the front window, watching fog rise up from the ground. It was a soothing and reassuring sight. He didn't know what this *thing* in the park now was, though, except that it wasn't a fog and it was neither soothing nor reassuring. Something about the way it seemed to change dimensions and proportions with ridiculous speed… Ashton shook his head. He'd both drunk and inhaled more than he should've done tonight. Hallucinating weird fogs in the park. Had to be fog. What else just hovered a couple of feet off the ground like that? So he went in, crashed out on the couch, and when he woke the next morning he'd forgotten the apparition along with much of the previous night. Which was fine until he saw it again.

The second time was early one afternoon when he'd gone out to collect his mail and then go shopping. There was noise from the park as usual, as it was Friday and that meant sports day for the kids at the school across the road. Except that, usually, when the kids were out playing whatever it was, they didn't have some evil-looking cloud, for want of a better word, hovering around them. And between them and through them. The *thing* just… lurked slightly off the ground, cycling through a range of colours that might variously have been green, brown, grey, maroon and a few others he couldn't identify without ever quite being any of those colours somehow, and floated around the teams of schoolkids in a way that was kind of gelatinous and gaseous at the same time. Ashton felt oddly nauseous at the sight, especially when he realised none of the kids over in the park were reacting to the *thing*'s presence. And that they had no idea it was, in fact, there. Plus it was broad daylight and he hadn't consumed anything for some days. So he couldn't blame it on that.

Ashton screwed his eyes shut and shook his head. When he opened them again the *thing* was gone. Fantastic, he thought as he walked down the road towards the shops, living here is driving me insane. He decided against telling his doctor when he went to get his prescription renewed. Somehow he felt no good would come of it.

The *thing* appeared to him a few more times over the coming weeks. There seemed to be no pattern to the apparitions, some of which came by day and others by night, sometimes he might see it two days in a row and then not see it for another week or longer, but always it loitered in Wakefield Park, visible by its own weird and faintly disturbing luminosity and in the street lights as well, and no one but Joel Ashton ever seemed to notice it. Sometimes he would observe people walking through the park while the *thing* was there, and he would see them just pass through it like it didn't exist. He came to realise that, indeed, it *didn't* exist as far as they were concerned; he was the only one lumbered with the dubious privilege of being able to see the *thing*. He wondered why it had to be him in particular.

Ashton was pondering this one night when the first migraine hit. He had noticed the *thing* becoming more agitated the more he saw it; sometimes as he would be walking home he could see it from a distance, hovering but quiescent, until as he approached it seemed to become more active, seething through a variety of loose shapes and forms and an obnoxious range of colours until he could get back into the house and no longer see it. He wondered about his own reaction to the situation, and was somewhat puzzled by his own acceptance of it. So, some sort of mental aberration he was oddly reluctant to seek treatment for was causing him to hallucinate this… whatever it was, and he was *fine* with that somehow. Well, not "fine" as such, but he'd accepted it as normal for him somehow, and in a way he was kind of impressed with himself for having done so, for having been smart enough to recognise it as a psychic disturbance and get on with things like a normal person instead of a lunatic (even though he supposed he technically *was* one even if he was aware of the fact). He was also kind of perplexed by the way he also attributed feelings to the *thing*, as if it were living and sentient and had specifically chosen him to be aware of its presence. Indeed, its increased activity when he was nearing home almost suggested a dog excited by its master returning from work…

It was in the midst of this thought that the migraine struck. Ashton was prone to tension headaches, but he knew this was way heavier than one of those. The odd thing about it was the *music*, or at least that was what he thought it was. Like distinct notes and tones, albeit not in any scale he would've recognised, but as he clutched his head in agony he began to discern some sort of pattern in the sounds. Atonal it may have been, but random it was not. And then realisation dawned on him, and he suddenly knew what was actually happening. He could not, of course, have actually described *how* he knew this, just that he did, and he knew that he was wrong was about two facts. One, this was not a migraine. Two, the *thing* was absolutely not a psychotic hallucination.

In terror, he looked out the window over to the park. The *thing* was there, and somehow he dimly recognised that it knew he was looking at it. It had gained his attention.

The *thing* was indeed living and sentient, he suddenly knew. It had targeted him specifically. And he was not even remotely the master of it.

Ashton spent the entire next day in bed, neither willing nor able to face the world outside. In time he dragged himself outside to collect the mail, and cast a fearful look over to the park where, to his relief, there was no sign of the *thing*. He went back inside to fix himself some breakfast, see what was in the news— no further stories of multimillionaire DJs buying homes in SE 36 at any rate— and then got dressed and went shopping. A pleasant stroll on a reasonably warm day, somewhat ruined by the fact that the *thing* was waiting for him on his return. He winced and tried to ignore the way it seemed to have grown. Damn this place to hell, he thought as he put the groceries away, suddenly hating the area more than he ever had. Bad enough it was so far from anywhere exciting, now it was haunted by... well, whatever the hell the *thing* was supposed to be. He decided he would sit out and catch a bit of sun in the backyard, which at least had the decency to be quite pleasant in the afternoon, and also he couldn't see the *thing* from there.

He woke up in the same place a little after dawn the next day, sprawled on the ground and a small amount of dried blood in the dirt near his face. What the Christ, he thought in horror as he suddenly realised where he was and just as suddenly realised he had no memory of what had happened to him. Creeping back inside the house, he struggled to fight through the haze of pain and remember. Gradually he pieced together images similar to the night of the "migraine", that same odd sense of something like music... but a different sense of the sound too, more like an approximation of speech. The more he tried to remember, the more he felt like it was his own name being called. Or someone trying with great difficulty to call it, someone not used to saying his name... or saying words at all. Someone not used to human speech. Some*thing*.

Just because Ashton couldn't see the *thing* from his back yard didn't mean that it didn't know he was there. And now it seemed to want to talk to him.

Damn this suburb? Damn this PLANET for harbouring such things, Ashton thought.

This pattern continued over Ashton's next few encounters with the *thing*. Part of him was, to be sure, impressed in a way by what had happened to him; it wasn't everyone (at least it seemed so) who found themselves connected to an entirely non-human entity like he seemed to be, even if he didn't even begin to understand how or why; indeed, he found himself wondering if even the *thing* understood how and why. On the other hand, part of him—probably the greater part, in fact—was simply aghast at the whole thing because he didn't understand it. It *shouldn't* be happening. Ashton was not a believer in the supernatural and, as such, rationalised that the *thing* had to be a properly natural phenomenon, whatever it was. Even so, he couldn't escape the feeling of something fundamentally *wrong* happening here. Entirely non-human entities shouldn't just be making connections with people like this. That sort of thing just didn't happen. Especially not in shitty suburbs like SE 36. And the fact that it was happening to *him* specifically and not someone else didn't help.

Ashton would sit cowering on the floor when the *thing* tried to reach out to him. It had evident difficulties with his mind, and he could never make anything out beyond vague emotions, and a curious sense that the *thing* had equal problems understanding him. The clearest sensation he got from it was one of sadness and disappointment. And the primary sensation he could radiate back at it was, purely and simply, hate. He already hated being in SE 36 as it was, and the one thing he liked about the place, i.e. Wakefield Park, had been pretty comprehensively ruined by virtue of the *thing* being there. Over time, Ashton stopped feeling wonder at his situation and simply came to hate it.

He would wake up in the morning and hate the very fact of his ongoing consciousness. He hated when the *thing* was there, though he almost hated it more when it wasn't because he'd woken up dreading the sight of it for nothing. He hated not knowing when he would or would not see it. He hated when it tried to "talk" to him, hated the hideous migraine-like sensation and the way it would leave him knocked flat for hours. He hated that he could not understand it, and somehow he hated more that it could not understand him, as if two beings entirely alien to each other *should* be able to naturally communicate with each other… he *really* and most irrationally hated the feeling of sadness the *thing* seemed to express when it didn't understand.

"WHAT THE FUCK DO YOU WANT FROM ME?" he suddenly screamed one night after a more than usually aggravating day when the *thing* had pressed on him with some heaviness. He did not particularly care that he was stark naked at the time and howling at it from his opened front door; damn the neighbours and let them think he was mad. Something odd happened, however, when he did this. The *thing* suddenly went dim, losing much of its own luminosity, and contracted to the shape of a sphere, hovering what appeared to be about ten feet off the ground and quivering slightly. And then its glowing outline slowly edged down towards the ground and seemed to surround something else. A *human* shape.

Ashton looked out at the park and realised *someone else* was out there that night, and for reasons he could not fully understand he felt they were not only fully aware of the *thing* surrounding them (unlike seemingly everyone else) but were connected with it in some way. At this distance it was impossible to actually make out the person's features, of course, even in full daylight they wouldn't have been any more than a silhouette against the background. Despite that, he could not shake the feeling, which he might even have called knowledge, that whoever they were they had some sort of relationship with the *thing*... which then abruptly shrunk to a point and vanished.

Ashton went back inside the house, shut the door, and suddenly found himself laughing at this episode. It had been more than usually perplexing, but when he came to realise what had happened he couldn't help himself. He'd hurt its feelings. And now it was sulking.

A few days passed in which time the *thing* made no appearances, and Ashton permitted himself the luxury of thinking he'd beaten it. One night, he accordingly took himself down to the pub at the lower end of SE 36, where he made occasional appearances in an effort to force sociability upon himself, and somewhat to his own surprise had succeeded in making acquaintances there. One of the latter had informed him there would be an "international guest" behind the decks that night, and since he was in a brighter frame of mind than usual, Ashton decided it might be interesting to see what that was all about.

When he got there he was greeted by Marcel Atlas, who sat at his usual table with a pint in front of him and waved Ashton over when he saw him. While waiting to be served his own beer, Ashton looked over at the DJ area in the far corner, where he saw a tall girl with the dark skin and intricate tattoos of one of the Old Tribes contrasting strongly with the canary yellow T-shirt and white pants she wore. She looked familiar but he couldn't say why. "Our international guest?" Ashton asked as he sat down, "She looks like a local."

Atlas nodded. "She is. DJ Alice Frampton. Plays a lot of big festivals and the like."

"And this place too? Seems like a bit of a comedown. Not going to get the sort of money here she'd get at the Pavillion or somewhere like that…"

"Mmm," Atlas agreed with a smile. "But she's Old Tribes, as you probably noticed. Boris who runs this dump has known the family for longer than either of us has been alive. She's doing this on the quiet as a bit of a favour to him."

Ashton took a swig of beer. "So how come I've never heard of her if she's world-famous?"

"Because you're a tedious middle-aged classic rock bore like me who stopped caring about new music about fifteen years ago and doesn't keep up with this sort of thing any more. Mind you, I don't think many people in this country actually do know her that well. She got discovered at some new year bash by some other DJ from overseas who was touring here, he got her a bunch of gigs in other countries. She's become one of those local folks who's fairly well known in the US and Europe but can't get arrested here." Pause for a drink. "You have, however, heard of the house of in Bardolph St?"

Ashton nodded. "That one that went for nearly two million a few months ago?"

"That was her that bought it."

Ashton's eyes went wide at this. Suddenly he recalled the details of that news story he'd read about that stupidly expensive house bought by some local person who'd made good overseas… and here was the local person in question. Looking back over at the DJ booth from his seat, he suddenly felt slightly odd and self-conscious about being in the same room as someone who clearly had more money than he was likely to see in his lifetime. Playing other people's records was evidently the ticket to fame and fortune for the lucky individual…

It was, in fact, a terrific night out; DJ Alice Frampton played a rock solid mix of 60s and 70s soul, lots of Motown and Stax and Philadelphia International and less-known labels, slipping in the occasional longer disco twelve-inch to take a quick toilet break, but otherwise keeping at it for what must've been four or five hours in total. Ashton enjoyed it immensely, and found the young woman fascinating for some reason that went beyond the mere fact of her attractiveness; she was, after all, perfectly fine on that front and Ashton had always had a bit of a thing for Old Tribe girls anyway, but there seemed to be something more to it than that, some sort of aura or something, he wasn't sure what the right word for it was. A certain luminousness he couldn't really explain. First rate taste in music, too. That was a vital consideration.

Once it was over he complimented Boris, the pub's owner, on getting an internationally renowned DJ to play music at his humble pub to a not especially large crowd—maybe forty or fifty people in the place—for what was no doubt a lot less than she was probably accustomed to. Boris nodded and gave a thin smile. "Helps being a friend of the family," he agreed as Alice came over to the bar for one last drink before the place closed. "Joel Ashton, Alice Frampton," Boris said by way of introduction. "Alice, Joel. Joel is kind of new in town and he occasionally darkens my doors and he is delighted to make your acquaintance."

It was quiet enough now that Ashton could hear Marcel Atlas gently laughing to himself, and he fumed silently at the old boy for dropping him in it like that. "Hi," he said in a way that did not fully disguise his discomfort. Talking to women never did come easily to him.

"Hi," Alice said in a soft voice and with a broad smile that indicated her full awareness and enjoyment of that discomfort.

"My, ah, friend Marcel over there," Ashton indicated the other man starting his own last pint for the night, "He tells me you're our local multi-millionaire." *Our*? he thought as soon as he said it, wondering if he had somehow gradually turned into a local himself... Alice nodded enthusiastically in response. "Why, though?" he asked.

She frowned at this. "How do you mean?"

"Well," he said, fumbling for a way to not sound offensive, "This... well, this place," with which words he raised his hands in a vague circle to indicate the whole area around them. "It doesn't strike me as the sort of place a multi-millionaire would, you know, choose to live. I mean, if I had the option I'd be living somewhere more exciting and that..."

"Family business," Alice said simply. "I've got a place in Europe too, but there's things need to be done here. Got to do my share of the work."

Ashton nodded. It was a fair enough answer. "What about *you*, though?" she asked. This was unexpected, and Ashton just looked at her confusedly. "I mean," she said, "Boris says you're new to the area—"

"Not *that* new," he interrupted, "About seven or eight months now."

She smiled at that. "Hardly anything," she said brightly, "But anyway, here *you* are for however long, but you don't seem to be... you know, much of a fan of..." She waved her lands much like Ashton had done a moment earlier. "This. So what does bring you here?"

Ashton shrugged. "Landlord emergency," he said, "Had to move quickly and my old folks' place was the quickest option. Pretty much living off their property and their investments."

Alice nodded. "Not really here by choice," she said sympathetically, "I don't think a lot of people who live in 36 really do so by choice, though." She turned her head to look out the pub's murky window. "An awfully sad thing in a lot of ways..."

Ashton nodded. By now he was reasonably intoxicated and somewhat desperate to get out of an encounter that had started awkwardly and showed no signs of getting any easier. "I'll, ah, let you finish your drink off," he said, knowing this was hardly the most graceful way to exit the conversation but it was the best he could manage under the conditions, "Nice meeting you."

"And you," Alice said with a huge and reassuring smile, then turned and walked back over to the DJ decks.

"Score," Marcel Atlas said with a unpleasant leer on his face. Ashton glared at him in response and said nothing.

The night ended as it had to do, people had homes to go to and all of that, and so the crowd gradually filtered out as Boris closed the pub and put the lights out. Atlas drifted off to his apartment while Ashton stepped very carefully outside. He hadn't been used to drinking quite that much for a while now, and it was affecting him considerably. Just as well he didn't drive, he thought, though he was also too late for the last bus that would've taken him home. Still, a good walk would clear his head…

Except the sight of the *thing* cleared it a lot quicker.

His jaw dropped open in horror as he took in the facts that not only had he not even remotely beaten it, it was also evidently not tied as he had somehow thought it was to Wakefield Park. It hovered over the intersection of Wakefield Road and Adams Street, the corner where the pub was located, about ten metres off the ground and bigger than he had ever seen it, stretching itself along the four directions from the crossing. Ashton could not escape the sensation that the *thing* was unimpressed with him as it rippled and steamed high above him.

"I don't think it likes you very much," Alice Frampton said as she walked past him and crossed over to the other side of Wakefield Road.

Ashton was stunned enough by the apparition of the *thing* and still sufficiently fuddled by the booze that it took him a whole minute to really register what she'd said, by which time it was of course too late to reply. But Alice Frampton could see the *thing*. She had seen it and she could read it. That much was clear. He turned in dread and began the long walk home, the *thing* remaining where it was but rising higher and higher in the sky so it was still visible. Always behind him, but always there if he turned around to look, and it was always there whether or not he did. It would *always* be there.

Ashton rarely left the house now unless he absolutely had to, getting groceries delivered rather than going out shopping himself, doing whatever he could via the Internet rather than in person, basically cutting off the already minimal contact he'd had with the world around him. Since he had comparatively few real expenses and could survive in relative comfort off an inherited investment, work was not a concern for him and so that was another thing he did not need to go out for. Even prior to this whole business most of his time was spent in reading and listening to music, substantial collections of which he'd accrued over the years, and he had generally found this sufficient along with the occasional bit of actual socialising. Now it was basically all he had, when the *thing* would let him do it. Whatever meant he didn't have to go outside and actually see the *thing*, though, was fine by him. Whenever he did have to go out (mostly to collect whatever mail may have arrived), he would look at it just long enough to observe how much larger it was getting and how much more it was encroaching upon his property before darting back inside to avoid seeing any more. The sole person he actually wanted to see was Alice

Frampton, to learn just what she knew about the *thing*, but he knew the likelihood of that happening was minimal at best even if he did venture forth…

The *thing*, of course, evidently saw no reason to leave Ashton alone just because he was doing his best not to look at it, and the random attacks of attempted communication like a fistful of white-hot knives being driven into his skull were harder and nastier than before, and more debilitating. But Ashton nonetheless felt something different about them. He had felt before that the *thing* was sad when he and it were unable to communicate. Now there was a much more marked feeling of anger and hostility emanating from it towards him—that feeling was now apparently mutual—but there were times he sensed that feeling was not aimed entirely at himself. And he gradually came to the realisation, even if he couldn't say how, that the *thing* was angry at *itself* for being unable to break through to him.

And when he came to this realisation, Ashton let his guard down for a moment and suddenly felt a sympathy for it he could not explain.

As soon as he did this, his head exploded as razor-sharp rays of impossibly coloured light and noises that sounded like a gigantic and reverberant legion of drums playing in the cavernous depths of Hell itself sliced and vibrated him into his constituent atoms, or so it felt. Through the excruciating pain Ashton could also sense something else. Laughter, monstrous alien laughter. The *thing* was taking the piss out of him, figuratively as well as literally, and in some corner of what was left of his conscious mind that it chose to let him keep, Ashton wondered if the *thing* were more capable of human emotion than he'd wanted to believe. It was as if it had tricked him into thinking it was frustrated with its own efforts so that he would open up and it could then come back at him like this out of sheer spite…

Ashton finally woke up two days later, drenched in his own sweat and urine and shit, feeling hollow as if he had been disembowelled and slightly surprised to find he had not in fact been. It would be a few more hours before he could find the strength to actually move, his own repulsion at stewing in his own waste finally proving too much , by which time it was dark and the only light in the room was that visible through the now rarely lifted blinds, a mix of the street lighting and the vile luminosity of the *thing*. Staggering to his feet, he drifted through to his bedroom for fresh clothes, and something else.

He had been startled to find the switchblade in what had been his parents' bedroom; it sat on the bottom of his father's old wardrobe next to a few old paperbacks. What the hell his father was doing with such a thing (actually, what if it had really been his *mother*? Now *there* was a thought) baffled him, since it was illegal to own and the old man had never exactly been prone to violence or breaking laws, and Ashton himself just felt weird seeing it there and tried not to think about it. Now he thought about it as he dressed himself, and retrieved it from the wardrobe, turning it over in his hand (nice bit of craftsmanship, he noted; Dad *had* always found that important), though he had no idea what he could possibly do with it short of stabbing himself. Which, at that moment, was a distinct option…

Clothed again, Ashton went back through to the front room to find the door lying open to the street outside and the *thing* pulsating away.

No longer even horrified by it, he went through the door, and the *thing* parted around him as he did so. Looking up, he saw it now occupied the entire visible space around him, covering the entire sky from horizon to horizon like some sort of revolting dome, stretching in all directions for an indeterminate distance and rising over him to what must have been nearly a mile in height. And looking ahead of him, out towards Wakefield Park, he saw that human shape again, the one he'd seen that other time, which he could now just make out in the small amount of light pouring onto the field from the street lighting, making odd poses by raising its arms into what looked like difficult positions, turning around as it did so, though at this distance and in this light Ashton still could not identify any features.

Venturing back inside for a moment, Ashton's not fully-functioning brain realised he might just have a better use for the switchblade…

The *thing* gave off a vague vibration that might have been concern as Ashton strode forth with remarkable purpose across the road to the park, but it parted into a sort of corridor for him to walk down as if it knew where he was going. The closer Ashton got to the figure, the more he could mark. They had their back to him, but he could discern the darkness of their skin, and the ceremonial garb of the Old Tribes that they wore. He had seen videos at school of the Old Tribes doing ritual dances, and he knew this must be one of those. As he approached, the figure's outline grew clearer. They were female. She lowered her arms, stood upright and turned around to face him.

"Hi," Alice Frampton said.

By now Ashton was no longer capable of feeling anything, including surprise, so he took her presence as somehow entirely predictable and obvious. It made as much sense as anything that had happened to him in recent months.

"The family business?" he asked, indicating the *thing* around them as it swirled through the sky.

Alice nodded. "Pretty much. My ancestors have… tended to it for centuries now. Time for me to do my share."

"But what *is* it?"

"It's…" She paused as if she were trying to find the right words, then waved her hands around like Ashton had done himself that night they met in the pub. "It's… this *place*. This whole area." She looked up at it with an expression of what could've been fear or reverence or both. "Kind of like what the Romans called the *genius loci*, a sort of divine presence in the environment. It's… well, it's kind of South East 36 itself, I suppose. And more…"

Ashton shook his head, trying to comprehend. "What, it's a sort of god?"

"Not quite," Alice said patiently, "Kind of a spirit of place. The sort of thing that gets called a god because people don't know what else to call it. It predates the Old Tribes, obviously, and it… well, didn't like us encroaching on it. But we used the land well and we paid it respect, and then… well, white European settlement kind of screwed *that* up over the last hundred years, didn't it?" She looked into the distance sadly. "It remembers what this area used to be like before there were people, even before the Old Tribes first came here. It's got used to people, it doesn't hate them as such, sometimes it even likes them, but it wishes things were like they used to be…"

"But it hates *me* as such," Ashton hissed, "What have I done wrong? Why's it picking on me?"

"Because you hate it," Alice said simply, turning back to face him, "You hate this place. It doesn't know *why* you hate it, but it's… kind of offended that you do. It just doesn't know how to make itself understood. Not your fault, obviously," she added hastily. "But you know what some families are like, they'll tear strips off each other but they'll shoot down anyone else that tries to do the same? It works a bit like that." She turned away again. "It doesn't really hate even you. Joel. It just wants a bit more respect."

Ashton's right hand started reaching around to his hip pocket, suddenly noticing he could feel hate coursing through him again, that the numbness was lifting.. "So *you* understand it," he said.

Alice nodded. "The Old Tribes have had thousands of years to learn how to deal with it," she said. "Not that it's easy to do so or anything like that, and we still don't know completely what it wants always, which is… well, *messy* sometimes." She gave a small shudder that was not entirely because of the coolness of the night. "But we know enough to be able to take care of it."

"So," Ashton said, pulling out the knife, "You can make yourself understood by it, too." Alice said nothing. "Make *me* understood, then. Tell it to leave me alone. God answers prayers, or so they say…"

Alice spun round, looking furious. "I can't *tell* it to do anything," she snapped, "It's not there to be *commanded*. I don't have any control over it…"

"*Well what fucking GOOD are you?*" Ashton screamed as he plunged the blade into her abdomen. She didn't see it coming until a split second before it entered her. Watching the blood flow from her and cover the ceremonial robe she wore, she turned her face up to Ashton with an expression of astonishment, and fell to the ground as his hand let go of the knife. As Ashton looked at the body at his feet, he was only dimly aware of what had just happened, still feeling only rage boiling within him, until he heard a sound coming from somewhere above him. He had never heard any sound like it, and yet he knew what it must be. He had offended the *thing* for the last time.

Joel Ashton looked up at the sky, which looked like it was seething with the same rage he felt. The mass of the *thing* convolved with fury, an anger he knew was directed at him and for which he had nothing but contempt. Fuck this place, fuck everything about it, and most of all fuck this *genius loci* or whatever the hell it was. As the *thing* rotated at terrifying speed it became a hideously red and violent-looking cloud mass like the top of a hurricane seen from space, emitting a thunderous noise composed of unspeakable hate that emerged from what looked like a mouth. And the mouth had fangs.

And Joel Ashton laughed, because he realised after all this he would never leave South East 36, and in a way he would be part of it forever.

The *thing* gave him just enough time to appreciate the irony.

SIGNALS
JOHN PAUL FITCH

Gus Dillon hadn't seen a storm this bad since the big one in '35 that killed his Pa. The old fool had gone outside in the swirling rain and thunder to make sure the barn door was closed. Lightning cracked close by and spooked the horses. He was caught in the rush when they bolted, his head crushed by hooves, bones shattered, flesh pulped to marmalade. He couldn't have heard Gus screaming and hollering as he watched his Pa being trampled to death.

Gus burned that barn to the ground after the funeral and shot those horses in the field, and let the pigs eat the corpses. This storm was worse.

Gus climbed the creaky stairs as wind shook the old wooden house. He stuck his head inside James' room. The boy was fast asleep. Gus closed the door softly and made his way along the hall. Lily was likewise fast asleep. He lay down on the bed and pulled the quilt high up to his chin and lay in the dark, counting the moments between the flashes of light and the rolling peals of thunder. At some point he began to dose, and soon was fast asleep.

If he'd been awake, maybe he'd have seen the streak of lightning that cleaved the sky in half. Maybe he'd have seen it strike the antenna of the TV station up on the hill above his farm, turning the mast white-hot. And just maybe he'd have gone up there to check if Tank Williams, the station's maintenance man, and Gus' drinking buddy, was okay. But Gus saw and did none of these things. Instead, he moaned and thrashed in bed, bound by slumber and dreaming of wind and thunder and crashing hooves and split skulls and blood on dirt.

George Elliot had been enjoying a peaceful cup of coffee and a slice of pie when the waitress called his name. The dozen or so patrons glanced around as he answered. He was used to the glare of crowds, of suspicious men, and flirty glances of women. He was a G-Man.

"Yeah, sweetheart. That's me."

"Phone call for you. Booth over there." She pointed to the glass booth to the back of the coffee shop. George buttoned his jacket as he stood, keeping the flash of polished gun metal from public eyes. The weapon snuggled against his ribs on his left-hand side. George sidled up to the booth and slid the door closed, lifting the receiver.

"Elliot."

"George, it's Fred Dekker. I need you to come in. We got something."

George shook his watch free from his cuff and checked the time.

"30 minutes." He hung up and exited the booth. George picked up his hat and coat from his seat and left a tip for the waitress before heading for his car. As he passed the counter he winked at the girl. She blushed and turned her head coyly. George smiled and pushed out into the cold Autumn afternoon.

Chief Agent Fred Dekker was pouring himself a drink when George entered his office. The old man loved a scotch in late afternoon, when the secretaries had packed up and left for the day and the junior agents were long gone, and he always kept a bottle in his desk drawer. He drained the glass and poured himself another while the ice was still cold. Fred offered the bottle to George.

"Drink? Good for what ails ya."

"No thanks."

"Suit yourself. This is the good stuff." He leaned back in his chair, the springs squeaking, and ran a hand over his white hair. George sat opposite him and crossed his legs. He placed his hat on his knee.

"What you got for me, Fred?"

Fred swigged the scotch. "Ever heard of a town called Calladen? Couple of hours upstate?"

"Should I have?"

"Not unless you're into pig farming."

"I like bacon, that's about it. So why are we interested in it now?"

"A few days ago, Calladen was the epicentre of some unusual electro-magnetic storm activity. The fly-boys in Nevada tracked the storm. Sent a spy-plane to take some aerial shots."

Fred opened the desk drawer and pulled a manila folder and tossed it onto his desk. Several glossy photographs slid out onto the desk top.

"The plane flies up around 14 miles in altitude. Takes great shots, don't you think?" He gestured to the photographs. George slid himself closer to the desk. Pictured was a dense mass of dark cloud, its innards incandescent with white-hot electricity.

"Nothing too unusual about storms, Fred."

"No. But this wasn't no ordinary storm."

Fred rummaged in the folder and pulled a graph from amongst the photographs. It showed a relatively stable line with small peaks and troughs, and one sudden sharp peak that almost went off the page. Fred continued, "This here is a graphic showing a burst of gamma radiation. This peak occurred when those boys out in White Sands set off the Trinity bomb."

George stared at the graph, at the spike that almost went off the page.

"Trinity."

Fred lifted a second graph from the folder. It showed a similar pattern as the first, small waves followed by one enormous spike.

"This here is the radiation released by the freak storm over Calladen, George. Most of it was thankfully jettisoned into the upper atmosphere and out into space." George could feel the icy fingers of foreboding worm their way through his chest.

"So why are we having this meeting, Fred?"

Fred gathered up the photographs and slid them back into the folder and closed it up. "Some of the townsfolk have disappeared."

George sat back and let the reality of the situation wash over him.

"So, you're sending me."

Fred nodded. "Right again, old friend. The fly-boys are paying close attention to the situation and the higher ups in Washington think a personal presence may be required." He nodded to the file on his desk. George reached for it and, lifting his hat, stood.

The drive took longer than George had expected. Narrow roads wormed their way through hills punctuated by blind corners and summits, and all the while he had to pull over to the side to let the never-ending parade of lumber trucks rumble past. The radio whispered static and hinted at snatches of Duke Ellington and the deep baritone of a radio announcer. George flicked the radio off and concentrated on the drive as a fully loaded truck barrelled past, kicking up clouds of dust and small stones which pelted the windscreen. He glanced at the map sprawled on the passenger seat, turning it towards him. The route was marked on its contoured lines in red felt pen. Lifting the map for a better look, he didn't see the buck till it was too late. The bang of heavy flesh on metal. The road twisted, and sunlight sparkled in glass rain, refracting into a thousand colours. The sky was beneath George. He felt himself soaked in hot liquid. The acrid scent of copper pricked his nostrils. And there came a screeching. George couldn't tell if it was he who screamed or the animal.

He inhaled quickly, pain stabbing his side. He was lying face down on soft grass in a field spotted with small yellow flowers, his arm pinned under his stomach. He rolled over slowly. His head spun as he tried to figure out where he was and why he ached so badly. A black Ford Fairlane, it's roof crushed, the hood buckled, lay on its side in a ditch. "That's my car," thought George. A stag, torn almost in half, jutted from the windshield. Innards spilled out over the Fairlane's tan leather interior. A shattered leg still kicked at the dark grey sky. The world became slippery and George let his head fall back onto the soft grass.

Rain pelted the window like a snare drum and wind buffeted the glass, howling under the eaves, and calling George from the peaceful depths of sleep into the pain of the living world. He cracked an eyelid slowly, the swelling on his face making this simple act an outright chore. Light crept through the gap between the bedroom door and the carpeted floor. His neck and body stiff from the impact and the blossoming bruises across his torso, George ran through his memories: a tumbling world, the crack and crash of shattered glass, a hooved leg kicking against encroaching death, the soft embrace of grass and the earth beneath him and the deep swimming blackness of oblivion. Springs squealed as George slowly sat up and swung his legs over the side of the single bed. He was dressed in a clean white tee-shirt and a pair of boxer shorts. They were not his clothes. Floorboards creaked as he stood on unsteady legs, the muscles complaining, spasming. A pair of pants hung over the back of a rocking chair in the corner and folded on the seat was a wool sweater. He took in his surroundings, a dresser, a wardrobe in the corner, and the bed. Someone's bedroom for sure, and by the look of the bottles of cologne on the dresser it was a man's bedroom, most likely an older gentleman. George dressed slowly and limped to the door. Muffled voices through the wood. Urgent talk, a man's deep baritone and at least one woman's alto tones locked in conversation. George cracked the door, hinges creaking. Then came the voice.

"Hello? Are you awake?"

George stepped out into the hallway and headed for the stairs. AS he turned at the top of the staircase, a smiling grey-headed man in a white shirt and black pants waited at the bottom, coffee cup raised. "You ready for a cup of black gold?"

Doctor Paul Banovich poured George a full mug of coffee and placed it on the table next to the roast beef and lettuce sandwich he had prepared for his guest. He took a seat beside his wife, Margaret. George scanned the kitchen, a large chrome sink under the window, workbench, yellow wallpaper, polished wood cupboards at head height, and a large lead fridge directly to his right. The door to the back porch stood immediately to his left, and a swing door to the living room behind him. The scent of coffee and freshly baked bread swirled in the air.

"Helluva bang you gave yourself, young man. Your car is completely wrecked."

"The deer around here are a menace. They jump out in front of you. I don't know how many times I've almost run into one." Margaret smiled. "Eat. You'll need to regain your strength."

"Thanks Doctor –"

"Paul, please."

"Thanks, Paul."

"The Sheriff called me when they spotted your wreck. You were lying out in the field. I got them to bring you here where I could keep an eye on you. You've been asleep for a good eight hours."

"Jesus. So how am I doing, Paul?"

The Doctor smiled. "Apart from some bad bruising you came out of that wreck in pretty good shape."

George nodded and bit into the sandwich.

"You'll be here because of the report I filed?"

"Missing people. You filed the report?"

Paul nodded.

"Why don't you start at the beginning." Said George.

"We had a big storm a few nights back. Took out the TV broadcast station up on the mountain. Real bad. Anyway, nobody seen hide nor hair of the station chief Tank Williams since then. Gus and Sarah Dillon and their boy, Little Gus. They've been missing since the night of the storm too. At first, we thought maybe they'd gone camping or something, but nobody seen them leave. Their animals are roaming around the fields. Didn't tell anybody they were going anywhere."

A gust of wind shunted the house, spraying the kitchen window with rain. "I'll need to speak to the sheriff."

"Not at this time of night. You best try to get some more rest and I'll drive you into town in the morning. Sheriff Barker will be there at some point. Depends on how much whisky he swallows tonight, of course. Oh, almost forgot." Paul stood and moved to the kitchen bench and opened a drawer. He turned and in his hands were George's badge and weapon, still in its holster.

"Agent Elliot," he said, placing them on the table. George finished the sandwich and swilled the last of the coffee in his cup. The doctor and his wife stood. "We best be hitting the hay. There's more coffee in the pot and help yourself to anything in the fridge." They moved towards the kitchen door. Paul leaned on George's shoulder and whispered.

"There's some scotch in the cabinet in the living room. Might help you sleep." He winked conspiratorially and was gone. George poured himself another mug of hot coffee and, savouring the roasted scent, he made his way down the hallway past the stairs. A bookcase nestled in the nook under the stairs and George bent to inspect the assorted novels and tomes. A flickering caught the corner of his eye as he ran his finger over the books, Steinbeck, HG Wells, Bradbury. The glare of a television lighted the lounge room to George's left. The living room was conservatively decorated, a small two-seater couch against the wall, a table with a lamp, a rocking chair beside the window, and against the far wall a small square television set on thin wooden legs. The screen was fixed in the centre of the set, knobs for adjustment of signal either side and a wire receiver atop the box. Static snow cast a blizzard on the small screen, bathing the room in hissing white light. George pushed into the room, closer to the television. Didn't the Doctor tell him the station was down? Why would the television set be on? George moved towards the static screen, hand out to turn it off when a shadow crossed the screen. George paused. Slow movement, rhythmic, hypnotic. It waved back and forth behind the static, hiding in the snow. Through the hiss George could have sworn he heard a voice, a whispering. He flicked the knob. The light reduced to a small dot, burning into the glass. He backed out of the lounge room, the small dot refusing to fade. It stared at him like a white pupil. He headed back to the kitchen where his wallet and weapon still lay on the table. George inspected his wallet, his credentials still intact. Then he checked his weapon and put one in the chamber.

The drive to town took less than ten minutes. Golden sunlight cut through the cold morning mist. George was dressed in the same slacks and sweater as the night before. Doctor Banovich lent him an overcoat and some boots.

"Margaret will have your suit cleaned and patched up good as new by this afternoon," he chirped.

"Nice country here." George gazed out at the fields. Insects still buzzed in the late autumn air, honey coloured light warming the surface of everything it touched, the last of the seasons fight against the coming winter. George cast a glance at the tree covered hills, densely forested, thick pine trees nestled together like the bristles of a brush.

"Yeah, it's not too bad to look at that's for sure."

"Ever have trouble before? People going missing?"

"This country is older and stranger than most people realise. I been here my whole life, seen a lot of strange things up there in the woods. Other folks seen lights, some claim to have seen Bigfoot. Can you believe that? Bigfoot." The Doc chuckled.

"You seen Bigfoot, Doc?"

"No. Saw the lights though, when I was younger. Up there on Widow's Peak." He pointed towards the highest point on the ridge where half the mountain sloped gently up and dropped off sharply, like it had been cleaved away.

"They'd come up at dusk, swirl around the peak. Whites, reds, greens, blues. They'd dance around in the sky, circling. Then they'd disappear before your eyes and you'd never have guessed they were there. I guess these days you'd call them Flying Saucers." George kept his eye on Widow's Peak until they turned the bend and it slinked behind a grove of trees.

They ate breakfast in Sissy's Diner while they waited for the Sheriff to show up. Sissy, a large motherly woman in her 60's, took their order and brought them their food with a smile. Paul didn't even have to order, Sissy bringing him his usual scrambled eggs on whole-wheat toast, and with it came a large pot of black coffee which came with a country wide smile and a grey bee-hive haircut for free. George lifted a complimentary box of matches from the ash-tray in the centre of the table. *Sissy's Diner – Best Eggs in The North.*

George was mopping the last of his egg yolks with a piece of bacon when the door to the diner swung open. Sheriff Barker swaggered in like he was John Wayne, cowboy hat tipped back on his head, badge shining in the morning light, hand on his weapon holster. He was tall and as wide as a line-backer. Pulling his aviator sunglasses from his face he spotted George and Paul, and ambled his way over towards their booth. He tipped a nod to Sissy who was already pouring coffee for him. He sat himself down in the booth opposite George, fixing him with a quizzical stare.

"Paul. How are you?"

"I'm good, Jack. This is Agent George Elliot." He gestured to George as the Sheriff removed his hat. The sheriff extended a meaty hand across the table, which enveloped George's almost completely.

"Agent of what?"

George cast a glance around the diner. People stared at them.

"We should speak somewhere less public. How about your office, Sheriff?"

Barker looked George up and down before nodding slowly. He half turned in the booth. "Sissy, make that coffee to go, would ya?"

"I'm a Special Agent of the Federal Bureau of Investigation assigned to work with the United States Air Force."

The Sheriff's office was cramped and cluttered and dusty. The black eyes of a wall-mounted stag's head reflected the light from the window. Barker squeezed himself into a swivel chair, the wood creaking under his weight. His large wide desk was cluttered with towers of paper and stacks of files. In the centre of the desk was a metal typewriter and a large desk lamp perched on the edge. Barker slid his hat from his head and smoothed his thinning hair back over his scalp.

"FBI. Air Force…what do you all want up here in our little town anyway?"

"Seems like you have a couple of missing people, Sheriff."

"You know, we can handle our own business here. We don't need the help of the FBI or the Air Force or even the lord Jesus himself."

George crossed his legs and smoothed out the material of his pants. "Fact of the matter, sheriff, is that a family is missing, and as the good doctor reported a certain Tank Williams also appears to have disappeared."

The sheriff eyed Banovich angrily before smiling from the side of his mouth.

"Look. They probably all gone hunting or something. They'll turn up. Mark my words. So why don't you just get the FBI to send you up a new car or whatever, and you can go back to investigating whatever it is you usually investigate. Hell, maybe the Air Force will send you up a chopper or something."

"Sheriff. I'm part of something called Project Blue Book. Have you heard of it?"

"Blue Book? What is that. Colouring book for little kiddies? You get crayons with that?" He started chuckling to himself, the chair groaning as he leant back.

"We investigate cases which show signs of extra-terrestrial connections."

"Extra-what-now?"

Doctor Banovich flinched visibly. "Aliens?"

"That's correct, Doctor." said George.

Barker cackled. "Little green men? Christ, I think he needs another check-up. Aliens!"

George stood. "I'll need to take a look at the Dillon household."

"I can drive you up there." Said Paul. George nodded and they both moved towards the door.

"Now wait a god-damned minute. There ain't no little green men running around these hills, there ain't no flying saucers, there ain't no aliens. This here is God's country, with a capital 'G'. Those Dillon folks are off having a good time somewhere. Gus and Tank are probably drunk off their asses right now. You just watch. Christ. See what you did, you gone and made me blaspheme the good lord's name."

George took a step back towards the Sheriff. "Tell me one thing. Did you even go up to their place to have a look?"

"No, and there wasn't no goddamned good reason to either."

George turned to the doctor. "Paul, do you own a firearm?"

"Yeah. I got a rifle in the back of the truck. Never know when you'll need one round here. There've been sightings of cougars out in the woods, big ones."

"Good. We may need it." He nodded to Barker as he turned to leave. "Sheriff."

Barker stood from his chair and puffed his chest out, sucking in his gut. He pulled up his belt at the sides.

"Now you just wait a goddamned minute. Nobody is going galivanting around my town without me." He muttered to himself as he fished on his desk for his car keys. George slid Paul a sly wink. The old doctor smiled back at him.

The drive up to the Dillon place was quiet and uneventful. Clouds capped the mountains, building high and dark. George stared at them, feeling that peculiar tension in the air.

"Yep. Looks like it's gonna come down heavy. Maybe even soon." Said Paul.

George pulled his weapon from his shoulder holster and slid the barrel back. A round was nestled in there like a baby.

"One in the chamber, as always. It's good practise for a professional." Paul said.

George put the gun away and sized George up. Paul smiled.

"101st Airborne," he said. "Screamin' Eagles. Of course, I was in service long time ago. Too old to go fighting Nazis. You serve?"

"Marines. 1st company."

"Guadacanal?"

George nodded. He stared straight out of the window.

"What you boys did was incredible. Just want you to know that." Paul turned back to the road. George shifted the wing mirror. Sheriff Barker's cruiser was still behind them.

"Anything I should know about Gus Dillon before we get up there, Doc?"

"Like what?"

"Is he prone to violent outbursts? Has he ever smacked his old lady around?"

"I been treating this town for twenty years. Seen a lot of bruises on women, hidden under make-up. Never seen a single mark on Lily, or their boy for that matter. Why do you ask?"

"I need to understand what kind of man I'm dealing with. Some men hide their nature behind a mask. A veneer of normalcy, or a shell that they put around them for other folks, but they always reveal themselves to those closest to them, those weaker. You can always tell what kind of a man you're dealing with by how he treats his lady."

"Well as far as I'm concerned, Gus is a good egg. He adores Lily and their kid. He's not dangerous." George stared up at the clouds again, they'd turned dark grey-blue. He patted his gun softly and nodded to himself. His gut was telling him trouble was coming. And it was never wrong.

The Dillon house sat at the end of a long gravel drive. Three storeys high with a long porch running around the perimeter of the house; and a set of wooden steps leading up to the front door. Trees on three sides, the beginning of the woods, and behind it, half-way up the mountain, was the broadcast station.

"This house has been in the Dillon family for generations." Sheriff Barker wheezed, the walk up the driveway stealing the breath from his lungs. "I remember Gus' Daddy living here, Big Gus."

"Imaginative choice of name for his son."

Barker shot George a look. "I'm named after my Daddy too. Most folks are."

"Even the women?"

Barker hissed. "Even the women…you goddamn city boys…always with the smart mouths." He sucked in a breath and cupped his mouth "Hey Gus!"

Barkers voice boomed out, despite his lack of fitness. No response came.

"Well, there goes the element of surprise. I doubt anyone is here anyway." said George, moving off to the side to get a better angle of the back yard, which looked deserted. Clothes hung on the washing line and a basket lay at the base of the clothes pole. When they'd come through the gate the mail box had been overstuffed with newspapers and letters, bills and brochures. They could hear the wind come down the mountain, rustling the trees, whispering through the branches. George listened to the woods.

"You hear that?" he said.

"Hear what?" said Sheriff Barker.

"Exactly. Nothing. No birds, no wildlife."

Doctor Banovich scratched his cheek. "Shit. Didn't Fred have a dog? Big old brown Labrador. You could hear that thing bark for miles on a bad day."

Barker took off his hat and rubbed his thinning scalp. "Probably took it fishing with them."

They neared the porch. George stopped and turned to the other men. "Sheriff, head around back, see if there's any movement, Doc, you're with me."

Barker pulled up his belt. "Now wait a minute, Agent Elliot. I'm Sheriff round here. I make the calls."

"Okay, Sheriff. What's your call?"

"Well…" Barker blinked, "I'll uh…head around back and check it out. You two stay here." He pulled his service revolver and crouched and slowly crept around the corner. George waited till he was out of sight before moving up the steps onto the porch with Doctor Banovich close behind him. The Doc peered in the window beside the door. George could see the drapes were drawn from where he stood. Doc shook his head.

"Can't see a thing."

The door was solid wood with a frosted glass pane and a heavy brass knocker. George jiggled the door handle.

"Locked."

"How do we get in?" said the Doc.

The door frame shattered on the third kick and the stench hit George as soon as the door swung open. Musty, fruity, rotten. A black tornado of flies buzzed inside the hallway. George and the Doc covered their faces with their hands.

"Oh Christ." said Banovich. Stepping onto the hallway rug they spotted a pale looking Sheriff Barker move into the kitchen with his handkerchief over his mouth and nose.

"Somethings dead in here fellas," he said. A staircase stood to the right and a doorway to the left led to a lounge room. A rocking chair and couch stood near the window. A bookcase and a glass cabinet full of plates and crockery lined the far wall. Pictures of the Dillon family adorned the walls, and against the opposite wall stood the television, or what had been the television. Presumably it had once been a regular sized plastic and wood television had warped and distended, like something had melted it and stretched it out across the wall, *smeared* it. It looked organic, like it had begun to grow, swelling and contracting like flesh. The screen was gone, replaced by a pulpy orifice, the inside red and glistening. Ropey tendrils extended from the television stretching across the floor to the source of the stench. Flies covered the prostrated bodies of the Dillon family like moving fur. They lay in a heap before the television, bodies limp and empty as deflated balloons. The tendrils punctured the bodies of Gus, Lily, and the boy in half a dozen places. The family reduced to empty husks.

"What in the lord's name?" Barker moved towards the family, reaching his hand out towards the boy. The kid had slumped over, his head touching the floor. A tendril ran taut from a large wound on his neck, the blood dried to a crust where the fleshy tube had pierced him.

"Don't touch him." Said George as he circled the family, his eyes narrowed on the crimson strands stretching out from the television. They glimmered in the light. Barker's wet eyes were fixed on the boy, his mouth working, but no sound came from his lips except the quiet hiss of breath. Barely a step from the boy, Barker reached out to touch him. The tendril quivered. George didn't even have time to warn Barker. There was a soft smacking sound, like lips kissing as the appendage released its bite on the boy. The head of the appendage peeled back revealing layers of flesh opening and closing, and underneath the flaps, two white bony protrusions worked like a beak. It reared up like a viper and lashed out at Barker, striking him in the stomach. The Sheriff hollered as the tendril pierced his torso, his shirt seeping red around the wound. The tendril pulsed as it began to suck at the Sheriff, filling itself with his blood. In the chaos, George watched as the other tentacles detached from the Gus and Lily and began to wave and flick in the air around Barker.

Tendrils whipped towards George and the Doc tendrils, eager to taste fresh victims. George bundled Doc Banovich out of the way, the spearing tentacle missing him by inches. Barker screamed as three tendrils shot into his body, two in the chest, one in the upper leg. They pulled taut and Barker's feet went from under him. He slid towards the television, grasping at furniture as he went. His fingers clutched the leg of the couch and held. His skin tore where he had been speared, spilling blood onto the floor, as the tentacles pulled at his flesh.

"Oh Christ. Help me."

"Hang on." George scoured the lounge room, looking for something to help him, his eyes only finding ornaments. Seeing nothing he spun back towards Barker just as the Sheriff's fingers slipped from the table, and he shot towards the television. George did a double-take. The screen of the TV had become transparent and soft, like jelly. Behind the opaque liquid was a moving shape, curved and sharp. It broke the surface of the screen and opened wide. A toothed mouth opened wide like a flower, rows upon rows of short pointed teeth which ran in circles down the things dark gullet.

George's hand moved in a slick manner, the result of thousands of hours of practise. In a flicker his weapon was in his hand. He raised his arm and fired at the cavernous mouth, bullets popping the flesh of the creature. A high-pitched noise came from the thing as the bullets struck its pink flesh, but it didn't stop pulling Barker towards its maw. The Sheriff's fingers gave out and he was hoisted from the floor. He screamed as the lips of the creature closed around his abdomen. The Sheriff began to kick and thrash. Blood gurgled from his mouth and ran down over his chin and neck. George ran to him, covering the steps to the television as quickly as he could, yet he may as well have been running through treacle. There was a crack as Barker's back snapped and he folded backwards in half. Barker's arms went limp and his head dangled towards George as his heels came up to meet it and he slid into the maw whole. A burst of electricity came from the television set. George could have sworn blind that a blob of light ran from the back of the box and along the coaxial cord to the wall socket. The screen went dark as the glass returned to normal. Barker was gone, leaving George shaking on the floor amidst the hollow bodies of the Gus and Lily Dillon and their son.

George blinked, his breath coming in gasps. Somewhere, someone was saying his name, but it sounded far off. All he knew was the dull grey glass of the television screen, the white dot in the centre shrinking to nothing.

George and the Doc sat in the truck in silence and stared at the Dillon house as the sun died behind them. Doc Banovich turned to look at George. His face was carved from granite, the jaw tight.

"You ever seen…?"

"No."

"anything…?"

George shook his head.

Silence.

"How do you suppose…?"

George nodded up the mountain towards the bent and scorched radio mast, and the lines of soldered copper wiring that spread out from it like veins and arteries.

"Didn't you say that the broadcast station got hit by lightning during the storm?"

"Yeah, so." The Doc's face slackened as he realised what George was getting at. "You don't suppose it's somehow…?"

George turned to the Doctor.

"It wasn't an ordinary storm. Also…last night. Your television was on. I thought there was something in the static. A shape moving behind the glass. I shrugged it off as a symptom of the accident, but what if that thing…" he nodded towards the darkened house. His eyes followed the line of the telephone wire which ran from the roof of the house and over the top of the truck.

"If it's travelling through the wires…"

The Doc gunned the engine of the truck and slammed it into reverse. Tyres kicked up dust as they spun.

"Margaret."

Her shoes were all that was left of her, and the still-wet puddle of blood on the carpet. The television hissed static. Doc Banovich collapsed to his knees on the floor and wept. George let him sob. He went to the cabinet and pulled the bottle of scotch and popped the cork. The whisky's scent was sharp and pungent, peat and ash. It stung his throat, burning its way down to his stomach. When the Doc was finished weeping he stood and dried his eyes with his jacket sleeve. He took the bottle from George and gulped several large mouthfuls before handing it back. George stared at the old man, his eyes crimson and puffy.

"We gotta get this sonofabitch, Agent Elliot."

"It's moving through the transmission wires. Whatever this goddamn thing is. The radio station. That's got to be the source."

The Doc turned back to the television and with a guttural howl, swung his boot straight through the screen, which exploded in a shower of glass and sparks.

"We'll burn that bastard outta there."

With two full gas canisters clanking in the back of the truck, filled from the pumping station on Main Street, George and Doctor Banovich tore through the town. Houses flickered with light, lounge rooms strobing with television static.

"The whole town. The whole damn town."

They swung the truck up the tree-lined road to the TV station. The silver moon rose quickly behind the mountain.

"When we get there, I want you to stay outside. I can't risk another member of the public being hurt. It's my job to take this thing out. You hear me, Doc?"

"I hear ya. But I ain't listening." Doc drove on, his face like granite. "That son of a bitch took my Margaret. I'll have my vengeance. Ain't nobody gonna deny me that."

George sighed. "If you say so, Doc."

The station loomed out of the darkening tree-line. A simple squat rectangular building with a towering red and white strutted mast, anchored to the ground by metallic guy ropes. The windows were dark, and the front door stood ajar. There was no sound at all in the woods, no evening birdsong, no hum of insect life. The clouds above the station swirled. The wind carried the musty scent of coming rain and no sooner had George noted it than the first drops began to fall.

Doc Banovich hoisted the gas cannisters from the truck.

"How do we go about this, George?"

"I say we toss the gas inside and light the place up, unless you got a better idea, Doc?"

"You'll need this." Said Doc Banovich. He tossed something small and metallic to George. Light glinted off the lighter as it arced through the air. George caught it and held it up.

"Can't beat a zippo, can you, Doc?"

George slipped the lighter into his pocket and relieved the Doc of one of the cannisters, hauling it across the dirt lot towards the front door. Reaching the threshold, George pushed the front door open with his foot and peeked around the frame of the door, trying to get a look inside. As he bent to unscrew the cap on the cannister, he became aware of a shape inside the station, barely visible in the gloom. George dropped the can and reached around for his weapon.

"Show yourself. I'm a federal agent. I am armed."

The man stood in the shadows facing the door. George drew a bead on him and pulled back the hammer on the gun. He heard Doc Banovich approach behind him. Doc craned his neck over George's shoulder.

"It's Tank Williams. Holy hell!"

The Doc dropped his cannister.

"Hey, Tank. Come on outta there. You been hiding up here this whole ti--"

George reached inside the door and hit the light-switch, illuminating the station control room. Doc Banovich stopped mid-sentence.

A muscular man of maybe thirty was suspended from the ceiling of the station by a sheet of flesh which had been stripped from his frame and stretched up and away from his body.

"Oh Christ. Tank…" Doc Banovich made the sign of the cross. Tank hung limply, his face bloated and grey. Tendrils, the same kind that had taken Sheriff Barker to his death, and presumably Margaret Banovich, extended from the walls around Tank, from the radio equipment, from the tape banks, from the monitors and television screens that were stacked in corners. The walls themselves were upholstered with pink and red skin, veins underneath pulsing with fluid.

"Doc. The gas."

They both reached for their cannisters. George began to toss the petrol on the walls closest to him, pouring gasoline on the desks, the chairs, filing cabinets. He was careful not to touch the fleshy walls. Doc Banovich likewise avoided the tendrils which pulsed like veins. George tipped his cannister upside down, emptying the last of his gas onto the floor. Banovich poured the last of his near the body of Tank Williams, some of the petrol splashing on the man's legs. Tank kicked at the touch, his body spasming. He let out a moan, a low guttural sound which came from the depths of his body.

"Holy hell. He's alive." Banovich dropped his cannister, the contents spilling out onto the floor. He went to the suspended man, whose head hand lolled backwards. "George, give me a hand to cut him down."

The Doc ran his hands over William's torso checking for his vitals, Tank head lifted again, and his flesh quivered like jelly, the eyes long since turned to mush and run from the sockets. Williams body began to shake, the tendrils attached to him quivering. Doc Banovich realised his mistake too late. George didn't have time to warn him as Tank's arms slipped around the Doc's body. The sheet of flesh tensed like a muscle and Tank was hoisted up towards the ceiling, taking the yelping Banovich with him. George went for his weapon. By the time he raised his arm to fire, Tank's body had opened, and the stomach peeled back like lips, the insides lined with rows upon rows of teeth. Banovich screamed as he was pulled into the body of what had once been Tank Williams, which quickly closed around him, the teeth slicing into his flesh, tearing the meat from his bones. In an instant he was gone, Tank's pale skin closing over him, sealing him inside. The old man struggled beneath the surface. Tank shook from side to side violently, and the roiling inside him stopped.

George emptied his weapon at Tank. The bullets tore holes in his torso, and George hoped he hit the Doc to save him from suffering. The bullets made no difference to Tank who moved quick as a spider. Tendrils tightened and slackened, pulling him across the ceiling like wires. Tank trembled, his limbs contorting, arms bending backwards at perverse angles. The stink of gasoline was almost overpowering, George spluttered as it caught his throat.

He staggered backwards, away from the creature, and turned to run for the door, but the thing was too quick and too smart. It scuttled across the ceiling over George's head, swinging its tentacles at him. George sprawled in the petrol, gagging as it splashed on his face, feeling it burn his tongue and lips and eyes. The creature had taken up a position above the door, blocking the only exit. George scrambled to his feet as the creature detached itself from the ceiling, sliding its way down the wall. The seam on its body peeled open, its maw gaped and the eruption of red flesh beneath glistened.

George wiped his streaming eyes and felt in his pocket for the lighter that Doc Banovich had given him.

"If I'm going down, you're coming too, you ugly sonofabitch." George flicked the lid of the zippo as the creature began to advance on him. The spark caught flame first time. George tossed the zippo at the thing.

The gasoline ignited with a loud 'whoosh', the wall of heat knocking George several feet backwards, stealing the wind from his chest. He slammed into a filing cabinet against the far wall. The world winked out for a moment and when it came back the room was an inferno. Black smoke billowed near the ceiling, thick and nebulous and somewhere up there was a knot of tentacles and roiling flesh. George heard it scream and thrash against the ceiling, trying to break through. In a blur of motion, it swung down from the ceiling and barrelled past him, slamming into the wall. The plaster crumbled and cracked under the impact but did not give way. The creature lurched backwards, tentacles firing out in every direction seeking purchase. It tore itself away towards the door which splintered as the creature burst through. Wind rushed into the inferno, fanning flames either side of the door, which rose up hungrily. For a second the fire parted. George took his chance and ran for the door. Every step was an eternity. He heard a low groan from above him as the ceiling sagged. The flames closed in. George covered his face with his sleeve and dove through the open doorway.

He lay in the rain for a moment, feeling the water soak his clothing. cool air on his face. Electricity cut through the sky, the air booming. George rolled over and pushed himself up to his knees. Rain came down heavier as another crack of thunder boomed, shaking George to his bones.

"Where the hell did you go?" he glanced around. Lightening shot between clouds and George spotted the steaming creature as it made its way up the bent transmission mast. Flames licked the base of the metal structure. A groan came from the building as the ceiling gave way. The antenna wavered for a moment, the thing wrapping its tentacles around the main strut, clinging to the structure. It was only a matter of time before the heat softened the steel sufficiently for it to collapse. George would watch it fall and he would make sure the creature was dead.

"You ain't got nowhere to go, you ugly bastard."

The metal began to buckle, the towers apex slowly leaning to one side. Framed against the sky, the creature clambered to the top of the antenna as the clouds opened once more. Lightning rippled in a split second across the sky, sparking the clouds up from the inside like lanterns before unleashing one almighty strike of white electricity down onto the antenna. Electricity shot down the mast and down the guy lines. Transformers on the side of the building exploded, bursting with electrical charge, the lines of telephone and television wiring that fed the town glowing white hot as the charge dissipated through them, firing off in a thousand directions at once. The mast turned molten, white fading to red, then to orange. The creature was gone.

George watched the fire burn all night from the cab of the truck. It burned itself out around dawn. The storm broke soon after.

He took the truck back down into Calladen and parked on the silent and wet Main Street as the sun rose behind Widow's Peak. Not a soul stirred in the town, not a light flickered. George glanced up at the contrail of a jet high up in the early morning sky. His arm began to ache and when he looked at it he realised he'd been burned quite badly. It'd need looked at, but not here. He couldn't wait to get out of this town. George slid himself back into the cab of the truck and made to gun the engine when he heard the ringing of a telephone nearby. It was a payphone outside Sissy's Diner. Then came another phone ringing from the hardware store nearby. Then the faint sounds of another, and another, and another. Telephones like a chorus of chirping crickets. George limped over to the phone booth and slid the door shut behind him. He sucked in a breath before lifting the receiver and the sound of screaming and chaos filled his head.

FROM LITTLE ACORNS GROW
BRENDA KEZAR

Bones piled on blue tarps filled the floor of the hangar-sized warehouse, and long tables draped with white plastic tablecloths rimmed the perimeter. Men and women in white lab coats and mud-smeared coveralls scurried among the stacks, some adding bones to piles, some removing. A woman in a white lab coat stopped before a pile, frowned, and studied the clipboard in her hand. Her face lit up, and she teased a bone from the pile, Jenga-style, and trotted away with it.

Dr. Sheppard turned and faced the tour group, spreading his arms wide and beaming like a proud father. "Every one of these specimens was uncovered in the same mass kill site at the base of the bluff. Mammoths, bison, and saber-tooth cats made up the first layer, and then we dug deeper and found ancient bears and woolly rhinos, and then," he shook his head, laughing. "It's like digging into a timeline. It's astounding! They are stacked like cordwood built up over millennia, and we're still digging!"

Nikki tossed her long, blonde hair and batted her eyelashes. "So Jurassic Park is next? When a wooly mammoth strolls through Times Square, you'll be the man behind it?"

Dr. Sheppard chuckled. "No, I'm afraid not. I'm a lowly paleontologist, not a geneticist."

Kate rolled her eyes. Typical Nikki, always had to be the center of attention. "How did so many fossils end up in this one spot?" She tried to pull his attention back to the science. Jurassic Park? Honestly! She shot Nikki an exasperated look.

"The theory is that a tremendous flash flood--or more accurately, many floods, over many years--washed them over the bluff. It's the only explanation for such an astounding number of specimens all at the same site. The numbers rival even the largest of Paleo-Indian buffalo sites," Dr. Sheppard said.

Nikki gave Kate a sour look and then turned her thousand-watt smile on Dr. Sheppard. "Could it have been Paleolithic man?"

"No, these absolutely predate man."

A short man with oversize glasses ran up to them, waving a clipboard. Before he could say a word, Dr. Sheppard cut him off.

"Mortie! I'd like you to meet my students." He gestured to the two younger men in the group first, "Jake and Ryan." The two men held out their hands. Mortie squirmed impatiently but dutifully shook their hands.

"And," Dr. Sheppard grabbed Nikki's shoulders and brought her in front of Mortie. "This is my star student, Nikki. I'm hoping she will join us here." Dr. Sheppard gestured toward Jake and Ryan again. "Hoping they all will; they'll be excellent additions to our team."

Mortie tilted his head toward Kate and raised his eyebrows. She smiled sheepishly in return.

Dr. Sheppard smacked his forehead. "Oh, sorry. This is Nikki's friend ...," he snapped his fingers three times.

"Kate." She held out her hand. "Also one of Dr. Sheppard's students, but I'm just here for moral support, not to join the team." Mortie shook her hand and gave her a pity-filled smile.

Dr. Sheppard either ignored her comment or didn't catch the sarcasm. He took the clipboard Mortie held and studied it, frowning. "What's up?"

"I'm missing half my Elasmotherium." Mortie stabbed his finger at the clipboard accusingly. "What am I supposed to do with half an Elasmotherium?"

Sheppard grinned and handed the clipboard back. "Relax. They're still digging--."

"Yes, but they are in different strata than my Elasmotherium. They should have found it by now." His voice rose two octaves. "I'm going to be stuck with half an Elasmotherium."

"Don't give up hope. The rest of your Elasmotherium might have washed farther out. Just be patient." His smile broadened and his eyes twinkled. "And half an Elasmotherium is better than no Elasmotherium, right?"

Mortie scowled and sagged dramatically.

Sheppard sighed. "Give me a second, folks. I'll call the diggers and find out if anyone's uncovered more of Mortie's Elasmotherium."

Mortie fluttered behind Sheppard as he followed him out of the warehouse.

Kate watched them go. <u>She</u> wanted to dig for Elasmotherium parts, but no one was falling all over himself to recruit her. No, she was a boring, average, blend-into-the-background kind of gal. And when she was with Nikki, Miss-Shines-Brighter-Than-Venus-on-a-clear-night, she really faded into the background. It was no surprise that Dr. Sheppard couldn't remember her name!

Jake walked to a table where smaller specimens were laid out for sorting. He picked up a silver-dollar-size fossil with the perfect imprint of a daisy in it and brought it to Nikki. "A beautiful flower for a beautiful lady."

"Why thank you, sir." She curtsied, took the fossil, and dropped it into her purse.

Kate gasped. "What are you doing?"

Nikki shrugged. "Picking up a souvenir."

"Souvenirs are postcards and snow globes," Kate hissed. "Tchotchkes, not research specimens!"

"Come on!" Nikki rolled her eyes. "We're in Russia, for Christ's sake. You know you're probably never going to be here again, so you have to take back something that really means something. Postcards and snow globes won't cut it."

"I didn't want to come in the first place," Kate muttered, folding her arms.

Nikki had guilted her into coming, insisting it would be dangerous to travel internationally alone. And who knew what Dr. Sheppard's intentions were? Sure, he had been their professor, but what did they really know about him? He could be some kind of pervert, luring young women to foreign lands to have his way with them. Kate had to come and keep her safe.

"Put it back, right now. I'm serious," Kate said.

Jake grabbed a four-inch-long bone from the nearest pile, held it up defiantly, and slid it into the pocket of his faded jeans. "You aren't going to rat us out, are you?"

Nikki giggled at the outline of the fossil in his pants pocket. "Is that a metatarsal in your pocket or are you happy to see me?"

"My turn." Ryan walked to the table, grabbed a small trilobite fossil, and slid it into his pocket. Jake joined him, examined the fossils for a moment, then selected one and returned to the girls.

"Here," Jake held his closed fist out to Kate.

Kate backed up. "Forget it."

"It's just a fricking rock!" Nikki rolled her eyes. She snatched the fossil from Jake's hand and shoved it into Nikki's sweater pocket. "Live a little."

Kate laid her hand over her pocket and felt the hazelnut-size rock inside. The three others glared at her, daring her to take it back out of her pocket. She glanced around. All the nearby researchers were absorbed in their work, and the warehouse had no cameras. No one would ever know they'd taken the fossils. And she did deserve to get <u>something</u> out of this trip. What could be the harm?

She had thought she would have a heart attack going through customs, worried they'd see the rock and ask questions. She hadn't believed her good fortune when she passed through security without a second glance, but she spent the agonizing moments before takeoff expecting the police to come running across the tarmac.

As soon as she was home and in her apartment, she locked her door, drew the curtains, and jumped on the couch. She pulled her suitcase onto her lap, pawed through the clothes inside, and pulled out her secret treasure.

She opened the tiny plastic bag she'd stored it in--the kind, she imagined, that drug dealers delivered crack in--and dumped it into her palm. The fossil looked like a giant, petrified rabbit turd. She pinched it between her thumb and forefinger and rolled it, as if the mystery of what kind of fossil it was would be revealed in the tiny bumps on its surface. Her heart hitched when it crushed between her fingers.

"Damn!" She dropped it into her other hand and wiped her fingers on her pants. The damage wasn't as bad as she thought; only the outer shell had come off. What remained resembled a small almond, and--she scratched it with the edge of a fingernail--it was soft! Her fossil was a seed encased in a hard rock shell.

She sighed and closed her palm around it. If it was soft, it meant it would probably rot without its protective shell. Her souvenir of the once-in-a-lifetime trip would waste away and leave her with nothing.

Unless …. She opened her palm and studied the seed. How amazing would it be to have a long-extinct plant growing in her ratty little apartment? It probably wouldn't grow, but what could it hurt to try?

"Why not?" She went to find a flowerpot.

A month later, she grabbed a bowl of bran flakes, curled up on the couch, and flicked on the television. It was tuned, as usual, to CNN. They wrapped up a lighthearted story about a sixth-grader raising funds to help a devastated animal shelter, and the anchor's face grew serious.

"Arson destroyed a research facility in Siberia overnight." The screen cut to the smoldering ruins of a building. "The Koehler Institute in Kamchatka, Russia, had recently celebrated the discovery of hundreds of prehistoric specimens in the Siberian ice."

Kate nearly dropped her bowl of bran flakes scrambling to turn up the volume.

They cut to a live shot of a man with tear-filled, bloodshot eyes, his gray hair fluttering in the wind like goose down. Behind him, smoke rose from the ruins of the building. The text at the bottom of the screen read, Doctor Ned Beadle, founder of The Koehler Institute. "We are devastated by this tragedy. So many bright minds lost, so much research wasted."

The camera cut to the reporter. "Any clue how this happened?"

Dr. Beadle shook his head, his mouth set in a grim line. "No. By the time fire crews arrived, the building was a total loss. The only thing we know for certain is that the fire was set by one of our own researchers."

The reporter nodded sympathetically. "Do you know why?"

Dr. Beadle sighed. "No. We can only surmise he suffered from cabin-fever induced delusions. He seemed to believe one of the specimens was trying to kill him."

Kate's eyes wandered to the tiny plant in the blue flowerpot on her computer desk. "Oh, my gosh! Good thing I got you out of there or you'd be a crispy critter."

Her heart skipped a beat: Dr. Sheppard! What had happened to Nikki's beloved professor? She picked up her phone and sat at her computer desk. While she waited for Nikki to pick up, she shook her mouse to wake up her computer.

Nikki didn't answer, nor did her computer wake up. With her luck, something had gone wrong in the building's electrical system, and the computer was fried. Every time it stormed, the old building creaked, and the lights flickered. If it had fried her computer, she was out of luck. Her bank account still hadn't recovered from the trip yet.

She peered under the desk and frowned. Funny, she didn't remember any green, fuzzy cords coming out of the computer before. She stood and pulled the desk away from the window. A green, hairy vine thick as her pinky led from the dirt in her plant's pot and out a chink in the window frame. She squished herself between the desk and the window and tried to push the window open, but it was painted shut. Outside, hand-shaped leaves--larger versions of the ones on her small plant--fluttered in the breeze.

She grabbed the vine and grimaced at its hairy warmth in her hand. She pulled gently, and the vine slid an inch into the apartment then hung up with its leaves bunched against the glass. No matter how hard she pulled, the vine wouldn't budge.

"Dang." She let go of the vine. "How far did you grow?" She'd have to survey the problem from a different angle.

She ran down the stairs and outside, to the overgrown vacant lot next door, and picked her way through the thistles, broken bottles, and trash snared in the weeds. She looked up to her apartment window and froze, her jaw hanging open.

From the cracked, white paint of her window, one green vine protruded. As it trailed down the three stories below her window, the vine fanned out and branched like a river delta. At ground level, the vine-covered twelve to fifteen feet of the building in hand-shaped, hand-sized, leaves so thick, not a single brick showed through the curtain of greenery.

She ran her hand through her hair. So much for keeping the little plant hidden. The best thing to do now would be to cut the vine down, get rid of the evidence, and pretend the whole thing never happened. She ran upstairs, grabbed her scissors, and cut her little plant free from the vine. The moment the vine was cut free, it slid violently through the hole and out of sight.

"Sorry, little guy, but keeping you is too risky." She grabbed the little plant, tossed it in the kitchen trash, and tied the bag. Then she grabbed the only thing she owned that might work for disposing of the evidence: a meat cleaver. It wasn't a machete, but it would have to do.

She grabbed a handful of garbage bags and the cleaver in one hand, the kitchen garbage in the other, and struggled down the stairs. At the bottom, she peered out the front door. The street was empty, but she wrapped the empty garbage bags around the cleaver, just in case. No sense in panicking anyone on the street. She pushed the door open, set the full bag into the pile at the curb, and picked her way through the lot next door to the wall below her window.

She raised the cleaver, then stopped and cocked her head, not quite comprehending what she was looking at. A dead bird lay tangled in the vines. <u>Several</u> birds, actually, and a couple of squirrels, and a cat, all sunken and dried like mummies. Beetles crawled over the matted fur of the cat, and maggots squirmed in its empty eye sockets and open, snarling mouth.

She tucked the garbage bags and cleaver under one arm and checked her free hand for any sign of a rash from touching the vine earlier. Some plants secreted chemicals to keep grazers from eating them, though that wouldn't explain the cat!

Her hand looked fine, but she still had the creeps. She wished she had thought to grab gloves, but there was no time to go back now.

She took a deep breath to steel herself, hacked off a three-foot section of vine, and stuffed it into the garbage bag. She wrinkled her nose, cut off a two-foot section all the way around the cat, and carefully slid it into the bag.

Something buzzed past her ear and she cringed, waving her hand by her head in panic. She hated bees. Another swing of the cleaver and a hunk of vine with three birds in it fell by her feet.

She heard another buzz and thought, I've found a bee's nest, and then a sharp, fiery, pain bloomed in her thigh.

"Damn," she said, dropping the cleaver and grabbing her thigh. She jerked her hands away when something hard and sharp pricked her palm. A white shard, two-inches long, stuck out of her thigh like the broken-off end of a knitting needle. Her jeans darkened with blood around it.

Her throat felt like it was closing. She turned toward the deserted street to look for help. Her legs were made of lead, but she managed to shuffle one foot slightly forward, but then her legs froze, and she toppled into the weeds, crushing an old bag of beer cans under her cheek.

She fell facing the wall of vines and blinked twice, trying to figure out if her eyes were playing tricks on her. One of the vines appeared to be moving. It pulled itself away from the rest of the vines and fell to the ground. It slithered side to side toward her, like a green, hairy snake, its leaves whispering as it slithered.

She squeezed her eyes shut in denial; she had to be hallucinating. When she opened them again, the vine had reached her foot. She opened her mouth to scream, but no sound came out. She concentrated all her effort on moving her arm toward the fallen cleaver, but she could barely wiggle her fingertips.

The vine wrapped itself around her ankle several times, its bristles scratching her skin. It tightened like a noose and yanked. She slid closer to the main plant. It yanked again, and her ankle popped.

The vine yanked again and her shirt rucked up, and rocks and bits of broken glass scratched her back. The next tug pulled her another foot or so, and then she hung up with her butt resting against something hard. No matter how much the vine struggled and jerked, she wouldn't move. A second vine wrapped around her other ankle and the two vines tugged in unison. The joint effort worked, and she winced as she scraped up and over whatever she'd been hung on.

Three more vines slithered out, and she held her breath, expecting their hairy touch, but they slithered past her, out of her view. The other two vines continued jerking her toward the wall.

Something popped and clattered beyond her view, and her heart leapt: someone was coming to save her! Another pop rang out, louder, closer, followed by more rattling, like ball bearings dropped on a hardwood floor. Something rolled into her field of vision: an almond-sized ball. A seed!

The plant yanked again, and she hissed as her legs slammed into the wall. A delicate tendril crept from beneath the leaves of the main plant. The last three inches of it were white and sharp, like a shard of bone. Her eyes went wide, and she willed herself to kick and flail, but her arms and her legs still wouldn't move.

Another vine slithered out from the main plant and wrapped itself around her arm. While the bone tendril slid closer, the vine holding her arm twisted, exposing the white, soft underside of her arm. She squeezed her eyes shut and tried to scream as the bone tendril slid into her skin like an IV needle. Fiery pain bloomed and wetness trickled down her arm. Her eyes flew open at a stab in her neck and another in her ankle. She screamed silently, her eyes rolling in desperation and pain. By the time another bone tendril found the soft skin of her belly, she had passed out.

😨😵😈

Johnny untied the garbage bag at the curb and nudged Maddy. "Look what somebody tossed out."

Maddy looked over from the trash bag she'd been rummaging through and scowled. "Can't eat a houseplant." She grabbed a handful of soda cans from the other trash bag and threw them into her rusted shopping cart.

"Don't let her get to you," Johnny told the plant. "She's always cranky when she's hungry."

He pulled the plant out of the bag and smiled. "You can come home with me. I've got myself a cozy little spot in Central Park. Lots of trees and squirrels and sunshine. You're going to love it there."

WITH ALL HER TROUBLES BEHIND HER
S.L. EDWARDS

Pan peered through the sights of her rifle.

The boy she rested her bead on couldn't have been older than seventeen. Scraggly, ragged brown hair and a scowling mouth full of half-teeth. He paced slowly at the mouth of the mine, swatting his gloved hands against his pants and periodically spitting out something black and viscous. The men around him had the blackness pouring out of the corners of their eyes like charcoal tears, streaks going down their faces and across their lips. It seeped from their ears and noses, from every exposed orifice of their bodies as diseased war-paint.

There was no hope for them, and only one cure.

She sighed, shook her head and put the carbine across her lap.

The winters were colder in Utah than San Francisco, and the Rockies had been one hell of a hike. A train ride to Salt Lake, a three-day horse ride and a day's hike. For what? She wasn't a *hero*. At least, not one that she would want on *her* side any way. This didn't concern her, she shouldn't have to kill a bunch of men who until a month ago had been church-going, god-fearing innocent husbands and sons. She shouldn't have to play the sinner again.

She cursed and picked up her rifle again.

The wind blew across the pines, batting her face in cold, searing snow. She lined her sights on the boy. He'd be the first, but he wouldn't be the last. She wanted to say a prayer, to say *something*.

But she didn't believe in God, just *gods*.

And they weren't worth praying to.

She squeezed the trigger.

"I'm so sorry."

The gun bucked and the boy's head splintered open. He fell to the ground slowly, his knees folding in as his neck wobbled under the shifting, wet weight. A roar went out from the others. She reloaded her weapon quickly, even they though would be slow to find her, weighed down by the snow and blinded by the pestilence that had overtaken them. She waited for another, a balding man with a scraggy, grey beard. She fired into his stomach and he fell to the snow as dark, infected blood bled through his fingers. A third, a tall man with onyx black hair and shoulders as wide as the world grunted and growled as he recognized the glint of her rifle.

She gritted her teeth. Standing so that she could run towards the man, matching his careening momentum with her own. Her hands went around the barrel of her gun, turning it so that she could launch the stock into his jaw. There was an ugly snapping sound, a twig splintering into shards. The man fell back, and before he could stand she put a bullet right into the center of his forehead.

Crack.

The birds scattered, crying out in panic. The winter was wild around her, masking her sight in a flurry of snow as the wind rose furiously against her.

She squinted through the snow. Two dark silhouettes made their way through the flurries, circling her like angry, lonely animals. As the storm calmed she could see their glinting, barred teeth. They came close enough to see, hissing and moaning as the black pestilence bubbled from behind their teeth. They were beyond speaking now, beyond reasoning. Their bodies did not belong to them. Their minds were long gone.

They moved slowly, waiting for her to respond. Their eyes were red with burst blood vessels, probably leaving them nearly blind.

Pan shook her head, reaching for the knife sheathed just outside her coat.

"Come on then."

A man got near her, a short fat man who probably smiled at his grandchildren and told his wife dirty jokes. Maybe he was a blacksmith, maybe a tailor. Whatever he had been, he didn't deserve this. He lunged at her and the knife went into his neck with little resistance. Just a wet slip, as if it was *meant* for him.

The other ran at her, and the knife pierced his stomach before digging across his chest.

The black gore cascaded down on her.

She panted, looking around one more time. There were no signs of a fire, no coals or pots to cook with. They didn't need to eat, not since what was down in that mine took over them. Pan resisted the urge to cry. She was doing her part, doing what was right, even if it didn't look at way.

She wiped the snow away from her face.

The mountain air howled. The entrance to the mine was wide and dark. Something drafted up from within, charging the air with all the anger and cold of a wrathful, hungry panther.

She slung her single shot rifle over her shoulder and sheathed her knife. There was no telling how many more dead men there would be before this was over.

Her hand came to her chest, where a little box just big enough to hold one cigarette rested. Reminding herself that the box was there reassured her.

The odds were already stacked in her favor.

It wasn't just a bunch of diseased miners she needed to worry most about, after all.

Pan sighed and let her hand slip from her box and the thin cord that kept it around her neck, stepping into the mine resolute to finish her work.

II.

"I don't understand why you're here. Or even how you knew how to find me."

The woman in Pan's office was petite, no older than 17. She was mousey, with a narrow nose and a downward eye which told Pan that she was not someone who was comfortable here. Her flowery, too-heavy dress was no fit for a San Francisco summer, and outside the growing city was heaving with a sultry, humid fog.

Pan's office didn't help. A plain, wooden room with a wide window facing towards the Bay which capture all the moisture and heat the breeze could bring. It rested in a two-story brownstone, with grey-brown wooden floors and empty walls. Only Pan's desk and one single bookshelf were visible in the yellow-blue light of an oceanside day.

"I'd heard that there might be bounty hunters in San Francisco."

Her accent was atrocious and unidentifiable. But people often said that about *Pan's* accent, who still had trouble with American pronunciation even after all these years.

"Yes mam, that's true." Pan lifted her boots onto her desk. "You can't sling shit without hitting a bounty hunter. Gold dries up and what's a boy to do? There ain't much gold left, but plenty of bodies. Real good money to be made in bodies, let me tell you."

"But I-" the woman paused, twiddling her thumbs and looking down to the floor.

"You what, sweetheart?"

The woman stopped, giving Pan a sour look.

"Abigail."

Pan laughed. "Alright, you *what,* Abigail?"

Abigail resumed her sad, reluctant look, "I heard about *you.* About a problem you solved outside of Carson City."

Pan narrowed her eyes. This wasn't a normal job then. She was perfectly content killing criminals. Your murderers, rapists, hell, she'd even killed her fair share of spies in her life. But that wasn't going to be what this was. This would hit closer to home.

She opened her desk drawer. The whiskey flask was a tall one, so she heaved it up onto her desk and dug for two glasses. She poured a fist of rye into the first glass and then motioned to Abigail, who shook her head and crossed her hands.

Pan took a sip, letting the slow burn rest just behind the back of her lip.

"Yeah…that was a railroad man." Pan sat down and thought about Carson, about the dusty town surrounded by smooth, dry mountains. "He came back from some expedition to Egypt with something he thought was a genie. Something he thought he could use. But it wasn't a genie. And it used *him*. So."

Pan put down her glass and looked at Abigail head on.

"What am I dealing with?"

And Abigail told her story. The story of a mining town in Northern Utah, about a mine drying up and a group of men who were desperate to feed their families. Men who dug deeper and deeper, men who sometimes stayed up in the mountains for weeks and wouldn't come down until they had *something* they could sell.

The story of the day they all finally *did come back.*

Men who had loved their families were suddenly cruel, men with newly evil eyes who came at night to rob their own sons from their beds. Men who at first hit, and then tortured the ones they love. And then there were the women, the women who escaped that dead mining town, who left the men to their mountain in the hopes that they could find someone who could help.

The story of a girl named Abigail, who after hearing stories in Carson about "young woman bounty hunter" who dealt in "spooky shit" in San Francisco, came all this way just to see her.

Pan nodded solemnly, looking out the window and on to the ever-growing city below. Her faded reflection didn't betray her secrets. Her tan, smooth skin was as olive-colored as the day she was born, without blemish or mark. Her fiery raid hair was cut short, her deep brown eyes sad and dark.

"How old are you, Abigail?" Pan asked.

"Sixteen."

Pan snorted, wondering what would happen if she revealed her age to the young woman. Would she leave, offended and angry? Would she scream and run away, screaming "witch" or "demon?" Or would she just sit there, in silent disbelief until Pan abandoned the subject?

Pan would leave it. The poor girl had already been through enough.

"Your husband," Pan reached into her desk drawer and brought out a large flask. She poured herself a fist of rye into a highball glass. She motioned to her flask, but Abigail shook her head.

"Was your husband one of the men who…*changed.*"

"Yes mam." Was all she said.

Pan nodded, deciding not to say anything further.

"I can help you," she paused, taking a draught of rye that slid down her throat in thick, playful burning streams, "But I have to tell you, there's no saving them."

"What?"

"I hate to say it." Pan stood from her desk again, leaning over it so she could look Abigail squarely in the eyes. "But if they've got what I think they've got, there's no getting them back. They died up on that mountain. What came down," she tried to think of a delicate way of saying what came next, "What came down wasn't them."

"Then how are you going to 'help?'" Abigail's face was angry, desperate and confused. Poor girl.

Pan stared at her, waiting for Abigail to figure it out herself. When she did, her eyes widened and mouth formed a listless "O."

"Do you think you could point out where they are on a map for me?" Pan let a little affection back into her voice.

Abigail nodded, and Pan unfurled a map on her desk. It was marked with x's and lines, traces of one-woman massacres across the continental United States. For a moment, she was wrecked with pains of nausea and sadness.

She swallowed her rye and grunted, handing Abigail a pen.

A little circle in the mountains Northern Utah.

A little circle surrounding those poor, damned bastards.

III.

Pan wondered if she had already killed Abigail's husband. A young girl like that could have been married to any one of those men. People that far away from civilization tended to not care about things like age. Love was love and they would take it where they could get it, even when it wasn't love at all.

The mine was dark and frigid, colder than the air above. Her heavy hide coat was weighing her down, slowing her movement and making loud whooshing sounds with each stride. This sort of work was easier in the summer. Her mind drifted back to the last time.

To Carson City.

She had stopped keeping track of how many people she had killed. She probably stopped counting after she turned fifty. Hundreds of years later, the number became even more irrelevant. But it didn't stop hurting each time. If anything, her immortality made her see life as *more* precious.

She was always amazed at what people were willing to throw it away for.

Footsteps plodded ahead of her.

She unslung her rifle.

He was a big boy, almost seven feet tall. He growled, throwing his head around like a bull as he quivered with blind, animal rage. If he could get his hands on her, he would rip her to shreds.

Pan pulled her trigger and hit him squarely in the chest. He fell, and before he could get back up she planted bullet between his eyes.

Her ears were ringing with her rifle's echo. She swore, not sure if she could handle another shot without going deaf. Further down in the mine an angry, shocked scream rose from a gurgling throat. She should have brought a sword. Swords were good weapons for this sort of thing, long enough to give a bit of range and quiet enough to not go deaf. But all she had was her rifle, a revolver and a knife.

She would've thought it would have been easier by now, that guns would make it faster than spears and swords. But blood was blood, no matter how it was spilled. She'd been doing her work for centuries, first with iron then with steel and now with gunpowder. The alcohol was getting weaker though, and sleeping was harder each night. Would she have nightmares after this, or would she just forget?

The possibility scared her more than anything else. Every now and then the vivid memory of a life she took would boil up and overtake her, paralyzing her as she relived the murder. She would be sick with herself, wondering why she was allowed the temporary mercy of forgetting her life. Of forgetting her sin.

She wouldn't forget. She would try to remember these men, to remember Abigail and the duty that brought her down into the belly of the mine.

She stopped and reloaded her rifle, just in case. Then she reached to her right side and drew out her revolver. It'd be just as loud as the rifle, but the walls were getting narrower, aiming would less difficult. Six bullets. If she was lucky, that's all she would need.

She could still see in the dark, one of the many "gifts" that her gods gave her. They "didn't want her missing a minute of it," they had explained to her through tears. She was not proud of what she did on that day, how she had thrown herself at their mercy and begged for a death and an end. But her begging had only fueled their sadism. A never-ending life, never-dimming sight and an increasingly high tolerance that would not even allow a reprieve in drunkenness.

Pan hated her gods. Hated them for controlling her life, for making her kill even now.

But, she had to admit, they made her good at it. Better than any Achilles had ever been.

A draft rushed with a form that slammed against her. In surprise she dropped her revolver, screaming as a hand forced her face into the rough wall, cutting her skin and sending a trickle of tangy, copper blood to her tongue. She bit down her anger and surprise. An opponent even only a little bigger than her would have an advantage, and the man who pinned her was well over twice her size.

As his teeth reached for her throat she brought her foot between his legs.

The man roared in anger and pain. Though the pestilence had overtaken him, his body was still a man's, with all the weaknesses that came with it.

She lifted his neck gently, exposing it so her knife's incision was neat and long. The black gore poured out of him, and after a long minute his corpse was paling into the dark pool beneath him.

She was panting, stomach churning and back aching from the fight. Hand-to-hand was not her specialty, though she had been taught by a few masters in Africa and East Asia. She found it too messy, too uncertain and unreliable. Uncomfortable and intimate, she preferred her opponents to keep their distance whenever she could help it.

She leaned against wall of the mine and breathed slowly, quieting the roaring drum in her head. She lifted her hands, watching them shake in electric panic.

Breathe.

She could hear the furious wind far away, the flurries of snow and frost that had kept all this sickness buried for centuries. The wind blew through the tunnels, coming from behind her and boring down into the caverns below. There was no response, no shuffling of feet or unthinking, reflexive grunts. Even though she knew it was too naïve, too hopeful, she allowed herself to believe that she was alone.

She smiled, bowing her head into her gore-crusted hands.

The black ichor was too thin, too scentless to have come from anything living. Or maybe the air was too cold for the rot to stink. Whatever it was, she was glad for the small mercy.

She lifted herself up and away from the wall.

She picked up her revolver and moved forward alone, with no other sounds than those of her boots grinding against the dirt with staggering, uneven steps. She hummed to herself an old song in a language no longer spoken. The walk lasted miles, the men must have been desperate to have dug so deep.

They should have known better.

Then she came to it, the spot where the mines ended and the tunnels began. Pan wondered what they thought they found when the discovered this patch of hollow earth, when their picks struck a stone wall only to crack through to open spaces. A ruined mine wall hung open, stones haphazardly moved to the side so walking through was easier.

The walls of the tunnels were smooth, made by natural erosion and the burrowing of some gigantic worm. What made them had probably been there for thousands of years, biding its time before breaking the surface.

She wondered how many troubles were writhing down there, and if she would have to hunt them down more often as mankind continued to assert its ambition over a world it had no chance of controlling. Immortality would be even more exhausting if that was the case.

Her boot slipped beneath her, sending her sliding down the tunnels. Her hands shot out, but only found cool, smooth tunnel wall.

"Shit! Shit!"

She spread her arms and legs, hoping to slow herself as wind roared in her ears. The water clung to her coat, but here were no stones to catch. Finally, her hand hit a groove in the tunnel floor and she grabbed it at once, jerking her shoulder as it snapped back the weight of her body.

She hissed, pausing for a moment before she stood.

She was only a few feet away from an edge, though she couldn't see how steep the drop was. Carefully, she lifted herself and took a single step forward.

She would have fallen about forty feet.

The ground below was covered in loose pebbles and black mud, washing against the shores of an underground lake. The surface was flat and still. She picked up a stone at her feet and tossed it into the lake. It entered the water with a gentle "plop" that echoed for minutes in the yawning cavern.

The surface of the water began to move, boiling and writhing in fury.

"Right then."

A long, sharp head emerged, glowing and bulbous blind eyes lined against pale, scaled skin. Its long, serpentine body was as dark as the cavern around it, giving its head the appearance of a floating cow skull. The spikes across its back were jagged and uneven, and at the end of its long, narrow mouth it hissed to reveal rows of narrow angler-fish teeth.

Black gore leaked from between them as it turned towards her. Its bulbous eyes widened.

It wasn't blind at all.

Before she had time to shout the trouble rammed its head into the cavern wall beneath her, sending her wobbling as she slipped to meet the ground forty feet below.

IV.

Through the dim hum of her head voices were laughing at her. Beautiful wind-chime laughter, playful and innocent, laced with the venom of a sardonic and cruel joke. Loud, bellowing laughter of deep lungs and immeasurable power. She was running, pleading, screaming and crying across an unseen and never-ending canvas.

"You're even better than I expected." A sonorous, velvet male voice purred.

She bolted up in the mud and grime, panting furiously as she realized the voice was a memory.

Only a memory.

The trouble towered above her, leering as her bones snapped back together and bleeding flesh sealed itself shut. Its white wide eyes watched curious, in reverence and awe as Pan put herself back together. She winced and cried, electric fires spewing from her joints and small vertebrae across her neck. Hot tears welled up, uncontrollable and unstoppable as they broke the dam of her screaming.

It'd be easier to die, she thought, than put herself back together.

"Awww…" the trouble proclaimed above her. Its voice was high-pitched and grating, the voice of a sore-throated child.

"So, that is what this is."

She picked herself up and moved her arms, making sure that her body still worked. She looked up, standing straight as possible to consider the trouble.

Pan had never encountered one that could speak before.

Maybe she could reason with it.

"I was a small thing when I first escaped."

She let it speak, feeling her neck to make sure the real weapon was still where she left it. But her neck was bare. The thin chain of her necklace must have snapped in the fall. She'd need to stall the trouble so she could look for it, otherwise she wouldn't stand a chance. She began pacing, pretending to listen intently to the trouble as she scanned the ground for a small, ornate wooden box.

"Set loose into a wide, open night. My brothers and sisters…gods…we were *legion*, writhing into the open air to set loose our divine duty upon mankind. I buried myself deep, waiting to gain strength and power. I knew I'd be found eventually, mankind is self-destructive after all. I only wished to aid them in the endeavor."

It laughed, and Pan shuddered.

"Of all the things I expected to see when I was finally unearthed, I never expected it would be you, *mother*."

She stopped looking for the box and froze. The word was accusatory, a lash against her very soul. She turned to the serpent defiantly, pointing a finger to its too-pleased-with-itself skeleton smile.

"Don't call me that."

It laughed again, shaking the roof of the cavern above it.

"What would I call you, then? You were the one that set us loose on the world, the one who sent us forward as emissaries of divine will." It lowered its head to her level, closer to examine and mock her, "You unleashed us to do good."

She shook her head, scanning the ground as she talked.

"There's nothing good about what you do."

It paused and twisted its head to the side, questioning and inquisitive.

"Is mankind not too aspirational for its own good? Do they not damage their only and sacred world? Are they not vainglorious and cruel?"

"No more than their gods," Pan spat.

She still could see them when she closed her eyes. They were beautiful beyond words, which it only made their cruelty more pronounced and evil. They had adorned her with gifts, showered her with love and praise. Lovely, kind Aphrodite. Apollo, moving in the graceful, dancing moves of a warrior-poet. And Zeus, whose smile glistened like dew and lightning.

And then they gave her the jar.

"You speak blasphemy." It seemed frightened and indignant, an innocent being challenged and shaken.

"No, just telling you how I feel. Maybe you can sympathize. What is it that you do to people? Spread sickness? How is that a good thing?"

"It's what they *deserve*." The trouble hissed.

"We shouldn't get what we deserve," Pan responded. Her eyes fell on the box, no bigger than a pen-case, lodged between two pebbles. The thin chain which had kept it around her neck had been broken in the fall, strung out in flayed angles around the box. But it was still intact, the painted wooden surface covered with oils that made it nearly indestructible.

"Justice is never pretty." She added, moving towards her weapon as she kept her eyes on the monster.

The trouble watched her slowly, its eyes shining in the dark like portals to Hades. It hummed, seeming to consider her words. Pan thought of how long the trouble had been in the dark and began to pity it. No doubt it had grown mad, angry. If it was anything like her, it hated itself.

"And the ones who deserve justice rarely get it anyway." She added softly.

The monster shook its head.

"You're *lying*. The gods created me for a reason. Just as they created *you* for a reason."

She shook her head, only a few steps away from the box. If she didn't get it, she'd be down here forever. The trouble could spend eternity tearing her apart, just like poor Prometheus.

"They didn't have a *fucking reason* for making me. They were just *sadistic* and *bored*."

"NO!" It roared, rearing up its neck and arching it for a strike. "They made you what you are so that you could *suffer*. Because you *deserve* it!"

It lunged at her, its ways open to expose all its long, needle-teeth. She fell to her knee and drew her revolver, firing two shots into its left eye. They eye burst like a rotten orange, spilling luminous white blood into the water below. The trouble reared backward, screaming and crying out in pain and terror. Her hands came down on the box, and without taking a moment for pause, she opened it.

First there was nothing.

Then a small rectangle of light.

The rectangle grew brighter and larger as the cavern burst into a blazing fire. The walls shook, setting stones and stalactites crashing down. The trouble screamed in terror and pain. A stone cracked against its back and it fell, its mouth falling open as it cried out.

"You monster!" It roared out.

"Get in the box, you spooky shit!" She roared back.

It wept, the suffocating, stifling crying of a horrified child that could not understand its suffering. Its form collapsed, fading away as it folded on itself. As the light consumed it the trouble became a shadow, growing narrower and narrower until it was little more than a dark, long worm.

Little more than a black, writhing thread.

There was a final, weak whisper.

"You *deserve* it."

She snapped the box lid close. The cave around her was quiet now, and above her the mineshaft loomed high.

'She deserved it,' it had said.

She gritted her teeth and placed the box in a coat pocket, throwing herself at the stone wall and gripping her hand against a jutting stone.

V.

Abigail did not respond when Pan finished her story.

Outside the trolleys moved slowly, their mechanical creaks rising into the air to match the cawing of the seagulls above. Pan's hand was itching for her flask, and she strummed her hands nervously waiting for Abigail's response.

"They're *all* dead?" Abigail finally ventured, allowing a little hope to penetrate her voice.

But Pan nodded.

"They all died when the monster died. It grabbed on to them, made their lives its own. They couldn't survive without it."

She wouldn't tell Abigail how many of the men she killed herself. There was no need to get into the gruesome details.

"What should I do now?" Abigail asked.

Pan laughed, perhaps a bit colder than she needed to be.

"Go back, go forward, it doesn't matter. Just put all this behind you. You're young, you've got a whole life to live."

Abigail nodded, mustering a weak smile.

"Thank you, for whatever you did out there…"

She slid an envelope across Pan's desk. Pan contemplated not taking it, feeling some level of revulsion from taking a bunch of money from a newly minted widow. But she needed to pay bills, and any money would do.

Pan slid the envelope into her shirt pocket.

"Nothing to it. Just try your best to be happy, Abigail. It's important."

The young girl nodded, "Well, thank you anyway."

Abigail's flowery dress left and closed the door behind it.

Alone at last, Pan drew her flask from her desk. Its grey surface showed her reflection. A pretty face with sad, deep eyes. Tired eyes.

Considering those eyes, the flask felt heavier in her hands.

She wondered if she could put it away, leave it back to its prison desk-drawer. She could go for a walk and take her own advice, maybe watch the sunset and flirt with some kind man who could help her forget her problems for just one night. One good night in a long, long life.

She could take her own advice and live her life, put all her troubles behind her.

But then the reflection in the glass changed. Instead of a beautiful young woman, a bearded man looked back at her, white eyes and black gore bleeding from between his lips. A corpse-white man, choking as his neck was collapsed by strong hands. The illusion faded, and her own face returned.

Still beautiful. Still unscarred.

She didn't bother with a glass.

CHAOS AND VOID
DEBRA ROBINSON

I met him on the way to a gig. He was the epitome of every old biker stereotype I'd ever seen. Tall and skinny, so thin his jeans flapped against his sticks for legs. Long, stringy, gray hair, with some sort of dangly black earring peeking through on the left side—a Maltese cross, it looked like. The de rigueur black leather vest with patches, worn over an old frayed jean jacket, cemented the overall impression. There was some kind of crusty, dried, banana-pudding-looking stuff on one shoulder. His face was crazy; seamed and furrowed, stretched tight over high cheekbones and brown from years in the sun. His eyes darted continuously, and his mouth worked. He stood just outside the Circle K, shuffling from foot to foot, looking out of place.

Too much Meth?

I hoped he was harmless. I'd dealt with a thousand of his type in my world.

I eased out of my car, planning to slide past him, get my soft drink, and get out of there. I was already late for the gig.

I've been a musician all my life. It's an easy, fun job; you only need to work a few days a week, and a bit of talent puts you at the top of the musician food chain. For this girl, it's perfect.

Tonight's job was an engagement party, a shindig for the couple's friends. A full band was booked for later; but because the older relatives would be there early, they needed mellow, acoustic music. That's where I come in.

I wasn't always a female musician pushing middle age. I spent years in rock bands, playing van-in's, kegger's, and frat parties, fending off the best and worst, long before aging-biker-dude showed up.

I kept my head down as I passed him—always avoid eye contact is one of the rules—and pulled open the door. It was on the way out, soda in hand, that he stopped me.

"Aren't you Kerri?" he asked in a deep, gravelly voice that didn't match his spindly frame.

I turned to face him, pasting on the noncommittal smile.

"Yes, I am."

The thing is, in my business, I meet thousands of people each year, sometimes *thousands* upon thousands. They come to see me play, and if I've done my job well, they end up feeling like they know me, since all night long they listened to my lame jokes, and silly stories. The irony is, I don't recognize *them* at all. Sometimes, one may look a little familiar, but that's rare. To musicians, the audience is invisible, interchangeable, and homogenous. Our focus is the music. So I'm often caught out unawares by nice people who act like they're my best friend—and I automatically assume they know me from seeing me perform. Disconcerting sometimes, but it's an everyday occurrence for me.

"I'm Smokey," he said. "You played for my brother's wedding."

"Oh, okay."

He drew his cigarette up to his mouth, and his hand was shaking badly. I mean, like *really* shaking.

"Are you alright?" I asked, concerned.

He blew out a cloud of smoke and shook his head.

"I ain't been alright since I saw the truth."

I let this pass, not really wanting to get involved. Somehow I had to escape without causing offense.

"Well, I'm almost late for my show, so, I hope everything's okay, but I've gotta go." I ran all the words together, easing away from him, my car only feet away.

He took another drag, looking down at his boots, nodding his head. A hopeful expression lit up his craggy face. "My brother and his wife still talk about their wedding, and how great you made it."

Shit. Now I have to do something.

"Oh, good. I'm sorry I didn't recognize you. What's their name?"

"Turner. I'm waiting on a ride right now, as a matter of fact, I'm going out to his house."

Double shit. The Turner's paid me a LOT of money for that gig.

They also had a nice home and were not serial killers or anything. So he somehow appeared a little less weird by association after divulging this. In all honesty though, the money aspect mattered, as it always does. It has to.

I smiled. "That was a beautiful wedding, really gorgeous. I'm headed out past the Dam, and their house is right on the way. Would you like a ride?"

"I sure would," he beamed. He walked to the passenger side and opened the door.

I slid into the driver's seat, not real happy about this turn of events; not that I didn't want to help someone out, it's just that he was so strange. *And* he was shaking so badly! Luckily it was only a few miles to his brother's.

He blew a big cloud of smoke into the windshield, and it bounced right back in my face. I coughed a little as I eased the car out of the space, trying not to be impolite.

"Oh, sorry," he said, noticing. He rolled down his window to flick the burning end from the half-smoked cig.

"I quit years ago, mostly for my voice," I offered.

He reached for a pocket on his vest to save the rest of the cig. His hand shook so badly, he could not undo the button. I couldn't help but stare. He noticed that too.

"If you'd seen what I've seen, you'd shake too."

I nodded, as noncommittal as possible.

Yeah, I'm totally regretting the ride offer.

"You know in the Matrix, where you can choose that red pill or the blue one? *I* chose the red."

Well, here it is, might as well jump right in.

"Yeah, I usually seem to choose that red pill too. You said you saw the truth? Is that The Truth with a capital T?" I joked, desperately trying to keep it light.

I felt him staring hard. I glanced over and a slow smile was spreading on his face, an evil smile.

Kind of freaked me out, and a cold chill ran up my spine. We were turning onto route 800.

Only a couple more miles.

He leaned in closer. "They're all around us," he whispered. "*We* don't really want to *see* them. *They're* The Truth."

A niggling little worm of fear squirmed its way deep into my spine, down low in my back, like the feeling you get when you're too high on the ladder and sure you'll fall.

A nervous laugh escaped me, I couldn't stop it. I glanced over, and he was staring at me, stone faced.

"You have to know about them first, and *now* you do," he said. "They open up your third eye—so you can *see* them. They open it *for* you, because they *want* you to see them." His grin started again, splitting his face as wide as could be.

I was stunned into speechlessness, and believe me, *that* doesn't happen often. We drove under a streetlight and I looked across at him, trying to gauge if he was joking, high, or what.

In that brief moment, as the light above shone a vertical bar across his upper body, then his face, then on to his other shoulder, I saw it.

In the middle of his wrinkled brown forehead, a fat, thickly-rimmed eye blinked, slow and sleepy-like. Yellow, gummy, matter hardened in the corners, and a fresh film of it dripped off onto his leather vest, adding to the golden crust already there. And his legs, so stick-like before, looked huge now, giant tubes bursting at the seams of his jeans, barely squeezing into the car seat.

My breath stopped. The car veered, and I fought for control. His brother's house was ahead on the right. I hunched over the steering wheel, unable to look at him, terror freezing my very soul.

Our Father who art in Heaven…

I started praying, an automatic response to the pure evil I felt in that car with me.

He began to chuckle a little. "What's the matter? Did you see The Truth too?"

I couldn't speak, I began hyperventilating. I didn't want to look, in case that hideous eye was gazing back at me.

I pulled the car parallel to the house, hanging over the wheel, staring straight ahead. I heard the door open.

He leaned back in.

I refused to turn his direction.

"I guess maybe you didn't *really* want that red pill after all," he said.

The door slammed. I hit the power locks, and only then did I turn slightly to see him shuffling up the sidewalk toward the house. I couldn't see his face and I didn't want to. I stomped the gas, rocketing away, tires screeching. I tried to calm myself. I couldn't.

I don't know how I got through the gig. Professionalism has its rewards, I guess. I kept touching my forehead, but it felt just like always. I sang my songs, but I found myself searching other people's heads and staring at dark shadows in corners. I couldn't help it.

On the way home, passing the Turner house, I sped up.

My little dog Bo greeted me at the door, jumping frantically, and my unease slipped a little further into the background.

"Do you have to go out?"

He did.

Far too many shadows lurked in the back yard, so I took him through the house to the front porch, where I keep a dog tie fastened to the glider.

At 3a.m., the main street I live on is quiet, no traffic at all. I hooked Bo up, and stood, glancing up and down the wide street as he sniffed at the lawn below me, while traversing the perimeter of his leash.

It was eerily silent.

That same feeling started at the base of my spine, way down where our earliest primitive warning system develops; that tingle of fear.

Something's wrong.

I turned to my left. I could see all the way down the street past the red light on the corner, a mile of dark houses side by side. Nothing there. I turned to the right, the distant fluorescent sign of the Circle K, where all this started, visible a half mile down.

The tingle in my back grew. My head felt funny.

"BO!" I hissed, as quietly as I could.

He bounded up the 3 cement steps and I scooped him to my chest, unbuckling the lead. From the corner of my eye, I saw movement.

A figure on a bicycle flew down the sidewalk across the street. A black leather vest flapped out behind him. Long dark hair, white oval of a face was all I could see, and oddly shaped legs, very thick, like black stovepipes pumping up and down. He looked like a young version of Smokey-the-Biker.

His bike's front wheel dropped over the curb and bounced back up on the other side.

There's no sound.

No rattle of the metal, no flapping of the vest, nothing. I know the sounds a bike makes as it drops over a curb— a sound as familiar as my own name.

I watched the figure continue down the street, blocked briefly by my large rhododendron. I stepped back to catch a glimpse of him coming out on the other side.

But he didn't.

I moved to the end of the porch, hugging Bo to my chest, expecting to see the bike heading off towards Circle K.

But it was gone.

That just can't be.

I opened the door and took Bo inside. As I put him down, I saw a thick, viscous, yellowish glob on his back.

Panic.

I ran to the mirror. No eye, but a strange set of lumpy lines lingered on my forehead for a full five minutes as I rubbed and pressed, trying to make them go away.

I slept fitfully that night and had terrible dreams. They seemed so real.

I woke with a start, groggy, and with a headache.

There was thick, yellow gunk on my pillow.

My horror was complete.

I felt my forehead; smooth.

I raced to the basement to wash the bedclothes, Bo at my heels, and used bleach to kill any third-eye germs. I stayed there, leaning against the dryer, sick to my stomach, staring at the wall, until the laundry was done.

Bo followed me back upstairs.

I went over it in my head. How did this start? Did I really see that eye on Smokey the Biker? Or was he somehow able to *make* me see it? Was the soundless bicycle rider a trick played by my ears? Was the nasty yellow custard on Bo's back and my pillow able to be explained any other way than third eye seepage?

I'd never felt so unsure of myself, like I was losing my mind.

I stood at my window thinking, picking at a nail, looking out over my backyard, which bordered my neighbors' with an unobstructed view. At the rear of their lot, something was forming out of thin air: a huge cone-shaped mass.

An incredible, pulsing brown cloud, taller than my house materialized, swirling and rotating, transparent, yet with shapes moving inside it—a hundred objects at least. It rose up on the neighbor's side, weaving and bobbing, lumbering upright to a gigantic height. Creatures, big and small twisted within it, smashing into each other, spinning and bouncing off, separating, only to collide again with others.

A black, cow-shaped animal with a gaping orange mouth at the end of its neck instead of a head, slavered and chomped at a fat, two-legged, goat-headed humanoid beside it. This thing had the same thick legs as the bicycle rider—and Smokey the Biker's-*post*-third-eye appearance.

Clear, amorphous blobs spun and trembled, like gobs of jelly, splatting into thick tube-shaped creatures with long arms. These last had demonic features, with pointed teeth, and huge lidless eyes, which rolled as they clutched at any creature passing nearby. One seized the goat-headed human by its thick leg, then gnashed its teeth in rage as the vortex sucked away its purchase on the distorted appendage. All the while, my eyes fought with my brain at the incongruent images before me.

The cloud moved directly at me.

I shrieked, and Bo started barking.

I reached for my forehead, afraid to turn away from the terrifying cyclone threatening my home. I felt for the third eye, and my fingers came away wet with yellow slime.

I *willed* it to close. I *raged* and *cursed* at it. But it obviously didn't, because I could still see the violently rotating abomination heading straight for me.

I watched in horror as the gyrating cloud spewed monsters from centrifugal force. An angry demon-tube thing landed across the fence separating my yard from the neighbors. It squirmed and rolled off, righting itself, and moving in a snake-like manner, toward my back porch.

A blue, jelly-blob, with large, black, doll eyes, squooshed flat, then round again, as it progressed slowly forward, compressing and expanding in an up and down motion, and propelling itself by this means. It crossed the alley behind my house, and entered my yard, leaving a wide, shiny slick behind it, like some kind of depraved slug.

Other monstrous atrocities were being birthed from the spinning funnel, spit out at high velocity, landing, rising, shaking themselves, and setting off towards me.

I was riveted to the window, terrified, wondering whether the monsters crossing my lawn or the massive, twisting cyclone would reach my house first. Would the cloud obey the laws of physics? Would the things inside the vortex be deposited into the room with me, or would the physical structure of the house split the funnel somehow, diverting it, causing it to dissipate?

I was frozen to the spot, watching the horror unfold. But a part of me wished I could run to the mirror to look at myself, to see the proof of my third eye opened. My shock and disbelief warred with terror, as each revolution of the spinning monstrosity brought new, horrifying sights rotating into view.

The writhing cloud of monsters approached until it undulated a foot outside my window, collision imminent. I shrank back, bracing for impact. I could not close my eyes against the sight of the horrific beasts spiraling within.

Then I blinked—and it was gone.

It vanished with a small *pop*, like the sound of a thumb pulling from a beer bottle. The crawling, undulating horrors on the lawn, the gigantic brown tornado, everything—all just disappeared instantly.

I stumbled backward, burst into tears, and collapsed on my bed. Bo immediately scrambled up, frantic, licking at my face, at my forehead.

I immediately realized why.

I grabbed his tiny body, spotting a vile, straw-colored glob of the viscid stuff around his mouth. I reached for a tissue and wiped it off, gagging. Then I ran for the bathroom mirror.

There was more on my forehead. The ridges were there again as well; the last vestiges of what had recently been there.

I ran hot water, and scrubbed my forehead so hard, it turned bright red. I couldn't think anymore. I couldn't cry. I was numb.

I stayed curled up on the sofa with Bo all day. I found Joel Osteen sermons on You Tube and watched them, one after another, needing the positive comfort of my childhood religion.

As evening approached, I shut them off. I had to decide what to do next. Bo needed to go out, but I didn't want to open the door. I peeked through the blinds, afraid to see anything but my usual back yard. But everything appeared normal, so I finally opened it.

I hooked Bo to his lead, mustered up my courage, and walked toward the neighbor's fence, to the spot where the tube-creature had landed after being flung from the cyclone.

There was a mark, a scuff, a few shards of wood bent forward, and a slick track in the grass, where it had righted itself and begun to move toward me, pulled like gravity seemingly, to my humanness—as though I was the center of its universe, the sun in its Milky Way.

A sick, wet feeling flopped in the pit of my stomach

Were they were coming FOR me? To kill me, eat me, or absorb me somehow?

My imagination ran wild. I tried to calm my mind.

Maybe they were sent to bring me back? To where?

Dear God, no.

I shut that down instantly. But the thought struck me with dread, the way real-life awfulness always did.

Was the funnel really Smokey's red pill? Or mine?

I barely slept that night. Bo curled up in the crook of my knees, shifting himself each time I turned from side to side. My racing thoughts did help me though—I found a possible temporary solution for my immediate problem. Although I couldn't predict when the third eye would *open*, I could possibly shut it down by *covering it up*.

I was about to find out.

I dug in my closet for an absurd pink *Hello Kitty* beanie my Grandma had given me for Christmas. It was standard wear for a nine year old, bless her heart, but it was also tightly woven, and long enough to pull down over my forehead.

A final glance in the mirror told me I looked ridiculous, but I had a feeling it just might work. The first thing I planned to do, was go to Smokey's brother's house, and try to get to the bottom of this.

The ride out there was tense. I found myself focusing on each side of the berm, once jerking the wheel into the other lane at a rabbit hopping along in the culvert. I touched the beanie constantly, reassuring myself it sat well below my eyebrows, completely obscuring my forehead.

So far, so good.

I didn't know what I would say to the Turners. I could barely articulate this experience to *myself*. I knocked and took a deep breath as Gail Turner opened the door.

She recognized me after a moment, a disdainful glance at my beanie giving away her opinion of either *Hello Kitty,* or my fashion sense.

"Hi, Gail! Excuse the beanie, bad hair day, and all that."

"Well, hello Kerri! What brings you out here?"

"A couple nights ago, I gave your brother-in-law a ride out to your house, after running into him at Circle K. I guess you could say his conversation was a little unsettling. I hoped you could tell me where to find him, so I can ask him about it."

The puzzled expression on her face told me something was wrong.

"Smokey? You couldn't have given him a ride here—because he *wasn't* here—in fact, he went off to Sedona to find himself the week after we got married, and we haven't seen him since."

"I dropped him off out at the road," I said, inclining my head in the direction of my parked car.

She continued shaking her head no, baffled. She wasn't faking; I could see *that* much with my own *two* eyes.

"My husband talked to him a few times over the past year, and to be honest," her voice dropped to a conspiratorial whisper, "he sounded unhinged."

Suddenly, she seemed alarmed. She stepped back just a bit.

I pulled at the beanie again, patting at the pertinent area, afraid she'd see *it* sticking out. My fingers came away wet, and I began to panic. I grimaced at the gushy mess before I could stop myself, and wiped my hand on my pants. *Now* she was staring at my forehead.

"I don't know. All I know is, I need to talk to him. He told me something scary. I need to understand it."

I sound insane.

She backed up further and started to close the door.

"I'm sorry, he hasn't been here. My husband thought he'd had some sort of break with reality. He was spouting crazy things last time we spoke to him—about other dimensions, and how our true natures are not revealed until *they* reveal them to us—real paranoid stuff."

"I'm not making this up, Gail. Smokey told me who he was, how else would I have known to come here?"

She shook her head more violently, frowning and easing the door further shut.

"I believe you. But if he was in town, and you dropped him off here, he never came in. And just between us, I think he's dangerous. Something's not right there," —she tapped the side of her head with an index finger—"and that's been the case *way* before *this* nonsense came up. I'm sorry I can't help you more."

I knew she was done.

"Okay, thanks. You might want to lock *your* doors, too."

She agreed, obviously shaken.

The door closed, and I heard the lock snick.

I was back at square one.

In the car, I stared in the rear view mirror at the growing discharge on my forehead, seeping through the stretchy pink material and congealing there. But at least the hat was working. It kept me from seeing anything abnormal.

I'm gonna need more beanies.

I ran into the dollar store on the way home, buying all the $1.99 hats they had. I also bought a box of thin, extra-absorbent panty liners.

On the way out the door, a millennial was coming in, wearing the ever present beanie pulled low, the signature coonskin cap of his generation. It had a large wet spot in the middle of it. He nodded at me, his eyes drifting to *my* wet spot—in recognition? I froze.

I haven't got time to think about this now.

Back in the car, I got everything ready. I knew I had to take off the disgusting, sopping wet beanie and replace it with a dry one, and I wanted that switch to be as fast as possible. I didn't want to see monsters.

I opened the box of liners and peeled off the no-stick strip on the back of a pad. I pulled the price sticker from a black beanie, and stuck the pad about two inches up inside it. I held it beside my face, checking the level of the pad placement against the slimy, wet, yellow goo seeping through the pink beanie, then adjusted the pad a little higher.

It was time. I took a deep breath, steeling myself.

I pulled off the wet hat in a quick motion, flinging it onto the passenger seat floorboard with one hand, clutching at the dry one in my lap with the other. In that moment, with the third eye exposed, I saw four things:

1. The whirling brown tornado rotated five hundred yards away, casually sucking up a millennial with huge tube-shaped legs, whilst spewing out blobs with lidless round eyes, creatures of every fantastic form, and giant-legged, demonic fanged, tube people.

2. Normal folks were approaching the store totally oblivious, but a couple millennials, also with wet beanies, stared directly at me, seemingly co-conspirators in this Salvador Dali-esque nightmare.

3. The sopping wet hat I'd thrown in the corner had sprouted a three foot in diameter, rapidly expanding, round-eyed, quivering blob, apparently growing from the thick yellow liquid saturating it. The yellow goo was reproducing—self-replicating. This blob-creature would overtake the car's interior within seconds at the rate it was growing.

4. Lastly, and worst of all, as I scrabbled for the fresh hat in my lap, I could see my own gigantic tube-shaped legs. I was becoming one of them.

I pulled the black beanie down tight, and everything went away. I patted and adjusted the pad into perfect alignment.

Then I lost it.

I pulled to the far side of the parking lot and cried, hunched over the wheel so no one would notice me. After a good five minutes of soul racking sobs, I felt ready to proceed with some kind of plan.

Find Smokey the biker.

Before I pulled out of the parking lot, I assembled another stick-on panty liner in a fresh beanie, ready for the next quick-change. I tossed the wet one on the floorboard out the window, wondering briefly if the expanding blob on it still existed simultaneously in the other dimension, even though I couldn't see it.

It was mind boggling, really.

I decided I would go home, rest up, and figure out the logistics of my next step—making the rounds at all the local biker bars, in search of Smokey. I wiped my eyes one last time and started off towards home.

As I navigated the familiar streets to my house, I kept watch for Smokey, saying a silent prayer. I needed to find him, to have him shut off this horrible affliction, to show me how to go back to the blue pill life, to explain why the millennials seemed to be in on this nightmare.

I was almost to the Circle K when I saw someone leaning against the building beside the door. It was Smokey—in the exact spot where I'd first met him. Fear took over this time, because I knew he was pure evil. Maybe even the Devil himself.

As I pulled into the parking space directly in front of him, he saw me, and that satanic grin split his leathery face. My legs were shaking, but anger was replacing my terror, and I slammed the car door and stalked over to him.

"What have you done?" I hissed under my breath. "Fix this! Put me back the way I was!" I could feel the pad in my beanie sticking to my gooey forehead, sliding a bit in a fresh flood of banana-yellow third-eye mucus.

Smokey held up both hands, palms out, as though to say *whoa*. I noticed his teeth were very bad. But I didn't feel sorry for him. I wanted to hurt him. Maybe kill him.

"It's a construct. We all recycle. We all renew and change," Smokey said.

"What the hell are you saying? I'm seeing monsters. I *am* a monster."

"No, the monsters are the lower energies, not you. Let go. Don't fight it. It's good, very good, when you let go," he cooed.

"You're insane. Just like Gail said."

He laughed, throwing his head back. He didn't wear a hat, so I assume he somehow had control over *his* third eye.

"Take the hat off. Let the whirlwind absorb you and spit you out. The cycle is never-ending. And we are all one," he said, closing his eyes in some crazed, Zen-like imitation.

I stared, trying to comprehend. I couldn't.

"How do I stop it, I don't want it, I can't take it!" I screamed.

A man coming from the store frowned at my outburst and edged away sideways.

"Accept reality. Take the hat off. Let it pull you in. Let it recycle you, change you."

It was hopeless. I started to cry, stumbled back to my car and looked up in time to see Smokey fading away, right there in front of God, the Circle K, and everyone.

Then he was gone.

Maybe the brown tornado sucked him up. I assumed so; since it would be invisible to me, with *my* third eye covered.

I could barely see to drive, the tears wouldn't stop, and sobs shook me. I pulled into my driveway and hurried in to the comfort of Bo. I hugged and cradled him until the grief passed. I took him upstairs to my bedroom and sat him on the bed. Then I kissed him goodbye.

The questions were unanswerable.

It was all unknowable, until it was known.

I pulled off the hat, half stuck to my skin with dried yellow matter. I stared out the window at the funnel forming, towering up, flinging horrendous creatures in all directions. I fought the fear as it approached my house. I tried not to stare at the limping, dragging, sloshing monstrosities crossing my lawn, coming for me. I didn't need to worry about them anyway; the cyclone would reach me first, long before they did.

I watched the spinning things inside the vortex smashing together, struggling against one another for supremacy. I imagined myself among them, and what *that* might be like. Smokey said no—not me, only the lower energies. But how could that be true? If I could *see* them, why wouldn't I *be* with them?

Look how crowded it is in there.

God help me.

The monstrous brown tornado lumbered closer, breached the outer corner of my house, and entered my room. I heard Bo squeal, behind me on the bed, and then the Behemoth sucked me up, entered me, as I entered it.

A million pinpricks of energy surged through me, thundering across my nerve endings, pulling me into the vortex with a grunt of pure ecstasy and surprise. I saw no creatures, I struggled with none. I basked in the throes of its perfection—until we were one.

It was glorious.

Some time passed, I don't know how much. I found myself outside the funnel, flung out, and landing across the street in front of my house, spent, yet invigorated.

I crossed the two lanes and reentered my home, finding Bo safely asleep on my bed.

My mind was clear. I understood.

I ran to the mirror.

Yes. The years, washed away.

I know why Smokey changed me. I now feel compelled to change others.

We look old.

We are not.

We are young, younger each time we are sucked into the Behemoth, the Construct.

We shall open every eye.

Recycle every human body.
And dry every tear.
We are the Millennials.

THE RIVER RAN RED
CaLVIN DeMMeR

The river ran red. It wasn't the first time Asani had seen the peculiar occurrence, but it transfixed him all the same. He'd once gone upstream in search of what caused the crimson color. Angry voices and the pounding of spears on shields had stopped him from quenching his curiosity.

Not this time.

He moved between the branches of the trees along the river, inhaling the plethora of aromas from citrus sweet to damp and musky. The humidity of the Western African atmosphere caused salty perspiration to run down his face. It didn't bug him anymore. This was his real home, and he loved the jungle.

His mother had taken him away from here after his father's passing. The village they'd moved to bored him. There was even a school now, and his mother had forced him to attend from the first day it opened. It wasn't for him. Asani longed for the old ways. The stories his uncle had told him captivated him. He wanted to be like the village's warriors. He wanted to learn the old methods of doing things, as well as to hunt animals, and fight enemy tribes—the last wish was really a dream because such violence had stopped many years before. Getting to visit his uncle, who stayed in a village in the jungle, a village that still had some resemblance of their ancestor's ways, was heaven.

A harrowing scream caused him to pause.

Asani's intestines knotted. It was a male, but the man was either so scared or in so much pain that he didn't sound too far from being a pig when slaughtered. There were many different predators within the jungle, and many of them could do a man harm. Reaching toward his hip, Asani retrieved the knife he'd brought with. The handle was rough, and a splinter pricked his thumb as he tightened his grip. Rays of sunlight piercing the canopy of branches overhead reflected off the blade, shining on the trunk of a nearby tree.

There was a handprint on the trunk.

It shared the crimson color of the river.

Something disturbed the bush to his side. A branch snapped. Asani didn't see anything moving and kept low, making his way toward the sound. If it was an animal, and he caught it, he'd gain some much-needed respect. Putting the man's scream to the back of his mind, he inhaled deeply. Straight for the throat was the advice he'd received when asking about how the tribe had become such proficient hunters, killers.

He came out from a bush covering him, stumbling across an open path.

The path was man-made, created by his village, and Asani looked ahead, wondering where it led.

Figures came into view. Asani's heart shuddered, and his mind commanded him to take flight. But, it was too late. His uncle had seen him. His uncle saw everything. The seconds that passed as the men approached him were insufferable. Asani feared his uncle would send him straight home, or worse, scold him in front of the group.

His uncle did neither.

He waited for the rest of the men with him to walk ahead. None bothered to look at Asani, as if he didn't exist.

With no witnesses in sight, his uncle placed a hand on his shoulder, gripping down hard. 'What are you doing here?'

Asani needed a satisfactory answer and fast. His uncle's eyes burned his own. 'I was hunting.'

'So far from the village?'

'I didn't realize I'd wandered so far.'

His uncle frowned. 'Did you hear or see anything?'

Asani wasn't sure if his uncle meant animals or something else. Was it a test? He tried to remain calm, hoping no tells surfaced. The man's scream came to the fore of his mind, but he hastily searched for another thought, one of a jungle, serene and still.

'Nothing,' Asani said.

☻☻☻

The following morning, a gentle breeze danced around the village. Asani stepped out of his uncle's hut, knowing that the cool atmosphere wouldn't last long. He walked past one of the elder women, who tended a fire she'd made.

'You hungry?' she asked, stirring the black pot that hung over the flames.

Asani shook his head.

He wanted to return to the river and find out what had happened to the man there the previous day, but he couldn't see his uncle anywhere and was afraid of running into him again. The aroma of porridge and fresh bread flooded his sense of smell. Maybe something to eat wasn't a bad idea while he contemplated a course of action. There would be daily chores lined up for him, but they were the furthest things from his mind.

He turned back to the woman, but she'd left with her pot.

Asani took a seat by what remained of the fire, hoping she'd return. The sensation of a centipede crawling over his back tickled, and he looked around the village, searching for anything out of the ordinary. All he saw were the villagers doing their chores: women preparing breakfast, men sharpening spears, women washing animal furs, men adding wood to various fires, and kids running around.

Yet something wasn't right.

The sounds of hundreds of birds taking flight came from the trees on the perimeter of the village. They ascended into the pellucid sky. Then came screaming, much like the man Asani had heard the day before. He looked ahead. A man came out from the tree line, wearing nothing but some animal fur over his lower half.

Blood covered the man's face.

Asani moved to his right, sensing the man would run straight into him. But instead, he turned and ran away from the village, screaming and thrashing his arms about as if something was eating him alive.

Villagers moved out of his path.

Asani stood in a trance. The man vanished from his view. No one in the village paid any attention to him, apart from moving out his way. And then they carried on with whatever tasks they'd been doing.

It didn't add up.

'Psst… Over here.'

Searching for the voice, Asani looked at one of the girls from the village. She indicated for him to follow her as she ducked between two huts. It hadn't been the first time he'd noticed her. It had, however, been the first time she'd spoken to him. She was by far the most attractive girl he'd seen in the village with her toned, slender limbs, and long black hair. Her eyes softened as she gestured again with her hand for him to follow her into the jungle.

Asani obeyed.

They walked for about twenty minutes before her pace slowed, and she stopped abruptly, turning to him.

She placed her index finger over her lips. 'Shhh.'

Asani didn't hear anything but obeyed.

'Okay.' She stepped toward him. 'I saw you were surprised by the man running through the village. I'll tell you about him. But first, I'm going to show you the circle of madness. Have you seen it before?'

Asani shook his head.

'Good. I'm Fahimah. I've seen you around. You come and go. Your uncle is the leader of our tribe. You must be special?'

Warmth rose from the base of Asani's neck. 'I-I'm Asani. I usually stay in another village with my mother. I visit here every now and again.'

Fahimah nodded, indicating for him to follow again. She stalked her way past low growing bushes and trees with narrow trunks. The normal sounds of the jungle had disappeared, making the silence an unusual event.

They entered a clearing where the sun warmed Asani's face. He looked around. Oval-shaped rocks formed a circular perimeter around them.

'That man you saw running through the village was not cured.' Fahimah pointed at one of the rocks. 'Do you see the drawings?'

Asani walked to the rock. Someone had painted a creature on the smooth gray rock. It was unlike any animal he'd seen with its saber-like canines, scales over its body, and a long tail. It's most intimidating feature was the horn on its head. Around the monster, severed human limbs floated.

'What is it? What is this place?' Asani asked, looking to the rock on his right, where he saw a river painted red.

'That is the Dingonek, or as some people call it: The Jungle Walrus. It lives somewhere in the river far from the village. This place, as I told you, is the circle of madness. It is where some warriors come if they have side-effects from the ritual. They draw on the rocks, scream, and do other things until the evil and madness has left them.'

Asani remembered the crimson section of the river and the man who screamed. But, surely this was all just a tale. A creature in the river? A ritual? The tribe had stopped a lot of the old ways. Hadn't they?

'You don't know about the ritual?' Fahimah asked, walking toward him.

Asani shook his head. 'No. I also find this monster hard to believe.'

'I can't speak confidently about the Dingonek, I've only heard the tales. But, the ritual? That's very real. It's going on this very week. The man you saw running through the village must have failed. Not even the circle of madness will be able to cure him, I think. He'll never become an elder in the tribe now. Might even be sent away…if he ever returns.'

Asani strode to another of the rocks. This one had a man holding a skull high into the air.

'Why is the skull red?'

'Some say it's because the water stains it after a while, others say it's because of the evil of the creature, and some say it's from all the blood spent in the river. The ritual is not always passed.'

'What is the rit—'

Fahimah pulled him down to the ground, hard, before he could speak further. She held her hand over his mouth. The skin on her fingers was soft, yet her grip firm.

'Quiet,' she said, 'someone is coming. We must go. Follow me.'

Asani crawled behind Fahimah until they reached the safety of the jungle. They then hid behind some bushes, waiting to see who came.

His uncle and other men appeared.

They huddled in the clearing, near the circle of rocks, but no one entered the circle as he and Fahimah had. Asani could hear them talking. It was hard to understand exactly what they said due to the distance and the return of the jungle's sounds.

'…tomorrow…he will do us proud…' someone said.

'…today was bad…barely got in…'

'…he didn't die…'

'…death may have been better…'

One voice was clearer than the rest. Asani's uncle said, 'I have no doubt tomorrow will be a good day. Tumo's son is brave. He is fighter. He will pass the ritual.'

💀💀💀

Asani woke up in darkness. He'd willed his mind the night before not to let him oversleep, and it had listened. It didn't take long for the early morning to illuminate the dark hut. His uncle got up, fumbling with something in the shadows.

Asani tried to watch his uncle under almost shut eyes.

His uncle reached for his spear and then attached a knife to a band around his waist. Beneath his breath, he prayed, kneeling in the pale light.

After parting ways from Fahimah yesterday, after seeing the circle of madness, the ritual ruled Asani's thoughts. What was it? And could he pass it?? Would they allow him to attempt it? Would he gain the tribes respect then? He sometimes sensed how they looked at him and what they thought. Coming from more modern ways, he didn't doubt they thought him weaker, maybe even unworthy of the tribe.

He'd told Fahimah he'd join her later that day. She was beautiful, intriguing, and he enjoyed the moments he spent with her. But, having the entire tribe respect him was a stronger pull. He just needed to know what the ritual was.

His uncle grabbed his shield and exited the hut.

Asani slunk out behind him, carefully, so as not to draw attention.

His uncle moved fast and splashed his face in a large bowl of water, before accepting some porridge and something to drink from one of the women seated at a fire. Clearly not wanting to waste time, his uncle downed the drink and finished breakfast with large, fast gulps.

Asani's stomach groaned as he followed behind his uncle. He ducked behind a hut, sensing his uncle may look back.

A group of men, also armed with spears and shields, joined up with his uncle, including a younger looking man, who his uncle patted on the back. The warriors around him obscured the man's face.

The group then headed into the jungle.

Asani followed, reaching down for his knife. He felt nothing but air where the weapon should be.

There wasn't time to fetch it from the hut.

He wandered into the jungle, where a mystical quality mesmerized in the early hours. The sun hadn't heated the world to unbearable temperatures yet and shadows created the illusion of secret realms hidden from the urban world. The earthy smell was strong, but so too were the other spicy and sweet aromas of the natural world. Every unexpected sound could potentially be a wild animal. It was a world where anything could happen.

Things changed when the men continued on the narrow path Asani had discovered yesterday. Now, he had to keep well back from his uncle and the other men. With no trees or bushes to hide behind, any mistake would give him away. Sometimes, he had to hold back until he could just make out their voices. Fortunately for him, the men had begun singing once out of earshot of the village.

They disappeared ahead, taking a left off the path.

Asani pursued them, cringing every time he stumbled on the uneven ground, as each ill step or shuffle caused the earth to moan, whether it be leaves rustling or branches snapping underfoot. Eventually, he was near enough to observe where the men had gone.

They stood around a part of the river that had almost formed a circle, surrounded by tall trees with hanging branches. It was a peculiar sight. Asani had become so accustomed to the narrow snake-like shaped river that the new spot came across like a little paradise hidden away in the jungle. He imagined how blissful it would be to swim here.

His uncle and the other men aimed their spears at the water's surface. Their shields were in place, protecting their bodies. Asani ignored the wobble in his knees. The younger man, Mwamba, Asani believed his name was, had not done as the rest. Mwamba stood, praying.

'Mwamba, are you ready? Are you ready to be an elder and pass this ritual?' Asani's uncle asked. 'You only have to retrieve one skull, and you're one of us. We've all done it before. We know you can do it.'

Mwamba nodded.

'It's morning. The Dingonek sleeps. He only wakes in the evening. Do not be afraid, Mwamba, son of Tumo. Are you ready?'

Mwamba nodded.

'I said are you ready?'

'Yes,' Mwamba muttered.

'Go now.'

Mwamba dived into the river.

Asani wanted to laugh at the silly myth created as part of the ritual. This couldn't be easier. The images on the rocks had reminded him of the drawings of kids in his school, and he wondered if the circle of madness was also an invention to add to the mystique of the ritual. The monster meant to inhabit the river was the most ridiculous of all.

Mwamba splashed around, forceful, not the sound one would associate with normal swimming.

Asani stood, stealthily, trying to see what had caused the man's actions.

'Just relax. Get the skull,' his uncle said to Mwamba.

Mwamba ducked below the surface.

When he came up again, he wasted no time swimming back to shore, where he fell to his knees and raised the reddened skull above his head. Asani's uncle and the rest of the men patted him on the back, whispering congratulations.

'Let's go,' his uncle said. 'The Dingonek will be upset at someone disturbing the balance of death in the river. We will celebrate properly back in the village.'

Asani had seen and heard enough.

He creeped out from his hiding spot. 'Uncle, I wish to perform the ritual next.'

His uncle's eyes widened, his mouth opened, and Asani realized it was a look of shock—a look he'd never seen on his uncle's face. His uncle became reanimated and indicated for the rest of the men to leave them.

'What are you doing here?' he asked Asani once they were alone.

'I want to do the ritual.'

'That's not how it works. Only those invited may attempt it. All the men have now seen you here, breaking our ways. You're a real embarrassment, Asani. This is sacred.'

'That's stupid.' Asani stomped his foot. 'It's so silly I could pass it in my sleep.'

His uncle pushed him in the chest, hard, sending Asani reeling backward until he lost balance and fell onto his rear. Tears built up in his eyes. Denied the chance to do the ritual and then the physical contact brought feelings of anger and shame to the surface.

'I can do it, uncle,' Asani muttered. 'And then the village will respect me.'

'No.'

His uncle reached down, grabbing Asani's arm, and yanked him up.

'Come, we're leaving this place. You are never to come here again. Do you understand, Asani?'

Fearing more punishment, Asani nodded.

A tear streaked down his cheek.

The afternoon heat was particularly unforgiving. Asani didn't mind. It reflected his inner turmoil. The anger, humiliation, and pain feasted like maggots inside of him. The first of his punishments was to help clean some of the pots used during lunch. This would have tipped him over the edge had a switch not flicked within his mind once he'd arrived back in the village. He was biding his time, waiting for the opportunity to head into the jungle.

Nothing would stop him performing the tribes' silly ritual.

He'd retrieve one of the red skulls, and everyone would respect him.

When some of the elder people began heading into their huts, to take naps before the evening's festivities in honor of Mwamba, Asani dropped what he was doing. He retrieved his knife and headed into the jungle, watchful for prying eyes.

He didn't know the exact route. But knew that if he followed the river upstream he could check for the path that led to ritual's special place. Feeling better than he had all day, he couldn't help but chuckle. He imagined the villagers faces of shock and awe when he returned with the skull. He didn't wish to spoil the festivities for Mwamba, who seemed nice, but the village and his uncle had brought it upon themselves. They would respect him and celebrate him as well. Maybe he could even convince his mother that this was the place for him.

He'd be an esteemed elder after all.

Maybe one day he'd even replace his uncle as the tribe's leader.

Asani's cheeks felt sore, and he noticed he was grinning. Pausing, to look around, he decided to move away from the river, hopeful he'd come across the path.

He did.

It was all so easy, as if the gods had already written his destiny in stone. Ignoring the usual precautions of being in the jungle, Asani started jogging up the path. He wanted it all, now.

When he came across the river, he didn't wait.

Asani dove right in.

The water was not only warmer than he expected, but it was also clearer. He glanced down, then lowered his head into the water, wondering where he'd find one of the skulls. Scanning the rocky river bed, it occurred to him he might not find one. Maybe they were placed here before the ritual?

He cursed himself as he raised his head above the surface.

Biting his tongue, he decided it best to look around before conceding defeat. It remained possible a skull had been forgotten. He submerged himself again, seeking an area to inspect before kicking himself to the bottom, where he swam, searching the rocks on the river bed for anything that stood out.

It didn't take long for him to notice red become the dominant shade in the river. Looking ahead, Asani realized he'd have no problem finding a skull. There were many. Along with the skulls, there were other bones dyed with red, most of them shattered. He needed to breathe, but the urge to grab one of the skulls was stronger.

He stuck his fingers into the eye sockets of the nearest skull and headed back to the surface, now wondering why there were so many—at least twenty to thirty of them were visible. He could understand why the village would want to make it easy for the challengers doing the ritual, which really was just an elaborate ruse to scare the men and test their bravery, but where would they find so many skulls and why were other bones scattered over the river's floor as well? Were they animals?

Surfacing, he looked at the skull in his hand.

It was human.

When the river was shallow enough for him to walk, he decided not to worry about the amount of human bones in the river. Maybe the tribe had some strange ritual after all, like instead of burying their dead, they dropped them into the river. Whatever the reasoning behind the bones, it didn't matter. He'd retrieved one of the skulls. He would gain their respect and become one of the elders.

Asani got down on one knee and raised the skull when he stepped on land, mimicking Mwamba. No one patted his shoulder or congratulated him, but he imagined them doing so.

He stood, as heat, like someone starting a fire, erupted over the back of his right leg.

Something white and sharp, protruded through his right thigh.

Asani looked at the object in disbelief. His world wobbled like the time he'd drunk alcohol for the first time. He touched the object, which now looked like an animal horn, and as he did, pain exploded from the wound throughout his body.

The horn disappeared, leaving a hole in the middle of his leg.

Asani braced himself by widening his stance and trying to find equilibrium as his body swayed like a small tree hit by intense winds. He heard splashing as he turned back to the river.

Asani stared upon the Dingonek.

The drawing on the rocks did not do justice to the true horror of this creature.

Deep-set crimson eyes, raging with the intensity of freshly lit Hell fires, stared at him. The horn on the top of the creature's head was sharp, large, and stained red. Was it from the blood of its victims? Was it his blood? The scales that covered its body were thick, like armor. They'd be impenetrable to any weapon Asani could think of. The creature was broad, rivaling hippos Asani had seen in the wild. It was long as well. He guessed at least eighteen feet. Razor-sharp teeth backed up two distinctive white fangs. Even the creature's tail, which had a barb, reminding Asani of those on scorpions, had evolved with the purpose of killing.

Asani screamed, knowing it was pointless. The villagers were too far away, partying, and enjoying Mwamba's win.

Asani threw the skull he held at the Dingonek, but he didn't have the strength required, and it plopped into the river a few feet from him.

The Dingonek sprung forward, landing just before the water's edge. It swung its scorpion-like tail.

Asani couldn't dodge it in time, and the blow sent him flailing through the air, where he crashed into the trunk of a tree. He'd heard one of his arms snap before dropping to the hard, unforgiving earth. The hurt had become so unbearable, it was almost as if it couldn't be real. But, it was. Sharp stabs of pain appeared randomly all over his body.

A stinging bite, from one of his feet, spiked next.

Fighting against blacking out, Asani discerned the sky above shifting. The beast dragged him somewhere. When he felt the water over his feet, he knew he was about to become sustenance for the creature of the river.

The Dingonek was real.

He'd failed the ritual.

It was heart-breaking enough that he couldn't pass and that he would die, but what crushed his heart further was the fact that he would not see Fahimah again, nor have the village celebrate him.

But soon, maybe even the next morning, another member of the tribe may retrieve his very skull when passing the ritual.

Asani had to accept it.

His head was now below the surface. The Dingonek was taking him deeper into the river. His lungs burned. He had to breath. The water tasted like metal as it filled his lungs.

His view darkened.

By attempting the ritual, with or without his uncle's permission, he'd already become a member of the tribe.

Not everyone could be the hero.

Some had to die for there to be skulls.

This was the way of his people.

EXTINCTION IN GREEN
KURT FAWVER

Day 1: We cannot leave this windowless basement room, for the emerald light outside has become too fierce and the noises we hear within it have become all too unfamiliar.

Day 2: We do not know the source of the light, only that it began yesterday morning when it washed over us in place of dawn and, brighter than the glint in a god's eye, blotted out the world.

Day 3: Our dying phones find no reception, so our messages of panic and confusion go unsent and unread.

Day 4: Water continues to flow from the pipes and electricity continues to twist through the basement wires, but for how long and to what end?

Day 5: Muffled chitterings and moans from beyond the ceiling filter down to us and make us dream of anthills high as skyscrapers and infirmaries staffed by roach physicians—images from a world we no longer understand.

Day 6: The basement is divided into three sections: a storage area stocked with canned goods and bottled water, a laundry room we've converted to a bathroom, and a rec room replete with couch, billiard table, and minibar.

Day 7: There are five of us, all strangely nondescript beyond our skin tones and our performed genders, all without significant external markers that might lead to deeper characterizations.

Day 8: We refuse to reveal our names to one another, as naming ourselves would provide too much reality to a situation we pray might yet be nothing more than an exceptionally vivid nightmare.

Day 9: We spend too much time inside our heads, constructing meaning for the incessant scratching on the walls above us and envisioning the innumerable ways we will all suffer before we can finally rest.

Day 10: We are lucky that the basement is well stocked with beans and dried fruits and all manner of nonperishable foodstuffs, otherwise who knows what measures we may have had to take.

Day 11: Our cycle of night and day has been replaced by a cycle of general exhaustion and complete collapse.

Day 12: Silence rules our waking hours, as there is little to speak of other than our fears, and the proper words do not exist to give them voice.

Day 13: This afternoon we noticed that a strip of searing viridescence now outlines the basement door, a fact which leads us to believe the light has grown even stronger, even brighter since we took refuge here.

Day 14: Are our families and our friends still alive somewhere and, if so, are they still human?

Day 15: Today we heard footfalls above, followed by a single, hollow scream that quickly faded to a rubbery squeal, as if from a punctured balloon in its final exhalations.

Day 16: Many of us murmur the names of our loved ones in our sleep and grasp at empty spaces where warm, knowing bodies once nestled against us.

Day 17: If five random passersby become trapped in the home of a stranger for the rest of their lives, does it make them a family?

Day 18: We debated the virtues of unlocking and opening the door to the basement for a momentary peek outside our safe haven, but decided that the reward of knowing would not have outweighed the consequence of seeing.

Day 19: I must force myself to keep these records short, given that there is only one small notepad in the basement and I intend for it to last as long as we do.

Day 20: A pungent odor as of burning wires entered the basement this morning, accompanied by a chorus of feverish clicks and disjointed groans from above; hours later, neither has dissipated.

Day 21: We wonder what project is being undertaken in the world beyond this basement: war, assimilation, extermination, or an enterprise so alien that we cannot begin to even grasp its edges?

Day 22: All the canned food we eat tastes of salt and rusted metal—the flavor of survival, of desperation, of unremitting imprisonment.

Day 23: A brief flash of darkness broke through the green light today, a beacon to remind us that safe harbors may yet exist where the light does not hold dominion.

Day 24: We've taken to playing a word association game in which we try to relate objects in the basement to memories from our former lives—either of which might be illusory at this point.

Day 25: One of the men in our enclave broke down today, repeatedly screaming the phrase "Extinction in green" and pounding his head against the concrete floor; though we tried to restrain him, he still managed to injure himself so severely that he lost consciousness and has remained catatonic ever since.

Day 26: This evening, after the man who beat himself senseless stopped breathing, we stuffed his body into the dryer in the laundry room and recited a liturgy of broken prayers.

Day 27: The light that seeps in from around the door seems to obey no rule of physics, twisting and turning like a snake seeking purchase on a tree limb or a tentacle sneaking toward prey.

Day 28: A terrible, low rumble like a million mountaintops collapsing in tandem has shaken our walls and bludgeoned our skulls all day.

Day 29: One of the women in our group volunteered to scout beyond the basement door, but we value companionship more than freedom at this point, so we declined the offer; time and pressure, however, may very well change our estimation of worth.

Day 30: The other man, the one who didn't beat in his head, tried to charge his phone with a bare wire and burned his hand to the muscle—proof that ingenuity born of ignorance will not save us as it did our cave-dwelling forebears.

Day 31: We have lived in the basement for one full month, but time has no relevance where cataclysm is concerned; days, months, or years cannot adequately measure the full dimensions of terror.

Day 32: The emerald light slithered farther across the floor today than it ever had before, backing us all into a corner in the rec room where we hugged one another and confessed our sins.

Day 33: We remain huddled in the now urine-soaked corner, packed tight as cattle on a killing floor and perhaps just as frightened.

Day 34: The woman who volunteered to scout beyond the basement stuck her foot into the light, where it began to contort and elongate like chewed bubble gum stretched between two fingers; she flinched away almost instantly, but her foot remains changed.

Day 35: The light finally receded to its usual orbit around the basement door and granted us a temporary stay of execution.

Day 36: Yesterday's entry may have been preemptive, as a plague of bulldozer-sized locusts—or something far more unimaginable—has chittered at an unbearable volume all day, making it impossible to hold a thought for more than a few seconds.

Day 37: The chittering abides, has increased in scope and magnitude, causes us intense nausea and uncontrollable vomiting as blood leaks from our ears.

Day 38: The insectile assault continues, the air thick with vibration and difficult to breathe; is this the mocking laughter of the light?

Day 39: Hard to concentrate through the many-legged hallucinations, the dark spots skittering at the corners of my vision, the dry heaving of pink-tinged phlegm and bile.

Day 40: Finally blessed silence has regained control and we have regained some semblance of bodily function, though we are dehydrated and starving.

Day 41: We slipped in and out of sleep all day, but during our brief bursts of awareness we saw willowy silhouettes dashing through the light on the opposite side of the door; none of us had the desire to investigate further.

Day 42: After counting the cans of food left to us and determining our current rate of consumption, we've concluded that, with tighter rationing, we can survive for approximately 120 more days if we so choose.

Day 43: A fact none of us realized until the woman who rarely speaks mentioned it: we haven't heard the patter of rain against the house's siding since we retreated to this enclave.

Day 44: On a whim, we tied a clothes hanger we found in the laundry room to a piece of string and slid it under the basement door; by the time we reeled it back a few minutes later, it had acquired a pearlescent greenish-black hue and serrated edges, transforming into an object that calls to mind alien weaponry and predatory biology.

Day 45: Neither the single pop of a gunshot nor the desperate howl of a siren has reached us in our prison, which leads us to assume that rescue is, at best, a comforting fairy tale.

Day 46: The emerald light has surely burned away everyone we loved or wished we could have loved, everyone we hated or should have hated; perhaps it burned away our capacity to ever love or hate again as well.

Day 47: The woman who volunteered to go outside stares at her misshapen foot for hours at a time then examines her opposite foot and her hands, which forces me to wonder whether she takes comfort in the normalcy of these other appendages or wishes that they, too, would be stretched into the strange new future of the world.

Day 48: The man with the burned hand proposed a theory: that beings from another realm of existence have come to terraform our galaxy and develop it in the same way construction crews develop untamed fields and virgin forests; he suggests that we are the ants populating those natural spaces and the light, with its attendant noises, is part of indifferent machinery too complex for our understanding.

Day 49: I've considered the man's theory from various angles, but cannot ascribe to it for one reason: "development" as a project is a human construct and I see no reason to believe that what lies beyond the basement door has any relationship to humanity or its inconsequential motivations.

Day 50: We cry frequently, over nothing in particular and everything in general, and we laugh at inappropriate moments, like when someone bumped the ON button of the dryer and the dead man within spun head over heels for a full three minutes.

Day 51: There have been too many consecutive days without notable sounds or changes in the light's behavior; this serenity disturbs us more than the tortures we've already endured.

Day 52: We worry about the ways we will die, as all of us agree that we would prefer to meet our ends from familiar reapers like knives, guns, ropes, and drugs; none of us has the courage to mention old age or natural causes, even as vague possibilities.

Day 53: The woman who volunteered to go outside suggested we remove the basement door from its hinges and push forward, into the light, using the door as a shield—a bold plan, a desperate plan, but an untenable plan, given that the light seems to shine from every direction.

Day 54: Today, the faucet in the laundry room shuddered, moaned, and spat a gelatinous, forest green liquid that smells of freshly mowed grass and ammonia.

Day 55: Because the pipes continue to produce only the dark green ooze, we have been forced to open our stores of bottled water, which we saved for an eventuality such as this.

Day 56: Something heavy landed on the roof and moved about in rapid, seven-step jitters for part of the day; we believe it is gone now, but, for all we know, it could still be resting atop the house.

Day 57: Another observation from the woman who rarely speaks: despite the fact that we live in a basement, we have seen no mice or spiders or ants or roaches or any other common denizen of dark corners—an implausible coincidence at best.

Day 58: The light has found a way to climb the length of the ceiling; it hangs above us, threatening to fall like a final curtain and finish its work.

Day 59: We fear to stand, nervous that the light may somehow reach down and pluck us from our shaded preserve, so, instead, we have begun to crawl along the floor on hands and knees, like infants learning to navigate the intricacies of bodily motion.

Day 60: Due to our need to conserve water we have been unable to wash ourselves for almost a week, thus the stench of stagnant flesh and overheated crevices has become the better part of our atmosphere.

Day 61: The man with the burned hand pulled the billiards table across the basement and enlisted our help in flipping it on its end and propping in front of the door; he imagined that it could block the cracks along the doorframe where light sneaked in and, so far, it has.

Day 62: We woke to a tremendous crash and found the man with the burned hand crushed beneath the pool table, blood foaming from his mouth; he couldn't tell us what had happened, but he did wheeze an too-familiar phrase to us before expiring—"Extinction in green."

Day 63: We held an impromptu funeral for the man with the burned hand and shut his corpse away inside the washing machine; we didn't discuss where we will store the next one of our dead.

Day 64: We're bothered by how the man with the burned hand came to be positioned under the table and we're suspicious of the reason it tipped over; we agree that the light is responsible for both, though we cannot prove its crimes.

Day 65: Without the extra barrier of the pool table, the light has again swept across the ceiling and shines brightest above the spot where the man with the burned hand met his end, as if in mockery.

Day 66: A question I cannot help but increasingly entertain: is the light alive and self-aware?

Day 67: Our experience no longer contains the capacity for reasonable explanations; whatever happened to the world brought with it an alternative system of logic and a strange, new set of physical laws.

Day 68: The woman who volunteered to scout beyond the door spent the entire day in the laundry room, turning the faucet on and off, staring at the dark green liquid that flows from the pipes.

Day 69: For several hours, I watched the stream of liquid with the woman who volunteered to scout beyond the door; I have to concede that I, too, am mesmerized by the way the liquid catches the emerald light and transforms its bruising glare into a river of impossible stars.

Day 70: It's becoming ever more difficult to remember the excited trill of birdsongs in the morning, the venerable musk of old books pulled from a dusty shelf, and the silken heat of our lovers' lips against our throats.

Day 71: For no reason we can discern, the light above us now ripples like the surface of a lake blown anxious by gusting winds.

Day 72: We continue to lie in the laundry room and gaze at the stream of liquid; occasionally, one of us will ask a rhetorical question like "What happens when our water runs out?" and expect the viridian ooze to provide an answer, but it never does.

Day 73: Today, the woman who volunteered to scout beyond the door ran her hands through the flow of dark green liquid—an action that caused her fingers to lengthen, narrow, and fuse together in a raptorial claw similar to those of mantises.

Day 74: The woman with mantis hands insists that they cause her no pain; in fact, she says that her hands feel stronger, more dexterous, and more a part of herself than ever before.

Day 75: We watched the woman with mantis hands snap a steel pipe in half with a flick of her wrist and silently considered how easily those alien hands could break a neck, a skull, or a spine.

Day 76: Is the liquid a condensed form of the light or a tool of the light or is it a medium that allows the light to be what it is?

Day 77: The woman with mantis hands decided to run her feet under the green liquid; her already elongated foot changed rapidly, gaining needle-like bristles, sharp talons, and two additional toes.

Day 78: In the woman who volunteered becoming the woman with mantis hands, we have crossed over a line that should demarcate reality from fiction but, clearly, no longer does.

Day 79: Everywhere the woman with mantis hands crawls, the light brightens above her.

Day 80: The woman with mantis hands scaled one of the basement's concrete walls and, laughing all the while, hung upon it for half the day.

Day 81: The woman who rarely speaks drew me aside and asked how long we could safely reside in the same space as the woman with mantis hands; I answered that the time for safety was already long past.

Day 82: Part of me wants to see the woman with mantis hands finish whatever metamorphosis she's begun; another part of me trembles to conceive of that metamorphosis's final result.

Day 83: Something like an air raid siren, but much deeper and more hollow, echoed through the basement three times today.

Day 84: The woman with mantis hands says she's going to drink the green liquid; she says she'd rather keep changing and live than stay boxed in this basement and wither away.

Day 85: To protect ourselves, we removed the knobs from the faucet in the laundry room while the woman with mantis hands slept--a cowardly act, perhaps, but at the end of the world bravado is sibling to death.

Day 86: When the woman with mantis hands discovered the lack of knobs, she eyed us with hatred, slashed through a case of our water with one of her taloned feet, and told us that we didn't understand "what sacrifice the future demands."

Day 87: The woman with mantis hands says she is leaving tomorrow, says she has new thoughts that cannot be expressed in words, says she cannot guarantee our immunity from her rage.

Day 88: The woman with mantis hands opened the basement door, flooding emerald light over all but a sliver of laundry room, and walked out, slamming the door behind her; we expected her to shout "Extinction in green" as she left, but, instead, she said nothing, her silence a reminder of how limited our powers of communication truly are.

Day 89: Less than three months since the light arrived, and only the woman who rarely speaks and I remain.

Day 90: I hope dogs continue to survive out there, somewhere; dogs were always the best of us.

Day 91: The woman who rarely speaks drew a circle on the wall and told me that it encompassed the remainder of the known universe.

Day 92: We argued religion today, with the woman who rarely speaks exhorting me to "trust in the Lord's plan" after I suggested that there might be no God watching over us; debate ground to a halt when I pointed to the light flooding over the ceiling and shouted, "Maybe that's God"--a possibility too close to our most worrisome suspicions for either of us to continue debating.

Day 93: Another day, another bizarre blast of noise—this time an earthshaking buzz like a rocket powered by a hundred billion bees lifting off its launching pad.

Day 94: The light creeped down the walls a few inches; even on our hands and knees, we no longer feel out of reach.

Day 95: The woman who rarely speaks told me a story about her five year old son and his first day of kindergarten—how nervous he was, how nervous she was, how letting go felt both entirely wrong but absolutely right, how his face lit up when he stepped off the bus and saw her at the end of the day, and how his face lit up when he talked about his teacher and all the new friends he'd made at school; she says she hopes he's found new friends again, wherever he is.

Day 96: I miss my husband, my dogs, my parents, and my friends; I miss the excited rush of wind against my face just before a thunderstorm and the bite of a freshly brewed cup of coffee in the morning; I miss not feeling scared every moment of my life.

Day 97: The light has pulled itself a few inches lower, so that if we did walk upright, it would graze the tops of our heads.

Day 98: If memory serves, today should be the first day of winter, yet the temperature in the basement hasn't dropped even a few degrees from when we first arrived.

Day 99: The woman who rarely speaks gathered the remaining food and water into a single pile and fell asleep atop it.

Day 100: Should we mark this centenary with song and dance or a memorial service?

Day 101: I tossed one of the billiards balls up, into the light above us, to gauge how quickly the light worked its transformation; it fell back into my hand as a deep green, metallic disk.

Day 102: The woman who rarely speaks is counting and recounting every last article of sustenance we possess; she hugs each can and bottle to her chest as she numbers it and gently stacks it among others of its kind.

Day 103: I've been thinking a great deal about the woman with mantis hands and the wonders and horrors she might be seeing now, if she is still alive; I find myself almost yearning to see them, too, if for no other reason than to break the monotony of cinder block cavern that surrounds me.

Day 104: The light dropped further today and now nearly touches our backs when we skitter about on all fours.

Day 105: We have taken to lying flat and unmoving, so as to not draw the light's attention.

Day 106: We squirm along the floor like awkward grub worms when we need water, food, and bathroom breaks; otherwise, we lie in our makeshift beds and let our minds drift to the edge of sanity.

Day 107: This is not a life we're leading; this is a form of death no one knew existed.

Day 108: Maybe I'm letting abstract thought run away with me, but I'm beginning wonder if the light is a mode of evolution rather than extinction—and I'm also beginning to wonder if, in this instance, there's any difference between the two.

Day 109: Transformation is the keystone of the universe and yet it's an unsettling concept for creatures such as ourselves, who cling tight to the notion of an unwavering essence at our cores.

Day 110: Apropos of our current situation, I recall one of my college philosophy professors remarking: "A thing has to stop being in order to become."

Day 111: I'm increasingly tempted to stand up and let the light burn my face into a new tomorrow.

Day 112: The woman who rarely speaks coos to individual cans of beans and jars of peanut butter as though they were pets or children.

Day 113: Chittering again today, but different this time—less raucous and more patterned, like speech from a mouth that cannot form human sound.

Day 114: The light gathered itself in a great wave and rolled over the pile of food and water the woman who rarely speaks assembled; she moved in time to be unaffected, but all our rations have mutated.

Day 115: Already, after only a day without sustenance, my head throbs from dehydration and my fingers shake with hunger. Our water has turned viscous and dark green, like the liquid from the pipes, and the canned goods have reshaped themselves into strange configurations that resemble squat bacteriophages. Within the cans, we've found translucent pastes that smell of copper, gelatinous ochre mounds that hiss when exposed to air, tiny spheres dark as midnight, and a fuzzy substance of many hues that swirls clockwise even when it's untouched. If this is water and food, it is not for us. At least, not yet.

The woman who rarely speaks is curled on the floor, chanting "We'll be fine." I tried to talk to her, to plan an escape, but she didn't respond. I believe she intends to stay in the basement and wait for miracles. I believe she will die.

As for the light, after transforming our supplies it retracted to its pool on the ceiling. There it remains, rippling contentedly.

I realize this entry is overlong, but surely there cannot be many more to come.

Day 116: I've made a decision, and the decision is mine alone. I will walk out of the basement, into the emerald light. The woman who rarely speaks can't be moved, though I've tried. Balled up in a fetal position, she's entered an unresponsive reverie. She whispers to herself a phrase that sounds too much like "Extinction in green" and whenever I touch her, she thrashes violently, as if in full seizure. I have no medical background, no psychiatric training, so I let her be.

I assume that when I enter the light something will happen to me. Maybe my flesh will grow sleek and hard and powerful. Maybe I will acquire new senses that reveal so much more of the world. Or maybe I will simply crumble under the light's intensity and there will be no more "me" to worry about my fate.

Whatever the case, this is the only option. I must go.

Day 117: Last entry. Vision spins. Stomach feels torn in two. It's now or never.

I hope I find my husband.

I hope I can breathe fresh air again.

I'm excited.

I'm terrified.

I'm tired of being.

I'm ready to become.

CHOSEN
AARON J. FRENCH

Rosa emerges alone, Tom still asleep in the tent. She's gorgeous in the dawning light, black hair spilling down her shoulders. "How's the watch?" she asks. "Any trouble?" She brushes her teeth using water from a canteen.

"I saw a weird green light streaming across the sky. Do you know what it was?"

"A UFO?"

I chuckle. "It landed by the mountain. The undead have gathered along the peaks."

She stares at me, a smear of toothpaste on her chin. "You sure?"

I offer binoculars.

"There's so many," she gasps, peering through the lenses. "Should we check?"

"Let's get the others."

"I'll wake Tom." She disappears into the tent.

Rachel's standing in the trees looking at me. Seventeen, blonde, thin, was a cheerleader at her high school, has said only a handful of words since we found her outside Wichita cowering in a garbage can. Her parents tried to kill her.

"Sleep all right?" I ask.

She marches off to brush her teeth and comb her hair.

Big Mike appears. Burly, bearded, muscular and wearing a flannel coat and a cowboy hat. He adores Rachel. "Another fine morning in hell," he says. "Don't tell me you sat there all night?"

"Crapped my pants," I said. "I'm too ashamed to move."

He howls with laughter. "Figures."

When we're all together, I recount my observation of the green light. There's some debate. We pack our things and head out, Big Mike in the lead. His large pack encompasses his back and shoulders. The big silver .44 Magnum he carries at his waist seems even larger. He's got an ammo belt slung around his hips.

Conversation is scarce. We must be aware at all times. The dead attack suddenly, without warning. When they do, you better be ready. Will they attack on our way to the mountain? Likely. I scan the endless rows of pine and spruce. Something tells me they went to the mountain after the crash. Like an exodus.

As we approach, I see a shuffling figure coming up the road. By its gait, I would have to say *zombie*.

"Look sharp," Big Mike says. Rachel squeezes in close at his rear, as Tom and Rosa draw their weapons. I draw mine.

"Where there's one, there's many," I say.

Tom scoffs mockingly. "Naah, *really?* I thought these things came in nice pairs and family units—"

"Keep your eyes peeled," I snap, more harshly than I'd intended. But it gets the job done. We come up the road; just over the next rise, the mountain starts to incline. We'll find the remains of whatever caused that weird green light somewhere in the trees. But first, the zombies.

"Can you handle that one, Mike?" I shout.

He nods, cocking his gigantic .44 Magnum. All I can think about is Clint Eastwood in *Dirty Harry*. "My pleasure," he says, leveling the barrel at the advancing figure.

Having experienced the report of Mike's revolver several times, Rachel takes a step back and covers her ears. Mike pulls the trigger, unleashing thunder. The report echoes off the mountain and comes back, reverberating. My ears ring. When I can hear, I see what's left of the zombie, writhing in a pool of blood on the road, surrounded by spattered brain and bone. It's almost artistic in its arrangement.

Big Mike cocks the hammer. "Here they come."

"I don't see anything," Rosa says.

Then they're swarming all around us. The forest comes alive with movement. The dead fast-approach out of the trunks and branches, literally hundreds of them.

Rachel drops to her knees, curling into a ball with her ears still covered, while the rest of us begin to fire. She's only a child, after all. We don't hold her behavior against her. I try to focus on the ones sneaking up behind. Ten have appeared on the road back there, horribly twisted beings of undeterminable sex and age, crooked arms and legs, tattered clothes, and eyes like fire. They hiss at me, with cavernous maws.

I open up with my Heckler and Koch USP 9mm. I have learned through experience that it is better to take a breath and aim. The undead are slow. You've got plenty of time if you can just relax your mind and focus. In the beginning, I would let loose clip after clip in a mad frenzy, only rarely hitting anything. Now I take my time.

The first one's head parts like a melon. It takes a final step, drops. I fire again and hit the second one between the eyes. The bullet whips it around like a ballerina. I dispatch the other three in similar fashion.

I whirl around and see Rosa and Tom emptying their clips into the forest on our left. They fight like I used to fight: *hurriedly*. They've dropped a couple walking dead, but they've been more successful kneecapping closer ones. These drag their own ruined bodies through the dirt.

Tom and Rosa don't see two more approaching from the right. Big Mike is busy holding the front. His slow, methodical firing sounds like the end of the world. If I hadn't turned, Rosa and Tom would be dead.

I fix the first one in my sights. Female. Fresher, not like the others: long, matted blond hair, breasts, remnants of a ruffled dress. Her arms reach for Tom like Frankenstein's monster. She'll be on him in a second.

I take off the top of her scalp. Blood sprays down Tom's side, a gleam of skull reflects the sunlight, then the horrible, twisted woman-thing crumples.

Tom jumps back, his eyes wide. He notices the one at his feet and wheels, and I know he is thinking *Fuck, that was close!* He gets rid of the other advancing zombie, firing three quick rounds into its head. The creature's face unfurls like a blooming rose. Drops. He looks at me and mouths *thank you*.

I tip my head.

The firefight lasts another ten minutes. Toward the end we all wind up alongside Mike in the front. Most of the zombies are coming over the rise. By the time we finish, a mound of corpses lies in the road. The silence following is eerie.

Mike helps Rachel to her feet. We proceed with caution. She covers her eyes with her hands, and I can't say I blame her. The sight of so many bodies is repulsive. Not to mention the smell.

We mount over the rise and reach the other side. Now the wooded mountain rears up before us, peaks and crags jutting through trees. More zombies perched up there, silently keeping watch, blending with the landscape.

A moment later we come across the alien spacecraft. It isn't smoking or flaming, which seems odd because it crash-landed. It resembles every archetypal UFO I've ever seen: roundish, oblong shape, composed of silver alloy, with a symmetrical square protrusion toward the center (cockpit, I presume). It's covered with strange alien characters, like Mayan hieroglyphs. Cracked like an egg on impact. Fissures and splits reveal bright red wires, curious gadgetry, intricate circuit boards.

Big Mike sighs. "Great. Now aliens."

"There were always aliens," Rosa says. "I saw a UFO once. I was sitting on my back porch smoking a cigarette when it appeared overhead. Looked just like this."

"*Mmm*, cigarettes," Tom says.

My eyes scan the forest. I glimpse red orbs watching from the trees. We're surrounded by zombies.

"Why aren't they attacking?" I say.

They look around and suddenly notice the undead ambush. Handguns are pointed into the forest. We wait for them to advance, but they never do.

"I don't get it," Tom says. "They've got us surrounded, why don't they come?"

No one has an answer. Rachel does. In one of those rare instances when she speaks, the teenage girl says, "They don't come because they're scared."

We look at her.

Tom looks at her. "What do you mean?"

But Rachel has already withdrawn to her private world.

"She's right," I say. "They're *watching* us, waiting to see what we will do. I think they're guarding the ship."

"Come over here," Mike says. "Look at this."

We join him by the trees, where he's staring at something on the ground. When I get there, I see it's a set of crude tracks in the mulch. They lead away from crushed fern bushes.

"Is that alien?" Tom asks.

"More'n likely," Mike replies. "I used to do a lot of hunting back before It happened, and I never seen tracks like this from no animal."

"What do we do?" Rosa asks.

They're all looking at me. "We follow them," I say.

And we do. They lead into the heart of the forest, back around the side of the mountain. All along the way the zombies observe our progress, but don't attack. The tracks lead into the thickest patch of trees yet, and suddenly the sunlight is halved. Only tiny traces of it filter down through the branches.

At length we enter a clearing and everything changes. Noonday sun beams onto an expanse of green grass, where flowers and weeds and vinery grow in abundance. We all stop at the border of trees, breathless.

The alien is here.

The undead are also here. Dozens of them arranged in rows before a jutting rock outcrop, on which the alien sits. Cross-legged, like the Buddha. The zombies are either kneeling or lying prostrate, gazing at the gray alien as it orates in some subtle, peculiar language.

"My God, *do you see it?*" Rosa whispers.

I shush her. But it's too late. The alien notices us. It ceases speaking and lifts its triangular head in our direction. I'm amazed by its size. Although cadaverously thin, it has to be almost eight feet tall. Its eyes, lidless and inky, are the size of tea saucers.

Then it vanishes. The zombies grow tense, begin to murmur. An atmosphere of electricity crackles.

Then it's back, standing three feet away. From this close it's absolutely frightening, tall and gaunt and not of this world, an utter *fuck you* to everything we as humans hold dear and consider as normal.

We draw our guns, but it raises its arms in surrender. It absurdly resembles some politician, posing like that. Its long face, free of emotion, turns from one of us to the next and its tiny slit of a mouth says, in static-y English, "You not dead like others."

I lower my 9mm. "No, but you're about to be if you don't start giving answers."

Big Mike cocks his revolver loudly. "I don't see any reason to allow this thing's words to enter our heads." He fires and we all jump, but the alien quickly vanishes, then re-materializes a little further off. He skips almost ghostlike back onto the rock and turns to the kowtowing zombies.

A string of words delivered in that same curious dialect, and the dead start rising to their feet. We open fire, laying out the first dozen in seconds. From the corner of my eye, I see Rachel fleeing into the trees. I hope she can stay out of their midst. When we've dealt with the ones in the clearing, we turn on those who, over the last several minutes, have been creeping out of the forest. We move as a single unit, our backs to each other so that we face all four cardinal points. We fire and reload until the dead stay down.

We reach the rock outcrop, but the alien is gone. The forest seems unnaturally quiet after the gunfire. The only sound is the wind through the leaves.

"Where is Rachel?" Mike says, panicked.

I scan the trees but don't see her. "I'm sure she's fine."

"What if she gets lost?"

"There!" Tom points straight across from us. I expect to see Rachel, but instead it's the tall gray alien stalking across the grass. Covered from head to toe in foul, brackish liquid—zombie gore—and it doesn't look pleased.

"You kill mind-soul slaves!" it screeches.

We open fire, but it dodges our bullets, flickering in and out of reality. Finally, we stop. It doesn't seem as if our guns *can* kill it. A scary realization.

"You kill mindless. Now I need more mindless, at least two—you and you!"

At that moment the alien raises its arms, and Rosa and Tom lift off the ground. They start to scream and claw at their necks, as if they're being choked. Their feet dangle almost a yard above the grass.

"You son of a bitch!" Big Mike shouts. He rushes the alien, meaning to tackle it, but some invisible force field prevents him. When he connects with it, blue light shimmers around the alien's circumference. He flies backward, crashes into the rock outcrop, wincing in pain.

I fire again, but the bullet only triggers the shimmering blue light effect. The alien gives me a look that seems to say, *Silly human. What is your logic?*

I watch in horror as Tom and Rosa are dashed together like two rag dolls. Again and again, their bones cracking, their heads thumping on one another. A horrible sight. Tears well in my eyes. Rosa and Tom are my friends, and we have traveled many miles together. Now I'm seeing them bashed to smithereens.

I can't stand it. I shut my eyes. I cover my ears to block out the screams. When it's over, I chance a peek. The bodies of Tom and Rose lay on the grass, twisted around each other like a pair of pretzels. I can hardly look without tearing up. I notice the alien observing me with an inquisitive expression.

"I'm going to kill you," is all I can say. It doesn't respond. Big Mike manages to get back on his feet and stands beside me. I hear him crying.

"Now what?" I ask.

He shrugs. We both stand there, staring at the alien.

The bodies of Rosa and Tom begin to twitch. Mike shakes his head, sobbing, "Oh God, no."

Without thinking, I cock back the chamber of my 9mm and aim it at Rosa's head. "Not if I have anything to say about it."

The alien, alarmed, glares at me and raises its hands. "Not destroy new-deads. Is there a function of reality you cherish? I make that dead for you."

"What are you blabbering about?" I'm about to pull the trigger when it swipes its hands in a sweeping arc and dislodges my 9mm. The weapon lands some distance away.

"This reality"—the alien shakes its head—"not new reality. Is old one. *False* one. For the new one to come, we must exterminate you."

Big Mike raises his .44 Magnum. "What do you mean *exterminate?*"

With a flick of its wrist, the alien sucks the revolver out of Mike's hand into its own.

"Hey!" Mike shouts.

The alien studies the weapon with its cold gaze. "This how you kill mindless. It was once a metal, now a firing. Does exist in nature? No? Where exist? Mind?"

Mike darkens. "What the hell are you talking about? It's mine, give it!"

"Relax," I say. "Play cool."

"Hell with that. It's screwing with our heads, trying to mindwash us. Don't listen to it."

But I know better. And the fact that I know better chills my soul. The alien has asked us a metaphysical question. I feel obliged to answer.

"The revolver does not exist in nature," I say. The alien turns to me. "Metal doesn't exist in nature, either. Only the *potential* for metal."

It raises the gun, aiming it skyward. "The potential?"

"Right."

It studies the gun. "Where does image come from?"

I tap the left side of my head. "From mind."

If possible, the alien appears to grin. An expression of understanding spreads across its face. "Part of old reality," it says. "Must die like mind, like rest."

I feel as if we might be getting somewhere, but suddenly Mike pulls a snub-nosed .38 from his boot that I didn't know he was carrying.

"Mike, don't—"

"This is crazy," he says, and aims the .38 at the alien's head. He fires. The bullet stops in midair, hovers, drops to the ground. He fires a second time; same thing.

He looks at me. As he does, the alien pulls the trigger on the .44 Magnum. The sound of its report is deafening. The barrel flash blinds me, but not before I witness half of Mike's big, bearded face torn away. I'm pelted by blood and gore. Mike drops to the grass.

The world hums around me. I feel sick, light as a feather, and then I'm falling. Everything is a blur. I land hard on my backside then lie still, staring up at the sky. It breaks apart into nothing. I exist in total darkness.

Have I passed out?

With time, I'm able to sit up. What I see does not console me. The world is gone, replaced by endless black. I can't see my body. All I see is the gray alien.

"Am I dreaming?"

It contemplates me, tilting its head. "Yes. Old reality, always dreaming. That is why mine have interfered your reality. Why we make your species mind-soul slaves."

"You did this?" I can't say I'm totally shocked to learn that aliens caused the outbreak of undead and brought an end to human civilization. Still, hearing it packs a punch.

"Not me," the alien says. "My people. We come now, change your reality into new one. More oneness, less doubleness. No more... *potential*. Only infinite."

"We will resist," I say.

"Yes, we know. That is why we make mindless. You slaves, you all mindless soul slaves. We create reality for *all*."

It opens a circle in the darkness using its gray hands. At once I'm reminded of the black hole Mickey Mouse vanishes through at the end of Disney cartoons.

Beyond the hole I see the forest and the clearing. I see Tom, Rosa, and Mike, all undead, all zombies, standing in the grass, swaying. They're covered in gobs of dripping blood. Their eyes are bright green.

"I go with them and other mindless," the alien says. "We go past mountain on to nation's capital. You go other way. Into northern trees. You keep mind."

"You're going to let me live?"

I'm genuinely surprised.

The massive head nods.

"Why?"

"Because you connected to girl. You watch girl, keep safe. Girl important in future."

I'm stumped by this, then realize the alien means Rachel. "What do you need her for?"

The alien turns its black eyes from me and steps into the opening. I see the zombies that were once my friends gather around it. Together they stalk off into the trees. Soon they are gone.

I am propelled forward by an invisible force, drift in and out of consciousness. I see many strange things I cannot comprehend. Curious visions of reality that even my many years studying philosophy have not prepared me for. When I come to I am sitting back in the clearing, in the grass, alone.

No. Not alone.

Someone is standing in the trees. Looking at me. She looks scared but seems unharmed. I wave to her and she waves back. She joins me.

"They're gone," she says, her voice shaky.

"Yes, the alien and the zombies are gone. We're safe."

She shakes her head. "No. Big Mike, Tom, and Rosa. Our friends are gone."

All I can do is nod, once. She looks off sadly into the forest. Her blond hair falls like golden straw around her face.

"What do we do now?" she asks.

I'm pleased she is speaking so much. Quite a change from her usual reticence. "We keep heading north into Canada. Perhaps we'll find some folks to join us along the way."

I pause, wondering if it's wise to say what I'm about to say. Then I decide I don't give a damn.

"The alien let me live because of you."

This gets her attention.

"It said you had an important role to play in the future, and that it wanted me to look after you. Any idea why it said that?"

She shrugs her shoulders. "It beats me."

But I notice something strange about her eyes, some glimmer of understanding. Like she is hiding something. With a groan, I get to my feet. We spend the next twenty minutes gathering our things and pilfering through the packs of our former friends. The sun is descending fast.

"Ready?" I say, after we're loaded up.

She doesn't reply.

"I'll take that as a yes."

I start into the forest, heading in the direction which my compass claims to be north. Every so often I look over my shoulder to make sure Rachel is following.

She is.

Always.

BONE SEQUENCE

Duane Pesice

It didn't come all at once, but once it came, it kept on coming. The makeshift tarpaulin umbrellas and other jerry-rigged contraptions went almost immediately, and we were s.o.l.

There was nothing to do but go inside, hold our noses, and hope that we'd be able to dig our way out, after.

And it only took a week to fuck things up that much, and I wasn't even trying. You should see me on my best days.

It all started when the Russian came back from Giant Mart with what looked like an oval cake of Irish Spring...

"Da," he agreed. "Is rock. Looks like szoap though." His accent was thicker when he was drunk. "I keep it. May be lucky, some day."

The dog growled.
"Ivan, what?" The Russian said. "You no like?"

Ivan whined a little and watered the wall. The Russian held the door open for him. "Inside with you," he said. "Go lie down."

"So." He put the stone on the patio table. "I leave here. I make tea." He went inside, the door clicking behind him.

I put out a hand, stroked the stone. It was weathered, smooth. The resemblance to a cake of soap was only circumstantial. It had olive and black streaks in it as well as white. The color was a little more blue than the soap.

It warmed to the touch. A tiny glowing fractal appeared on the surface.

That gave me a start, and I withdrew my hand and skulked back to my place. I had been sitting outside, taking in some sun, but it was setting and I was getting hungry.

Brutus sauntered up, returning from wherever he'd been, the breeze ruffling his fuzz. "Moww," he remarked, stopping to wash a paw. "Rowmf."

"Mew," I agreed, opening the door to let Himself in. He curled his tail around my calf companionably and headed for the kitchen.

"Moww," he said from atop the table. He pushed an empty tumbler to the floor. Apparently the hunting wasn't very good, where he'd been, or he'd likely have

He's spoiled, of course. I like it that way.

I fed him half a can of gushy wet food and half a cup of dry, and gave him fresh water.

There was half a package of bologna and some bread in the fridge, and that and a package of ramen became my repast. I was just sitting down to enjoy my dinner when I noticed a single bass note, low and long, repeating every few seconds.

It was almost too faint to hear, but I could feel it in my chest. Brutus didn't like it and hid under the bed.

I sucked down the broth and spooned noodles. The note continued. I grabbed my sandwich and went to investigate.

It wasn't noticeably louder with the door open, so I locked the security door so that I could get some air and stood there munching and scanning the vicinity to try to determine the source of the noise.

Presently it stopped. Brutus and I watched tv for a while until that palled, and I thought perhaps I would undertake a walk for the benefit of my foot and general disposition.

The *shambler* was sitting in her usual spot on the walkway in front of her apartment door. She saw too, or at last, she was watching.

The *greengirl* that lives in the unit below her wasn't home. I took pains to hide my face, so that the *shambler* wouldn't notice me.

The barrio copter was making a pass overhead. It's usually not a good idea to be out and about when it's near, so I bided my time, sitting on the wrought iron rail of the futon, safe behind the black steel security door, in the shadow of the upper-floor walkway.

Upstairs and two down wasn't in, and the *shambler* had nobody to tease. She tired of that and went inside to watch tv. I could hear her tune it to her favorite channel, the one nobody else gets, and turn it up.

Soon she was shrieking with laughter. I shuddered, safe in my little place, and smoothed the fur on Brutus' neck a little.

The thrumming low note, almost too low to hear, sounded from the direction of the street. It dopplered and then returned, louder, somehow urgent, and then spiraled rapidly up the scale to a whine and was silent.

The Russian came into the courtyard, carrying a Giant Mart bag, the huge black dog trotting next to him with massive jaw wide open and its pink-and-grey tongue lolling.

He walked over to his patio table and deposited his parcel, unlocking the door so that the beast could enter. He picked the stone up from the ground and put that on the table, too.

"Da," he breathed, and unpacked the plastic bag, withdrawing a tub of sour cream, a big jar of dill pickles, a can of potato chips, and a package of hot dogs.

Also a quart of rotgut vodka, a Big Pop, and a plastic spoon.

Some of the pickle juice was spooned into the sour cream and stirred around. The Russian extracted some tiny salt-and-pepper envelopes and shook some of the contents in, re-stirred, tasted.

"Da," he said with evident satisfaction, smacking his lips. "S'good."

He proceeded to the methodical demolition of his meal, alternating eating hotdogs in two bites with crunching the pickles down, dipping the occasional chip in the sour cream, scooping up big waves of white goo and stuffing them into his maw.

Every second pickle or so he took a long pull from the vodka bottle and a swallow of the Big Pop.

It didn't take long, and he finished by putting the scraps and the garbage into the Big Mart bag, grabbing his glass, and repairing inside, shutting the door.

The 'soap' was still on the outer table.

That low note kept coming and going, so deep in the bass and so faint, but so pronounced.

The meal had made me somnolent, and I proposed to myself that I would walk later, and nap right then. I was agreeable to this, and took on the task with gusto.

The futon rattled too, but I reposed nonetheless, and presently drifted off into a troubled slumber, filled with visions of cyclopean architecture and huge dressed stone blocks and gigantic carven ice floes.

Some of the ice floes had passengers, horrible ones that looked like carrots with their clothes on, and even worse ones that were all eyes and mouths and possessed no real shape, and pursued the carrot-people unto their doom...

I woke gasping, sweating. Brutus was peering out of the security door, watching the flow of what looked to be antifreeze coming from the Russian's patio.

The bass note was much louder and had scaled up a bit. There was even the suggestion of drumming behind it.

The dog was whining and pacing, chained to the front gate, just out of reach of the slime.

It was consumed as I watched. The slime washed over the poor hound's body and the sizzle and stink made me retreat briefly. It happened quickly, and the dog made no noise.

When I could look again, all that remained of the grotesque tableau was a single leg bone lying on the concrete and the leash and collar still fastened to the wall.

A little of the slime adhered to the front step of the Russian's apartment.

The 'soap bar' was nowhere to be seen.

Mercifully, it was quiet.

The *greengirl* had come home while I was sleeping, and her wash fluttered in the breeze, suspended from a length of twine that she had attached to the palms that stood at the head of her hedges. She was watering her garden and talking to the plants. I could hear her but I couldn't make out the words.

The *shambler* was still watching tv.

Brutus wanted to go for the walk. He was a-scratching at the iron door and voicing his complaint, meow-meow.

"Come on, Boy," I said to the kitten. "Let's go up to the arroyo and watch the stars come out." I grabbed my pills and a bottle of water and stuffed them into my pack, along with my phone, and locked up real good behind me.

We walked slow, or, rather I did, with Brutus describing ever-greater circles around me as we neared his favorite hunting grounds. The locals were still out, queuing up at Giant Mart, buying sodas and chips and beer to help them make it through the night, and the barrio copter had risen and was flapping like a pterodactyl as it described lazy figure-eights up in the sky.

I stayed in the shadows. Eventually it deployed the spotlight, while I was sitting on a rock reading true-crime stories on my phone. The narrow beam captured bobcats, coyotes, javelinas, and a lone man in a tattered serape that trailed behind him as he ran, trying to outpace the pursuit.

His movements, deliberate, studied, were mute evidence of his crime.

I watched him disappear as I got up and leaned on my crutch, on the bridge over the dry wash, surrounded by the bats and cacti that serve as my retinue, there in the shadows.

The cat came and curled around my ankles, telling me he was hungry, but we bide, waiting until the threat has passed to return to our rooms.

The folks that person the barrio copter don't really care who or what you are — they just want to administer punishment. It's best not to attract their attention.

After a while, Brutus and I head back south, traverse the few short blocks back to our abode.

The bass notes have resumed in our absence. They're louder and lower, more menacing. There is definitely a beat, on the 2 and the 4.

There was another bone on the patio, a human femur this time. I was tempted to grab it and throw it in the air to see what would happen, but it's best not to tempt fate.

The lights were on upstairs and I saw Clairvius gazing out of the front window, watching as the *shambler* sat on her chair, on the right-hand side of the front door. Her roommate sat on the lefthand side and looked to be asleep – though with her it's hard to tell.

The *shambler* put her feet up on the rail and let her robe fall away. I couldn't see from my perspective, but Clairvius got an eyeful and turned white for a minute. His face disappeared from the window, and I could hear retching noises through the half-open door.

The *shambler* laughed, half-cackle, half-grunt.

I unlocked the door and we went inside. Clairvius' dog was barking overhead. I could hear him stomping around. "Oh my GOD," he was saying, over and over.

I could make out the words between the barks.

Brutus mewled for a can, curling around my ankles. I fed him and located more sandwich makings, fed myself too.

We settled in for the night.

That slow bass pulse was going when I got up to take a leak. I opened the inside door enough that I could see the lake of green slime reaching almost to my place.

The drums were louder, the snare rat-a-tat-tatting between the leaden beats.

One pseudopod spirited away my garbage can. I watched it dissolve as it traveled back toward the source. All kinds of flashing neon colors were coming from inside the Russian's apartment, and the smell of rotten garbage and rotting fish was distinct and pungent.

Distorted electric guitar began to sound over the top of the bass and drums. I closed the inside door and hoped that the tide was trending out.

That music was enough to give me bad dreams again, all ice cities and strangely ordered humongous stones and carrot-people screaming about their teakettles and being slaughtered by the amoeba-eyes.

The amoeba-eyes were all trailing the same neon-green slop as I had seen on the courtyard.

Some of the carrot-people had charms and key-fobs made out of the same kind of stone as the Russian had found, except that these were all carved into star shapes.

And their voices! Gods they were shrill and piping and irritating. "Teakettle-lee!" They cried, or something similar.

I woke up just as the penguins were arriving. Giant ones, with evil little black eyes.

The sun was coming up. I decided to get up with it and threw on some sweats and a t-shirt.

Clairvius, upstairs, was crying, softly. He did that sometimes, at night. His dog was pacing – I could hear its claws as it traveled. That wasn't unusual either. The dog was a huge Rottweiler, friendly as hell but a wound a little tight.

The greengirl was out on her patio, watering her garden and spraying some of the slime back toward the Russian's apartment. There was a hipbone by the patio table. Also the head of a javelina, teeming with flies.

I went out and walked over to retrieve my garbage can. The greengirl smiled at me. I nodded back, politely, and noticed that the door of the Russian's place was open.

"Okay," I told myself. "Be brave,"

I went in.

The stone was sitting in the middle of the living room, many times its original size. It had a few eyes and a dozen or so lamprey mouths and was eating the contents of someone's garbage can and the garbage can itself.

Why it spared mine, I've no idea. But that saved me from having to carry it out to the dumpster, so I was okay with that.

It was sitting in a pool of slime, stinking. I held my nose.

"Well, you'll make a good garbage disposal," I told it. "For a week or so, or until management wants their money. Cuz I assume that leg bone belonged to the Russian."

I was rewarded with a unison blast, loud enough to cause me discomfort. The distorted guitar faded away slowly.

"The septic tank is behind your patio," I said, backing away. "Just in case you feel snacky."

Yeah, just another day in Crazytown. Not as strange as the day the *shambler* arrived, with her peculiar gait and misshapen body and her magic television. Or when the sky turned orange, a couple of years ago. Or when Clairvius and his missus and their giant black dog showed up.

No, it was just an ordinary day, with a monster in the neighbor's apartment, weird and possibly inhuman neighbors, and all the madness I could handle, and then some.

I remember the old landlord telling me "this place, it was built on sacred land. The people that were guarding it were defiled and then slaughtered. Ever since then, it been, well, off. The slime of the years has soaked right into the ground."

It didn't take long to figure out what he was talking about...mind you, he was just explaining why the place was so cheap.

I remember coming to check the place out. Just off the corner of two main drags, it was, two adjoined two-story buildings, dusty clay in color, with a wrought iron fence with pikes on top, altogether uninspiring.

Which was just what I was looking for. Cheap, not too flashy, somewhere I could hole up and recover from my crash in.

I turned into the side drive and a hand reached out from the second window as a car pulled up to snatch the little plastic packet and exchange it for a bill.

The rental agent wasn't there yet, so I parked the car and sat watching as several more vehicles visited the drug drive-through, which apparently had a number of things to offer. I made a mental note of that in case I had the need, and presently the gray Toyota arrived.

"Hi," I ventured. We shook hands. Joe was a little taller and a lot wider than I was, had the look of a gone-to-seed defensive tackle and a cop haircut.

"Hey," he said. "Let's go see the place."

The apartment wasn't impressive, but it'd do. It had some odd little angles, and one of the rooms was a pentagon. Tile floors, easy cleanup. Individual water heater, no washer or dryer, no dishwasher. Little pentagonal patio with a palm tree on the right of the front door.

My unit has a back door, which leads out into a gangway bisected by the fence, with open desert on the other side.

"This used to be my office," Joe said. "I had that door put in so I could get away." He chuckled to himself.

"You're not trying real hard to sell me," I said.

He chuckled again, low in his chest. "Either you want it or you don't. I don't want there to be any surprises. It's cheap, it's clean, and it's out of the way. The owner owns the rest of this block and isn't interested in developing.

"It's low-income housing. You know what that means. It's not a bourgeois neighborhood." He shrugged and put a pinch of tobacco into his cheek.

"So, you want it? 250 deposit, 350 a month. 600 total."

I handed him the cashier's check I'd had made out. That wasn't my first mistake, but it may have been the biggest. Only time will tell...

I left the Russian's apartment open and headed back to mine. Brutus was out and about, so I had the place to myself. Took advantage of that and cooked some bacon, which he craves and will snatch away, added a couple of eggs, brewed up a pot of java.

There was a little metal table and chairs out on my patio, courtesy of a previous occupant. I took my plate and cup outside and ate.

The music had sped up enough that it was almost recognizable. Definitely a full band. The table rattled a little.

A little pseudopod or rivulet had stretched all the way to me. I tossed the remains of my breakfast into it, added the eggshells and coffee grounds from inside.

Those were absorbed immediately.

I went back in and got the litter box, dumped that into the neon-green stream.

Soon enough, that too was gone. The creature was still hungry.
It didn't get near the *greengirl's* plants. That meant that it had some measure of intelligence, or at least an urge to self-preservation. There's something *off* about their luxurious growth – they don't seem entirely *natural*.

Not that the amoeba-eye was natural, either, but the plants are clearly inimical. The eye-beast doesn't project the same kind of malign intelligence.

She watched as I fed the creature. So did the *shambler* and her roommate.

One section of the beast itself had found its way out into the patio area, where several of the lamprey-mouths were manipulating the bones it had left, whittling away at them, wetting them enough to bend into various shapes.

These shapes were then placed on the ground, the patio table having doubtless been consumed at some point. They were all identical, vaguely-Christmas-tree shaped.

Art? Or an attempt to communicate? I never did find out.

The *shambler* threw her garbage down from the walkway. The rivulet absorbed that all in a twinkling, and the band played on, slow and deep.

Her roommate took her garbage all the way downstairs, heaved it into the flow, which by now covered half of the courtyard. The pool reached out toward her.

She started, noticing that, her eyes growing wide, and made for the steps, but she tripped over a root that had grown there by the foot, and she fell.

The pseudopod extended six feet or so to grasp her, and her pain and horror were clearly voiced, and for quite some time as the lamprey mouths tore her flesh from her bones.

The *shambler* screamed as well, long and loud and way into the supersonic. Clairvius' dog howled. Clairvius himself came out and leaned over the railing, taking in the scene.

The *shambler* began shambling toward the staircase. The slime pool receded, though the pseudopod still quested. It ignored her. Whatever she was, it wasn't part of the creature's diet.

Instead, the pseudopod snaked around the side of the building. There was a quick thump and then bubbling noises and the smell of fresh raw sewage over the creature's native sewage-and--rotten-fish cologne. I took that to signal the draining of the septic tank.

Then the amoeba-eye *belched*, with a sound and smell so foul that it beggared description.

I could hear a creaking and a cracking, and suddenly, a pseudopod appeared in the window of the vacant apartment upstairs from the Russian.

The creature *belched* again, and the music got louder. Stinking slime erupted from the drainage grates at either end of the pool and then got loudly sucked back.

More crunching and cracking, and several eyes and mouths appeared on the roof. The creature was still growing. It had clearly filled both apartments and was behaving like too much batter in the bread pan.

[slow heavy metal music playing]

One more belch, and the creature exploded, taking the end of the building with it. The air was filled with odor and tiny droplets of thing-matter that looked and smelled like nothing more than shit, and the shit-rain just kept on coming.

THE BRIDE OF THE ASTOUNDING GIGANTIC MONSTER
BUZZ DIXON

He missed the medical officer -- barely.

Luckily the medic dived to one side just as the giant hypodermic came whistling past. The point missed him but the reservoir struck him a glancing blow, breaking several ribs.

But he lived, and that was important.

Consumed with rage, consumed with fear, his brain racing as his stretched synapses desperately sought new connections, The Astounding Gigantic Man went to town.

Las Vegas, to be precise.

You've seen the newsreel footage: The shock, the surprise, the terror.

Several people were injured, not directly by him but in accidents cause by their own blind panic.

The police pulled up with riot guns, but they hesitated, not because they possessed any scruples -- hell, they would happily gun him down in the blink of an eye if they thought they could get away with it.

No, they feared their submachine guns *wouldn't* kill him, and the relatively minor vandalism The Astounding Gigantic Man was guilty of would escalate to full scale carnage.

Directed at them.

Discretion proving the better part of valor, they opted to hold their fire until the Army deployed with their bazookas.

Meanwhile, The Astounding Gigantic Man roamed the Strip, driving pedestrians to shelter, chasing cars off into the desert.

He was very bad for business.

Being The Astounding Gigantic Man had its drawbacks, chief of them great physical stress and strain. He fatigued easily, and now, feeling exhausted, he leaned an elbow on a rooftop café' adjoining a casino and tried to catch his breath.

It was Vera's last day in the chorus. Long in the tooth for a Vegas showgirl (at 35 the other dancers referred to her as Grandma), today when her shift ended she would be hanging up her feathered headdress for good.

She had no idea what she would do next.

Her booking agent reported no gigs for her. The show director couldn't have cared less about her fate. The pit boss said she could train to deal blackjack or she could become a cocktail waitress.

A cocktail waitress.

A God damned cocktail waitress.

Still in full costume when the screaming crowds poured in from outside, Vera watched the TVs in the bars switch from ball games and horse races to news reports of The Astounding Gigantic Man "rampaging" through Las Vegas.

"He's right outside the casino!" somebody screamed and immediately the terrified patrons began fleeing the building.

Not Vera.

You couldn't say she had a real plan, a real *idea* what she was going to do. Somehow, instinctively, she made her way up to the rooftop cafe'.

The Astounding Gigantic Man was breathing heavily.

"Hey."

He didn't hear her.

"Hey!"

She thought he still didn't hear her but after a moment he ponderously turned his head towards her, huge feverish eyeballs *looking* at her but not really *seeing* her.

"Hey, you okay?"

He blinked, breathed heavily. "No. Who are you? Do I know you?"

"I don't think so. I'm Vera. What's you name?"

He looked at her, pondering the question for a moment. "Glenn. I think my name is Glenn."

"Hi, Glenn."

Another long pause. "Hi, Vera."

An awkward silence followed. The police established a perimeter around them, hoping they wouldn't need to move in until the Army arrived.

"So…whatcha doing? What brings you to town, Glenn?"

The hormone injection -- the one that initiated his so-called rampage – started to work. The previously uncontrollable cell growth slowly started stabilizing.

Mental stability returned as well.

"I…I really don't know, Vera. I feel very, very tired, very confused. I feel like I'm waking up from a nightmare, but what I'm waking up to is just as much of a nightmare."

In the casino, Mr. Squallido the manager pointed to the TV in his office and asked, "Who da hell is dat?"

The office staff and other employees who crowded into his office for safety said, "The Astounding Gigantic Man."

"No, not him -- *her*! Who is she?"

The show director, a flamboyant heterosexual with reserved parking at the Las Vegas STD clinic, peered at the flickering grey screen and said: "Vera. That's Vera."

"She work here?"

"She does. Did. Today's her last day."

"No, it's not."

On the rooftop, Vera listened sympathetically as The Astounding Gigantic Man unloaded his tale of woe: The nuclear test. The radiation. The atomic mutation. The growth spurt. The astounding gigantic size he became. The gulf that grew between him and other humans.

The gulf between him and his fiancé.

Vera listened carefully. She was calculating but not cold. She didn't know what was going to happen, but somehow she saw her fate tied up in his.

She would, to the best of her ability, look after his best interests since in the end that would be the same as looking after her own.

The door to the main casino opened behind Vera and Mr. Squallido stepped out, waving a white flag made from a bus boy's towel and a roulette coup.

"Hi! How ya doin'?"

The Astounding Gigantic Man looked wearily at him and asked, "Who's he?"

"I'm Mr. Squallido," Mr. Squallido said. "I'm Vera's employer."

Vera knew his name (vaguely) but had never seen him in person. Nonetheless she turned and nodded at The Astounding Gigantic Man. "That's right, he is."

"Can I get you anything?" Mr. Squallido asked him.

"I'm thirsty."

"Understood. Garçon!" Mr. Squallido turned to the casino entrance. "Pitchers of ice water for our guest!"

The remaining casino staff formed a champagne bucket brigade to pass pitchers of ice water to The Astounding Gigantic Man. Like trying to slake your raging thirst with thimbles, if you're thirsty enough you'll be patient enough and enough thimbles will do.

By the time The Astounding Gigantic Man's quenched his thirst, the Army surrounded the hotel. The Astounding Gigantic Man's former commanding officer came up to the rooftop café to talk to him.

"Hello, Glenn."

"Hello, general." A wary tone.

"You've caused quite a bit of trouble."

"What? Trouble? No, no trouble at all," said Mr. Squallido. "Our specialty is hospitality, an' Mr. Astoundin' Gigantic Man is our guest. Isn't he, Vera?"

Vera nodded quickly. She sensed where this was heading and like a surfer judging which swell would prove the perfect wave, started positioning herself for a ride to glory.

On his way up to the café to confront The Astounding Gigantic Man the general played out several possible scenarios in his head; this was not one of them.

"Well…ah…thank you, Mr…"

"Squallido. But you can call me Julius."

"Yes. Well, thank you, Mr. Squallido, but if Glenn will just come with us back to the base…"

"Mr. Astoundin' Gigantic Man is comfortable right where he is, right, Vera?"

"Oh, yes, yes, he is! Aren't you, Glenn?"

The Astounding Gigantic Man blinked, eyes a little more clear. He didn't want to go back to his spartan existence in a hot airplane hangar back at the base. At least here he could talk to somebody.

"I'm comfortable."

Mr. Squallido turned back to the general. "So dere ya go. He likes it here."

"I appreciate your concern, but we can best take care of him back at the base."

"Excuse me, general, but I think if a call hasta be made between U.S. Army accommodations" -- The general was an Air Force officer but Mr. Squallido neither knew nor cared -- "an' *our* hospitality, nine outta ten astoundin' gigantic men would prefer stayin' at our casino. Ain't dat right, Mr. Astoundin' Gigantic Man?"

The Astounding Gigantic Man nodded. He still looked weary. Vera stepped over and put her hand on his elbow. Her palm barely covered one of his freckles but he appreciated the gesture.

Mr. Squallido turned back to the general. "So dere ya go. Mr. Astoundin' Gigantic Man is gonna stay here wid us. Ain't dat right, Mr. Astoundin' Gigantic Man?"

The Astounding Gigantic Man nodded again.

"With all due respect, Mr. Squallido, I don't think you appreciate the… uh…*enormity* of the situation."

"I appreciate da enormity of Mr. Astoundin' Gigantic Man," said Mr. Squallido in a lowered voice, "an' will sue da fornicatin' excrement outta anybody who provokes him an' causes damage to my fine establishment. Capisce?"

The general capisced. In the end this was negotiated: The casino would provide a circus tent for The Astounding Gigantic Man to live in until permanent quarters could be arranged. The military would provide food and water and monitor his medical condition.

After the general left and the Army and police withdrew to a few blocks away, Mr. Squallido turned to Vera and The Astounding Gigantic Man.

"Thank you," said The Astounding Gigantic Man

Mr. Squallido waved dismissively. "No biggies," he said, irony not being one of his strong points. "But I gotta be honest wid ya, I ain't in dis business" -- He pronounced it "bid-ness" -- "fer my health. Meanin' how do you plan on payin' fer yer stay here?"

The Astounding Gigantic Man blinked. Vera saw the hairs on his arm rise like switchlades. "Mr. Squallido, you just can't throw him out."

"Who said anyting 'bout trowin' him out? Vera, as wunna our long term permanent employees" -- Vera sensed the new paradigm and shifted accordingly -- "you know we look after our guests *an'* our own around here. I was just wundrin' if Mr. Astoundin' Gigantic Man might be innerested in long term employment hisself."

And that's how The Astounding Gigantic Man became a casino greeter and Las Vegas celebrity.

The casino's lawyers hammered out a deal with the government. The Astounding Gigantic Man received 100% disability from the military, including food and medical care. The casino provided him with a job and clothing and built a house for him.

Of course it made all the news and special blue ribbon panels investigated the dangers of atomic testing and nuclear radiation but after that, once the initial hoopla and faux outrage died down, The Astounding Gigantic Man became a fixture on the Strip.

Vera stayed with him in her new position as Coordinator of The Astounding Gigantic Man Public Appearances. She became a minor celebrity herself, frequently popping up on local radio and TV shows to tell where The Astounding Gigantic Man would be appearing next.

It was not a smooth transition from career military man to minor show biz celebrity for The Astounding Gigantic Man. The break up with his fiancé proved particularly acrimonious and ugly, and she hurled many false accusations at Vera.

But not all the accusations were false.

One thing that did smooth over The Astounding Gigantic Man's transition from a military career to one in show biz ("Fewer clowns to deal with," The Astounding Gigantic Man joked years later) was the parallel transition from his professional relationship with Vera to a personal one.

A cruel cynic would say the personal was the professional in Vera's case but that's not true. Vera's from conventional morality always showed willingness to entertain a certain tit-for-tat when dealing with men who helped her, but never a bald faced quid pro quo.

Mr. Squallido told her, "See to it he stays happy, capice?" and she capiced and years later when a senate committee investigating Mafia influence in Las Vegas convened (they found none, by the way), both she and Mr. Squallido could truthfully say that at no point ever did Mr. Squallido pay her to have an intimate relationship with The Astounding Gigantic Man.

But still...

Rumors and crude speculations fueled the comedy rooms along the Strip but truth be told, it isn't as difficult to imagine as one might think. Certain things she let him watch her do, and certain things she did for him, and once the military medical officers felt satisfied the A-bomb blast radiation had rendered him sterile (couldn't have dime size sperm swarming the Strip; that *would* be a nightmare) they turned a blind eye to anything that might transpire between them.

They did monitor his health, and his health (never good after the blast) was failing.

Part of it was the radiation, part of it was the sheer strain of moving ten tons of flesh around with a skeletal / cardio / nervous / muscular system that hadn't been evolved to deal with such weight.

He walked less and less. The first few years as a greeter (wearing a huge cowboy hat and chaps) The Astounding Gigantic Man stood in front of the casino and boomed out his welcome to the guests, the tourists, the rubes, the marks.

Later they changed his costume to that of a friendly giant and gave him a giant stool to sit on. That made it easier for people to take pictures with him and a lot less stressful.

(Every now and then Mr. Squallido would bring one of his high rollers out to meet The Astounding Gigantic Man. Most of the time it was because the high roller wanted to meet The Astounding Gigantic Man but sometimes it would be so that once safely out of The Astounding Gigantic Man's earshot Mr. Squallido could tell the high roller that he better settle up his gambling debts muy pronto. And they always did. Neither The Astounding Gigantic Man nor Vera ever suspected this side use of The Astounding Gigantic Man's services, and that was probably the best for all involved.)

When he could no longer walk from his home to the casino and back, the casino customized an 18-wheeler as his personal transport.

Even with the truck, it became more and more tiring for The Astounding Gigantic Man to attend public appearances other than at the casino.

Vera kept him happy, and Vera kept him going, but Vera wasn't there when his heart finally said "screw it" and just stopped working.

She was on the air at a local talk show promoting casino stage productions when they abruptly cut to commercial and told her she better get home fast and brought out the next guest -- a juggling seal act -- to mask her sudden departure.

He was dead when she got there; while napping before his evening shift he simply stopped breathing and beating his heart. The end.

They wept for him -- Vera and Mr. Squallido and the general and all of Los Vegas -- because they might be crass but they certainly weren't callous, especially to anyone who made them a ton of money (even the general; he used The Astounding Gigantic Man's atomic mutation to get funding for a proposal to create an army of giant warriors).

In fact, only his ex-fiancé took any glee at The Astounding Gigantic Man's death since she wrote a tell all book that didn't sell because everyone wanted to read Vera's tell all book.

But Vera really told bupkis.

Knowing it was her last gig, Vera planned accordingly. She invested in real estate around Vegas; did well. She milked her fame as The Astounding Gigantic Man's widow (they were married? Oh, yes, they were married, and despite Mr. Squallido's blandishments to make it a big Las Vegas spectacle, they kept it very private and very small -- at least as small as a wedding involving The Astounding Gigantic Man would permit).

She paced out her TV and convention appearances, and every now and then she appeared at some event for an anti-nuclear or pro-disabled rights group.

For the most part, she stayed a fixture on the Strip, never announcing her appearance or demanding attention, but there to be recognized by those who knew.

And all in all, not a bad gig. Certainly better than being the widow of The Amazing Pus Man.

UNDERGROUND ROSE
Natasha Bennett

The cactus was gone.

David sat up on the edge of the bed, wiping away the last cobwebs of sleep. He hated the stupid thing but his ex-wife, the bitch of all bitches, demanded they kept it on the nightstand. He should have tossed it out, but…he couldn't bring himself to do it. Now it had disappeared, and he damn well knew it had been there last night because he had scratched his hand trying to water it.

He studied the carpet in case he had knocked it over in his sleep. Nope, no sign of it. Did someone take it? That seemed unlikely. Although his door was unlocked, he lived in a cabin in the middle of nowhere. Besides the fact that he had lived alone, there was a nice wad of bills on the nightstand which remained untouched.

Maybe she had done it. To mess with him.

A slow grimace spread across his face. That meant she was back in town.

He got up and dressed in the same clothes from last night-a flannel shirt and blue janes. Next was a pot of coffee. A customary look around the place told him that nothing else had been taken. He lived in a small town, at least three hour's drive from the nearest city. He enjoyed the privacy, and the property was dirt cheap. *She* had once insisted on moving back to the city, even throwing a vase at him until he agreed. He had even packed up half the house before…that night.

Shaking his head at the memory, he left the cabin and started his job as a tow truck driver. Sometimes he would help a stranded motorist, but the town primarily hired him to clear out the roads on a semi-regular basis or to make any manual labor a bit easier. He was currently working at a construction site, and the development moved slowly. No one was in any hurry to make a resort, but the mayor demanded one to increase tourism. It would likely be abandoned and demolished by the end of next year. More work for him later.

Once he was finished for the day he decided to go to the hardware store to pick up another cactus. He selected one from the shelf that looked in decent enough shape.

"You know, cactus plants usually last a lifetime. Or is this a partner for the other one?" An amused voice asked behind him. David turned around and saw the Sheriff with a cart of gardening supplies.

"Hey Roy," David greeted. "Busy day?"

Roy shook his head. "Just a few teenagers who decided to fight in front of the liquor store. They're cooling it off in a cell." He eyed the plant again. "How about you? I thought you hated that thing."

"Yeah, um…" David hesitated. "Do you want to grab a coffee?"

"So you think Rose is back in town," Roy said thoughtfully, stirring his coffee cup. They were in a diner just across from the hardware store. The two of them had been friends for a long time, ever since David had pulled Roy's police cruiser out of the ditch. The story of how it had ended up there, to begin with, was one David would never repeat to a living soul. "How do you feel about that?"

"I don't know," David admitted. "Worried, I guess. I was happy having her out of my life."

"That's understandable. The woman is dangerous, no question about that. She was mentally and physically abusive. Everything was a game to her, especially you. I still don't know what you saw in her."

"She didn't start out that way," David sighed, leaning back in the red booth. "She was funny. And sweet. But something changed after she moved here. I guess she still missed the city, and every time I fought back, the angrier she became. You know, I still can't remember a goddam detail the night she left. Not a single one."

Roy took a bite of his egg sandwich. "She put your head through a window, David. When I got there, you were covered in blood and needed to be in the hospital for a week. You were lucky-*extremely lucky*-that someone heard the noise and called it in. And Rose? I don't know, man. I couldn't find her anywhere, but judging from the note she left it seemed pretty clear she had skipped town. And now she's back." He stirred his coffee. "I'll keep an eye out for her. In the meantime, it might not be a bad idea for you to get some extra security."

"What, you mean like an alarm system?" David asked. "Shit man, there's no way I can afford that stuff."

"I'll buy one for you. The station could use an upgrade anyway after you're done with it. The mayor will approve it." Roy finished his coffee. "Come on. The hardware store is still open. I'll help you pick out a good one."

It took a few hours of installation and fiddling to get the cameras set up. He was completely clueless when it came to technology and relied heavily on Roy to get them together.

"All right, I got it set up so I can watch the cameras from my private laptop at the station. If anything happens tonight, I can see it right away."

"I really appreciate this, Roy. That being said, I can't say I exactly feel comfortable with the idea of someone watching over me," David admitted.

"Yeah, I get it. You like privacy. So does everyone else in this town, for one reason or another. But it should only be for a couple of days. And Rose is crazy enough for me to be genuinely concerned for your safety. Unless you would prefer to hang out at the station?"

"And hang out with your drunk teenagers in a cell?" David asked with a smirk. "I'll pass, thanks. You want to stay for a drink?" The town had no liquor store, but one of the residents, Andy, would brew a selection of various beers and deliver them himself. He didn't know how legal that actually was, but it did save driving a few hours to the city. Roy knew about it but didn't seem to care as long as it was kept low-key.

"Nah, thanks. I'm technically still on patrol." He waved his hand. "Sleep tight."

David watched him drive away, and the cabin became quiet again. He took out a beer and chugged it down. He always had at least one before bed. That done, he took the cactus plant out of a plastic bag and put it on the nightstand, exactly where the last one had been. That done, he laid back in bed. He thought it might be difficult to sleep, but he fell into a deep sleep.

She was chasing him through the woods, crackling in glee. He aimlessly ran through the trees, the branches scratching again his skin. Dirt caked his hands and clothes. Suddenly he tripped and landed in a pool of blood. Not his own, but-

"Hello, lover," her chilling voice said behind him.

David's eyes snapped open, and he jerked upwards in fright. He glanced at the plant. It was still there. Good. Wiping sleep from his eyes, he had a shower and dressed. The nightmare had woken him up an hour before the alarm was supposed to ring. He thought about it, then grabbed his keys.

Half an hour later the smell of hot coffee, bacon and eggs hit his nose as the waitress, Trish, set his plate on the table. "Thank you."

"I don't normally see you here this early," Trish said, refilling his coffee.

"I guess I worked up an appetite," David said with a smile, which was true. The two held eye contact for longer than necessary. He had always taken a liking to Trish, but the situation with Rose always kept that possibility from his mind. Well, how long was he going to keep that from living his life? "Listen, do you-"

Abruptly she turned away as a customer waved. "Excuse me."

David sighed as he watched her take another order. Oh well. He started digging into his food, and his eyes went to the missing poster of fourteen-year old Alicia Moss. The poster was old and faded. She would probably be a year older by now.

He remembered his dream and frowned. No, Rose was a lot of things, but she wasn't a murderer. It was just his imagination working overtime. He looked up at Trish, who was whispering with the line cook. For some reason both of them were frowning at him.

David finished his food, paid the bill, and left.

The sun was beginning to set as he drove up to his cabin after work. Usually, the quiet sound of nature would have calmed him, but now he could hear…nothing at all. No birds at all. He parked and got out of his truck. Someone had been here. Maybe they still were.

He opened the door to his cabin cautiously and could smell blood. "Rose?"

Every window in his kitchen was smashed, and the dishes were thrown to the ground from the cupboard. His microwave was caked in blood. Fighting a wave of repulsiveness, he opened it, and quickly looked away. A squirrel was stretched out, his entrails spilling out on the tray. Its tiny, beady eyes were frozen and looking at David in terror. Seeing it, David resisted the urge to wretch.

A note was written above the microwave. *See you soon, lover.*

The door burst open, and Roy entered with his gun drawn. "Get out," he ordered. "Now."

David didn't need to be told twice. He ran out of the cabin and sat down on a nearby log. It felt like a lifetime before Roy opened the door again and gestured David to come back inside.

"She was here, all right," Roy said. "Saw everything on camera. She had quite the mental breakdown in the kitchen."

"Are you sure she left?" David asked, quickly grabbing a baseball bat out of the cupboard.

"Yep. I've searched every corner of this property and there's no sign of her." He cracked open a beer from the fridge and handed it over to him. "David, look…it's not safe for you to be here anymore. I was kidding before, but now I'm serious. Come with me back to the station. I promise you that the cells are way more comfortable than they look."

"Thanks, but honestly Rose made my life a living hell in the last months I knew her. I loved her, but…every day I was too afraid to stand up to her. I can't let that happen again, even during this. She wanted to drive me out of this place, but it's not going to happen," David insisted, shaking his head.

Roy sighed. "Well, in that case…guess it's a good thing I brought an overnight bag."

David put his beer on the table. "You don't have to-"

"Don't worry about it. I'll put out an APB. We're going to catch this psycho."

"Thanks, Roy, I mean it," David said, feeling a bit less on edge.

Roy put the squirrel in a garbage bag. "I'll dump this and grab my things."

David watched him go and eyed the beer on the table. Without hesitation, he took a swing, then frowned. The beer seemed a little…off. Instantly he felt drowsy, even though he should feel terrified. He put a hand to his head.

What if Rose had drugged the beer?

He instantly set the beer away from him, only to grab it a second later. Were there any signs of any needle marks from the top?

No. Nothing.

David shook his head. He was on edge. Maybe Andy had just brewed a bad batch. He walked over to the kitchen, trying to ignore the smell. There was another six-pack in the fridge. He studied each one individually. Were they okay? Nah, he didn't want to chance that weird feeling again. Instead, he reached for a jug of water.

Suddenly a force yanked him backward, and a hand covered his mouth with a cloth. *Rose!* He tried to scream and fight off his attacker but couldn't seem to pull him off. Which seemed impossible. David had spent most of his life working in manual labor. Rose was a small woman, despite her temper. He should be able to fight her off. He looked down. The arm covering his mouth was large, and male.

Not Rose, Dave thought. *Then who…?*

It was his last coherent thought for a while.

"Oh god," David choked as he ran through the trees. It was too dark, and he couldn't see where to go next. Left? Right? He only knew that he was hurt, and it was bad. His side was numb and his clothes were soaked in blood. He needed a hospital. Quick.

Suddenly he tripped over something and landed face-first into the soil. His hands touched something wet, and sticky. The moonlight parted from the clouds, and he could see blood. Ring in front of him was Alicia's corpse.

"David!" Rose shouted from the trees. She was clutching her chest which was gushing with blood. "Get out of here!"

"Rose!" Dave ran forwards, and the air crackled with a noise. To his horror, Rose fell to the dirt, a bullet hole in her forehead.

"Ugh…" David weakly gripped a tree for support and turned his head. "Oh god…"

Roy stood in the clearing, a gun pointed at him. "I'm sorry, David."

David opened his eyes. He was laying in his bed, looking at that damn cactus again. How did he get here again? It was too fuzzy to recall. He ran a hand through his hair, trying to wake up. Suddenly he remembered the dream, and it felt as though a knife twisted slowly in his gut.

Roy. Roy had shot his wife. And maybe poor Alicia as well.

The Sheriff was fast asleep on the couch, wrapped in his old mother's yellow quilt. David moved slowly, fearfully. The top of his toe connected with a beer bottle, which rattled. David held his breath. Roy didn't stir.

He crept into the kitchen, grabbing his jacket and sneakers. He then shut the door behind him and changed outside. David walked to his truck and paused. There was a shotgun in his shed. He made sure to grab it as well and drove off.

He didn't stop until he reached the diner, crashing hard against the concrete stopper in the process. He ran inside, where Trish was pouring coffee. "Trish, you need to come with me."

"David?" Trish echoed. "What are you-"

"It's Roy. He murdered Rose, and he's going to come after me. We both need to get out of town before it's too late. I know this is sudden, but he knows that I like you and he might hurt you-"

"David, you're babbling," Trish interrupted, moving to the front counter. "Why don't I call Roy and ask him to come here? I'm sure he can explain everything."

"No, no, no," David said, shaking his head at the very thought. "Trish, he put a dead squirrel in my microwave!"

"Why would he do that?"

"I don't know! And there's more," David glanced at the poster, and his voice sped up in fear. "I think he killed Alicia too. Maybe, I don't know, maybe Rose found out and that's when he shot her and then maybe I found out but then I couldn't remember and now he wants to kill me too-"

A fork dropped against a plate. David noticed that everyone in the diner had stopped eating and was openly looking at them. For a moment, it was eerily quiet.

"I'm calling the cops," Trish finally said.

David reached for her arm. "Trish-"

Trish recoiled at his touch. "David, you're not well!" she snapped. "Just… sit down somewhere and don't go anywhere. It'll be okay. I promise."

David watched her go into the kitchen. No, it wasn't safe here. Or anywhere else in town. He studied the diners. "Tell Roy that I have a shotgun if the fucker comes anywhere near me. I'm leaving town."

He left the diner and grabbed his keys. He wasn't ready to go, though. Not yet.

David stayed out of sight at the old lumber mill, one of his former job sites. He had no reason to go there and figured it would be as good place as any to lay low. One time he saw Roy's police cruiser drive past, its lights flashing. Roy didn't spot him. David released a held breath.

After the sun set, he drove halfway back to his house before parking on the adjacent road. Luckily he still had his tools from work. He took out a shovel, a flashlight, and his shotgun. He then headed to the forest.

The dark trees were intimidating as hell, but he needed to press on. He knew he was right. He just needed to prove it to Trish, and the entire town. It took some searching, but eventually he found an area similar to the one in his dreams. Some of the trees had old blood caked on them. He set the shotgun against a tree and started digging.

Fifteen minutes later, he stopped, and set the shovel aside. He had found two bodies wrapped in blue tarp, one of them being the size of a small child. The other was Rose. Seeing it, his heart clenched. She was never here.

Suddenly, he heard a dry click behind his head. "The whole town is looking for you, David," Roy said softly, holding a gun. "We were worried. But I figured you would come here."

David was very still. The shotgun! It was propped against the tree. He could grab it, whirl around, and shoot. That would take two, maybe three seconds? Was Roy even a good shot? It's not like there was much crime around here.

"I took out the shells a few days ago. David, look at me. Don't even try it," Roy implored, reading his mind.

David gritted his teeth and ran for the gun just as Roy pulled the trigger. David felt something sharp pierce his neck. *Not a bullet*, he thought feverishly. *If it was a bullet blood would be gushing everywhere.* Rage overtook him. *Blood! Blood!*

To his amazement his hand thickened and grew three times the normal size. His fingernails grew larger, sharper. His muscles were thickening. He was growing, and it was a glorious feeling! With a roar he slammed his fists down upon the tree, causing it to fall.

Roy jumped out of the way. David eyes were changing as well, and Roy had become a fat morsel of food that was in his way. He jumped on top of him, about to sink his teeth into Roy's jugular.

Then Roy fired again, and everything abruptly went dark.

David. I'm sorry, I didn't mean to hurt you... Rose's voice whispered in the dark. Please come back.

David's eyes snapped open. He was handcuffed. Oh god, he was handcuffed to a bed in a cell. He gave it a feeble yank, but didn't have any... what was that, before? His hand looked completely normal. He studied it in acknowledgement.

"You're awake," Roy said quietly.

David turned slightly to face him. There wasn't any blood on his shirt at all. He felt swollen, his neck felt bruised, but...he was alive. "What the hell happened to me?" he asked. "Rose-"

"I'm sorry, David. I shot her, all those years ago. She was a monster, perhaps always had been. She killed Alicia and tore you up pretty bad before I was able to stop her. You were on life support for a few days, but then you started healing way faster than you should have. That's when I knew. Somehow she infected you."

"I don't remember all of this," David persisted.

"It's true. Every night, you change."

"Then why not get my blood tested? Why not call the health authority, or the government?"

"Sure, we could do that. And they would come sweeping in with helicopters and quarantine tape. And then they would find that Andy's alcoholic run was not exactly legal. And that Elizabeth has a son with a few outstanding warrants. They would pry open this town and leave nothing left. We all came here to get away from the big city and the government, and there would be *nothing left* when they were done. Understand?" His gaze looked at him imploringly.

"No," David said flatly. "If Rose isn't here, then who tore up my house? How did the plant go missing?"

"Oh, right," Roy sighed as he unlocked the cell door. "Well, we had a good plan at first. You didn't remember anything, and you were a creature of habit already. One beer every night. It was easy enough for Andy to lace your beer with a little sedative, then drop in around midnight to make sure you had taken your medicine."

"Wait, what?"

"He was on the mayor's payroll, so it was just another job got him." Roy waved a dismissive hand. "Except last time he got a little sloppy and broke your plant. Fucking idiot. We were hoping that you wouldn't notice, but well...

you suspected Rose was back and things escalated from there. I set up the cameras since it seemed necessary to keep a closer eye on you in the meantime."

David said nothing, thinking. "So why…what made you put that message in the kitchen?"

"We were planning to quit things after that, I swear," Roy said. "We just needed you to believe she was there for a little while longer, then I was planning to say I chased her off. Things were supposed to back to normal. But, well, I guess everyone got a little carried away. Sorry." He unlocked David's handcuffs. "Trish was pretty pissed off after you left the diner, believe me. Said she wouldn't be a part of this any longer unless I told the truth."

David couldn't believe a word of what was hearing. "So I'm just free to fucking go?"

"You're not a threat. Never were. You're just someone with a very manageable condition. Hell, maybe it's a good thing you do know about it, in the end. The point is…you've been in this town for decades. We're not going to let you stop living here just because of one minor problem. We all feel that way." Roy smiled. "Coffee later?"

A few minutes David sat in the diner, trying to wrap his mind around what Roy had said. It struck him how…normal everything seemed now. People greeted him. Someone from the construction yard told him to go back to the site tomorrow as they needed his truck. It was as though the last few days never happened.

But it did, David thought, miserable. *I'm a monster.*

He suddenly heard his coffee being poured. "So…" Trish began. "You like me, huh?" she smiled.

Despite himself, David smiled back.

Maybe things weren't so bad, after all.

THE PEPYS LAKE MONSTER
ORRIN GREY

The Wikipedia page for "Pepys Lake Monster," accessed 2015

Pepys (/ˈpiːps/ *peeps*) Lake refers to both a lake and neighboring town located in northeastern Connecticut, near the borders of Massachusetts and Rhode Island. Pepys Lake is best known for a series of monster sightings that occurred there in the early 1900s, and *The Pepys Lake Monster*, a 1963 black-and-white science fiction monster film directed by Graham Ward inspired by the sightings. *The Secret of Pepys Lake*, a documentary film about the monster and the making of the movie, was released in 2012 and won the Raab Prize at the High Strange Film Festival in Golden, Colorado.

Pepys Lake, 1959

Michael Deschutes was out too late on a rainy Sunday in his father's skiff when he saw the monster. It wasn't quite dark, but the thick, low clouds made it nearly so, and the rain that fell in a steady tap, like fingers on typewriter keys, made the early evening a miserable one. Mike sat near the rear of the boat, his shoulders hunched, the hood of his slicker pulled over his head.

He had heard stories about the monster since he was a kid, of course, but he had never seen it himself, nor known of anyone whose tales seemed more credible than drunkards seeing snakes. Yet here it was, rising up from the lake not twenty yards from the bow of the boat, rising and rising on a neck that was taller than the basketball goals at school.

Mike would later attempt to describe the creature. First to his father, then the police, and then the *Pepys Lake Observer* and even the *Padgett's Mill Herald*. The head was long and angular, almost equine. Had Mike ever seen a giraffe—even in a picture—then that's what he would have compared it to, save for the huge, froggy eyes that blazed like lamps. It made a sound like a train chugging along the track, and when it opened its mouth it spit forth a geyser of flaming sparks.

Somewhere in Germany, the 1940s

Reinhardt had been a puppeteer before the war. Every year, during the summer months, he had set out his little stage in the town square and re-enacted the story of *Der Rattenfänger*. The animatronic figure of the piper in his multi-hued clothes made of candy glass, belling out around his mechanical legs so that the light filtered through them. Inside the figure's back was a music box, a spiked cylinder that turned on a spindle as carefully-tuned metal fingers plinked over the raised knobs to create the tinkling music that summoned the rats.

Each rat was not distinct, but a single organism; a mass of rabbit fur laid over wheels and gears and red eyes that lit from within, all rolling along behind the piper as he led them out of the city and into the mountain, which opened wide on its clockwork hinges to receive them. And then the curtain closed, and when it opened again the piper was being denied his due payment by the townspeople, simple automata in black robes who bobbed their heads and held bags painted with *pfennig* signs so that the children would recognize them as money. When the piper reached for the bags, the townspeople pulled them away with a jerk, their arms bending backward on a hinge.

The curtains closed and opened once again, and there was the piper, once more leading a huddled mass through the town square to the hungry mountain. This time, the mass was made up of children. They spun on their bases, to indicate that they were dancing, though once again they were truly just one figure, like a wagon that the piper pulled behind himself, their wheels hidden in tracks sunk into the base of the puppet stage. They disappeared into the mountain and it snapped closed behind them, the piper's tune dwindling off gradually into silence. In the town square, the real children clapped and clapped, even though he had just shown them a vision of their own untimely deaths.

Reinhardt's father had been a shoemaker by trade, but a stage magician by choice. He had gone off to the bigger cities a few times a year, to perform tricks on disreputable stages for crowds of drunkards and harlots. In their rooms above his father's shop, the old man had created the tricks that he would perform. Mechanical birds and spring-loaded mechanisms that he tucked up his sleeves. Boxes with hidden compartments, and plants that seemed to grow in a matter of moments.

These had always been what fascinated Reinhardt. Not the tricks themselves, but their secrets. The mechanisms that made them work. He knew that for the children, the illusion was the thing; that's why he worked so hard to hide the mechanisms that drove his puppets. But for him, it was the building, not the performing, that gave him joy. He loved the secret gears and wheels that made his creations live.

As for the story, he never understood its appeal, not until the soldiers came and began rounding people up. Some were conscripted into the army, to serve the cause, while others were taken off to someplace worse. Once again a piper came and took the children of Reinhardt's town, though this time the mountains that opened wide to claim them had other names: Dachau and Buchenwald and Auschwitz.

When the first of the soldiers marched through the cobblestoned streets, Reinhardt hid in the rooms above his father's old shop, where he now made puppets and automata, instead of shoes. His father had been a cobbler and a magician, but he had also been a Jew. Fortunately, he was four years in the ground by the time the soldiers arrived, and Reinhardt hadn't kept the faith, had never been interested in miracles, only in the solid and the mechanical, what he could touch and build. Still, when he heard the gloved fist on his door, he was afraid that he had been found out. Instead of the camps, however, he was told that the Fuhrer required his special skills for a project that would help the war effort.

It didn't make much difference, as it turned out. He was taken away by car, instead of by train, but at the end of the ride he found himself no less a prisoner. He was given a workshop much grander than the one he had made in his father's old store, and he was given the tools and assistants that he would need to complete his labors—other Jews like himself, though ones who had been identified already, marked by their names and their features and the yellow stars that they wore on their sleeves—who were there to help him build mechanical monsters for the man who planned to exterminate them all, for the piper who would lead them into the mountain.

Soldiers stood outside the workshop with rifles in their hands at all hours, but Reinhardt was considered loyal, and so he was given much more leniency than he might otherwise have enjoyed. While he labored building infernal devices, he had an apartment nearby that was vastly richer than anything he had enjoyed in his home town, and he had the run of at least some parts of the city, though he seldom traveled far without seeing soldiers in their crisp uniforms.

He could almost have enjoyed the relative luxury, the work. Could almost have forgotten the purpose to which is labor was being turned, had it not been for the poor wretches who toiled alongside him, their ultimate fates written in every flinch when a soldier spoke, every line etched into their gaunt faces. Had it not been for the knowledge that he was like them, in the eyes of the men who kept him so luxuriously, and that one day they would realize it, too.

That was why Reinhardt used his father's show business contacts—such as they were—to eventually meet with an actress who was sympathetic to the resistance, and who was, herself, in contact with filmmakers in Britain and beyond, who saw the benefit that his work could bring to their ventures instead.

So it was that one night Reinhardt, who had been a puppeteer before the war, was smuggled out of Germany under the cover of darkness to become a puppeteer of a very different sort, on a very different stage.

Pepys Lake, 2010

The diving machine was named *Nemo*—not, its inventor was quick to point out in an interview to be included in the documentary, after the fish from the movie, but rather the captain from Jules Verne. It looked like an aquatic beetle, with a turbine on its back and a light in the nose and small arms that allowed it to manipulate, however crudely, any obstacles that it might encounter, all controlled by a bank of switches and joysticks floating in a rented boat on the surface of the lake.

Sealed inside *Nemo*'s watertight outer casing was a camera, the thing for which it had been built. The camera recorded everything that *Nemo*'s searchlight shone upon, broadcasting it back up to the waiting boat above.

The resulting footage appears almost colorless in the documentary, the only light that reaches the black bottom of the lake that which *Nemo* makes itself. The film seems grainy with all the particles and motes that hang in the still water. This effect, almost like looking through night-vision goggles, heightens rather than reduces the ultimate revelation, as *Nemo* drifts over a hillock of silt on the lake bottom and we get our first glimpse of the monster.

Pepys Lake, 1956

Reinhardt's workshop in the small Connecticut town was much different than the one in his father's old shoe shop, or even the big empty warehouse where he had toiled for the Nazis. Now it was a repurposed boathouse, long as an airplane hangar and low-ceilinged, hung with chains and tackles and winches that allowed him to move the various parts of the machine.

Down the center of the boathouse was a strip of open water, which he could hear at all times lapping at the pilings that held up the floor beneath him. Here and there this strip of water was crossed by small walkways of metal and wood that could be slid aside when they weren't needed, so that the thing he was building could be lowered fully into the lake.

His assistants were different here, too. A young man and woman, barely out of their teens, rather than the sallow-faced slaves who had labored for him in Germany, though, from what he gathered, the studio wasn't paying them a whole lot more. They worked with him because they wanted to work in the moving pictures, the strange and golden empire that had rescued him from beneath the boots of the Nazis more than a decade ago.

Though he tried to forget, he still had dreams of waking up on the hard wooden floor of a train car, surrounded by the gray faces and shining eyes of ghosts that stared down at him. The train, he knew, passed into the mountain, which closed like a mouth behind it.

Since coming to America, Reinhardt had built many ingenious devices for the motion picture studios. "Special effects," they called them. Everything from tables that were built to collapse on command to hanging harnesses, mock guillotines, and reproductions of torture devices from ages past. He had built creatures, like the puppets of his youth, which moved and acted at his accord, powered by wheels and pistons.

Even the engines of war that he had been asked to create for the Nazis were not as ambitious as the project he labored over in Pepys Lake, however, and it wasn't even going to be put on film. "Then why build it?" Reinhardt had asked, and the producer, a man named Marsh, had put his hand on Reinhardt's shoulder and pointed up into the sky, as though at something Reinhardt should have been able to see, but couldn't.

"We're going to stir up a little publicity first," he had said. "Give them a *real* monster, something they can believe in. And once there have been a few sightings of *that*, we'll make sure that the word gets spread. National newspapers, the works. And once everyone knows the name… bam! *Then* we make our movie."

To that end, Reinhardt and his assistants labored in secrecy, under strict orders not to touch a drop of alcohol, or to fraternize with the locals any more than was necessary. When asked what they were working on, they had been given falsified credentials claiming that they were civilian contractors for the Army Corps of Engineers, and that they were engaged in testing various materials for buoyancy. "Why not just say that it's classified?" Reinhardt had asked the producer.

"If it's classified, then people are curious. They'll snoop," Marsh had replied. "If it's boring, then they're much less likely to stick their noses in."

The Dark of the Matinee blog, accessed 2009

The Pepys Lake Monster (1963) originally showed as the back half of a double-bill with the spiritualism shocker *The Final Session*, but is mostly familiar to viewers today from its occasional appearances on Saturday afternoon monster movie broadcasts throughout the 70s and into the 80s. Ultimately directed by Graham Ward, it was originally intended to be produced by schlock movie legend Kirby Marsh, but by the time it finally went in front of cameras he was already in England directing a pair of British shockers, so his credit is that of executive producer, instead.

Three things distinguish *The Pepys Lake Monster* from its peers: its unlikely "inspired by true events" logline, a surprisingly restrained screenplay by Gavin Summers, and, perhaps more than anything else, its monster, created by the under-appreciated German special effects genius Carl Reinhardt.

The titular monster itself is pretty much all head and neck, though we do get a brief glimpse of a gigantic clawed paddle foot, and a tail fin in one shot. The neck is little more than a column of scaly darkness rising up from the water, surmounted by a long, tapered head with lantern eyes and knobby antennae like a giraffe. The eyes are, at first glance, the most striking feature. Round and bulbous, they give off a somehow pumpkin-like effulgence, even on the black-and-white film, and if you squint closely you can see that they are compound, like the eyes of an insect. Then you are distracted as the monster delivers its coup de grace: opening wide those horse-skull jaws and blowing out a spray of sparks.

Though obviously mechanical to our modern eye, the effect remains impressive, and precisely how Reinhardt pulled it off remains a mystery. One that he took to his grave only two years after the film was released. According to studio records, the monster mechanism employed in the film was sold for parts as soon as principal photography was completed, but documentary filmmaker Gale Chambers thinks that there might be another way to get an idea of how the effect was achieved.

According to the premise of her planned film, which is currently seeking funding under the working title *The Secret of Pepys Lake*, the spike in sightings of the Pepys Lake Monster in the late 1950s was not, as originally believed, the impetus for the film of the same name, but rather the other way around. She claims to have uncovered documents alleging that Kirby Marsh and Carl Reinhardt built a previous mechanical Pepys Lake Monster, one that they deployed in the lake itself for years to startle the locals and help build the legend, before filming of the actual picture got underway.

Her pitch email asserts that she intends to prove this hypothesis by using a newly-invented diving robot to explore the bottom of the lake and find the remains of the original "monster," which her records say was sunk there in order to prevent it ever being found once the picture was released.

Loch Ness, 1954

Reinhardt stood next to the American producer whose name had escaped him and looked out across the water of the lake, or "loch" as their guide had pronounced it. Behind them and to their right stood a small stone castle up on a slight prominence, and everywhere around them and across the flat gray water mist hung in thick clouds and in tatters. "They say there's a monster under the water," the producer was telling him. "A serpent, or a dragon, or even a dinosaur, surviving on to this very day. They've been talking about it since the seventh century, when a visiting saint is said to have driven it back with the sign of the cross."

"I've seen enough monsters in my day," Reinhardt replied, "and known enough men that I don't believe in saints."

"Still," the producer said, smiling out over the water, "you've got to admit that it would make for one hell of a movie."

Bartlett University, 2016

The documentary film *The Secret of Pepys Lake* ends with shots of the documentary crew recovering the head of the original Pepys Lake Monster, built by Reinhardt in a boathouse on the lake and used to create hoax sightings throughout the latter half of the 1950s. The head has been badly damaged by its time at the bottom of the lake—one of the eyes is cracked, a blackened chasm in the candy glass exterior through which the incandescent bulb that once illuminated it is now visible—but it remains mostly intact.

A text crawl at the end of the film assures us that the mechanisms inside the head have been examined by engineers and special effects technicians, but that they are too damaged for anyone to get a very good idea of how the creature must have originally worked. The text crawl is interrupted by a snippet of interview with special effects guru Scott Cole. He wears a red-and-black flannel shirt and is shaking his head, rubbing at his beard as he talks.

"There's nothing in here to indicate how it did any of the things that we know it did," he's saying. "Where did the sparks come from? And how did he provide power to it under water? The outer shell isn't watertight, and even if it was, there's no visible method of producing those effects. There must have been some additional mechanisms that were damaged or removed before the monster was sunk into the lake, so that other people who found it one day couldn't copy his methods. Reinhardt learned his craft from magicians, after all."

What the documentary doesn't say is what happened to the remains of the monster after they were recovered. Gale Chambers donated them to the Bartlett University Museum of History in Maryland, where they now lie in a wooden crate in the back to a storeroom largely given over to items of historical significance that are too damaged to make them suitable for public display. Two smaller crates—containing pottery—are stacked atop it, and several paintings packed in cardboard have been leaned against its front.

Because the storeroom is rarely entered except to add new pieces to its ever-growing stockpile, no one has ever seen the jack-o-lantern glow that sometimes emanates from the slats of the crate, or smelled the whiff of smoke as the sparks sizzle against the wood inside. But perhaps someday soon, they will.

THE BRIDE OF CASTLE FRANKENSTEIN
JILL HAND

During the whole of a dull, dark, and soundless day in the autumn of the year, when the clouds hung oppressively low in the heavens, Franz Wilhelm von Richter had been passing alone, on horseback, through the Black Forest.

Not a living soul had he seen for hours. Franz was beginning to think the directions the innkeeper had given him back in Freiberg were wrong and he would be forced to spend the night outdoors in this wild, mountainous region. He drew his cloak closer around him and touched the pistol he wore at his side, seeking reassurance from its presence. There were wild boars in the forest, and wolves. If he were attacked he would need to shoot, and shoot quickly. He looked around apprehensively.

Franz was a bookish young man, a recent graduate of the medical school at Heidelberg University. He had never killed anything larger than a partridge, and he was uncertain whether he would be capable of defending himself against a wild beast. Then to his relief he saw, up ahead, the bent figure of an old woman hobbling along the road carrying a load of firewood.

"*Guten Abend, Mutter*!" he said cordially, pulling his horse up beside her. "Can you tell me the way to the *Schloß* of Herr Doktor Frankenstein?"

She stared at him from pale blue eyes in a face that was a crumpled mass of wrinkles. To Franz's astonishment she spat a thick stream of phlegm, narrowly missing his left boot. "I can tell you the way to go to the Devil," she snarled.

She hiked up her skirts and bolted away. Running swiftly as a hare, she disappeared between the evergreens, their dark, sinister canopy giving the Black Forest its name.

"*Meine Gütte*! I have never seen an old woman move so quickly," Franz marveled to himself. "I wonder what got into her? Perhaps she was mad. The mad are capable of tremendous bursts of energy, or so Herr Professor Grappenkudgel said during one of his lectures."

Thinking of his old professor made him miss Heidelberg, its ancient university with its Gothic spires, its streets bustling with activity, so unlike this grim, silent wasteland. What jolly times he'd had there! Franz smiled, recalling the time he slipped an eye into his friend Schultz's bock at Der Rosenkavalier, a *Biergarten* the medical students used to frequent. The eye was a souvenir from the subject of their most recent dissection, the wife of a clockmaker who'd succumbed to an attack of gallstones.

Schultz didn't notice the presence of the grisly orb until the stein was two-thirds empty. His scream upon discovering an eye bobbing in his lager, trailing its optic nerve the way a child's balloon trails a string, made Franz and his companions

roar with laughter.

Franz sighed. Those student days had been pleasant, but now he must make his way in the world. Where was Frankenstein's damned *Schloß*, anyway? He'd been riding for hours with no sign of it. Then he was seized by a horrible suspicion,

making him jerk the reins so the horse tossed its head and snorted irritably.

What if there was no Herr Doktor Frankenstein? What if one of his friends (Schultz sprang to mind as the most likely culprit) had engineered the whole thing as a joke? Writing to him, pretending to be a scientist living in a remote castle who did some sort of unspecified research he claimed was highly important, even ground- breaking? The mysterious Frankenstein had invited Franz to be his assistant and he eagerly accepted, posting his response the next day. Looking back on it, the

salary offered was suspiciously generous for a recent medical school graduate.

Franz cursed. If Schultz had done this he was a wicked rascal. An eye in someone's beer was one thing, but sending him on a wild goose chase deep in the mountains, with night drawing in, a filmy white ground fog sending tendrils like cotton wool drifting between the trees, where he might be attacked by a pack of wolves at any

moment. That was something else entirely. It verged on criminal cruelty.

He was about to turn back and try to find refuge for the night in the last village he'd passed when he saw a flickering light bobbing toward him. It gradually revealed itself to be an iron lantern carried by a short, stocky man with a twisted back, a few straggling black witch-locks clinging to his nearly bald pate. What now? Franz wondered. First a mad old woman and now a dwarf. Was it one of the Nibelung that legends claimed inhabited these mountains, guardians of a

hoard of gold and magic treasures?

"Hallo there! Do you seek the castle of Herr Doktor Frankenstein?" the little man called as he got closer.

"*Ja, danke,*" Franz said, stammering with relief. It seemed he was not lost after all, and Frankenstein really did exist. "I am Franz Wilhelm von Richter of the Heidelberg medical college. I am to be the assistant to the Herr Docktor. I had a hunch that perhaps I had taken a wrong turn. It was so long after passing through the village back there. The Herr Doktor's letter said the turnoff to his *Schloß* was

not far from..."

He stopped. The little man was glaring at him, eyes narrowed, his massive brow furrowed.

"What? What is wrong?"

"Are you making fun of me?"

"No, of course not. I only said I was not sure of the way."

"No, you said 'hunch.' You were making fun of my back," the man said, scowling.

"I meant hunch as in inkling, a feeling or guess based on intuition rather than known facts," Franz told him. "Anyway I didn't notice anything wrong with your

back."

The man shook his head disgustedly. "Either you are lyingoryouareaterribledoctor." He turned around, presenting Franz with a good view of his back. Waggling his shoulders, he said, "Look! I have a really bad hunch. How could you not have noticed? It's practically the first thing people notice about me, that and the fact I'm so short and ugly."

"My apologies," Franz said.

"Don't bother apologizing. I'm used to prejudice. My name is Igor, by the way. Frankenstein sent me to find you. Follow me, this way, hurry up! They waited dinner for you. The meatloaf will be getting cold."

He turned to go, swinging the lantern in his powerful fist.

"Excuse me!" Franz said. "What is meatloaf?"

Igor gave a barking laugh. "I am beginning to think you are not only a terrible doctor but stupid. Meatloaf is a loaf made of ground meat mixed with a hen's egg, to which are added breadcrumbs and various spices. Meat. Loaf. It's self- explanatory."

"We are not familiar with that dish where I come from," Franz told him humbly. He wanted to stay on Igor's good side, at least until he learned where the strange little man stood in the hierarchy of the household. If he were a mere servant there would be plenty of time to put him in his place. He hoped that was so. He didn't think he could tolerate being bossed around by the sarcastic and insulting Igor.

He nudged the horse into a walk, following Igor as he lit the way through a break in the trees, past rugged stone gateposts on which a lichen-furred heraldic crest could be dimly made out in the gathering dusk. The ominous rumbling of thunder rolled through the mountains. It was followed by a flash of blue-white lightning, illuminating the turrets and battlements of a vast stone building.

"That's Frankenstein's castle. Impressive, isn't it?" Igor said.

It was, in a dreadful sort of way. The *Schloß* was immense, obviously ancient, built of rough-hewn stone. A multitude of towers sprouted crazily from its many roofs. It was perched on a promontory and seemed to look down on them with brooding enmity. A sense of insufferable gloom pervaded Franz's spirit. He had set out with high hopes, anticipating finding himself at the end of the journey among congenial company in well-lighted rooms where fires crackled merrily in the hearths. The desolate Castle Frankenstein failed miserably to live up to his expectations. It looked haunted.

The horse twitched its ears and stopped walking. Even it seemed taken back by the castle's inhospitable appearance.

"What's the matter? You seem kind of glum," Igor said.

"It is only that I have ridden a long way, and am tired, and hungry," Franz told him.

"Well, cheer up. You're here now, and you're going to have supper. Meatloaf and mashed turnips, yum! After you eat Frankenstein will probably want you to start right in and get to work. You'll be helping him with his big project. Lucky you! He's working on something that will astonish the world," Igor said.

"What is it?" Franz asked, intrigued.

Igor gazed up at him soberly. "Don't tell him I told you, but he's perfecting a new way of making sealing wax."

"What?" Franz said, startled. Sealing wax was one of life's staples. It came in sticks from the stationer's. Letters were sealed with it. Legal documents typically bore red wax seals to verify their authenticity. Franz had a signet ring inscribed with his initials which he used to make an impression in the carefully dripped wax that he sealed his letters with. Sealing wax had been around for centuries. So that was the Herr Doktor's big research project, making a new kind? It was a letdown after what Franz had been imagining: a scientific breakthrough involving miracle cures, or some new marvel like the ether used as a surgical anesthetic that had recently allowed surgeons at Boston's Massachusetts General Hospital to remove

a tumor from a man's neck without the usual thrashing and screaming,

Igor snickered. "I'm joking. You should have seen the look on your face!" He twisted his ugly face into an imbecilic expression of open-mouthed astonishment. "For a supposedly smart guy you're awfully gullible. It's not sealing wax. It's much better than that. Frankenstein will tell you all about it. Ah! There's Frau Gruber. Come on!"

A woman had appeared in the portico beneath a Gothic archway. She was tall and broad-shouldered, with the grim aspect of a prison matron. She and looked capable of chopping down a good-sized tree with a few expertly aimed strokes of an ax. Somberly dressed in a long grey skirt and shirtwaist, she wore a white lace cap over iron gray hair parted severely in the center. Franz's heart sank still further. The bunch of keys on the chain at her waist gave the clue to her identity: she was the housekeeper. She held a pewter candelabrum in which were white tapers, their flames fluttering and bending in the cold breeze from the approaching thunderstorm.

"*Wilkommen*," she intoned in a hollow voice. "Welcome to Castle Frankenstein. Come in before you are drenched by the rain and you catch the grippe and die."

"Go with Frau Gruber," Igor told him, reaching up with a thick finger and poking Franz painfully in the thigh. "I'll take your horse to the stable and bring your things to your room. You'll probably want to give me a tip now, to make sure I'm extra-careful with your belongings. You wouldn't want them getting torn or dirty or anything.

Franz swung down from the saddle and flexed his shoulders, relieved to be standing after his long ride. He reached into his purse and placed a coin in Igor's outstretched palm. Igor glanced at it and kept his palm out, wiggling his fingers. "More, or ink might get spilled on your nice books and things, totally by accident, you understand," he said.

Thinking of his treasured volume of *Faust*, a gift from his mother, Franz gave him another coin.

"Come inside," Frau Gruber told him, smiling horribly. "The master has been waiting for you."

Thunder boomed, making Franz jump. It was followed by a sizzling bolt of lightning that struck one of the massive evergreens at the foot of the drive with a sound like cannon fire. The tree burst into flames. Frau Gruber regarded it impassively. "Either it will burn itself out or it will spread and set the forest alight. Nothing we can do about it. Come inside."

Inside it was hardly warmer than it was outside. The floor was made of stone flags on which the heels of Franz's riding boots thumped noisily. He tried to walk more softly. *Lieber Gott*, the place was cold! Wall sconces fitted with wax tapers gave a feeble light to an echoing entrance hall that rose thirty feet to a vaulted ceiling from which carved Gothic doo-dads dripped, like stalactites in a cave. Franz counted a dozen suits of rusty armor. On the walls were ranks of wooden plaques with antlers mounted on them, complete with skulls. Age-darkened ancestral portraits in gilded frames sneered down at him, the faces indicating

their owners had been either haughty or dissolute, or both.

All the heavy oak doors beneath arched stone doorways were closed, except for one. It was open partway, enough for Franz to hear the plaintive strains of a violin

being played.

"They're in there," Frau Gruber said, jerking her chin at the doorway. "I must see to dinner. The cook is subject to fits and the kitchen maids are kept locked in or else they will run away. It is not easy finding help out here. The local peasants are ignorant and superstitious. They think the master is in league with the Devil because, well...never mind. They just do. Now in you go," she gave him a hard

shove, propelling him through the doorway.

Franz found himself in a drawing room decorated with old-fashioned good taste. A tall, thin man dressed in evening clothes held a violin. His prematurely white hair was wildly tousled. He looked to be in his mid-thirties and his long, intelligent face bore a resemblance to a number of the ancestral portraits in the

hall.

On a divan upholstered in dove grey satin lounged a woman. She wore a peach-colored gown with a square neckline and a high waist and was the most extraordinary creature Franz had ever seen, startlingly beautiful in a disturbing way. Young and slender, little more than a child, she reminded him of Schneewittchen, the maiden from *Grimms' Fairy Tales*, with her skin white as

alabaster, her hair black as raven feathers, and her lips as red as cherries.

Reading that description one would think that sounds rather delightful, but seeing it personified was troubling. Franz wondered if she might have consumption, she was so pale, but then her lips wouldn't be so red. Unless she painted them, as some women do, although not generally the type of young lady one meets in a castle. He realized he was staring. Collecting himself, he bowed from the waist

and clicked his heels together smartly.

"*Guten Abend*. I apologize for my lateness. I am Franz Wilhelm von Richter, and you must be..."

The young lady cut him off. Turning to the man with the violin, she said, "Look, Victor! He has golden hair, like my fiancé Johannes."

The man placed the violin in its velvet-lined case and advanced on Franz with a smile, a long-fingered hand outstretched. "I am Victor Frankenstein. So glad you're here! Pay no attention to Elsa; my poor wife is sometimes confused." He took Franz's hand and leaned close to whisper in his ear, his shaggy white hair

tickling Franz's cheek. "She reads novels. They fill her head with foolishness."

The young lady sat up, her hands clasped beseechingly at her breast. "When can I return to Johannes, Victor? He will be out of his mind with worry. I fell ill at the dance to celebrate our engagement. I seem to recall I died and was buried. Could

that be true?" Her hands flew to her pale cheeks and she shrieked.

With two swift strides Frankenstein went to a glass-fronted cabinet and removed a small bottle filled with a clear liquid. Pouring a little into a glass he added some

brandy from a decanter on a sideboard.

"I am your husband, *Liebchen*. There is no Johannes. Have some of your medicine; it will dispel these foolish fancies," he told Elsa, proffering the glass.

"I don't want it," she said, pushing it away.

Frankenstein shot Franz a swift look of apology. "Sorry, she gets like this sometimes," he said.

To Elsa, in the wheedling tone of voice used when speaking to a stubborn child he said, "You don't want me to summon Frau Gruber, do you? Drink your medicine

like a good girl."

Elsa wearily closed her eyes, her eyelashes like black feather fans against her white skin. She accepted the glass and swallowed the contents. Franz was fascinated. She was probably a madwoman, but if so, she was the most attractive madwoman he'd ever seen.

"Time for dinner," Frankenstein said to Franz as the sound of a gong came from somewhere in the distance. "You must be hungry after your long journey. Some meatloaf and turnips will soon fix that. No need for you to dress. We're quite

informal here."

"Meatloaf again?" Elsa murmured wonderingly. Her eyes were half-shut and she slumped against the arm of the divan.

"That's right, darling. Meatloaf again. Haha! Aren't we fortunate! Come along," her husband said, grasping her arm and hauling her to her feet.

"Take her other arm," he said to Franz, who did so. Between them they half- walked, half-dragged the semi-conscious Elsa into the entrance hall and up a flight of stairs where a black bear reared on the landing, its fangs bared, its eyes glaring menacingly. Franz was frightened for a moment until he realized it was

stuffed.

Frankenstein guided them into a baronial dining room with dark red walls. A table long enough to seat fifty was set at one end with three places. He inserted Elsa into a high-backed chair carved from dark-colored wood and indicated the

chair opposite it.

"Please, sit," he told Franz. "Have some wine. We have a good cellar here. You will find it makes up for our being cut off from the world." He poured wine into Franz' glass and then into his own. "Some Gewürztraminer, yes? Afterwards we will have a fine old amontillado. We are quite civilized here, far from the nuisances of city life, with its gossip, its police courts, its small-minded individuals who attempt to ruin one's reputation by claiming that what he's doing is...ah! Here is

Frau Gruber with our dinner!"

The housekeeper entered carrying a platter on which was a long brown thing with strips of crisp bacon on top: the meatloaf, Franz supposed. Igor followed bearing a white porcelain bowl heaped with an orange mound of mashed turnips. They

set the food down on the table and Igor proceeded to serve them.

Frankenstein accepted his portion and turned to Franz. "Try the bacon. Igor slaughtered the pig himself. He is quite handy, our Igor."

"*Danke*," Igor said, smiling modestly. "It's good to know I'm appreciated. I help Herr Doktor with a lot of things. For instance I helped him dig up..."

"Turnips," Frankenstein put in quickly. He gave Igor a warning look. "You helped dig up these turnips, isn't that right?"

"Yes, the turnips," Igor agreed. "What else would a reclusive scientist whom the local peasants hate and fear and his loyal manservant possibly be digging up?"

Franz found the meatloaf surprisingly good. The wine warmed him and he began to feel a bit more cheerful. Frankenstein was obviously a cultivated man, speaking learnedly of topics ranging from opera to fly-fishing. Franz thought he would be a good mentor, someone with whom it would be a pleasure to work, from whom he could learn much.

Meanwhile Elsa had come out of her stupor and was languidly making swirls in the turnips on her plate with the tines of a heavy silver fork.

"Eat your dinner, *Liebchen*," Frankenstein told her. "The dead don't eat," she replied.

Lightning flickered outside the leaded windows.

Frankenstein laughed. "But you are not dead, and so you can enjoy your nice dinner. If you don't want any meatloaf at least try the turnips. Then we shall have

pudding. Cook made vanilla *Kaesencremespeise*."
Frau Gruber stamped her foot. "She can't have pudding if she won't eat her meat.

How can she have any pudding if she won't eat her meat?"

Feeling embarrassed by this bickering Franz changed the subject and asked Frankenstein if he would show him his laboratory.

Frankenstein beamed. "I would be delighted. I am proud of my laboratory. It is equipped with the very finest in glass and porcelain vessels for chemical experimentation. You may find it resembles the laboratory of Robert Bunsen at Heidelberg, which is no coincidence because he and I carry on a correspondence. It is through Herr Bunsen that I learned of you, my dear Franz. May I call you by

your proper name, is that all right?"

"Certainly," said Franz, flattered. So Bunsen had spoken well of him! That was good to know. He'd found the florid-faced instructor, inventor of the Bunsen burner, to be lively and quick with jokes, even when he was recovering from the effects of arsenic poisoning which he deliberately gave himself not once but several times as part of his chemical research. Bunsen was courteous to students, unlike some of Franz's professors, who shouted at them and called them names

like "blockhead" and "stupid pig-dog."

Elsa leaned over the table toward him. "Victor keeps mice in cages in his laboratory, white mice. He does things to them," she confided.

There is nothing unusual in that, Franz thought. He didn't like the look of exasperation, even anger, in Frankenstein's eyes. It was there and gone in a split

second. Igor poured him more wine.

"Speaking of mice, or rather bats," the dwarf told him, "I put your things in the Blue Room. It's at the base of the east tower. Whatever you do, don't open the

connecting door that leads to the tower."

"There are bats in the tower, hundreds, possibly thousands of bats. You wouldn't think one tower could hold so many bats, but it does," put in Frau Gruber. The

thought of so many bats packed into a tower seemed to please her.

"There have always been bats in the east tower," Frankenstein said philosophically. He placed his knife and fork in the center of his plate with the handles resting on the rim, and folded his white linen napkin, leaving it to the left of his plate. "We don't bother them and they don't bother us. Now, let's have some of cook's

excellent *Kaesencremespeise*."

Late that night Franz fled Castle Frankenstein, terrified by what he'd seen in

Frankenstein's laboratory. It wasn't the glass beakers and retorts and the other equipment ranged on the stone-topped tables that frightened him, or the mice scurrying in their cages; he was familiar with those things from his work in Heidelberg. It was Frankenstein's shocking revelation that sent him running away in terror. He claimed to be working on the study of blood, in order to prove

that it came in different "types," as he put it.

That, to Franz, was utterly bizarre. It went against everything he'd been taught. Blood was blood. Red and sticky. The blood of a pauper was the same as that of a king. Transfusions were commonplace. Sometimes the patient died afterwards, but patients were always dying. The idea there could be different kinds went against accepted medical knowledge, indicating an unhealthy fixation with the stuff.

"I have taken blood from the housemaids, and from Igor and Frau Gruber. Perhaps you will allow me to take some of yours, my dear Franz," Frankenstein said. He advanced on him with a hypodermic syringe, a gleam in his eyes.

If he's not a vampire, he'd the next thing to it, Franz thought. He's a monster. I must get away from here without alarming him.

"It would be my pleasure," he told Frankenstein, smiling in what he hoped was a confident and relaxed manner. "But I am tired now. Tonight I must sleep. In the

morning when I am fresh you may have as much of my blood as you like."

He packed his things and sat up, anxiously listening at the door to his room until the castle was silent. Then he crept out taking care not to make any noise, like a thief in the night. He went to the stable and saddled his horse, tearing off down

the road, away from that nightmarish place.

"The young man has gone. He left this note," Igor told Frankenstein in the morning. He handed him a sheet of writing paper on which the following was scrawled: *Urgent business that I had forgotten about until this moment calls me back to Heidelberg. I won't be taking the position of your assistant. My apologies for any*

inconvenience. F.W. von Richter

"I counted the spoons. None are missing. He seemed like the type who might steal the teaspoons. His eyes were too close together," Frau Gruber said.

"It's a shame, him leaving like that," Frankenstein said. He speared a sausage and cut it into pieces with his knife. Elsa sat opposite him, looking off into space and humming tunelessly. Frankenstein went on, "He seemed like a nice young fellow. Once we became better acquainted I was looking forward to sharing with him how I was able to raise Elsa from the dead. Oh well, it can't be helped. Perhaps it's best if I carry on my research without an assistant. Young people are so unpredictable."

NO MORE IRON CROSS
JAYAPRAKASH SATYAMURTHY

He asked me to come visit him in his axe lodge. I didn't find that strange; after all we were at a metal concert and that is the sort of thing you will hear from metalheads. I met him because he was hanging out with an acquaintance I was trying to dissociate myself from. He was just a little older than me, this acquaintance, and I was nearly middle-aged myself. He attended metal concerts in full combat gear: camouflage jacket and trousers, calf-length boots. I didn't mind any of this, just the usual sort of posturing you see with metal fans, but he also wore a replica Nazi-era Iron Cross, complete with ribbon, and I minded that very much. Every time I met Iron Cross, it was at the sidelines of some noisy metal concert. He was always drunk and would always buttonhole me, telling me how much weight I had lost since we last met. It happened to be true, each time; I think that may have been the real reason I wished to dissociate myself from him. Precisely how much weight did I have left to lose? Not enough.

He moved in a pack, big burly men like him, all just a little older than me and wearing denim vests covered in metal band insignias or kitted out in combat gear. Lots of chains and boots. This particular fellow was a bit taller than me, and much wider, most of it muscle. He was wearing a black t-shirt with the sleeves cut off to reveal well-defined upper arm muscles. It was a Black Flag t-shirt, kind of an unusual choice for a metalhead in Bangalore. He also wore a jade pendant on a thin silver chain around his neck. Pale blue jeans and dark grey canvas shoes, none of the camos or boots or patches or chains his buddies favoured. Trying to escape from Iron Cross' drunken chatter, I struck up a conversation with Black Flag. It turned out we had friends in common and he used to play guitars for a thrash metal band from late 90s that I'd heard of, even watched once at a concert. Our conversation took on some momentum and Iron Cross drifted away into some other discussion, or maybe the band on stage had struck up a song he particularly liked.

Black Flag and I spoke a bit about punk rock, which I did not really know a lot about, but I had been listening to some Dead Kennedys lately and there was that first record by The Adolescents which had always been a favourite of mine. A gap in the noise from the stage provided a suitable juncture to conclude our chat. As I walked away, he called me back and pressed a piece of paper into my hand. 'Come visit me sometime in my axe lodge.' I believe I replied with some lame salutation like 'hails' before moving on. I glanced at the paper; it was a phone number. I scrunched it into a pocket.

I was not worried about being picked up; I had been propositioned by homosexuals in the past and this didn't have the same vibe. I wasn't sure, however, that I really wanted a new friend. Nonetheless, when I reached home, I pulled out the piece of paper from my pocket and keyed the number into my mobile phone and then forgot all about Black Flag.

Several weeks later, towards the end of a particularly tiresome week at work, my phone started ringing. The screen simply said 'Black Flag dude' and it took me a few moments to remember who that was. Curious, but also a little reluctant because I was in no mood for a conversation, I answered the call. 'Hey, Jay, it's me. Marcus.' So that was his name. 'Hey Marcus, how's life?' 'To be honest, it kinda sucks just now. So I'm taking off to the old axe lodge. Why don't you drop in, hoist a few flagons, slay some dragons?' I wondered if the last bit was some sort of drug reference, and I don't personally indulge in anything heavier than some whiskey and weed, but I was just jaded and frustrated enough to be up for a change, even if it was some lame wannabe-macho metalhead junkie weekend bash. 'Yeah, sure. Where is it?' He said he would text me a Google Maps link. The place was just outside the city, beyond Bannerghata Zoological Park. It was set back from the main road by about half a kilometer. I shrugged. A bit far to go, but well out of the city noise.

Marcus had called me at around 7 PM on a Friday evening. I reached his axe lodge three hours later. Following the directions given by the Google Maps woman, I turned off the highway and rode down a tree-lined dirt road with a wooden fence on each side. At the end of it, there was a large pair of wrought iron gates with spikes on top. There were already nine motorcycles, a couple of SUVs and a jeep outside. I parked my bike beside the others and went up to the gate. There was a door inset in the left gate. It swung open when I pushed it, so I stepped in.

Two dwarves holding those long-bladed knives with a hook-like curve at the end of the blade, what the newspapers used to call 'swords' when reporting on gang violence, marched up to me. They were wearing brown leather fringed vests and garish red leggings with salmon pink tubing down the sides. They looked like extras from some Kannada historical film which hadn't paid too much attention to authenticity. They held their knives up to – well to my midriff, they didn't really reach much higher. Not sure whether to be amused or entertained, I kept silent. 'You follow us,' one of the dwarves said in a deep, resonant voice. It seemed like too large a voice for such a small man. He glared up at me as if he'd been reading my thoughts, then he and his colleague started trotting down a path between two large hedges. I strode briskly after them. The path twisted and turned so many times it became clear that it was a maze. A hedge maze in this time and place! I was considering asking my escorts if they were lost when we emerged into a large clearing. At the other end of the clearing was a long, low wooden building, like a traditional Mangalore house gone feral. The axe lodge. It even had a pair of crossed axes above the doorway. The lead dwarf told me that I was to enter the house.

Inside, everything was dark. I could vaguely make out animal skin rugs laid out on the floor, wall hangings with crude geometrical patterns on them, low tables, boxes, sacks; a bit of a mess, basically. At the far end of the hall was another door; this lead out a place where I could see a bright, wavering light and many silhouettes moving about. I heard voices, loud and jovial. I was certain Marcus' voice could be heard amongst them. I walked through the second door and came upon something very like a banquet scene from an Asterix album. There was a huge, roaring fire in the centre with tables and benches were arranged around it in a rough circle. All around the fire was a fence made up of crossed axes, tied together at their heads.

The men seated at the tables could have been metalheads, or bikers, or village toughs. They had coarse beards and/or long hair, and large, muscular bodies. I am not burly myself, in fact I'd been steadily losing weight for a couple of years, but I am tall, and I had been going through a bearded phase for a few months, so I fit in reasonably well. As I reached the tables, I noticed the serving staff – youths and maidens in white robes, carrying platters of food or large jugs of drink. I thought I saw Iron Cross in the crowd. Seated at the head of an especially large table was Marcus. He spotted me and called out my name, beckoning me over. A space was found at his table for me. Someone passed me a tall clay mug - a flagon - of beer. Someone passed me a plate heaped high with roasted beef, liberally seasoned with green chillies.

As the night passed, the flames leaped higher and higher and so did my spirits. There was a steady sound of drumming from somewhere just out of sight, and sometimes I could hear the drone of a tanpura emerging between the beats. After an hour or so, the plates and flagons were cleared away. The servants damped the fire down to a small blaze, just a few feet high. They untied the axes brought them to us. A little drunk, mildly euphoric, I accepted an axe and joined in the circle the men were making around the fire. The drums locked into a steady, fourfold beat and flutes joined in, repeating an upbeat, insistent motif. We started to dance around the fire. I soon got the hang of the dance. I thought to myself that this must be some sort of Men's Movement thing, like in America, where stockbrokers and ad executives take off on weekends to form drum circles and get shamanic in smoke tents.

The men started to whoop and holler; I joined in. After a while, Marcus turned towards the fire, took a flying leap over it. We all cheered. The circle continued to move. Every now and then, Marcus would tap someone with the handle of his axe and they would leap over the fire. When it was my turn, I made the leap with inches to spare. Bellowing in triumph, I joined the circle again, ready to leap again if need be. A few turns later, one of the men fell short, right into the fire. I was about to run to his aid, but someone held me back. The music stopped. We watched in silence as he writhed and screamed in agony. At last, he dragged himself away from the flames and was lead away by the two dwarfs, who had appeared on the scene when the screaming began.

The drumming started again. Half a dozen or so of the assembled men had not yet made the jump. They all had their turn. No one else fell. Finally, we were lead to a spot a few meters away where a row of the servants knelt on the ground, their hands tied behind them. Marcus walked up to the first servant, pushed him so that he was bent over even more, and then, with a great swing of his axe, beheaded the man. I watched, too confused to register a coherent reaction, as each of the men followed his example. By the time it was my turn, there were pools of cooling gore on the ground, blood on the hands and faces of the men, and I was too terrified to refuse. It took me three blows to behead the servant, an eternity of loud, animal screaming before I hacked her head off and silenced her. I stepped away from the corpse and threw up. Marcus came over to me. He patted me on the back and smiled at me. He handed me a leather flask and asked me to drink up. I did. It was rice arrack, very strong and fierce.

Later there was more feasting. A little before daybreak, we were lead to a place within the building and told that we could sleep. I lay down on a piece of sackcloth and quickly fell asleep.

It was already afternoon when I woke up. I could hear bird calls, the wind rustling through leaves. The house was dusty, the air stale. Outside, there were very faint burned patches where the banquet had been. Decayed remains of what might have been benches and tables. At the killing place, no traces remained of the blood that had been shed last night. I walked back through the house, emerged on the other side. No dwarfs turned up to obstruct or escort me. I walked back to the gate, easily finding my way through the withered remains of the hedge-maze. The gate was also in a shambles, rusted and falling apart. Outside, several of the vehicles were missing, and of the ones that remained, only my bike was still intact. A couple of other bikes were still there, but gutted and rusted as was the jeep I'd seen last night. I walked up to my bike. My helmet still dangled from the handlebar, my iPod stashed away inside. I plugged in my earbuds, pulled on my headphones. The bike started smoothly, the engine humming, ready to go. I put 'Protection' by Massive Attack on repeat and headed out.

All the way home, the woman sang 'You're a girl and I'm a boy' in my ears. 'You're a girl and I'm a boy.'

I thought for a while that this was some sort of Rip Van Winkle deal and that a great many years would have elapsed since I had gone down to the axe lodge. Certainly, the state of things at the lodge had suggested as much. Out on the highway, it became clear that this was not the case. I recognised the same hoardings, the same political posters, the same buildings and signboards I'd seen last night. I stopped at a hotel for a meal, bought a copy of a newspaper. It was Saturday, the day after I'd gone to Marcus'. So I hadn't even lost a day.

Back home, I collapsed into bed and slept through the rest of the day and most of the night. I headed out for work as usual, trying not to think about what I'd been doing on Friday night. I settled in at my workstation, checking my office email, opening the layouts I'd been working on last week. Around me, my colleagues started drifting in, exchanging greetings, stepping out in twos and threes for cigarettes and coffee. I started revising a layout, using work as a substitute for thinking. So it was only around 11 AM when I finally looked up and realised Iron Cross was sitting next to me. He was wearing a light blue half-sleeved shirt and dark grey cotton trousers and had short hair in a conventional cut. I could make out a religious talisman worn on a black thread around his neck. No more Iron Cross. I tried to make conversation with him, but it turned out that even though he knew me well enough as a colleague, he knew nothing about attending concerts and listening to heavy metal music. I stepped out for a cigarette. I spotted Marcus in a nearby cluster of smokers, walked over to him. He greeted me with the air of a long-term acquaintance, but was genuinely bemused when I tried to raise the topic of the axe lodge. 'Axolotl?' he asked, confused.

Over the course of the day, I realised that a majority of my colleagues were large, stocky men with beards and/or long hair. They were vaguely familiar - I was sure I had seen them that night. They all gave the impression of having worked in the agency for a long time and knew me to a lesser or greater degree, but had no idea about the lodge or a banquet or any of the things I remembered and I soon gave up asking anyone about it. I had my biggest shock when my team had to present revised layouts to a manager who turned out to be a dwarf with a surprisingly deep, sonorous voice.

Time passed. It was as if life had returned completely to normal and everything was exactly the way it used to be, except that the cast had been shuffled around, extras from one production transferred to another. I stopped losing weight, and when I attended concerts I met some of my old friends from the scene, but never that particular set of acquaintances which used to cluster around Iron Cross. I had been trying to distance myself from that man and his crowd, anyway. I just couldn't remember for sure if they'd been the same lot as the crowd at the axe lodge, at my office now, apart of course from 'Iron Cross' and 'Marcus'. Nothing strange, nothing strange in that particular way, happened again.

Many months later, my department received a group email from management. We were being sent to a weeklong team building workshop. I reacted in my usual way - a little loath to be carted off to some place away from my comfort zone, a little pleased to be getting a free holiday. I didn't see the one really strange thing until I was in the bus with my colleagues and people started speculating about the name of the resort we were being taken to. It was in Chikmagalur and it was called 'Axe Lodge'. A few people made jokes about deodorants and sexually available women. I looked intently at 'Marcus' and the other burly men. None of them seemed to have any unusual reaction to resort's name.

I was in a state of heightened anticipation throughout the rest of the journey, waiting for everyone to revert to type, for the white-robed servants to appear, for moonlit revels, ghastly rites, ghastly nights of blood and booze, but the resort was the usual sort of thing: a swimming pool, tennis courts, manicured lawns and landscaped gardens, an outdoor bar and everything that went on there remained resolutely mundane. The workshop leader was a Parsi ex-military man, a jovial, bombastic, fiercely intelligent fellow who asked us to call him Sam. He injected a certain verve into the proceedings, and I was appreciative of a small speech he made about overcoming prejudices. It didn't play well with some of my colleagues, who felt he should have 'avoided sensitive topics', but I liked it, especially when he said that we should just rent a large arena and let all the fundamentalists and the chauvinists and homophobes battle it out for the entertainment of the rest of society. Well, it made sense to me, but I've never believed in much, myself.

I found the team-building activities refreshing. They were so amiable, civilized, they were predicated on such a fundamentally modern, humanist paradigm of humanity, even if intended in the service of corporate efficiency. As the days went by, I often took the lead in figuring out cryptic clues or finding a path through a maze or obstacle course. It helped that, although I was pretty skinny, I was in better physical shape than my colleagues, those large men brushing up against middle age, their youthful muscle mass was turning to fat. Only 'Marcus' and a couple of others retained their muscle tone and strength, but I was able to match them on anything that required stamina rather than strength. I had a distinct edge in the more cerebral challenges, although I sometimes got mathematical clues wrong. I didn't really learn anything new about myself or about teamwork, but I was not expecting to. It all reminded me of a game show I'd loved as a child, 'The Crystal Maze', even if the settings were less elaborate. That sense of being part of a game, part of a show, an entertainment, was soothing. I knew narrative logic would see me through.

On the last day, there was a campfire and we were given white robes to wear. These were familiar in design and my unease returned. I was on high alert all evening, but all that happened were a few speeches, awards handed out to everyone, a round or two of singing old Bollywood songs, dinner and drinks by the pool. No bonfire, no circle dance, nothing but a convivial night with colleagues.

Back at work, things went on as usual. My life went on as usual. I am tempted to say I sometimes found tokens of that night at the axe lodge - bloody rags in my bathroom at home, dry leaves spilling out of my desk drawer at work - but it never happened. I worked in an office staffed by a rather large percentage of big-built men with the appearance of bikers or metalheads or village toughs, but it takes all sorts to make a world. The only real difference was that I knew I could kill someone if I had to. At least, I was reasonably sure that I already had, and that should count for something if it ever came up again.

ADMITTED INHABITANTS
DOMINIQUE LAMSSIES

Ayaks stopped running at the edge of a clearing and pressed her hand to the tree next to her. The full moon gave her enough light to scrutinize her surroundings.

After the incident at breakfast she had started running northeast, but she did not know the forests around Hartford as well as she had those around Mystic. It had been a mistake to flee so recklessly. But her recklessness had drawn the Englishmen into an unfamiliar forest. This would allow her to finish them at her leisure.

She heard nothing and fretted that she had outrun them. The five men that had followed her were young and fit. They should have no trouble keeping up with her unless she had unintentionally lost them. She knew they would not give up. A Congregationalist would never give up so long as a Pequot was left alive.

Something caught her eye and she looked down. The white apron around her waist glowed in the moonlight. She was still dressed as one of them. She untied the apron, then pulled the collar and cuffs from the black dress, glad of the sounds the seams made when they burst. The coif came off last. She pulled apart the plaits under it until her thick, straight, black hair tumbled down her back. Now she wore only black, a fitting color for a night hunter.

A day, on foot, from Hartford. She had them where she wanted them. It was time to close the trap.

She gathered up the scraps of cloth and threw them into the clearing. She screamed, then crouched low to the ground and watched.

There was a moment of silence, then she heard brush being trampled. The sound grew closer and she heard whispering. She stared at the trees until two men came into view.

Beecher and Dyer. The group had separated. The others wouldn't be far away though. She smiled. Two of them would be much quicker work then all five at once.

The pair crept into the clearing. Eyes ever watchful, Dyer stepped forward to examine the scraps.

"Clothing." He straightened. "Do you think an animal took her?"

Beecher's gaze roved the forest. "It would be God's justice for killing Goodman Pitkin. Is there blood on the clothing?"

Dyer bent down and picked up a cuff. "Nay." He threw it back on the ground. "Had she been attacked we would have heard the struggle."

Beecher lowered his gun slightly. He smirked.

"I think Goodman Pitkin was a fool."

Dyer's brow creased. "A fool?"

"Aye. Thinking he could tame a savage was foolish. There is a reason the Pequots had to be slain to the last at Fort Mystic." Beecher seemed quite satisfied with himself.

Dyer's eyes widened when he caught Beecher's meaning. His eyes searched for movement as he said, "Nay, Beecher. Goodman Pitkin was a holy man. If anyone could have succeeded, it would have been him. The Pitkins took marvelous care of her. I dare not think how betrayed Goody Pitkin feels."

Rage surged in Ayaks. Her jaw set and her hand slowly slid the knife out of her boot. The scars the Pitkins had left on her back and arms burned. Her thigh muscles twitched to spring at them. She knew they were trying to goad her into revealing herself and it was very nearly working.

A gunshot and a man's scream came from the darkness beyond Beecher.

Beecher craned his neck to look. Dyer turned his back to Ayaks.

She slipped out of her hiding place. Her arm snaked around Dyer's neck and squeezed, pinning him to her. er knife hand flashed out and drove the blade deep into the small of his back. His legs gave out and his body slumped against her. She held him and twisted the blade deeper. Dyer screamed.

Beecher turned back and raised his musket in one motion.

"You filthy heathen," he spat. "How dare you murder one of God's chosen."

It was her turn to smirk at him. "A little poison in his breakfast and I gave him his wish. If he was as godly as he thought, he is at The Lord's right hand and your anger is unfounded." She let Dyer's body droop as if her arm was tiring.

Beecher pulled the trigger. Ayaks jerked Dyer's body up to form a shield. The man's head snapped back as the musket ball struck his forehead. Ayaks let the body fall.

"A fine shot, Goodman Beecher," she smirked. She sauntered toward him. "I can wait for you to reload, please you."

There was another scream and something splashed in water. Ayaks pointed in the direction of the sounds.

"Goodman Dyer was right. Had I been attacked by an animal it would sound like that."

Beecher did not take his eye off her as he loosened his grip on the musket and turned it in his hand.

"Goodman Pitkin gave you a good life, Ayaks. Better then you deserved," he spat.

She gave a mirthless laugh. "'Tis true. But a poor heathen can never understand the wisdom of an admitted inhabitant of Hartford." Her smile widened. "Pitkin said that to be admitted, you must be faithful to your god. You seek to be an admitted inhabitant of your colony," she hissed as she slithered forward. "But I shall make you a part of mine instead. We shall see if you are really among His chosen."

He growled as he swung the gun, cracking her across the face with all his might.

"I will not have a godless heathen preach to me of His will!" he cried.

An unsettling snap came from Ayaks's neck and her head dropped against her shoulder. Her body did not fall.

Ayaks lifted her hand. She pressed her chin up and to the right. There was another snap and her head rested normally upon her shoulders.

"Luck was on your side, Goodman Beecher. That was the old wound. It grows more feeble each time it breaks."

His eyes widened but he still had enough wits to pull his sword and slash at her. She dodged.

"I shall not preach to you. I shall educate you the way Pitkin educated me."

She rushed at Beecher, head lowered like a bull, and plowed into his torso.

He did not brace himself. Ayaks was slight and he did not expect her thrust to have any power behind it. But it was like being struck with a tree trunk. He landed on his back so hard it winded him. In the moment he struggled to get his breath back, she got in three blows to his face. Each felt like a boulder. He jerked his torso to buck her off, but her weight was so great that he could barely move.

She pounded his face as if she were grinding corn. The blood on her hands only stoked her wrath and her personal litany began to recite itself in her mind: *One blow for every day it had taken them to drag her as a frightened child from Fort Mystic to Hartford.*

When he reached up to stop her, she grabbed his wrist and used her free hand to punch his elbow. *One blow for each of the kin she'd lost when Fort Mystic burned.*

Beecher screamed when bone penetrated flesh. His other arm flailed involuntarily. Ayaks caught hold of it and broke it as well. *One blow for having to say she was "blessed" they had made a slave of her.*

He tried to steel himself the only way he knew how.

"My God," he slurred through bloody lips, "my Father and Preserver, who by your goodness…"

The garbled words pierced her mind like a well-shot arrow, freezing her fury for but a moment before an ungodly shriek erupted from her. She seized her fallen knife and rammed it up underneath his chin, forcing his jaw shut.

"Not those words again!" she howled, reverting to Pequot. *One blow for every time they had cuffed her to make her say those words.*

"*Never* those words again!" *One blow for every time that goggle-eyed wife of Pitkin's had watched her like a hawk, waiting for her to make a mistake so she could order another beating.*

She redoubled her efforts on his face.

A laugh that sounded like water falling over rocks checked her anger. She exhaled as she looked down.

Beecher's face looked worse than Dyer's after the bullet had hit it. She should have expected this. Beecher had been an infuriating child all the days she had known him.

She pulled her knife out of his crushed head and stood.

She took a deep breath to gather herself up and heard a man's death rattle in the distance.

She stepped away from the body and snarled as her dress flapped against her legs. She lifted a handful of it and forced the tip of her knife through it, rending a large gap in the fabric. She used the cut to tear most of it away and pitched it aside.

Without another thought she pushed deeper into the woods. She followed the rustling of something heavy being dragged across the ground. She stopped when movement caught her eye.

There was a monstrous snake on the forest floor, a darker black than the night itself. Her eye would have slipped right past it had she not known to look for it.

An Englishman was on the ground, his legs down the snake's gullet. Its muscles contracted, pulling more of its victim inside. It slithered back a little, its tail disappearing into a large puddle.

Ayaks bore her teeth at the serpent.

"The hunting is mine tonight! Give him to me!"

"Presumptuous beast," a smooth voice chided, the snake's red eyes focusing on her. "They all end up together and still you deny me my amusement? Such a human to be so selfish. I thought we were past that."

She rose her knife and jammed it into the snake. Its roar shook the trees around them. The snake's head floundered back, the Englishman's loose limbs thrashing in the air.

"Stop! Give him to me!" she cried, trying to catch the Englishman's arm.

The snake disappeared completely into the puddle.

"You took my knife! Tell me which way is northeast in return!" she insisted.

An icy gust of wind blew into her back and she knew northeast was straight ahead.

She did not walk long before she came to a clearing. Some Congregationalist looking for farmland had made it years ago.

A dirt path that had been inexplicably muddy and dotted with shifting puddles of various sizes since the day the land was cleared ran between a barn and a house. Both were rotted out, but the barn still stood. The house had collapsed in on itself. The field behind the house was overgrown with weeds.

She entered the house and ignored the shriveled, emaciated corpse that was slumped in the chair at the table. She had seen it more times then she could count. She cared only for the knife that rested in front of it. But before she could reach it, the dead man's hand scooped it up.

"That was unkind, flesh devil," the silken voice of the serpent said. The corpse sat up straight in his chair and crossed his legs, perusing the knife in his hand as if it were a jewel.

"Why do you inhabit that corpse so often? I am beginning to think you enjoy it." Ayaks leaned back on her heels and frowned. She would never say it, but she was glad enough to hear a voice speaking Pequot that she cared not if it came from The Dark One.

The dead face turned to her, but there was no life in the shriveled orbs in his eye sockets and his jaw did not move as he said, "but I do. Why do I do anything, my vicious little monster? Because it amuses me." The corpse threw his arms over his head and he bellowed, "I, Abbomocho, exists only for my own amusement! You, like all others, are simply my playthings."

The corpse turned the knife in his hand and offered the handle to her.

"Now I know you have spied on the Englishmen in their worship," she scoffed. She snatched the blade and turned to the window.

"I do not think I have met anyone quite as disrespectful as you." The corpse folded his hands into his lap. "You are blessed that you divert me so."

"Still your tongue. I cannot hear their approach."

"Ah, they are a few moments off yet. You need to learn to remain calm in battle. I gave you a rare gift. No matter what they do, you will get them in the end. That is why I allow you to be so insufferable. *I* will get *you* in the end. There is no reason to be impatient."

She heard feet sloshing through mud and she shushed the snake in human clothing.

Gideon and Adoniram, the last two of the group sent out to hunt her, crept cautiously down the path, muskets raised.

The corner of Ayaks's mouth twitched into a smile as she waited for it.

The face of both Englishmen twisted in disgust.

"What is that smell?" Gideon muttered.

"Rotten meat, I would think," Adoniram said.

Behind Ayaks, Abbomocho gave a laugh that sounded like air bubbles escaping the sea and the corpse collapsed against the table with a thunk.

Gideon turned his musket to the house.

But the door to the barn creaked open with a sound like a woman gasping, then footsteps hurried inside. Adoniram, ever the brave man with something to prove, marched to the barn. Ayaks would only have a few moments to finish Gideon before Abbomocho let the Congregationalist see what was in the barn.

Ayaks left the house. Gideon turned to face her, musket pointed at her.

"You forced us to do this, Ayaks," he said, and she could see in his eyes that he was unsure about killing her. "We tried to save you. We tried to show you God's light. None of us wanted to hurt you."

She bore down on him. "But he did hurt me."

"I am one of God's chosen people," he asserted. "He will not allow any harm to befall me."

She was close enough to strike him with her knife so he pulled the trigger.

The ball hit her in the chest. She did not cry out. Her face did not change. The wound did not bleed.

Fear seeped into Gideon's face. He dropped the musket and fumbled for his sword.

Ayaks shook her head. "You should not have been sent to hunt me."

He managed to draw his sword, but she slashed down on his wrist and he dropped it.

She scooped up the fallen musket and swung the butt of it, striking him across the face. His feet slipped out from under him and he fell. She pounced on him and slashed his throat. His hands flew to the wound as if they could keep the blood in. His mouth began working frantically and she knew what he was trying to say.

"Nay. This is a place of sacred darkness and we will not have your god of light desecrating it. None of your foul words here."

She turned him over so he lay face down and pressed a foot to the back of his head, forcing his face deeply into the mud.

His hands did not leave his neck and he did not struggle. Ayaks frowned, disappointed that he had given up so easily.

A bullet struck her forehead. Her head jerked back and when she straightened, Adoniram was in the doorway of the barn, musket smoking.

She took a step toward him and there was a subtle shift in his face. He knew what had happened was wrong, but he was not going to back down. He kept his musket in one hand, but pulled his sword with the other.

"Oh, Divine Father, in union with your Divine Son," he started.

Ayaks gritted her teeth. Another prayer she hated. But one that kept him from noticing that Gideon's body was moving.

"And the Holy Spirit, and through the Immaculate Heart-"

Gideon struggled to his feet. Adoniram went white. The body was covered in mud and blood but he could still tell it was dead. It lurched toward the barn and Adoniram backed away, step by step.

His face twisted as he covered his nose and mouth with the crook of his elbow.

"Come hither, Congregationalist," Abbomocho said from somewhere inside. "I wish you to admire my handiwork, please you. It was your kin that inspired it," the serpent cooed, its voice bouncing off the high wooden walls.

He was in an aisle between two rows of pews. The aisle led to an old, rotted wooden table that had sticks on it tied together in the shape of a cross. There was a book of some sort in front of the cross and a large puddle under it that took up the entire altar area.

The pews were full of corpses in varying states of decay, the source of the suffocating smell. Gideon's corpse shuffled in and sat on the back pew.

The door to the barn closed. Adoniram turned and saw Ayaks with her hand on the door. She moved toward him and a puddle bubbled up over the mud behind her. A black snake with red eyes emerged from the water and hovered before the door, blocking the exit.

Adoniram searched for a place to hide. There were a few candles offering feeble light. They created dark spots along the side of the building. He would have to cross one of the pews of corpses to get there. He decided to take the chance.

None of them moved as he passed and Ayaks did not follow. She walked up the aisle to the makeshift altar.

"Why do you seek to harm us? We offered you salvation!" he called as he quietly began to reload his musket.

"I know you are reloading. You do not need to hide the sound."

"Play along, wrathful fiend!" Abbomocho insisted. "Answer his question, please you!"

Ayaks rolled her eyes and sighed.

"Do you mean being beaten to death? That is the salvation Pitkin offered me. He beat me so fiercely my neck was broken. But Abbomocho was watching."

"This method of worship you Congregationalists practice seemed entertaining and I thought to try it," the snake interrupted.

"Abbomocho is a great one for pranks," Ayaks said. "I made him a bargain. If he kept this body moving until it rotted away, I would make him a congregation."

Adoniram peaked up over the pew next to him and saw her pacing in front of the table. She needed to stand still for him to have a chance of hitting.

"It has been a year since Pitkin killed me and I have almost filled his church. Tis mostly English, but there are a few Dutch, some Mohegan. Ah, and Narragansett. Every chance I get I take a Narragansett. It was they who killed my mother and father after we escaped the fires at Fort Mystic." She stopped at the head of the aisle and stared off in thought. He aimed his musket at her. "You call us savages, but you were trying to wipe us out, same as we wanted to wipe you out. Now I see it must be this way. You English had to kill every

Pequot. Because we would have harried you until you lay beaten and broken, the life slipping away from you, willing to ask the help of whoever, *whatever*, came along first offering. You were the ones to succeed though. That makes you the better savages."

He pulled the trigger. The ball struck her chest.

She sighed, annoyed. "You shot my head. Did you think shooting my chest was better?"

He stood. He dropped the musket. "I am one of God's chosen," he declared as he strode back to the center aisle. "I am an admitted inhabitant of the colony of Hartford. I do God's work and I will cast out you devils."

"You have always done God's work. Now come and receive your reward," she hissed.

Something reared up out of the puddle under the table. It was twice as large as the snake by the door. He could not see its head because of the great mass of stringy, shaggy hair that veiled everything underneath it but two bulbous red eyes. It stretched up until it almost touched the roof of the barn, then set down two long, thin arms that ended in knobby claws.

The corpses in the pews sat up straight and bowed their heads. Each one pressed it palms together in prayer and they began to sing. Adoniram knew it was an Indian prayer and the further blasphemy made his blood boil.

Ayaks started down the aisle and Adoniram advanced to meet her.

He did not hesitate. He swung his sword as soon as she was within reach. She twisted away, but he cut away part of her dress, revealing the rotting flesh underneath.

She swung her knife at his sword arm, but he was too quick on his feet. She hunched to charge him. He pivoted out of her path and she fell into a pew. Adoniram stabbed her in the back. She went flat against the wood as if the wound had hurt her. But as soon as he pulled the blade free, she rounded and planted her knife in his chest. She pressed her chest to his, both hands pushing on the knife hilt. She walked forward, forcing him backward.

He rose his sword, but before he could swing she twisted the knife. He cried out and his arm fell but he did not drop his sword. She gave him begrudging respect for that.

She pressed him back until they reached Abbomocho. She gave Adoniram a shove and he fell back. She straddled the body, removed the knife and stabbed the Englishman's chest several more times, spending the last of her wrath.

"I like this one," Abbomocho cooed in Pequot. "He will make a fine addition to the congregation."

Ayaks stood as Adoniram's corpse got to its feet. It shuffled to the back pew and sat next to Gideon. As soon as it did the other corpses slumped and fell silent.

"You cannot go back to an English colony looking as you are," Abbomocho pointed out.

"I do not need to. The Narragansett need thinning." Ayaks dug two fingers into the wound in her forehead and pulled the ball out. "How much longer will this be amusing to you?"

One of the serpent's long arms went out and its claw nudged the head of a Dutchman to watch it wobble. "Awhile yet. Your body will not last much longer after the punishment it took tonight. Then no one will fill my congregation and I will grow bored and find a new plaything. I think I will mourn you though. You have been one of my favorite toys."

"You are the only one who will be sad I am dead. I will see to that." She turned away from the serpent. She left the barn, closing the door firmly behind her.

BITTER WATERS

Daniel Brock

Liza squeezed her eyes shut, causing more tears to streak her face. Her father, who had consoled her throughout most of the night, begged her not to come with him to the grave. She didn't listen. She followed him out the door and into the field.

The field was beautiful this time of year. Bright flowers inched their way towards the heavens, the trees were budding with pink and white blooms, and the sweet smell of new life swirled on the breeze. Yet instead of playing in the grass and enjoying the spring, Liza marched towards death. Ugly, horrible, death.

She spotted a dandelion in the grass, stout with a thick white bloom. She picked it, thinking in a roundabout way that it would be perfect to lay at her brother's grave. Dandelions were Liza's favorite. She liked to pick a whole handful of them by the river, mush the fluffy white tops together, and pretend the great white mass was a cloud, all the way from heaven that she was lucky enough to have caught.

In those moments, listening to the soft roar of the river, she felt like she was looking down from heaven. Her breath became the wind, her eyes the sun that overlooked it all.

But now, watching her father shovel dirt over her brother's handmade coffin, all she could do was weep. Once the final shovelful fell, Liza's father patted the pregnant looking mound of earth and went to fetch the tombstone, leaving Liza alone with Miller.

She sat in the grass next to the freshly turned dirt and placed the dandelion on top of the grave. She was almost cried out for the moment, but not for lack of sadness. Miller had been more than her brother, he had been her best friend, the only real company she had in their secluded corner of the woods. At the tender age of fourteen, he had caught a strange plague and died within the week. One day he was out hunting, doing chores, playing, and the next he was locked in his room. Liza wasn't even allowed near the door for fear of catching his disease.

It wasn't fair.

Papa came back and dropped a large stone at the head of the grave. Miller's name and birthday had been chiseled across the stone earlier that morning. Liza had added her own touch; an ink heart drawn below the letters. She added it not because she loved him, which she did very much, but because deep down she thought he would come back. When he did, she wanted that heart to be the first thing he saw. To show him he hadn't been forgotten.

When he came back he would pick her up and swing her in the air like nothing had changed. And while she flew through the air like dandelion clouds, they would laugh.

-1-

Weeks went by without sign of Miller, but Liza watched for him every day. From her room, from the kitchen, the porch; anywhere with a view she watched, knowing he'd come back one day. He loved her too much to stay away forever.

When she played outside in the shorter grass near the house, she listened for his arrival. Any twig snapping or crunch of last year's fallen leaves was met with the eager gaze of a hunter waiting for a called deer. Her patience endured, but the only thing to turn up during her time outdoors was a rabbit, hopping from the back yard. It was a cute rabbit, brown and white with a pink nose. Miller had always liked chasing rabbits. Wouldn't it be a surprise if he came home to find Liza had caught one all by herself?

The rabbit bounced lazily from here to there, in no big hurry as Liza snuck up behind it. She came within two feet and pounced. It raced away from her, and she gave chase. Across the yard, past the trailhead that wound back to the river, and on to the big field.

The rabbit vanished into the tree line, but Liza had stopped chasing long before it reached the safety of the forest. The path to its escape lead right over Miller's headstone. Liza stood in a wild patch of dandelions, staring at the oddly weathered stone and the faded ink heart upon it. Her eyes fell to the date on the stone. Not of birth, but the other.

Had it really been that long?

Tears welled up in her eyes, threatening to carve fresh trails of pain down her cheeks, but she blinked them away.

Miller would be back. He would. He just needed more time.

Retracing her steps through the head high wheat grass until she could see her house in the distance, she hesitated. For the last few days, Papa had been trying to fool her. He kept asking why she was looking out the window, even though he knew very well why. It bothered her that he kept trying to make her to forget about Miller.

The trail came up on her right and she decided to go down to the river and let the breeze from the water cool her off. It was a wide trail, free of brush and easy to walk. Papa had blazed the path years ago, and Miller always helped him clear it whenever it started growing wild again. Last time, Liza had helped too. She remembered the day clearly because it was the first-time Miller had shown her what happened when you blew on a dandelion.

It had been a long morning, spent hauling fallen limbs for Miller and raking leaves and pine needles for Liza. They were taking a break and resting by the river while Papa hacked some of the tall grass away when Miller had picked a dandelion and passed it to her.

"What do I do with this?" she had asked, smelling it. It tickled and didn't smell good like the red and blue flowers she had picked with Mama.

He laughed when her nose started twitching. "No, you wiggly bunny, you don't smell this one, you blow it."

"Why?" she said, looking at the flower like it was suddenly on fire or covered in bugs.

"Try it and you can tell me."

And she had. She remembered the seeds exploding off the stem, floating softly to the ground like tiny angels coming down from heaven.

"It's too bad we can't do that," Miller said when the seeds settled over the grass. "Disappear on the wind. End up somewhere far away, something completely different than before. Different, but still the same."

Liza had no idea what he meant and she didn't think he had either. Still she remembered it, even after all this time.

A pinecone crunched behind her, drawing her out of the memory. She looked back, expecting to see Papa. She stood at the end of the trail where a small shed full of fishing poles, hunting knives, and arrows stood. She thought maybe Papa had decided on fish for dinner, but he wasn't there. Nobody was there.

Something struck her then, thinking about Papa and the hunting shed. Miller had always loved to hunt and fish, but one day he'd been upset when he shot a deer and lost its trail in the woods, and he ran off. Disappeared for hours. Liza had found him later that night, in the shed.

Before the idea could finish forming, she was at the front of the shed, pulling the door open. He had to be inside, of course he was. He was just mad and wanted to hide in the shed like last time.

The door swung open and she peered inside. Aside from Papa's tools and work bench, the shed was empty.

She looked back and wondered for the first time what had crunched the pinecone. Another rabbit maybe. Or a squirrel. She couldn't see anything up the trail. In fact, there was nothing in the woods at all.

There was, however, something in the water.

-2-

"I'm worried John," Constance said to her husband. Supper was cooking on the stove, Liza was out playing, and John was filling his pipe with tobacco on the porch.

He mumbled a response through his pipe until the smoke finally began to billow. He inhaled once, then removed it to speak. "She'll be fine, she just needs time to grieve," he looked out towards the field where his only son lay buried, "and learn."

"I found a necklace in her room the other day. She said she was making it for Miller, for when he gets back. It was braided twine with a cross pendant of wood."

"Time will heal all our wounds. It always outlasts the pain."

"I suppose." It was quiet for a moment, only the birds chirping and the distant static sound of the river could be heard. Then she said what was truly bothering her. "I heard a rumor in the village yesterday. Mrs. Mathers in the market told me."

"Oh? Do tell," John said through the haze of smoke around his face.

"I asked her why the town was so quiet, so empty, and she said that three people have died since last we went to church. She said the men think it's some sort of animal that's been hunting people in the night."

"Why do they think that?"

"Because," Constance said, lowering her voice as if afraid said animal might be listening, "They said their throats had all been bitten, practically ripped out in the last instance."

"A mountain cat then? I've seen them before out hunting. They seemed to be skittish, at least the ones I've seen."

Constance nodded, absently fiddling with the strings on her apron. "Maybe one has gone rabid. Or perhaps it's something else."

"A bear?"

"No, something else entirely." She paused and John raised a questioning eyebrow.

"A madman you mean? Nonsense, we know every person in the village and not one of them have even a flicker of evil in their eyes." He settled back into his chair and puffed on his pipe. Constance remained silent again, though her apron was balled up in her fists.

"You know, my mother used to tell me stories when I was a girl. Stories from the Old World. They were dark, meant to scare a lesson into you, but she would always say that they were just make believe. But what if they weren't?"

"Whatever do you mean darling?"

"What if those creatures really do roam this world. You know, monsters, that steal children and kill innocent people. Doesn't it scare you, to think that you could meet one of these creatures?"

John shook his head. "Constance, there's a reason those stories are from the Old World. People were afraid of what they didn't understand, so they took what they did know, the animals that scared them, the demons from church, a grand mix of both, and they used them to explain the horrors they saw. There are no monsters in the New World dear, only those men who try to emulate them."

"I suppose," Constance replied. "But isn't there a grain of truth even in the wildest legends?"

John took another long puff on his pipe. He was tired of the conversation. He had conquered his fear of the dark long ago and reinforced it not four weeks ago, when he laid dirt over his own son. After that nothing scared him. Except Liza. She was too naive, and from the swing of this conversation, he saw where it came from.

He opened his mouth to say as much, but the words never left his tongue. A shrill echoing scream cut him off, forcing him to his feet. The sound brought to mind, for both John and Constance, the sound of a child being attacked by an animal.

What was worse, it came from the river.

-3-

The scream had been building inside of Liza from the moment she came across the coffin on the riverbank.

With a knife from the hunting shed, she had pried the lid open and toppled it into the water. It sailed away on the brisk current.

The man inside was dead, that was certain. From the looks of his pale, mangled body, it appeared he had been beaten to death, maybe even stoned. His limbs were broken, both of his arms and legs stuck out at unnatural angles. The sight of those ugly breaks made something else rise in Liza's throat that she only just managed to keep down. The worst part, even more upsetting than the dead man's open eyes, was the garlic. His mouth was stuffed so full of the smelly white orbs that his jaw looked like it had broken.

Still Liza didn't scream. Given the last person she'd seen in a coffin, she felt she could handle the sight of a stranger, no matter how gruesome his death may have been.

What she couldn't handle, though, was when the clouds parted and a bright beam of sunlight fell on his eyes, and the dead man blinked.

Then moved.

The scream ripped through Liza's lips like thunder on a warm summer night, and she ran. Ran to find her father, her mother, anybody that could keep the stranger with the garlic and broken legs away from her.

She was at the head of the trail when she saw them, running towards her from the house. She ran right into her father's arms and buried her face in his chest.

His voice was shaking with terror. "What is it Liza, what's happened? Are you okay?" He checked her arms and legs for bites or scrapes and hugged her tighter when he saw none.

"He was dead!" was all she could manage.

"Who is dead?"

"I don't know," she sobbed, "but he's not anymore."

Constance put a hand on Liza's back and stroked her soothingly. "Where is he darling?"

Liza stuffed her face back into her father's chest and pointed down the trail. She couldn't bear to say the coffin was in her favorite spot, next to the tree by the dandelion patch.

They started walking, either towards the house or the coffin, she couldn't tell at first. Only when the sound of the river grew louder did she realize they had chosen to investigate. The water was almost all she could hear when her father said, "This is curious."

Liza dared to remove her face from the safety of her father's chest and turned. The coffin was empty.

"Is this what you saw, Liza?" her mother asked.

Liza shook her head no. "There was a boy inside. He was all broken and there was something in his mouth."

"Well there's nothing here now except a box full of rose petals."

Liza looked over the edge and sure enough the only thing that remained in the box were hundreds of red petals, covering the bottom like the wine-colored carpet in the pulpit of the village church. "Are you sure you didn't just imagine a body? You know, because of..."

"No, Papa, no, I wouldn't make believe something so scary. It was the worst thing I've ever seen." She stuck her head back into his chest and he shrugged.

"Ok. Let's try and forget this whole thing," he said, hitching Liza back up on his hip and turning to leave. "I'll come back later on and get rid of that crate."

-4-

It only took Liza three days to finish the necklace for Miller. She started it the day before she had seen the bad thing by the river and stayed in her room the next two days, working on it and thinking of her brother and how much he would like it. It seemed the more she worked, the more she thought about him, and the more she thought about Miller, the less she could remember about the bad thing. By the time she emerged from her bedroom with the wooden cross dangling beneath her neck, she couldn't even remember what had been so bad. It was just a box full of flower petals after all.

Papa went back down to the river the next day and dislodged the box, but before he could haul it ashore, the current caught hold of it and sent it sailing down the river. Probably hit the waterfall, he'd mused, whistling as his hand floated down an invisible river and fell off the edge.

Liza had laughed and felt better. With the box gone, she felt no trepidation in walking down the trail and visiting her favorite spot, even if it was after supper.

The sun was sulking beneath the treetops and from the looks of the sky, it would probably rain again before full dark, but she couldn't stay in the house. Something told her today was the day Miller would come back, careening through the woods, breathless in his excitement to see his family. She walked the trail, smooth now that the rain had come and washed away the tracks (and the bad thing's box) and hummed until she reached her spot. She sat down with her back to a tree, staring out over the river. She only realized something was amiss when she leaned over to pick a dandelion.

On the day the box of roses had come, a grove of calf high dandelions had stood in the shady patch of earth between her tree and the water's edge. Today, however Liza had to nearly stand up to reach the closest one and even it had lost half of its seeds. What few remained were bent at the stalks, crooked like (the bad thing's) broken limbs.

A loud *CLANG* came from the old shed, causing Liza to jump with sudden discomfort. It sounded like a rake or shovel had fallen from the wall. The sudden, prickly fear in her spine surprised her, almost like she'd been expecting the noise.

"Papa?" she called.

No answer.

She approached the front of the barn. She found it stranger sill that her hands were trembling as she reached for the door. It took all her strength to open the shed door and look inside. Papa wasn't there.

But there was a boy.

"Miller?"

The boy stirred but didn't speak. He was sitting in the far corner of the shed in shadows, a pick axe on the ground next to him, his hands resting limply on his raised knees. Excitement took place of her fear.

"Miller!" she said again, taking a few steps forward and removing the necklace from her neck.

Hearing her approach, the boy flinched and held up one hand to stop her. Water dripped from his palm, like he'd just taken a long drink from the river.

Liza ignored the hand and walked further into the shed. She was so excited to finally see him and hug him and give him the necklace that she didn't notice the tip of the pick axe was also wet like the hand that begged her to stop. It was only when she got close enough in the dim light that she saw the water was not water at all.

Her breath caught in her throat and she lunged toward Miller and kneeled beside him. "What happened? Are you ok?"

The boy's shaggy black hair hid his face. He whispered something Liza couldn't hear and moments later Liza became aware of a strong odor on his breath. It reminded her of Mama's kitchen. It also frightened her. "Miller?"

He spoke again and this time she caught what he said.

Her brow furrowed, but she held out the necklace for him to take anyway. He did so gently, without looking at her, or even raising his head. The wooden cross was instantly stained by his bloody palm. "What do you mean you're not Miller?" she asked.

"I'm not Miller," he repeated in a harsh strangled voice. It sounded like he'd screamed himself hoarse the night before. "My name is Ethan."

"Oh. Ethan. Are *you* ok?" she asked, fighting the urge to take back Miller's necklace. It was ruined now anyway.

"No," he said, choking even more on his words than before. "I'm not. I haven't been for a while." He held up his bloody hands as proof.

Goosebumps rose up Liza's arms. "What's wrong?"

"I can't describe it to you. Only that it's horrible," he fumbled for words beneath his shaggy hair, "like a Call that I must answer, a thirst that I have to quench. Only it ruins me every time. Ruins...and satisfies." He shifted a little to wipe his face, and Liza saw something that she somehow expected to see. At his wrist was an ugly purple bruise, like the flesh around a torn ligament that was just starting to heal. There was another on his neck and chin, a great patch of discolored flesh that started just below his jaw. She imagined there were similar marks around his knees and ankles.

"You're the boy from the box?" she asked. Her voice was flat even though her insides were churning with fear.

The boy nodded.

"You were dead."

"No, but I was close. No, I can't die."

"Everybody dies," she paused for several heartbeats. "Who did those things to you?"

The boy sniffled, what might have been an attempt at laughter. "The villagers. They think I'm dangerous. Unnatural. I suppose I am, but I'm not what they think. Garlic and roses. Coffins and running water, it's all from a story. From the Old World."

"A vampire?"

Ethan looked up for the first time. His eyes were golden brown, red-rimmed, and moist. They showed emotions as clear as day, one of them being surprise.

"My Mother knows the stories," Liza shrugged even though she was pleased to have surprised the stranger. "They missed something," she added, jabbing her thumb over her heart.

Ethan sniffled again, then dropped his gaze to the pick axe. "Didn't work." He wiped his bloody hands on his pants. Liza could see now his shirt was soaked and clinging to him.

She wished Miller were here.

"If you're not a vampire, what are you?"

He was silent for a long time, as if he were trying to piece together the proper words. Liza couldn't tell if he was crying or smiling, the sunlight was all but gone outside and there was even less inside the shed. It was going to be a cold night.

"Where did you get this?" he said, dangling the cross from his hand.

"I made it. My brother had one just like it before, but he lost it one night hunting." She watched him as she spoke and saw his eyes express another clear emotion.

"You have to go," he said suddenly, climbing to his feet and standing over her. He was a lot bigger on his feet than he looked on the ground.

"Why?" She jumped back, startled.

"It- it's coming again. Just go, please," his hands began to tremble, "Please go!"

"Are you..."

"GO!" Ethan screamed in a voice that was not his. It was more a growl than anything. The scream that Liza had suppressed from the beginning now boiled in her lungs, the same way Ethan's skin seemed to be boiling before her eyes. It writhed as if some angry serpent beneath it was trying to climb free. Ethan doubled over and something inside him snapped loudly. Even through the darkness, Liza could see Ethan's body being ripped apart and reformed into something horrible.

She trampled the remaining dandelions on her way out, running home, blindly thinking that Papa would know what to do. He always did.

Over halfway up the trail, she heard the shed door ripped from its hinges and thrown into the water. Ethan, or whatever he had become, tore through the woods, covering ground faster than humanly possible. Liza dared to look over her shoulder and screamed at the sight of an enormous black beast chasing after her on all fours. It was close enough to see its eyes were red as the blood on the rusty pick axe.

She burst out of the trees, feeling the creature closing in on her as she made her way into the yard. The wind was howling, an orange moon glowed full, still low in the evening sky. Liza could see candlelight in the distance, could barely make out two figures standing on the porch.

Behind her, the creature made the same sound as the wind.

Oh no, she thought, I'm leading it right to them!

Just as the thought occurred to her, the creature took a great bound and leapt into the air. It soared over Liza, landing just in front of her, its back legs knocking her to the ground. It rolled to its feet, and stood over her, black claws raised in salute to the night, snout huffing in the cool air.

Liza closed her eyes. Miller had taken too long. Not only had she lost the necklace, but now she wouldn't be there when he got back. The beast bared down on her, saliva dripping from arched fangs.

Another howl ripped through the air, marrying with the sound of a gunshot. The creature leapt again, this time away from Liza and away from the house. Another rifle blast rang out, but the creature was gone, slipping away into darkness.

Liza followed its lead.

💀💀💀

It was daylight when she woke. She was inside, lying in her bed with her parents sitting over her. Mama held her hand, Papa stood behind her.

"What happened?" she mumbled.

"You were attacked," Mama said through tears. "An animal has been attacking people in the village and it came after you. Your father shot it and gave chase once you were safe."

"Did you kill it Papa?" she asked. She winced in pain after trying to sit up. A large bandage was wrapped over her shoulder; the inner wrappings were tinged with pink.

"No," he said, coming to her bedside. "I carried you in and set you in bed before I went after it. I thought it would be gone, but I came up on it in the field, by the woods." He blinked rapidly before looking down. "Liza, there are things in this world that can't be explained. Things so terrible they should be left to stories."

"I know Papa," she said.

The look on her Father's face told her that he knew she knew, and that was the worst part. There was more though, and he placed something on her stomach. It was the necklace she'd made for Miller.

"I came up on the creature at your brother's grave. It had been digging and by the time I managed to drive it off...well it had gotten what it was after." He cleared his throat. "This was on top of Miller's body. I'm just glad no one else saw what I saw. It was hard enough to bury him once..." He acted like there was more to say, but it didn't come out.

They all had a vague idea of what they had seen. In fact, Constance knew exactly what she had seen. A creature that was impossible to kill, that howled beneath a full moon, and snacked on recently deceased corpses. She knew the name, the story, the curse, but she kept it to herself. Glad that she, like her husband with Miller's corpse, was the only one to truly know.

Liza knew *who* it was that had chased her, but she also kept the information quiet. The beast was truly bad, but the boy inside hated it more than they did.

The necklace she had made for her brother rose and fell with her breathing. Dirt and blood still clung to it. Stuck to the crusty red-black liquid on the cross were little pieces of white dandelion blooms.

Her parents were silent, thinking about their child, about her safety and theirs. Constance wondered about the scratch on Liza's shoulder, and how much of the stories were true. Her father wondered how they would ever move on from this. Both feared this was impossible.

For Liza, however, it was simple.

She picked up the necklace, held it to her lips. With her eyes closed, remembering the day by the river with Miller, thinking about his life, and hers, and about all that he had meant to her, she blew on the crucifix.

The dandelion pedals drifted into the air, caught on a breeze, and disappeared.

MRS. DOOGAN
Lana Cooper

"You better stop making that noise or else I'll call Mrs. Doogan!" yelled old Mrs. Walsh from her porch. The gaggle of kids playing ball in the park across from her house immediately went silent.

Every kid on Oak Street had heard those words at one time or another. Their parents had heard them. And even some of their grandparents remembered the name that struck fear in the hearts of boys and girls: Mrs. Doogan.

No one had ever seen Mrs. Doogan, but whenever a child misbehaved, adults would tell them that Mrs. Doogan would come to take them away if they didn't get their act together. According to grown-ups, Mrs. Doogan lived in a big house in the middle of the woods and made bad children scrub her floors and eat cold oatmeal. There was no internet or video games at Mrs. Doogan's house. And no one who had ever been taken away by Mrs. Doogan had ever come back.

It was unfortunate that the best playground in the neighborhood was directly across the street from mean old Mrs. Walsh.

"I said break it up or else I'm going to call Mrs. Doogan!" she screeched yet again. Mrs. Walsh held up an old phone receiver. Its long, curly cord swung back and forth like a threatening pendulum. It was as much of a relic as she was.

Old Mrs. Walsh was Mrs. Doogan's biggest fan. It didn't matter if you rode your bike past her house one too many times or stood directly on her porch and played "Mary Had a Little Lamb" with armpit noises, Mrs. Walsh would immediately threaten to call Mrs. Doogan to take you away.

"Looks like Mrs. Walsh is at it again," sighed Mike. "You all want to meet back here Saturday when she does her weekly shopping?"

"Sounds good," replied Billy. Sidney, Chris, Greta, and Hannah all nodded.

Billy looked at his phone and hopped on his bike. He'd be 20 minutes early to help Sarge mow his lawn and tend to his garden, but he knew the old man always appreciated punctuality.

"See ya later!" he called, speeding down Oak Street to Sarge's house.

Bob "Sarge" Elmsford was a nice old man who lived across the street from Billy and his family. A favorite with the neighborhood kids, Sarge would often tell jokes, play ball, and give the neighborhood kids ways to earn pocket money by helping him and his wife with chores. In addition to pocket money, they'd also come home with fresh muffins or cookies his wife – affectionately known as "Mrs. Sarge" – made.

"Hey, Sarge!" Billy called. "I'm a little early!"

"Excellent," he declared, poking his head from the living room. "I thought you and the gang were at the park today?"

"We were. But crazy old Mrs. Walsh started yelling she was going to call Mrs. Doogan on us," Billy explained.

"Yeah, don't give her any excuses," Sarge inhaled sharply and shook his head.

"Aw! You really don't believe that whole Mrs. Doogan stuff, do ya, Sarge? I think Mrs. Walsh is just a big, stupid liar who hates for kids to have any fun. I mean, if you hate kids so much, why buy a house across the street from a playground?"

"Oh, I'm sure there's a good reason for that, Billy," Sarge said, the sparkle dimming from his eyes as he sat back in his easy chair. "I don't like that woman very much, either. But I would not test her."

The boy looked concerned. "You okay, Sarge?"

"I'm fine," he waved it off. "How 'bout we get started on that yard?"

Billy helped the older man mow the lawn and yanked several weeds from Mrs. Sarge's flower bed before the couple sent him home with a bag filled with chocolate oatmeal cookies.

"See ya this weekend," Sarge called as Billy pedaled away on his bike. "You can help me with the mulch pile on Sunday!"

"Sounds like a plan!" Billy called over his shoulder as he zipped across the street to his house.

That Saturday, the Oak Street kids congregated at the playground. It was sunny and peaceful since Mrs. Walsh wasn't there.

The kids were in the middle of a game of pickup when the old woman arrived home with her purchases.

"Uh-oh," groaned Chris under his breath. "Fun's over."

Mrs. Walsh glared at the children. "This little game better not continue. I just got home and want to sleep."

"But it's two in the afternoon, Mrs. Walsh!" whined Hannah.

"Don't you sass me, young lady!" she howled.

Hannah bit her lower lip, trying not to cry.

"Chill out already, Mrs. Walsh!" Billy yelled back. "We're not doing anything wrong. We're just playing. On a *play* ground."

The old woman gave them the stink eye from the pavement. Then, the bottom of her paper grocery bag gave way. A glass jar of spaghetti sauce hit the ground and splattered bright red goo across the sidewalk.

"Look what you made me do!" the old woman howled. "I've had enough of these shenanigans from you rotten kids! I'm calling Mrs. Doogan!"

"I'm sure you will." Mike shook his head and laughed. "Come on. We'll find another place to play."

Mrs. Walsh scrambled to collect her groceries before stumbling indoors.

Without warning, a heavy rain burst from the sky and thunder rolled in the distance.

With the hard rain falling, Billy and his friends disbanded for the day. They hopped on their bikes or trudged back to their houses as Mrs. Walsh made a big production of dialing her old rotary phone from her front window and speaking in a loud voice.

The next day, Billy was across the street helping Sarge prune the lilacs. It was still too wet to mulch anything as planned, but they were able to dig some of the beds for new flowers and fall vegetables.

Billy felt his phone go off in his pocket. It was a message from his mother. A little long-winded, as usual, but always very sweet.

"There's a Mrs. Doogan here to see you. Isn't that funny? Like that creepy old lady story. Are you helping her with her lawn, too? Let me know. Love you!"

Billy felt a chill go down his spine as he stared at the text message.

"Everything okay, kid?" Sarge aske.

"Yeah," he said. "Just got a text from Mom saying a Mrs. Doogan was there to see me."

Color drained from Sarge's face. He ran inside the house to peer through his front window. He stared through the blinds at Billy's house two doors across the street and saw the boy's mother talking with a tall, slender, elderly woman. She had pointed features and steel grey hair pulled into a severe bun.

To Sarge's old eyes, Mrs. Doogan looked exactly the same as she did over 60 years ago.

"Jane?" Sarge called to his wife. "Do me a favor and do not open this door for anyone. Especially a tall, old broad. Promise?"

"Sure," Mrs. Sarge replied. "But why? You didn't snooker this woman's husband at your card game again, did you?"

"No," Sarge said, shaking his head. "I think Billy might be in trouble. Just trust me on this one."

"You got it," she affirmed, giving him a playful salute.

Billy wiped his feet on the mat outside the sliding glass door that lead from the backyard into the house before re-entering.

"Everything alright, Sarge?" he asked.

"Come here, kiddo," he said quietly, still staring out the window. "Just stay out of sight."

Puzzled, Billy approached the window.

"See that woman over there?" Sarge asked, peering through the blinds.

Billy nodded, spotting the tall, grey-haired woman speaking to his mother across the street.

"That's Mrs. Doogan."

"You're not pulling my leg, are ya, Sarge?"

"I wish I was," the old man replied. "Be very careful, Billy. Do not let her catch your scent. That's why she's staying there for so long, gabbing with your mother. She's trying to catch your scent."

"Huh?"

"Is your mother doing laundry today?" the old man asked.

"Yes. She is, actually," the boy replied.

"That's why she can't get a good whiff."

"Sarge," Billy blurted "You're being weird."

"I don't care," Sarge said, uncharacteristically terse. "I'm telling you this for your own good. I don't want what happened to me and my friends to happen to you and your friends."

Suddenly, Billy understood why Sarge seemed to have all his energy sucked out of him whenever someone mentioned Mrs. Doogan – or Mrs. Walsh, for that matter.

"What happened?" Billy whispered. "If you don't mind telling me."

Sarge nodded and sat down in his chair near the window, still keeping an intent eye on Mrs. Doogan across the street.

"It was 1959 and I was ten years old," he began. "A lot of us kids on Oak Street would play at that same playground you and your friends visit. Only, in those days, we didn't have a Mrs. Walsh to yell at us. We had a Mrs. Leery, who was just as fond of threatening kids with Mrs. Doogan as Old Lady Walsh is.

One summer, my friend Petey mouthed off at Mrs. Leery when she yelled at us. A few days later, he went missing.

And a few days after that, an old woman I didn't recognize saw me riding my bike. It started raining and she asked me to help with her shopping bags. I left my bike and carried her bags into the house for her.

'Petey,' the old woman called behind me. 'I can still smell the last kids on the floor. You need to scrub harder.'

And that's when I saw Petey. He was scrubbing away at this old woman's floors. He had small punctures all over him and his ankles were shackled together. He tried mouthing the words 'run' to me, but couldn't speak. She'd cut out his tongue.

Then, I looked closer. I got a good look and realized Petey wasn't scrubbing her floors with his hands. His hands had been cut off and replaced with sponges."

"Was this Mrs. Doogan's house?" Billy felt sick to his stomach.

Sarge nodded. "It looked like any normal house, except she had small windchimes made of bone hung around the place. I realized those were her 'trophies.' The remains of children she murdered over the years – or centuries. Who knows."

Billy felt his stomach flip. "How did you get out of there?"

"I dropped the old woman's bags and tried to free Petey from his chains, but they wouldn't budge.

Mrs. Doogan ran at me and I tripped her. She hit a table and knocked a vase to the ground and it shattered. Petey was able to use the chains from the shackles on his feet to strangle her, but with no hands, he didn't have much leverage. She threw him off and took a broken shard of glass from the vase and slit his throat right there.

I was ten years old and watched my best friend bleed to death.

I had to act fast. I wanted to kill Mrs. Doogan for what she did to Petey. How she made him suffer. How she probably made countless other 'missing' kids suffer for God knows how long.

I think it was just pure rage that made me run at her. I took another broken shard – a big one – and shanked her right in the back. Her head swiveled around 180 degrees and I saw rows of sharp, silver teeth.

She wasn't just an evil old lady. I don't know what she was. But she wasn't human."

"Holy shit," breathed Billy, clasping his hands over his mouth at the words that escaped his mouth. "What did you do? How did you escape?"

"I just kept stabbing her. Stabbing and stabbing. She let out horrible screams and I ran like my shoes were on fire.

I jumped on my bike and took a shortcut through the woods.

No matter how fast I biked, I could feel her following me. And I could hear her.

'I can smell you, Bobby' she called. 'Don't think you'll get far! I know that little boy smell!'

This will sound even screwier, but I heard my grandfather's voice in my head. He was in the service, too. Years before me, obviously.

One time, he told me, 'The way we would hide from the dogs they sent to sniff out camp was to roll in the mud. It masked our scent if we coated ourselves in mud.'

And that's what I did. I was lucky. Because of the rain, there was a big patch of mud in the middle of the woods. I threw myself and my bike into the mud and rolled around in it.

I stayed there for a good hour. Waiting and hoping I'd thrown Mrs. Doogan off."

"What happened after that?"

"I went back home and told my parents about everything that happened. We called the cops and they went with us – and Petey's parents – back to that awful place.

Turns out, it wasn't even her place. There was no record of a Mrs. Doogan ever owning the house where I found Petey. The previous owners left town three months before. Just picked up and went to the West Coast."

"Did they really? Or do you think something else happened to them, too?"

"I wondered about that myself," Sarge replied. "But I was too young to know any better.

That same week, Mrs. Leery died in her house. Mrs. Doogan's biggest fan dropped dead of a heart attack. Supposedly."

"Good," Billy replied.

Sarge nodded. "That summer haunted me my entire life. And I'll be goddamned if I let that happen to you or any of the other kids on this street. I owe that to Petey.

You're good kids. All of you. And I'm going to make that miserable old bitch pay."

For a second, Billy didn't recognize Sarge. This wasn't the man who always had jokes and candy for the neighborhood kids or the old man who played ball with them or taught them to ride bikes. This Sarge was darker. Angrier.

Then again, maybe it was this dark side of Sarge that was what made him the kind old man the Oak Street kids knew and loved.

The protector.

Sarge rose from his chair and looked out the window again.

"She's still there," he said. "Still talking to your mother. This old bag doesn't leave."

Billy looked out the window with the old man. "What do we do?"

Sarge thought for a moment.

Across the street, Billy's mother cheerfully waved goodbye to Mrs. Doogan and shut the door.

"Okay," Billy heaved a sigh of relief. "I think she's leaving."

Just then, the old woman's head swiveled around. She opened her mouth and began sniffing the air with a long, serpentine tongue. Her mouth opened wide. Her jaw unhinged like a snake preparing to gobble a giraffe. The summer sun glinted off several rows of sharp, silver teeth that lined her gaping maw.

She smiled – the look of satisfaction of a person who sees a waiter bringing them their food.

"Holy shit!" Billy exclaimed, clapping his hands over his mouth again.

Sarge kept staring from behind the blinds. The old man wondered if Mrs. Doogan could still smell him all these years later. If his scent had changed with time. If maybe she could smell him and not Billy.

Outside, Mrs. Doogan turned her head to face back in the proper direction and began to walk home – wherever she called home now.

Just as the old woman faded out of sight, thunder roared in the distance and the clear summer sky cracked open with a torrential downpour.

"Call your mother and tell her you're staying here for dinner," he said. "I don't want her getting your scent in case she's still around."

Billy pulled out his phone and called his mother.

"Hey, Mom! Sarge and Mrs. Sarge invited me to stay over for dinner. Yeah, we didn't get as much done as we wanted to because of the rain, but we'll do more tomorrow."

"Okay. Please thank them for having you over. And don't stay too long," his mother replied. "Oh! Before I forget. You might have a new customer. That Mrs. Doogan lady I was telling you about is new to the neighborhood. She's friends with Mrs. Walsh, who recommended you help her with her lawn."

"Oh," replied Billy, doing his best to hide his anxiety. "Cool."

"I thought you said Mrs. Walsh was mean? That was nice of her to suggest you."

"Yeah," said Billy flatly. "That was nice of her. Where does Mrs. Doogan live? What did you chat about?"

"Oh, she lives a couple streets over. Where the Williamses used to live. I told her you'd probably be around later in the week since you regularly help Sarge with his lawn."

"Thanks, Mom," Billy replied. "I'll tell Mrs. Sarge you said hi, too."

"Love you."

"Love you, too, Mom," said Billy as he hung up.

"All clear, kiddo?" Sarge asked.

"All clear."

"Any recon on the old lady?"

Billy filled him in on Mrs. Doogan's connection to Mrs. Walsh and that she was supposedly living in the house the Williams family moved out of about two months ago – right before school ended.

"Prime time to find kids," Sarge suggested. "I've been doing some research over the years. I was never sure Mrs. Doogan was still around or if she was just something parents used to scare their children. But ever since I heard about Old Lady Walsh threatening to call her, I wanted to be ready."

"Ready?" asked Billy.

Mrs. Sarge brought a stack of books from the other room along with a colorful folder of pages that looked like they'd been printed off the internet. She set them down gently on the table.

"Thanks, sweetheart," Sarge said, giving his wife a peck on the cheek.

"Bob's been doing research for years trying to find out what he could about what happened to his friend Petey all those years ago." She patted the folder brimming with printouts in front of her. "The grandkids showed him how to print things off the internet and he's been assembling quite the dossier."

Billy thumbed through some of the printouts and flipped open a book with several Post-Its and sticky flags marking pages and passages.

He noticed a strange word repeated in all of them: Lamia.

"What's a lamia," the boy asked.

"I think that's what we're dealing with in Mrs. Doogan," Sarge replied.

"It's a half-woman, half-snake demon that eats children," explained Mrs. Sarge. "By the way, do you want ranch dressing or bleu cheese with your chicken wings?"

"Bleu cheese, please," Billy replied, slightly rattled. "So, she's a demon? What about Mrs. Walsh? Is she a demon, too?"

"I think Mrs. Walsh is human," said Sarge. "Remember when I told you about Mrs. Leery?"

"The woman who would always threaten to call Mrs. Doogan on you and your friends?"

"Bingo. I think Mrs. Doogan needs a human to help scout kids for her."

"Well, what does she get in exchange?" Billy asked.

"Who knows? Longer life? Money? A steady stream of oiled-up cabana boys willing to hump a dried-up old stove like Mrs. Walsh? I don't know," Sarge threw up his hands. "You don't sell your soul and have horrible things happen to children on your watch for nothing. But, it's a safe bet that with Mrs. Doogan being a demon, there has to have been some sort of exchange."

"That's legit," sighed Billy. "So, how the hell do we take out a demon?"

"With this," answered Sarge, pulling a long, silver knife from beneath the pile of books. "It's real silver and blessed by a priest. I'll stab her with this – which should work. But if she's a lamia, that means she's part snake. So, I'm probably going to have to cut her head off just to be sure."

"In broad daylight? We're just going to walk to her house or see her in the middle of the street and say, 'Hey, Mrs. Doogan!' and WHOOMP.... Just lop her head off?" asked Billy. "How are we going to do that?"

"Not 'we.' Me," explained Sarge. "I'm not putting you in any danger. You're just a kid. You shouldn't have to see what I've seen."

Mrs. Sarge came in from the kitchen and put her arms around her husband's shoulders. Sarge didn't readily show emotion, but after nearly 50 years of marriage, his wife knew how to read him.

"I want to help," Billy said.

"And you can," Sarge offered. "Call your friends. Or text them. Check in with them. Make sure they're safe. And make sure they don't leave their houses until we get this sorted out."

Billy nodded. "I'll do that right now."

"Good," Mrs. Sarge said. "When you finish, we'll have dinner."

"What do I tell them about Mrs. Doogan?"

"The truth," replied Sarge.

"Okay," he hedged. "But only if they ask. That's a lot to text."

"Just tell them Sarge said to lay low for now," he suggested. "They'll understand. And it'll save you some time."

"Got it."

After checking in with each of his friends and getting replies, Billy dove into the plate of homemade chicken wings Mrs. Sarge had prepared, dunking the spicy delicacies in blue cheese dressing.

"Everyone's accounted for?" Sarge asked.

"Yep," Billy confirmed, wiping sauce from his fingers. "Greta was the last to text back. But everyone agreed to stay inside for the next few days and not go anywhere without an adult. I told them I'd explain once we had the all clear."

"Good man!" Sarge exclaimed. "I'm going to scope out the Williams place tomorrow morning and see if she really is staying there."

"You're not going alone," said Mrs. Sarge, tapping her fingers on the table.

"I'm not putting you or Billy in any danger," her husband replied.

"Trust me," she said. "I can handle myself."

"I know, but I work better alone."

"Fine," the older woman huffed. "But just make sure you drench yourself in cologne in case she can smell you."

"I'll splash on a healthy dose of Aramis before I go. Happy?" Sarge said, putting his wife at ease and grinning at Billy. "Now, let's help Mrs. Sarge with the dishes. We can plan more tomorrow once I've gone on recon. It's getting late and you should probably be heading home."

"Thanks, Sarge," said Billy. "And thanks, Mrs. Elmsford. Dinner was great!"

"It was our pleasure," she smiled. "Oh! And don't forget the blueberry muffins I left for you and your parents in the kitchen!'

"Thanks again! See you tomorrow? Around 11 A.M.?"

"Sounds like a plan," Sarge smiled. "Text us before you're coming over so we can make sure you get here safe."

Billy nodded. The old couple walked the young boy to the front door. They stood watch across the street, making sure his parents were there to greet him and he was safely inside.

Once they were sure, Sarge and Mrs. Sarge gathered up the books, papers, and silver knife from the kitchen table, taking them back upstairs to the library before they retired for a good night's rest.

The next morning, Billy texted the Elmsfords and got the all clear to come over. He parked his bike on the porch, walked inside the house, and through the patio doors out back.

"How did recon go?" he asked Sarge, who was already outside, continuing to dig a trench around the perimeter for his wife's flowers and fall planting. The yard still had piles of mud from last night's storm.

"Confirmed," he sneered. "That's her new home base. I didn't see anything really strange out there. But she had her old, bone windchimes on full display on her front porch. We know where she lives, but I'm still working on a plan."

Billy's stomach lurched. Just then, he felt his phone go off in his pocket. "'Scuse me," he said, taking a look at its screen.

It was a text from Mom. As usual, it was long and detailed. "Hey, sweetie! That Mrs. Doogan stopped by again. She's pretty pushy about getting you to do her lawn. I told her you didn't call last night since you got back late. I told her you were still doing Sarge's lawn. She's on her way over to introduce herself to the Elmsfords and talk to you. Don't feel pressured to do her lawn, okay?"

Billy felt like he was going to power vomit against the fence.

"Ok," he texted back. "Thx Mom. <3 U."

"I don't think we have time to plan, Sarge," Billy said. "Mrs. Doogan is on her way over right now."

"What?" the old man's eyes bulged as Billy showed him the text.

Suddenly, the door bell rang.

The old man and the young man looked at each other.

Inside, they heard Mrs. Sarge open the front door. Just as Mrs. Sarge opened the door, lightning streaked across the sky and thunder rolled. The sky cracked open in a soaking downpour.

"Quick," Sarge said, shoving Billy into one of the flower bed trenches. "Roll around in the mud. Don't let her smell you. Just stay here 'til I come back for you!"

Sarge ran inside the house just in time to hear Mrs. Doogan say, "It's awfully rainy out here. Aren't you going to invite me inside? That would be the neighborly thing to do."

"Of course." Mrs. Sarge didn't even flinch as she ushered the thin old woman into the living room.

"What a lovely home you have," she declared. "It smells delightful in here. Like something very familiar."

"I bake a lot," Mrs. Sarge shrugged disarmingly.

"So do I," Mrs. Doogan smiled, catching sight of Sarge standing near the patio doors. "And this must be your husband! The one who works Billy so hard! Where is the dear boy? He's not gardening outside in the rain, now is he?"

Sarge and his wife shared a sidelong glance.

"Oh, we both are," he forced a cheerful tone. "I just came inside to use the bathroom. 'Scuse me."

He started to go upstairs to the library to get the silver knife. Mrs. Doogan stopped him with more questions.

"It's good to know Billy's such a hard worker. I could use his help around my house."

Sarge's blood boiled, knowing full well what the old woman meant. He wondered if she recognized his scent from all those years ago.

"I'm new to the neighborhood and have no children or grandchildren of my own."

Yeah, bitch. Because you eat them, thought Mrs. Sarge, eyeing the small hatchet mounted on the wall next to the kitchen fire extinguisher.

"That's a shame," Sarge's tone was pointed. "We have our own kids, our grandkids, plus the neighborhood kids. We love them and keep watch over them."

"That's a wonderful thing, Mr…… Sergeant, I presume?" prodded Mrs. Doogan. "Everyone refers to you as 'Sarge' and 'Mrs. Sarge.' I assume those are nicknames?"

"No," Sarge replied. "I was in the military in my younger days. The name's Elmsford. Bob Elmsford. And this is my wife Jane."

"Bob Elmsford," she replied. He swore he could see her tongue flick against her lips.

"Yeah. Bobby Elmsford. That name must sound familiar to you, Mrs. Doogan," he fired back. "How about Petey Garvey? That sound familiar, too?"

Mrs. Doogan's cold eyes flickered. "I thought I smelled something familiar."

Without warning, Mrs. Doogan lunged like a coiled snake at Sarge, her mouth opening wide to expose her rows of silver fangs.

Mrs. Sarge screamed and made a dash for the hatchet. Sarge grabbed one of his wife's knick-knacks from an end table and bashed Mrs. Doogan in the head with it.

Suddenly, her old lady guise had fallen away to reveal her true form. Her lower legs fused together to form a scaly tail with a rattle on the end. Her wrinkled face morphed into a mass of scales. Her eyes were cold, black, and glassy. She still had arms, but they terminated in sharp claws instead of frail hands speckled with liverspots.

The lamia glided across the floor to escape Sarge's wrath before doubling back and lashing at him.

Billy heard screams from coming inside the house. He knew Sarge told him to stay put, but he just couldn't. What if they were in danger?

He sprang from the mud and ran inside, the rain washing away some of the earth that covered him. He froze in terror at the sight of the giant creature in his friends' living room.

"Billy!" shouted Sarge, snapping him out of it. "Upstairs! Library! Top drawer! The knife!"

The boy made a mad dash up the stairs, ran down the hall and flung open the door. He found the large rolltop desk in the library, opened the drawer and saw the silver knife.

He ran down the stairs. The hardwood floors were slick with blood.

Mrs. Sarge had finally gotten in a clean whack, lopping off the end of Mrs. Doogan's tail, buying her husband and Billy more time.

Sarge had a large slash across the front of his workshirt, but was still fighting.

Billy tucked the knife into his belt loop and ran at Mrs. Doogan, disorienting the lamia and knocking her to the ground.

She thrashed around, her stubby tail wrapping itself around Billy and squeezing while she flailed her claws to keep Sarge back.

Mrs. Sarge – seeing she had a clear shot – heaved the axe above her head and brought it down across Mrs. Doogan's neck. There was a sickening squish as the axe cleaved through tendons.

Although her head was partially severed, Mrs. Doogan still had a tight grip on Billy.

But not that tight. The boy reached into his belt loop and slid the silver knife across the floor to Sarge. He picked it up and rushed at the creature, stabbing it in the heart.

"That's for Petey," he spat.

The foul creature wheezed and shook on the ground, life pouring out of it.

Once more – for good measure – Mrs. Sarge raised the axe above her head and brought it down, severing the lamia's head from its body.

Finally, Mrs. Doogan was dead.

Exhausted, the trio sat down on the blood-soaked floor.

"Well," replied Sarge. "At least they're hardwood floors. We can mop this up inside an hour."

His humor barely masked the surge of emotions he felt.

"How are we going to get rid of the body," asked Billy. "I mean, we can't call the cops."

"We have that nice new fire pit in the backyard that the kids got us for Christmas," Mrs. Sarge offered. "We can burn her in chunks and bury the bones in the backyard?"

"That's true. We already have flower beds dug around the perimeter," mused Sarge.

"And hey, it's not like she's human," shrugged Billy. "Even if anyone dug them up, they'd just think it was a really big snake – not like we're psycho murderers or anything."

Sarge stood up and helped his wife to her feet. She eyed the slash across his chest.

"Ouch," winced Mrs. Sarge. "We need to clean that wound and put some Neosporin on that."

Outside, the storm had cleared and sunshine restored to the summer sky.

The calm was broken as sirens screamed in the distance.

"Oh my God!" yelled Billy. "What are the cops doing here? How did they know?"

Mrs. Sarge ran to the window. It wasn't the police. It was an ambulance charging further down the block.

Suddenly, Billy's phone buzzed with a text from Mike.

"Yo!" Billy read aloud to the couple. "Old Mrs. Walsh dropped dead from a heart attack."

Sarge walked out his front door, breaking out into a run down the block with a speed uncommon for a man his age. Mrs. Sarge followed suit with a still muddy Billy not far behind.

Neighbors were gathered outside their houses, watching as EMTs pulled a white sheet over Mrs. Walsh's face and loaded her into the ambulance.

Standing outside the house was a muscular young man in his mid 20s – tan with tousled blonde hair wearing nothing but a pair of zebra-print briefs. One of the medics draped a towel with the words "Oakmont Hospital" around his shoulders. He looked shaken and confused.

"Well," Sarge chuckled. "I guess we know what Mrs. Doogan gave Mrs. Walsh in exchange, now don't we?"

Billy spotted Mike, Hannah, and Chris down the street and waved them over.

"I think we can tell the rest of your friends it's safe to play outside now," Mrs. Sarge grinned at Billy.

"Maybe we invite the kids over for a little barbeque after we clean the place up," Sarge suggested. "What do you think, Billy?"

Billy smiled back as he watched the rest of the Oak Street kids pour out of their houses as Mrs. Walsh's body was carted away. There were still a few more glorious weeks of summer left for all of them to enjoy.

"You got it, Sarge."

"I hear it tastes just like chicken," Sarge said with a wink.

FOR WHOM THERE IS NO JOURNEY
JOHN LINWOOD GRANT

Illinois, 1975

There came a time when I wanted to be forgotten again, no record of where I was going, no trail of hire-car receipts or plane tickets. New York was brittle and bankrupt, an atmosphere of savage self-harm at every level, from the street junkies to the Teamsters and the City Council. And I'd been noticed more than once.

I needed out.

I chose the open road, seeking some kind of quiet. I crossed Ohio and Indiana on foot, taking my time, avoiding attention. Cleveland saw me through Fremont,

Defiance and beyond, until I reached the edge of Chicago.

That was where I met Ella.

Ella was one of the truly lost. If you can have any sympathy for our kind, then she deserved it. I came across her just before dark as she shivered on a back-street, waiting for a clean, all-American husband to come driving slowly past and wave a handful of dollars at her.

"Hey, little kitten." they would call. "Daddy needs some lovin'."

Daddy, of course, had a wife at home, two kids and a scamp of a dog in the yard. He raised funds for the party, and went to church scrubbed up every Sunday...

She sensed me instinctively, clutching at my jacket before I could get clear of her. She emanated loneliness, a hopeless revenant with no clue as to her nature. She must have been about sixteen when she was Returned, and this close I caught the nature of her own hunger. She needed what the men gave her. Desire, disgust, even self-loathing, if they had any. Those base feelings that set their loins

pumping in filthy alleys. She didn't want those things, but she had to have them. "I've not seen you before," she said, reedy and desperate.

"No." I was already regretting that I had strayed into the city.

"You... you're like me."

"In a way." I peeled her thin hands from me. "I'm sorry – I need to go."

She was shocked that I might leave like that. She pressed me with a babble of questions, most of which boiled down to the simplest – what was she, and why was she like this?

I didn't have answers. She had been cast back, Returned, as had I, left trapped alone and ignorant in a body which was essentially dead. As to why, some talk of retribution, a divine plan far beyond our understanding. Others rage, or sink into madness and catatonia. I'd seen it all. None of the Returned remember what made us what we are.

I did wonder what this girl could have done to end up like this at sixteen, seventeen years old, working the cold suburbs of Chicago.

"Can I come with you?" she said, when she realized I really was leaving. "You could, y'know, do me, if you want to..."

I wouldn't be able to help her. Some of us are stuck, and Ella was one of those. She argued with me, called me cruel to talk about walking away, but the real cruelty was when I gave in. I told her she could tag along for a while, and in the early hours of the morning we headed out of Chicago.

In less than twenty minutes, she began to stumble. "I feel... sorta sick."

"You will."

Another mile went by. She was staggering now, looking back as if something was following her, a small figure in sixties clothes struggling along a seventies road. Ten years too late for Ella. Near where I'd found her there would be a grave, the epicenter. It might only be a scratch of dirt in a disused car park, but i intended to hold her close.

Eventually she was crying dry tears and clawing at the road, unable to go on.

"Something happened." I said, head bent. "You died, Ella, and you're meant to be here. We're all bound, trapped, in some way."

"You're not," she whimpered.

"Places don't trap me. If you head back, it'll get easier."

There was no point in waiting. Maybe she would stay there until she starved, faded to a shadow with no sense of who or what she was. But the odds were on her being where I'd found her by morning, her sandals scuffing the kerbside as the big, low cars went by, waiting for the one that slowed down. Hey little kitten, they would call, and she would come.

Meeting Ella had unsettled me. I left that place to trudge the highways, refusing lifts, and I grew hungry in my own way.

A week later, when a staggering, pock-marked junkie drew a knife on me in a truck-stop restroom, I didn't hesitate. I'd only gone in to wash the dust from my face, but it was pointless to miss this opportunity. It would have to happen, sooner or later. I ignored his blows and clamped my hands to his temples, taking what little he had to offer. I left him unconscious, slumped in a cubicle. I needed a coffee, to take the taste away.

A woman was hunkered down at the counter next to me. Broad shoulders, wiry gray hair and an easy smile. She watched me sink two cups of black coffee. It

would come up later, but I relished the caustic bitterness of it.

"Travellin'?" There were only trucks on the tarmac, and I was dressed low, a nobody on the road.

"Always."

I put her in her early fifties, a trucker. I wondered aloud at a woman taking up that line. Not an easy choice.

"Lost my man couple o' years ago. Business is business. I keep the rig running, and the bank from the door."

We took refills, and I chewed on an apple pie with too much cinnamon.

"Headin' up through Wisconsin, if you want a ride," she said, draining her cup.

I liked her confidence, that she thought she could handle me if she needed to.

"Sure. That would be – what do you Americans say – swell."

She laughed. "Do we say that? Name's Marge."

"Benedict." It was a name that had seen some use over the years. We shook hands, and I felt her strength – not sinew and bone, but deeper than that.

Her rig, as she called it, was patched and filthy. No sign of rust, though, and no clatter of gears as she pulled away from the truck-stop.

"She's a Peterbilt 351, solid," she said as she slid into lane. "You know much about truckin'?"

"No." I settled down into the cracked leather seat. "I don't drive." "Crazy English, huh?"

"It's what we're known for."

Marge respected a comfortable silence. Her husband Ed had been taken by the Big C. She'd driven supply trucks towards the end of the war, and had a daughter somewhere out West. She was alone in Wisconsin with her truck.

When we broke down twenty miles out of her home town of Eau Claire, I watched as she stripped the hot engine, replacing parts from a tin box in the cab.

"I'm haulin' another load straightways." "Do you still want company?" Marge closed the big butterfly hood. "Nowhere to go, no one to see?"

"That's the size of it."

She grinned. "Might as well ride along, then. You can learn one end of a spanner from the other."

We hauled containers, what she called trailers, for almost a week. I wasn't keen to go too near Minnesota – I had history there – but she mostly stayed inside the state line. Marge was on the edge of the system. She rarely asked what she was hauling, always just a half-step ahead of the debts her husband had left, but she

wouldn't quit.

"You're a puzzle," she said, one evening as we dined on the worst burgers I'd ever tasted. It was a shack near Winona, just over the state line.

I waited to see what was to come.

She spat out gristle, not looking at me. "Here's this English guy. He's wearin' an outfit you wouldn't use to wipe snot, but he's lick-spit clean." She put one big hand near to mine. Her nails were filthy with diesel and dust, the skin cracked and red. My slim, scrubbed fingers looked like a child's next to hers. "He's no hobo nor student, no gape-eyed tourist Up Nort' for the Spring. And he's in no

hurry."

She attacked the coleslaw on her plate. Apparently she had nothing more to say about me. I excused myself and threw up the meal round the back. You learn

these tricks after a few decades.

We were back in Eau Claire the next morning. Clean clothes for Marge, and off to a slaughterhouse, where we picked up a rusting trailer full of pork bound for

Marquette, Michigan, by Lake Superior. I'd never been to the Great Lakes.

"Don't think much o' this." She slapped the dilapidated trailer, and flakes of paint came away. I had to agree, but we hitched it up anyway.

Northern Wisconsin was sparse on people, a rolling landscape of forests and marshland. Lakes and smaller bodies of water glinted in abundance on either side of the highways, mirrors which caught a pale sun and threw it in our eyes.

"Be a tight run," said Marge as she charged up with coffee at a truck-stop off Highway 51. The rig was being examined by two other truckers who had offered

to look at it. The refrigerated unit was beginning to fail.

"Might see you to Marquette, lady," said one of them, wiping oil on his dungarees. "Might not."

"Don't have much choice, fellers. Can't go missin' a single contract these days." They nodded sympathetically, and returned to their congealing breakfasts.

"Gotta make it through," she said to me. "The bank's tightenin' up."

We were on State Highway 70 when Marge's creased face grew new lines. She'd been using the CB radio, though I could make little sense of the exchanges. The truckers had a code or cant all of their own. I heard someone called Grey Greaser talking about a rolling refinery, and had to brace myself as Marge pulled the rig

off the road without warning.

"Been a real bad fender bender ahead o' us. A gas truck's burnin', and a couple others overturned." She had maps out. "We won't be getting through before

noon, at least."

"Isn't there another route?"

"Plenty, but they'll be backing up. There's a weak section on Highway 17, and I doubt they'll let us over 'til that's fixed. Anything else is a long swing round." She fingered one of the maps, hesitating. "Ed knew a way. Least, he told me one. East

o' Eagle Lake, and up through Blackjack Springs." "So we take that," I said.
"I'll drop you off, next stop we see."
That came sudden and gruff, surprising me.

"I'd rather see the run through. Or do you think I'm bad luck?" That brought a sour grin to her lips. "Luck's not my best suit."

We stared at each other, long moments of nothing.

"It's an old lumber road," she said at last. "Doesn't have a good name. Hell, doesn't have a name at all." She was holding something back, but I knew that it

would come out along the way.

She started up the Peterbilt, and we turned north onto a long road flanked by trees. A lot of trees. Spruce and sugar maple, all in Spring clothing. I passed her

the flask of coffee.

"Used to be Meninomee country, this," she said. "Indians, you know? Native Americans. Lot o' stories about it."

I was disappointed. I'd met others who liked their mock-tribal tales, apologetic nods to the people they had almost exterminated. They varied between romantic hippy notions and cheap horror stories – there seemed to be more native burial

grounds in America than there had ever been natives.

"Is that what bothers you about Blackjack Springs?"

"Too many skeetos up there, which don't help. But that road's been no good for a while. Heard talk."

I held my tongue, and ten minutes later she opened up more.

"They say the lumber folk gave up on it, and that every year or so someone goes missin' round there. Maybe a tourist, maybe a backpacker. Couple o' years ago, a family came back early from campin' out. The grownups were fine; the kids couldn't speak. They'd been playing on the lumber road, and just come back like

that, struck dumb. Never heard no explanation."

"Your husband used it?"

"Ed went up there in seventy one. Found a deer, deader than Moses. That's all he'd say. He turned back towards Anvil Lake – wouldn't go this way again." She

shrugged. "It'll save two, three hours."

Rumors and a truck driver who'd been spooked. There were black bears in the area, Marge admitted, and yes, they could get riled, if startled or hungry. That

wasn't enough to worry me.

We were off tarmac by now and onto hard-packed earth, passing between stands of thick forest. Clouds of mosquitoes splatted against the windshield in tiny suicides, and found their way into the cab. Marge swatted them; they stayed clear

of me. The 'skeetos' knew what I was.

Water in ditches, in ponds, in creeks and lakes. Water and trees, but the way we needed was still there, straight and broad. When Marge stopped to relieve herself, I slipped off the rig to get the feel of the forest. Lumber trucks had beaten this road down, and here it was. I heard woodpeckers in the distance, and the bell-like call of the frogs Marge called spring peepers. I knelt and let other senses

taste the thin breeze.

As far as I knew there was no such thing as a 'cursed' place. I'd never found one, in nearly two hundred years. There was a taint on the air here, though, an

indefinable wrongness. I began to consider Marge's tales more seriously.

We drove on steadily, the tips of tree branches slapping the cab, and the Peterbilt kept going until we saw a tree down ahead of us, halfway across the road.

"Shee-it. Might be able to nose it aside, if I take it slow," said Marge. "Would pull round, but I don't know what's under those ferns – might be bog-land."

"I'll go and see." I hopped down from the cab, and made a show of straining at the tree trunk. It wasn't a recent fall, and I heaved it aside easily.

"Almost hollow," I shouted over. "One winter from being sawdust. That leave enough room?"

"Yep."

Her smile was off, somehow. Moving the tree so quickly had been a mistake. I had puzzled her again, which wasn't good.

A few more miles, and she stopped to check the trailer generator, which sounded on its last legs. Clouds were gathering, with rain to come. I went among the trees again, wondering if I could have been wrong about the presence by Blackjack Springs. The memories of my kind are complex, and moments can get confused.

I'd almost persuaded myself there was nothing there, until I found the deer.

It had been a white-tail, and young. Scavengers had left the body well alone. It was crumpled in the undergrowth, mummified despite the damp, but I could make out the dark imprint of a hand on its side, seared into the hide. It was a fair bet that Marge's husband had come across something like this, and made a sensible decision.

Like knows like. One of the Returned was here, somewhere. Ella outside Chicago, and now this. I had to wonder, as I crouched over the deer, if there was some subtle and terrible reason for us to keep encountering each other. Father Alun in the wilds of the Welsh Marches, locked in centuries of philosophical combat with a God who might not exist. The deluded creature playing vampire films to drugged teenagers in Chelsea, before I broke and drowned him. And the long- rider I'd watched as he slaughtered a bar full of people. Almost a year since

Minnesota...

"What happened to that?"

I'd been too engrossed to hear her approach.

"I don't know," I lied. "Best we get going, though."

"Bears don't have hands."

"No."

The rain came not long after, turning the sun-dappled road into a wet, dark tunnel. At my urging, Marge switched on the headlights, and added speed, risking the axles. I could feel a sliver of darkness out there, closer now.

She could see the way I was staring out of the cab windows.

"An hour," she said, straining to keep the rig steady as she avoided a set of deep, water-filled ruts. "We can cut across the State line and it's plain sailin' from--"

Something heavy crashed against the windshield, a glancing blow, and then was gone, lost in the rain.

"Uff-da!" Marge was rigid at the wheel, her face white, but we didn't slow down. "Deer."

It had been no deer, and she knew it, though not much more. I had seen the wiry limbs, and picked up the reck of need...

"Could we turn back?" I peered through the downpour.
"Nope." She jammed a cigarette between her lips, taking three goes to light it.

"Ain't enough room, and Marquette's waiting."

We managed a couple of miles before we saw the second fallen tree. This one was fresh, still covered in new leaves, and directly in our path. I shouted a warning, and she slammed on the brakes, skewing the rig. The Peterbilt settled at an angle across the road, hissing and creaking.

Marge looked at me. "You're strong." It was an accusation, not a compliment. "Can you move this tree, like the other?"

"I doubt it."

"Least that's a straight answer. How about I - we - get chains round it and haul it off the road?"

"Marge, there's something out there. We both know it. It's out-paced the rig, and I don't think it want us to leave."

If I'd liked her before, I liked her even more when she spoke again. No panic, no babble.

"What does it want?"

"You, most likely. I imagine it's hungry."

"So the stories are true." She took that in, chewed on it. "Why'd you say it's after me, not us?"

"I wouldn't taste so good, believe me. But it might not be fussy."

"We talkin' bigfoot, some Indian critter, or what?"

"You'll have to settle for 'what'."

Marge had a shotgun, and six cartridges. She held it up, a questioning look. "Every little helps," I said.

It probably didn't, but there was no point in saying so. Barring incredible good fortune, a shotgun blast would be a 'skeeto' bite. Marge, by her own account,

wasn't awash with good fortune.

I could walk away, as I had in Minnesota. It might bother me for a while, but I'd left people behind before. I weighed the matter up, my gaze on the edge of the trees. The cab was too small, its own trap. I opened the door on my side.

"More room to take a potshot out there," I said.

She hauled a yellow mackintosh from behind her seat, and we slithered down onto the road.

I could feel what was coming quite clearly now. There was a dead thing on the old lumber road. Isolated, and maybe insane. Some revenants hunger for memories to replace what they have lost, others for emotion or for something ludicrously

specific. This one drew on base vitality – animal or human - to sustain itself. I'd rather have met a monster from some native legend.

The rain was heavy, but I could sense it by more than sight.

"Over there."

Undergrowth crackled in the direction I pointed; Marge fired. Five cartridges left. When it stepped out onto the road, I really did wonder how fast I could run.

There had been a man there once. Naked, his eyes as black as his straggly hair, as his dirt-encrusted feet, he walked marionette-style. Any attempt to keep a semblance of his former life had gone, along with any clue as to who he'd been.

A soul Returned to its body, abandoned and left to eat into itself.

He came forward on an unseen wave of need. Those children must have come close, and been touched by a fraction of what we were receiving. Marge staggered, feeling it, but fired again, hitting him in the shoulder.

He jerked, the flesh torn, but kept coming. For a moment he looked at me, but what could he think, if he still had thoughts? Another of his kind, nothing to do with him.

His hunger was so powerful that it distorted my senses. Sweeping the rain from my eyes, I let Marge empty her shotgun.

I let her yell for help.

I let her be terrified, be that prey which he sought.

The revenant leaped, driving her down, his attention on nothing but his hunger. His crooked hands grasped her shoulders, tearing the mackintosh to touch bare flesh, and he began to feed on her. I measured myself, tested the limits of my loyalties...

I couldn't do it to her.

With the creature's attention on Marge, I took him from behind, trying to break his neck and slow him down. It turned out there was too much sinew and whipcord muscle for that. I had his attention, though. He twisted and raked at me, nails ripping my face. He fought more like a bear than a man, swiping, clawing and grappling, and we rolled away into the wet ferns, entangled.

I saw no shred of sanity in those eyes, only the psychotic loneliness of one who was bound to this road. He must have died around here – fifty years ago, or five hundred. It didn't matter. He was what I might have been, might yet become, stripped of the mock-existence that I had so carefully constructed. So many years of trying not to be this.

He had only one gift, to feed, and so he did, engulfing me in numbing blackness. He was physically stronger than any I had faced for years, an animalistic strength. I shuddered as the rest-room junkie was stolen from me, and more. The creature searched deeper, his hunger seeking out any vitality I had hoarded. He couldn't kill me – I don't believe a revenant can die – but he could leave me drained and helpless.

And that might be right, might be proper. I saw two centuries and one fleeting second at the same time. To give in, to find some empty rest, at least for a while...

"Bastard!"

The gun-stock slammed into the side of his head, breaking his feed. Marge stood over us, swaying. She struck again, breaking the shotgun over his head and then she staggered back. Given that he'd started feeding on her, I'd assumed she was already out cold.

For a moment I felt her anger, not his needs. Her husband, her truck, her life. So many disappointments, and yet she struggled. Of the three of us, she at least deserved a chance.

"Another day," I said.

Lifting my face to the rain, which knew nothing of need or fear, I broke his grip with one whiplash movement. "Today I have to go to Marquette."

I had been around a long time. I took hold of his naked body, fingers sinking in where the shotgun had ruined his shoulder. I stood astride him and became as he was - Returned, revenant, edimmu, whatever you choose to call the damned.

I fed, and his skin crumpled and darkened where I touched it. He tasted of the beasts, and of despair. And when I had done, I broke his spine and the bones in his arms and legs, leaving a broken puppet in place of a monster. At the end he was motionless. I'd taken everything that I could take.

Marge was unconscious at the foot of a spruce. No permanent damage, as far as I could tell.

I'd told her that I didn't drive, not that I couldn't. I threw the revenant into the trailer with the pork, and propped her in the cab. There had been an animal strength in him, and now it was in me, so I moved that tree. And I drove to Marquette.

The men at the receiving depot were unhappy. The refrigeration had cut out half an hour before I pulled into their yard, but I lied and told them that the doors hadn't been opened. By then I'd strapped a thin, senseless body, wrapped in spare rugs, to the back of the cab. No one had any interest in the bundle there, if they noticed it at all.

Marge came round as I pulled the truck into a roadside joint.

"You need coffee," I said. I wondered if she'd scream, or run from me.

"Where is it?" Her voice was hoarse, cautious.

"Tied up.

"Is it dead?"

"It always was," I said. "But it won't be able to move for weeks."

That wasn't enough for her, but I hustled her inside and forced her to eat. She needed to regain some of what had been taken.

"You delivered the load." She had finished off half a dozen eggs and a heap of bacon. "I owe you."

We'd lost the easy comfort we'd had before. If she didn't quite fear me, she didn't trust what I was any more. If she'd been conscious to see the final moments where I fed on the revenant, I doubted that she'd be sitting there at all.

"You owe me nothing." I placed two hundred dollars on the table. "There's one more run we need to do. I need to take a bundle to Chicago."

She agreed without asking why. When she dropped me in the Chicago suburbs, we said an awkward goodbye. It was for the best. Rather one moment of fear and doubt about the world, than with all the horrors that I carried.

The creature was near mindless, and I'd damaged it even more. It would be my gift to Ella. Ripped so far from the lumber road, it would bind to her small existence, and they would feed off each other's pain. It was the only way I could think of freeing Blackjack Springs. I knew the abject loneliness in Ella and in whatever

was strapped to the cab. They could turn inwards together, and do less harm.

They wouldn't – couldn't - be happy. There can be no such emotion in the Returned. Whatever we have done, can it be worse than this judgment of a strange, vindictive God?

Ella had forgotten me already, as I'd expected, but she stared in wonder at what I had brought her. She dragged the bundle out of sight, to a crumbling underpass,

and I left her pawing at the creature with thin, inquiring hands.

By that evening I was in a diner, drinking strong coffee, and I was alone again. I lifted my cup.

"Good fortune, Marge."

I was finished with Wisconsin.

NORMAL
JOHN CLAUDE SMITH

Cherie told me the realtor said our new neighbor was from Florida, but he's got Georgia plates on his car, a beat-up Buick that, I'm sure, swallows more gas on a trip to the grocery store a couple miles down the road, then my Honda does while running three weeks on a full tank. The only reason either one of us noticed him beyond taking stock of a new neighbor was that the dented beast of a car didn't sleep in the empty driveway, it lounged on the front lawn. The Henderson family, who owned the house before he did, kept the greens in immaculate condition. No matter the weary state of the rest of the houses slumped in this cul-de-sac, Vic Henderson was out there every Sunday after church, mowing and sprinkling like his life depended on it. It may seem humdrum, but it was a source of comfort for the rest of us.

But that was beside the point. The new man, no name attached to him yet, looked just like his car, half falling apart, the other half angry about it. I'd seen him a handful of times late in the evening stalking his front porch, chain-smoking with abandon. I watched him three times one night pop an unlit cigarette in between his lips to keep the dying one company, before taking the stub and lighting anew. Cherie and I, we don't really care about this kind of shit, but this man, he'd broken through the monotony of living here already, setting himself up and dismantling whatever the Henderson family had established as part of a routine we had acclimated to. Like the lawn-mowing deal.

This man, he didn't fit in, and I felt it in my bones, my belly, a seed of discomfort set to plant roots and blossom in the back of my brain with the what-haves and who-knows about him and his trespass on the normal group mentality everybody along our street was accustomed to experiencing.

Something was going to have to be done, Bob Franks from next door said to me, about two weeks after the man had moved in.

"He's making me uneasy, Phil. And Barbara, she can barely look at him--'something about him ain't right'--and I think her observations are correct."

"But what can we do? What <u>should</u> we do?" I didn't want to go there again. "He bought the house. It's his to demolish, apparently. If not demolish, well, it's his to alter—"

"That's the point. We don't like what he's doing."

Playing devil's advocate for a moment, but knowing what Bob meant, I asked, "What is he really doing that's so bad?"

Bob gave me a look like I was a traitor to something I wasn't sure I was even a part of; something I wasn't sure any of us was truly a part of.

I left it at that. I knew what he meant, even if it was draped in ambiguity.

A few days later, past midnight and I was anxious, couldn't sleep. Again. I gazed out from behind the curtains to see the new man working under the hood of his car, a portable lamp the size of the moon glaring down on him and into the open hood. I watched as he leaned in underneath, did whatever he did, and leaned back out, a displeased look on his face.

"What's he doing?" Cherie asked, her too large cat pajamas signaling her entrance into the front room, the frayed hem shush-shushing upon the hardwood floor in need of waxing.

"What are you up for, hun?" I said. She only looked at me like I was a dimwit. I knew.

It was him. The man across the street. Something about him had thrown all our lives out-of-sync. To confirm my suspicions, I noticed a light go on in the upstairs house next to his, the Bale's house, and a silhouette of what looked like Lucy Bale peering out toward the commotion, which was silent yet somehow startlingly felt by all. Heard, in a way, the psychic pathways perhaps filled with bleating warning alarms from one to the other within our little cul-de-sac. I knew if I stepped outside, I'd see Bob from next door watching from a shadowed window as well. But there was no way I was going to step out front. It would draw attention I did not want. Safely secured behind the dark curtains would be fine for me, peeking out as I wanted, the slit not open enough for anybody to notice. Anybody being the man from across the street.

The stranger who we all wanted to disappear.

It was getting to the point where something really would have to be done about the situation. Bob and Barbara Franks, Richard and Lucy Bale, Cherie and me – those of us who had decided to make this place home, had taken turns dealing with the unwanted. Five long years attempting to blend in, to belong, yet people like this man, they made it impossible.

It was not something we relished, dealing with the unwanted elements. But it had to be done. Yet, I could not imagine starting up again, another round commencing, and one after that, ad infinitum. Couldn't other people simply fit in? That's all <u>we</u> wanted. To fit in. To be seen as normal.

Cherie stuck a mug of water in the microwave and the hum of operation filled the empty spaces in the room. After spooning some instant coffee into the hot water, she moseyed over to me.

"So, what is he doing up at this hour?" she asked, leaning into me and peering outside. After a moments observation, she said, "Out of respect you'd think he'd pull the vehicle into the garage. Especially with that lamp."

"What should we do?" I asked, and knew I needed to follow up. "Bob's brought it up already. Something needs to be done."

Cherie, never one to cut corners said, "What needs to be done is what's always been done. His presence is wrong. He doesn't belong here." I looked at Cherie and, even though she didn't look back, I could see the resolute determination in her hard eyes. The time was approaching when action would become necessary.

I had to wonder if the six of us would ever fit in.

I peeked out again and watched as the man backed away from the car. Though there were a couple of large, red tool boxes next to the front left tire of the car, he tossed his tool on the grass which had, at this point, grown longer than it ever had before. The Henderson family, who had been here long before any of us had moved in, at least practiced a form of unobtrusive benevolence that did not irritate. Much like the Connors and Sanderson families, who also resided in our little cul-de-sac. They were all affable to the point of being dull, but we did not mind. That's all we needed from them. Though it may seem bland, that was our goal; that was why we had picked this cul-de-sac in a nondescript town in the middle of nowhere. It was a way to never raise suspicion. As if we did anything to raise suspicion, except on rare occasions, which were swiftly swept out of consciousness, appraisal turning to dust, to nothing; to never was...We did not want to make a scene, we just wanted to live our lives in calm seclusion.

If the man just mowed the lawn and parked in the driveway, his presence might be less…upsetting. But he's done nothing to indicate he'll be anything less than a form of subtle to glaring nuisance during his stay here. Glaring, just like that damned lamp. What if he sticks around for a year, two years, five years? Already sleep habits were being disturbed. Cherie being up right now and drinking coffee, she's done that a few times already since he got here. Me, I haven't gotten a full night of sleep since the day he showed up and parked his car on the lawn. I can only imagine what the others were experiencing.

Like now.

"Fuck," I said, and Cherie leaned into me to look outside again. "What… What's Bob doing? There's a process to undertake before anything can be done. What's he doing?"

"I don't know," she said, mesmerized by the scene taking shape. There was a slight upward curl at the corner of her lip.

Bob crossed the street with obvious resolve in his strong stride. He wore black sweats, no shirt, no shoes, not even any socks. The light from next to the car the new man was working on glistened off his sweaty skin. Tall shadows stretched out behind him.

"Maybe you should stop him—"

"No. No. He's made a decision we'd have to make anyways." My jaw clenched as I gritted my teeth.

"But he looks like he's not in the right mind to handle the situation discretely." As much as Cherie might like Bob's motives, she had a point.

I glanced around the cul-de-sac. There were no lights on in the Connors and Sanderson houses. No indication they were interested in what the man was doing. I turned my focus to the right, to the intersecting cross-street, and darkness was all I saw in the windows there as well. The people quietly slept in their slumbering abodes.

We watched as the man picked up whatever tool it was he'd dropped at his feet, a screwdriver or something like a screwdriver, and held it in his hand in a defensive manner. I wished I could hear Bob, to know what he was saying, to put the edge into the man.

Just then, though, the man yelled loud enough for me to hear him say, "It's none of your fuckin' business. Go home, fat boy." I wondered if his raised voice would awaken others, but could not pull myself to look away, to check the other houses.

Out of all of us, Bob had often exhibited the least amount of patience. It was noted in group sessions he'd acclimated best to the human experience.

The man raised the tool in a threatening manner. Cherie said, "That's it," and turned away. She knew what was coming. I knew what was coming.

Bob's body bloated like a water-balloon being filled to the bursting point, the skin stretched taut and cracking, before splattering in strips across the unmowed lawn, the street, the car, and the man.

This allowed Bob to take his ultimate form.

I sighed heavily as Cherie paced behind me.

The man's features flushed pale, blending with the lamp behind him. He almost got lost within the whiteness, though I could still see his mouth, and it was opening and, I'm sure, about to scream. Bob stifled the man's intention as one of his many limbs shot out and clamped over the man's whole head. Bob's bulbous body quivered, all lines of definition gone blurry. He floated toward the man, tethered *to* the man, though the man could not see this. He struggled, desperate fingers attempting to tear the pulsing orifice that encased his head from around his neck, so he could see, or breathe, since that would be an issue shortly.

Not that it would matter to the man. His struggle for survival was just that: a struggle, which he would not win.

Even though I could not see it clearly, as Bob was turned away from me, it was clear enough: his torso had opened, and the architectural structure of grinding gear-like bones and teeth were set to the task at hand.

It's how we feed, from where we come from.

Bob was going to devour the man, clothing and all, before doing the same with the vehicle, the large, red tool boxes, the annoying lamp—every iota of the man's existence would end up inside Bob. It would take mere minutes in the front yard, before he would head inside the house, the front door left ajar, and complete the erasing of the man. There would be nothing left, no evidence of his ever having been here, besides vague memories quickly fading among those in the neighborhood who may have seen the man.

This was how it always went. This is what we deemed necessary.

That's when I let out a startled gasp as Bob seemed to deflate, disconnecting from the man, who was no longer human. What stood in his place seemed more crustacean, which meant he was a—

"Plutonian. Why would a Plutonian want to live here?" Cherie said. Under different circumstances, I might have laughed at the hypocrisy suggested by the question. Cherie was back at the window, standing beside me. She let out a snicker, which crawled into my belly and nudged me there, like a dog might do to one's crotch.

"I need to stop this." I headed for the door as the Plutonian raised one of its many bony claws, about to smite Bob to smithereens, though Bob looked as if smithereens would be a step up.

"I suppose you should," Cherie said, but her voice was already diminishing as I dashed out the door.

"Stop," I said, waving my hands, trying to get the Plutonian's attention. "Stop!"

It worked as the Plutonian halted, looked askew at me, and said in the gurgling intonations of its language, and swiftly translated by the buds implanted in my ears and wired into my mind, "Why should I not annihilate this disgusting creature?"

"Phil," Bob said, a brittle whisper, like ice cracking.

"Phil," Barbara screamed, as she ran toward us. She was also wearing black sweats with no shirt, shoes or socks.

There was laughter from our doorway, Cherie taking it in, when she should be helping me.

Barbara started to shift, to bloat as Bob did, as if she was going to attempt to do battle with the Plutonian, who now stood there, bony claws resting on what might be its hips, though it might be its shoulders, the displacement of body parts rather perplexing.

As Barbara passed by me, I grabbed her and said, "No." She slipped on the long, wet grass, and landed next to Bob, who seemed to be slowly inflating himself again. As if he'd just had the wind knocked out of him and was now reversing the process.

The Plutonian said, "I don't want any trouble from you. I came here to scout out this planet, to see what its inhabitants were like. To study them and fit in as well as possible. To see if it was feasible as many on Pluto are looking for a change of scenery."

Cherie laughed loudly as she approached us. "He's just like us. He just wants to fit in." We all turned toward her as she sipped her coffee.

I turned back to the Plutonian. "If you wanted to fit in, what the hell have you been doing?"

Something about the way his face moved suggested confusion.

"I had studied a random subject, one of the males of the species, and have been following his lead. What you see me doing is what he always does. I just wanted to be normal."

"Normal," Bob said. "If all you want to be was normal, you obviously need to expand on your research methods, because nothing you are doing qualifies as normal."

"At least as far as we know," Cherie said.

"Well, I mean…" Bob stammered, sat up, almost fully filled in as the strips of skin he'd worn scooted back toward him. They were assuming their ultimate form as well.

"What makes us think what we've witnessed…" Cherie said, then paused as I approached her. "What?"

I whispered to her, all heads turned toward us and perhaps Bob and Barbara and Richard and Lucy Bale, too, from their perch in the upstairs room in the house to our left, understanding me, while the Plutonian stared, his body also shifting back to a semblance of human. A rather revolting choice he made, but human, nonetheless.

It's not as if any of the humans were appealing, but in order to be here, to fit in, to be normal, as the Plutonian had said, we had to put away our prejudices and make the appropriate adjustments.

After I whispered to Cherie, she smiled wide and laughed with such gusto we all joined in. Even the Plutonian, who was about to get an earful about what it meant to be a human. We spent the night chatting away, only hoping our words would make a difference.

As things settled down, the first steps toward successfully incorporating our new neighbor into the neighborhood were obvious. The Plutonian at least parked in the driveway.

Perhaps he would fit in.

"What's that sound?" Cherie said, early Sunday afternoon. She said this, knowing what the sound was, nodding her head before visually confirming. We both scrambled toward the front window and pulled the curtains aside.

There we saw a Plutonian wearing the skin of a human as he acquainted himself with what looked to be a shiny, new lawnmower.

SOMETHING HUNGRIER THAN LOVE
Aksel Dadswell

1

Rain and mist pull back over the mountains' jagged darkness like the snarl of lips over teeth. Everly's insides toss and swill as the ferry climbs a wave. She retches into her sick-bag's mouth, braces herself as the downward tilt drags, drags . . . and smacks back down with a hard fleshy *thwack*. Seaspray hits the windows, turns the world to a momentary blur.

Everly takes a slow breath, runs her tongue along her teeth. Her mouth feels chalky, tastes sharp. The mother of all acid reflux, she thinks, with a dark little burp of laughter. Her heart's a caged bird, weak and panicked. She just wants this to be over.

She rests her head against the window and looks out at the rain-dimpled water, the endless dark crush of it surrounding her. She closes her eyes, tries to focus on the sounds around her; the clatter of cutlery and the voices of children roaming the aisles, playing their games and telling their jokes in a language she can't understand. She listens to its guttural harmony, drifting to its rhythm, and the waves'. Her breaths are even, heavy. She slips in and out of bilious sleep, her dreams sharp and slippery and motile.

The ferry's mooring when she wakes, eyes sticky, throat a dry knot. Everly checks her pocket, makes sure her precious cargo is still there. Her fingers touch the fold of paper and she slumps with relief. Every second without her hand on it, paranoia convinces her it's lost.

She makes her way downstairs with the rest of the herd, past the cars lined up inside the ferry's guts.

Outside, the rain makes a haze of everything.

Everly sees the lift she's arranged to the accommodation waiting for her in the pocked bitumen of the parking lot. It's a battered red van, a cigarette flaring like a languid SOS as whoever's behind the wheel sucks at it and exhales endlessly.

She trots through the rain, gives a stunted wave. A woman gets out and opens the trunk. She's wearing a bobbly polar fleece jacket and the extremities of her face are red raw. She looks like a grazed knee, something you wince at and quickly cover up.

The woman takes Everly's suitcase, plasters on a limp smile.

'We should get out of the rain.'

Everly gets in the passenger seat and the woman climbs in next to her.

'Welcome to Moskenes,' she says, and her eyes are dead, ink-blot-dark. 'My name is Britta. I own the cabins down at Sakrisøy. I drive, I cook the breakfast, I check you in.' Her voice's rhythm rises and sinks in a lifeless but carefully enunciated singsong.

'Yes. Hi. I'm, uh, Everly?'

Britta raises an amused eyebrow. 'Is that a question?'

'No. I'm definitely Everly. I know that at least.'

'You must be. You are only person staying for two weeks.'

'Oh. Slow time of year?'

'Tourists, they do not come till spring, till everything is green.' Her gaze skims flat over the landscape outside. 'No green yet.'

Everly makes a show of mimicking Britta's gaze. The woman's not wrong, but Everly already knew that, and she's not really thinking about seasons now. The paper getting damp with her sweat, softening like marzipan as she folds and unfolds it, folds and unfolds it, her fingers procrastinating while her mind races.

'I'm not a tourist.'

Britta doesn't blink. 'So I remember from your email. Shall we go, then?' she says, starting the car.

They set off along a narrow unravelling road, dwarfed by mountains and ocean, the odd barnacle of civilisation clinging to the land or leaning out over the water, finding purchase where it can.

The mountains are all slick dark rock, sloughed of snow as winter slinks away. The sky's pale-bright but everything else outside looks dull, desaturated, like the colour's had its volume turned down.

The earth swallows them as they enter a tunnel that worms its way through the mountains' roots, and them worming through it in turn. A rough stone oesophagus, lit by a dim nicotine glow.

Driving through this gullet, she wonders what other things are squirming through the earth around her, the size of them, the proximity. A world busy with unknown life. Everly knows that feeling.

And then they're out again, Everly squinting as the sky rips open, sketches out the landscape for her afresh. Her hand in her pocket again without conscious thought.

Over another bridge connecting these fragments of land and Britta slows, pulling up in the muddy grit outside a cluster of mustard-coloured buildings no more or less remarkable than the others they've passed. In the photos Everly looked at before she booked the trip, everything seemed bright and inviting. Here in the flesh, the gap between advertising and reality glares.

Britta cuts the engine. The rain drums its fingers on the roof.

Everly's sweating beneath her jacket suddenly, despite the cold. That caged bird in her chest is at it again, but not from nausea this time. She fingers the paper in her pocket, folding and refolding it in the dark, runs her thumb over its torn edge.

'Do you have it?' Britta asks.

'Yes.'

Everly takes the paper out, unfolding it with a surprisingly steady hand. She doesn't look at it, can't. Her eyes on Britta instead. Everly hands it to her, an offering, a plea, barely daring to breathe.

She waits as Britta scans its contents, silent and inscrutable, seconds that feel like hours.

Then: 'What if I said that this is not for you? Not for me to give.'

'I'd call you a liar,' says Everly.

'And would I be? I did not confirm anything in our emails.'

'No, you were careful about that. But it was still an invitation. Why let me go to all the trouble just to reject me?'

Britta just looks at her. She cocks her head. Everly wants to scream.

'You are Australian, yes?'

'Yeah. Why?'

'You have come all the way over to Norway for this. There are things you did not say in our emails, also. You are running from something?'

'What makes you say that?'

'There is a sharpness to you, and you fidget always. You are... on the edge. Whatever you are running from, it will catch you.'

Everly's eyes slip around the scene, finding no purchase. She reaches up with her left arm to push her hair back, and her sleeve slips down a little. She sees the other woman notice. 'Maybe I want that. Maybe I'm not running.'

'I see. This place marks the end, you know this? From the Mouth and the Matriarch there is no returning. You will not leave unchanged.' Britta shrugs. 'Maybe you will not leave at all.'

'I understand. I've read about it.'

Britta laughs, the first genuine emotion she's shown, though it doesn't blunt her sharpness. 'You have read about it.' The grin dies on her face. 'And you have a gift?'

Everly nods.

'Something precious. Something close. Alive.'

Another nod. She coughs, swallows the bile rising up through her, clenches her stomach and tries not to vomit.

Something in Britta shifts. She refolds Everly's precious paper and hands it back to her.

'Shall I show you where you will stay?'

The cabins sit out over the water in a neat row. Everything's calm here, quiet and waiting. Britta unlocks the door of the fourth cabin down. A seagull the size of a cat paces the railing outside, fixing a lazy eye on Everly.

The cabin has two levels. Basic amenities crowd the ground floor. White lace curtains dilute the light. To her left, the steepest flight of stairs Everly's seen leads to a bed wedged under the angle of the roof. A small window set into the ceiling looks up, unblinking, at the wash of sky.

'Here we are.' Britta sweeps her hand across the room. 'All the facilities you need. Kitchen, bathroom. You can make a wood fire or use the heater by the window. And the lovely view.' She turns to Everly. 'Do you know when it will arrive?'

Everly shrugs. 'A few days, maybe? Can't be exact.'

'That will be fine. When it does, we will know. You must wait. You are lucky we are helping. Not many find us here. Even less still live. Most would not understand. Most would be afraid.'

'I am afraid,' Everly says, her voice turning brittle.

Britta steps towards Everly and takes her hand, traces a spiral on the palm. Her finger's cold, almost damp. Everly thinks that maybe Britta's eyes look softer, but that could just be the light.

'Not a soul has bothered us in years. And here you are, thanks to an old book. And you. Do you really know what this is all about?'

Everly doesn't know what to say.

'You could not know. You could not fathom Her.' Britta's eyes flick down. 'But you will. She is beneath us, beneath us all, and She is hungry. Always, always hungry.'

After the woman's left, Everly undresses and goes straight upstairs. She lies in the low bed, staring up through the window and the slow twilight beyond. She brings her left arm up to eye level, looks at the bruise there like a dissipating oil spill. She touches it, brushing it with her fingertips at first and then pressing and pressing until she feels the dull pain, right up against the bone.

When the light finally dies, she turns on her side and closes her eyes and doesn't fall asleep.

2

'You know, I feel like an arsehole for not asking you this on the first date, but what do you do?'

'Well you're definitely an arsehole and I already made a note of that, so strike one, buddy.' Everly makes a gun with her thumb and index finger, cocks it at James, closes one eye and makes a cartoony shooting sound. James laughs, plays dead.

'It's okay,' she says. 'I never asked you either. And, I guess I'm still technically a student.'

'Technically?'

'I'm doing a PhD.'

'Wow, really? I've never met someone who did one of those.'

'You seem genuinely impressed?'

James laughs, rocking back in his chair with his hands planted firmly on the table. His arms are taut, and muscular enough for Everly to notice.

'Course,' he says, the laughter still in his eyes as he looks at her, always so direct. 'Why wouldn't I be?'

'Honestly? Most people aren't. I don't have a "real job" in the "real world".'

'Who the fuck wants that? Plus, reality's subjective.'

'It is, is it?'

'Yep,' he says, like it's the final word on the matter. 'And I wanna know all about Everly's. What's your doctorate on?'

'Fertility cults. Their origins, history, evolution, geographical spread, their impact on modern religious frameworks . . . I mean, the jargon's pretty boring, but the research is much cooler than it sounds. *I* like it, anyway. I'm a history nut. That was my major. Well, ancient history.'

Everly stops, momentarily breathless, sweaty in the night's heat. She drains what's left of her pint. It provides a little relief and hides her embarrassed blush.

'Sorry,' she says. 'I don't normally talk about postgrad shit this much. Ooh, I'm doing a PhD. Big deal.'

'Yes big deal. I could listen to you talk about this postgrad shit all night. As if *cults* are boring, Jesus.'

Everly pauses, assesses him. He *seems* interested. The eye contact, the smile, all of him bending eagerly towards her.

'In that case, I can tell you all about it after you've bought me another drink.'

'Cheeky,' he laughs. As he asks her if she wants the same again, Everly wonders if he's ever not smiling or laughing, or both.

While he's at the bar, Everly flicks through her phone without really looking. She gets bored after a minute and sets it down on the table.

She's stifling in her leather jacket. Even out here, the night's so hot and close. She's uncomfortable in this boisterous press of people, hedged in by all the other tables crowded with makeup-caked girls and beefy, sweaty guys, all louder than each other in the swell of voices and music.

James is coming back. She watches him as he weaves his way towards her, a full pint balanced in each hand. He seems so contained but so comfortable, at ease just being himself.

He doesn't spill a drop before he sets the glass down in front of her.

She starts struggling out of her jacket.

'Don't know why I wore this bloody thing,' she says, while the sweat beads on her forehead.

'I think you look great. In or out of it.' James ducks his head, shy or embarrassed by his own compliment.

Everly finally manages to unpeel the jacket from her flesh, pulling it off like a hunter skinning a rabbit.

On the table, her beer's sweating about as much as she is.

'So,' says James, leaning forward. 'You were telling me about cults.'

They don't have everything in common, but the conversation never slows or falters. He really is interested in her, asking so many questions and contributing enough to each subject that she doesn't feel like she's in an interview.

They have a couple more drinks and a lot more conversation, and the world closes in around them. They lean in close as they talk, every other noise reduced to peripheral static.

At some point she realises she doesn't really know what they're talking about anymore, the words on flirtatious autopilot while she silently wills him to kiss her.

Everly can't remember when it happens or who makes the first move, but at some point they leave the pub, her hand sweaty in his. Above them, the star-pricked summer sky yawns. James takes her to his car, and they stand there looking at each other for one awkward grinning moment before he pushes her against the door and kisses her. She sinks into it, into the bright details. His thumb brushing her cheek. The press of him against her almost tender. Her dress sticking to every inch of her. Her skin sticky-hot like melted plastic.

His lips are cool, his tongue too.

Their mouths pull apart so slowly, and James looking at her the same way he has been all night, except softer, slyer, almost triumphant. He keeps trying to push down his grin.

'My place,' he says, his voice wet with spit, inflection lacking a question mark.

Everly just looks at him and they get in.

The drive's electric, the lights all stretching out, the road liquid black, his hand slipping over her bare thigh now and then. They snatch glimpses of each other, almost shy now in the eager silence.

Time passes in fragments, in slow blinks. A lightning-strike of colour and sensation, then down into dark and quiet before it starts up again.

The swing of headlights as they pull into his driveway.

James leading her by the hand again, through the dark of his house.

In his bedroom and Everly squinting against the shock of the light as he flicks it on. Her hand on his chest, pushing him back against the closet, and him pushing back, his face so close but teasing, drawing away and then close, and finally he's kissing her again and even though she told herself she wouldn't do it, it's happening and actually she likes it, likes the way he tastes, the sandpaper scratch of his stubble and his hand on the back of her head, holding her there, pressing their mouths together.

They undress in a clumsy rush and then they're on the bed, hands and mouths on each other, her hot and soaking wet, James pushing up and in. His hand on her arm, his thrusts, all of his contact with her creeps up to the very edge of painful, teeth all but biting, skin so close to bruised, but he finds her bright hot centre and works it so softly behind the calculated roughness, finds it like almost no other guy has done before him, that it contributes to her bliss.

When it's over they lie side by side, glistening and panting, barely a point of contact between them in the almost unbearable friction of their post-coital heat. The air's moist, ripe with the smell of the sex. Everly can almost taste it.

'Wow,' she says, her mind racing, wandering, but her tongue too thick for more syllables.

James runs a finger up her sweat-slicked thigh. He looks at her and his eyes burn.

'Does that mean I get a third date?'

3

Time drags. Every day, counting through each like it might be the one she's waiting for, feels longer than the last, but that could just be spring crawling closer. There's still no discernible change in the landscape, drab and distant as it feels.

She tries the local pub one night but everyone keeps their distance. She can feel the men staring, their slow sharp smiles sliding over her skin despite her layers of clothing. Not an unfamiliar sensation, never unfamiliar but never less than skin-crawling. A meal, that's what she feels like under that licked-lip scrutiny. Food on a plate.

She goes for a walk most days, for the fresh air and something to do with her time. She buys food at the small supermarket about thirty minutes away, and cooks by herself in the cabin.

Everywhere she goes, everywhere she looks or turns or thinks, the mountains loom, slick dark blemishes that never budge from her line of sight. The weather shifts from rain to sun, the moon pulls at the tides, and life moves about, and those mountains sit surrounded by it all, implacable.

Everly wonders what goes on beneath the skin, what their vast honeycomb insides might hide. Images of close, moist, coarse spaces fill her head. A pulse in the rock, the nurturing slosh of darkness all around.

💀💀💀

She gets back from her walk late one day with the sun still endless in the sky to find her cabin door sitting ajar by a sliver. A dull thrill spills through her, but it's not surprise. She's known this was coming. She's counted on it. She takes a breath and rubs her palms, already sweaty, on her jeans. Another breath, and another. Seconds stretch loud around her. Gulls crying. The beating of blood in her ears.

She pushes the door open all the way. For once it doesn't creak.

He's sitting there on the couch so casually, one leg crossed over the other, an arm slung up along the backrest like this isn't the first time he's seen her in over a week. She feels the memory of faded bruises on her skin, an itchy flush blooming on her arms and face. There's something else under there, too. A little electric thrill, like when she was a kid on Christmas Eve, that buzz that wouldn't let her sleep, her eyes closed but her brain still working, working. So much anticipation she could scream.

But she swallows it, says 'Hello,' instead in as calm a voice as she can manage.

'Hi,' James smiles. That's what gets her, the ease of his tone, the confidence.

'You found me.'

He leans forward. 'A three hour ferry, Ev. What the fuck? Why couldn't you've "escaped" somewhere a bit less out the way, eh?' He clicks his fingers in quick succession, pulling that I-fucked-up face that always foreshadows danger. 'I forgot, you love to complicate shit, dontchya?' His mouth blooms into a grin and it's all teeth. 'That's my girl.'

She wants to snap at him, get in there with a sharp retort, but her head's all in a jumble and the words won't come. She thought it would be easier after being away from him, but those awful familiar sensations are rushing back into the hole she exhumed them from.

Before she can drag a word out he's standing up and he's talking again, talking like he always does, over her, through her, his voice surrounding and corralling her, twisting her shape like wet clay.

'Why'd you run off? It was going so well. We had everything we needed, and more. And when I say more, *Everly*, I'm talking about the good news you never. Even. Shared with me. My god, what am I supposed to think?' He steps closer, hands held out towards her. '*I just want to keep you safe*. It'd be one thing if you fucked off alone, but in your state? Thought you could go running off to fucking *Norway* and I wouldn't find you?'

His backhand comes out of nowhere, erupts from his monologue's flow, its bite so familiar it tastes almost sweet. She stumbles back but doesn't fall, the weight of the moment keeping her on her feet. Her lip's split, but it's nothing she hasn't experienced before. She sucks at the blood, another familiar taste.

Before the moment can fizzle down, James is on her again, pinning her to the floor with his arms and knees. Late to the party, late to her life, Everly finds her fight. She wriggles backwards from of his grip and kicks out at him, hard. Something cracks under her heel and nothing's ever felt so good to her, the blood on his face so cathartic after all this time.

James reels back with a wet scream more surprise than pain, Everly scrambling back over the floorboards away from him. Her back hits the wall between the stairs and the door and she pushes against it, gets to her feet.

The door swings open.

It doesn't burst in or slam open or even creak. The silence of its entrance and the four masked, robed people who slip inside push the noise out of the room. Everly's holding her breath, relief flooding through her at their timing while her nails dig into the wall behind her.

'Who the *fuck*—' James starts to say through the ruin of his nose. He tries to stand, but the figures surround him, hold him. One presses a cloth to his mouth and his struggles slow before he goes completely limp. Two of them hoist him up from either end and carry him out of the cabin without a glance at Everly.

After a moment of breathless terror, she follows.

They move like a snake through the streets and the day's lateness. Every second figure carries a flaming torch as the long procession winds across the bridge and down the road's descending curve. It looks like the whole town's laid out in a line. Beyond that she can see the faint burning trail of the serpent's head, squeezing into the edge of town and up through the steeper incline between the mountains, where civilisation ends and everything else begins.

As if in a dream, Everly joins the slow trail, her limbs heavy and trembling, still coming down from her adrenaline rush.

Outside, the world's quieter than when she just left it. Cloud hangs low, hugs the mountains. Everything seems so small suddenly, and through it all the wordless march of robed figures, carrying James' body and bearing Everly along with them in single file.

Through the old mundane neighbourhood, lace curtains in every window. The ground rises as they move up through the edge of habitation, up into the mountains.

They head deeper, their way lit with the bright unblinking eyes of the torches. The path slopes up. Clouds occlude the sun, sharpening the wind's edge. The light's hazy, suffused in a soft fuzz through sky and air. Everything seems too bright and blurry, like she has a floater in her eye.

Up ahead, the dark glob of a cave mouth through which the procession files, silently and willingly devoured. Its opening is surprisingly smooth, lips parted in a scream or a yawn or a greedy gulp. Everly can't decide. Either way, she realises, this must be the Mouth.

Somewhere inside, the Matriarch.

She steps over the lip into a world where shadows swoop and flicker in the torchlight, make monsters of the rock's contours. Her mouth's dry, tongue like sandpaper. She doesn't dare swallow.

Somewhere, deeper, a slow eternal drip breaks the almost cloying silence.

The air inside is colder than out, somehow older, washed in and out by the torches' warmth. Everly smells damp, and something like moss on stone. There's a spice to the air not just from the fire.

Down they go, and down, and down some more, the air needling her skin.

Not a word is said, nor a breath heard except her own.

In the torch-light she can see tiny growths on the rock walls the further they go, little clusters of pale things wavering, shrinking against the flames. Motile shapes, some with legs and some without, evade the procession's descending glow.

Eventually, when they're so far down beneath the mountain Everly wonders if she'll ever see the sky again, they come to a set of steps cut into the rock, busy with carvings that adhere to some pattern she's not privy to. They're worn smooth in places from the tread of many feet. They feel old, older than everything here but the mountains, and perhaps whatever waits at their foot.

Everly takes them slowly, easing herself down one cold step at a time, those anonymous figures behind and ahead of her.

A lifetime later they reach the bottom. The acolytes leading her fan out to line the edges of a cavern so vast she can't see how deep it goes. Laid out like this, everyone fits comfortably shoulder to shoulder.

Everly looks up, almost surprised when she can't see stars in the sky.

Those carrying James lay him out on the floor, holding something to his nose that makes him stir and slowly come to. They leave him there and take their places around the cavern's edge.

While James fidgets into wakefulness, something looms in the dark, beyond the torches' reach. A statue, twice, three, four times Everly's height and breadth. She strains and stares into the dark, slowly piecing its shape together even though she knows it in her head, its broad contours licked by firelight. A fertility goddess, bulging at the breasts and hips.

The Matriarch.

James struggles to his hands and knees, gagging and coughing. The blood he spits glistens against the rock. He raises his head, looks at her, eyes reflecting the circle of fire.

'This is nice. This is great.' He wipes at the blood on his face and winces when he catches his broken nose. 'Jesus Ev, what'd you, join a cult?' He jerks his head at the impassive figures, each one indistinguishable from the next. He dribbles a bit of crazed laughter. 'The fuck're they waiting for?'

Everly steps forward, and it feels like the hardest approach she's ever taken in her life.

Finally, she finds a voice.

'I realised something recently. I always felt like the bruises gave me a shape, made me someone to see. But they're nothing to do with me. It's just you. Your fingerprints all over me. I don't need them.'

He snorts, but there's less edge to him. His eyes dart about, messily checking and re-checking their surroundings.

'But I love you,' he says.

'I don't need that, either.'

'Yes you do. We need each other.' So much conviction in his voice, like it's all so simple.

Her cut lip's oozing again. Tears sting her eyes in the smoky cavern. She casts her arms wide, and the smile she throws him is colder than the rock and earth that hems them in.

'Don't you see where we are? Where all this has taken us? We're down past the Mouth now.'

There's nothing behind his grin. He hasn't heard her, can't hear a word now over the roar of his own need, the smell of blood, the raw panic rising through him that he keeps trying to deny. He gets to his feet, breathing hard.

'Hope you had a nice holiday, Ev. Out here in the middle of buttfuck nowhere. You're a little bitch, you know that? All the shit you put me through. But that's over now.'

'I know it is,' she says. 'See behind you?'

He half-turns, suspicious. When he sees it he stumbles back, almost falls again.

'What the *fuck* is that?'

Impossible, but the idol seems closer now. Everly can make out more of its shape as it rises glacial in the foreground. Its curves glisten and almost shift, and Everly's gut drops as she realises it's not a statue at all. It's wet and moving and . . . alive, somehow. It seems to be breathing. She doesn't know why she didn't see it before, but there's a slow rise and fall, a soft weight to the breasts and belly that stone just can't convey. Everly trembles, all of her clenched and on the edge of a scream.

4

The bathroom's her only real sanctuary now, with its lock and running water to drown out the sound of both him and her screaming thoughts. Even when he's out she never really feels comfortable in the rest of the house, can't shake the feeling that he's hiding somewhere, waiting to jump out and scare her, grab her, kiss her.

Tell her he loves her.

Everly sits on the toilet, toes pressed against the cool tiles, wincing as she pees. She wonders if it'll be laced with blood again, like the last time he punched her in the kidneys.

She remembers James last night after a hurried, tender fuck she didn't really want but couldn't refuse, holding her and saying it over and over again in a breathless string: *I love you, I love you, I love you, I love you*. She thought it was an apology at first, him pleading with her to forgive him, showing her that he did care after all.

It's never an apology. It's an affirmation, a full stop on the end of a sentence. A violent, dark sentence with dirt under its letters.

She used to wonder how deluded he must be to think that he loved her after the things he did, or that maybe he was just a liar. But the problem was that he *did* love her, and that was so much worse.

She holds the paddle under her stream, panic seeping through her system, her life teetering on the edge of dreadful possibility.

The waiting's the worst part, that agonising space of time when it could go either way.

She checks her phone for the fifth time. She doesn't want to touch the plastic again. She wants to throw it in the bin and leave, just run out the door no matter the reality and never come back.

She plucks the test off the sink's edge and it tells her the one thing she doesn't want it to.

Bile tastes sharp and bitter as it rises at the back of her throat.

Even if it wasn't him, even if he wasn't the father she can't imagine this being a good thing. Every component of her life slipping down, turning and recalibrating to fit around this tiny new thing she doesn't even want. She'll love it, she knows, but only because she has to. She feels bad for it already, with a father like that. If it's a boy, will it be like him no matter how she tries to raise him? Is his dad's filth in him already, carried through from his seed?

She imagines it swilling around inside her like a worm in a bottle of tequila, but no, that's not nearly as intimate or horrifying as it actually feels. Something connected to her, growing *out of* her, *in* her. Everly shudders, hugs herself. She wants to run from this but she can't. There's no escape, except maybe one. She feels mean for this, wonders for a moment if she's a monster, but she can't think of it with affection or she might waver. And she can't waver, can't bring something of his into the world. There's too much of him in hers already.

She has a quick Google on her phone, reads about Doctors' referrals and finds the number for her GP. When she's booked an appointment she stands in front of the mirror with her jeans still peeling open and her shirt pulled up under her bra. She runs her hand over the deceptively flat surface of her belly, imagines she can feel it curled inside her already, hungry and growing down in the warm wet dark of her, filling up all the spaces inside.

She can't handle it in there anymore so she walks out into the backyard, looks at the man-made horizon of roofs and TV aerials, the odd stifled palm tree or peppy. The sun's sliding down behind it all, dragging its bright orange glow with it. Everly stands out there as the fire dies and the air cools and the mozzies come out. She wishes she could sleep, can't stand the thought of another day in this life of hers, this life with *him*. Another day, and another sunset and another day, and on and on until she's dead.

5

James has gone quiet, but Everly's forgotten he exists, forgotten everything here exists except this living, pulsing idol. It is a goddess after all.

There's a voice emanating from it, corkscrewing into Everly's head, a sound like whispers drifting through miles of pipe. It's thanking her, crooning, laughing a little. It tells her its story, whispers it in sharp words, the history of the world, the blind pale secrets that crawl in the deep. Its words trickle down inside her head, boring down through her soft parts, exploring her.

She's aroused and revolted. She wants to run, to die, to step closer to this glabrous giant. Her head's a noise of needles and voices and her own thoughts scrabbling for purchase. Nothing exists anymore except her and the Matriarch, and Everly's not even sure of herself anymore.

She gasps as something like a strip of skin unpeels from the glossy mass. It coils and uncoils, brushes the air in a gesture almost tender.

And then she sees it. This goddess isn't a goddess, or at least this voluptuous body isn't hers. Just a shape to take, a mould to fill.

It's a worm, some huge invertebrate, the longest Everly can imagine and longer still, coiled and folded into the shape of fertility itself.

'Ev, what is this? Ev help me. *Fuck.*' James' voice pierces her bubble and everything comes leaking back in. The acolytes are chanting now, a bass drone that rises endlessly as each member takes up the last one's slack. Round and round the circle they go.

James collapses to his knees, whimpering while the worm's head weaves towards him, more of it uncoiling as the main mass loses some of its cultivated shape. Its tip opens and a mass of pale tendrils unfurl so fast it looks like a magic trick. They fill the air, surrounding him and rippling with prehensile life, animated with a hunger Everly can't even imagine.

James turns his head to her, such a slow and deliberate motion, and the look on his face, more raw and agonising than she's ever seen before, almost makes her feel for him.

Almost.

The voice thanks her, and then the tendrils are on him, and it's pulling him apart, tearing him to so many bloody screaming orts of matter as the chanting of the acolytes rises and rises through the endless mountain hollows, through Everly's bones.

6

Pregnant women always have their hands on their belly, subconsciously feeling for a bump, soothing the small bundle of joy inside.

It's too early for even the beginnings of a bump, but Everly avoids all contact with hers, recoils every time she accidentally brushes against it. She doesn't touch it, with her hand or her thoughts.

She sits in a waiting room adorned with generic landscape paintings, the speakers oozing syrupy music that's supposed to be relaxing but only grates on Everly's nerves. While she waits, and to take her mind off everything, she sifts through some research material, a newly acquired book she had shipped over from a library overseas.

A handful of sad or anxious looking women go in before her, and Everly wonders about their circumstances, if they're here as a last resort, in desperation like her. At her stage she knows the termination will probably be medical rather than surgical. Just a couple of pills and some nausea, and she can flush it out of her forever. Like an exorcism, she thinks, but with more fluid.

She concentrates on the book, flicking through the pages, her brain barely retaining what her eyes are taking in, and then it's just there, shining out at her. Ancient practices, a stone idol, a handful of places puncturing the world like giant pins stuck in a map. She's seen things like this before, an accretion of clues, scabs and dribs and bits, moments always an ant's length away from some obscure revelation, if only the reader knew what they were looking at.

Everly keeps reading. She's forgotten where she is, what she's here for. There's not much information in the chapter, and the author's style is so labyrinthine it takes her a few times to catch their drift. But a hook has caught itself in her, this familiarity, the sense of something she knows or should know or might have forgotten, the big reveal on the tip of her tongue. It's been building in some neglected corner of her head and she hasn't even realised.

Some part of her has known about this ever since she saw that fertility idol somewhere, a museum or a magazine or maybe someone's house, a variation on the usual curvaceous goddess, a headless thing all breasts and hips. This one was different, she remembers, its surface busy with a dense tangle of carved lines, knotting and fitting together like a maze for the devout to follow.

Her heart's racing. Someone steps into the waiting room and calls her name but she ignores it.

She keeps reading, unpicking the thicket of prose. A statue or idol, a representation of their goddess that takes away a woman's pain, eats it, eats all their problems. There's no mention of the group's name, but there is a map, and some other diagrams.

This book, this page, cements it all. A mosaic of fragments useless on their own, not even really clues on their own, but together they point to something. Not just research, but maybe a solution to all her problems.

Everything just clicks down into place.

She leaves the clinic, drives home in a haze. James is still at work and she took the day off to take care of her problem. An excitement builds in her, a consuming buzz that won't go away.

Deep down, she doesn't really believe there's any goddess or that her pain – her mistakes – can simply be consumed by another. But she's so knotted up in her research, in the past beading up through the present, that she doesn't much care.

Maybe part of her just wants a holiday, a last peaceful place to spend some time before he kills her. Because he will, she knows that.

Either way, she wants to see some mountains before she dies.

7

Blood-mist is all that's left of him, so thick she's almost choking on it. It condenses in too-warm droplets on her face, the rest of him a squirming lump pushed down the worm's great endless throat. It's all throat, Everly thinks in some small corner of her mind. What does someone look like when they come out at the other end?

Is that what Heaven is? she wonders.

A hand falls on her shoulder and Everly jumps. Britta behind her, her mask lifted off a sweaty face. 'Now the sacrifice,' she says, her eyes fervent. She steps back into line.

Everly's caught in its regard. It sways and croons and that voice pesters at her, begging her in wet glottal syllables for the next thing to sate its awesome hunger. This next meal that pays for the first.

Everly undresses. Her jacket and her top, shoes and pants. Her skin bristles in the cold but her hands are sweaty.

Flesh, older than stone, than life, than Cambrian seas, greets her, caresses her. She closes her eyes and imagines the touch as tender kisses on her thighs and belly, kisses that converge towards a common destination. Everly feels the warm pulse of life between her legs, and she's wet despite herself. A few playful prods and touches, and then it's in her, this endless worm, and as it delves deep for its meal she imagines it filling her up, mincing all her insides and dwelling, coiled and contented, in her skin, and she its new living idol. It feels like that now, the agony of it, this thing delving where things ought not to delve.

A sharper pain as something's wrenched from her, plucked out like an unripe fruit. Bright spots populate her vision, the pain spilling wet and hot all through her, a kind of emptiness or hunger following it. The goddess retreats, emerging from the mouth of Everly's cave all wet and bloodied, something caught in its tip. The moment swells. This tiny thing held between them, connecting them, the span of its life stretching from mother to Mother, and Everly can't help but smile.

E

Jeffrey Thomas

Sitting at a table in their little afterthought of a company cafeteria, the sleeves of her blue smock rolled up plump forearms, Stella held open a battered and food-crusted copy of the magazine *International Gazetteer*, which the cover proclaimed was "Our Race Issue."

"Is that issue, or *issue?*" Georgina, sitting opposite her, asked while provocatively cocking an eyebrow and taking a sip from her paper cup of coffee. It was first break, nine AM.

"I'd rather read 'Our *Racy* Issue'," said another of Stella's coworkers, Lonnie, who had looked up from the even more stained sports page he was reading. "I haven't seen one of those in years. Do they still run photos of topless colored girls posing around in the jungle? Those were *very* educational to me as a boy."

"You can't say 'colored,' Lonnie," Georgina warned him, glancing furtively around the break room. At another table sat two workers from Ghana, but they were caught up in their own conversation, in their own language. "And the answer is no. Back in those days they thought it was okay 'cause they saw those folks as, you know, less than human. Like animals."

"I don't think it was that," Stella said, making a wincing expression. "I think they were just trying to educate people, and show them places they never saw before...and would never get to see. It was important, to teach us about other cultures. It opened our eyes. But now look at this." She turned the glossy magazine around to face the others, and paged back to an essay written by the venerable publication's new editor, at the front of the issue. At the essay's head was a decades-old photograph of a white man showing his 35mm camera to a number of ethnically garbed black men. "The new editor of *International Gazetteer* writes this long-ass introduction apologizing for the whole entire past of this important magazine that's taught generations so much about the world, and made us understand about other races. It's like she's trashing this magazine that she *heads!* It's all this crazy self-hatred...hatred at herself, even, for being white. Look, she apologizes for pictures like *this* –" she tapped that image of the photographer "– that she calls racist, because supposedly it implies the white man is superior and he's showing off to these poor ignorant savages."

"He's just showing them something they never saw before," Georgina said.

"Ex-*act*-ly," Stella hissed. "It isn't any more racist than if these guys showed him how they...I don't know, shoot a monkey out of a tree with a blow dart. It's just *people*, coming together, learning about each other."

"Natives killing and eating monkeys is how HIV got started," said Lonnie with authority, having returned to his sports pages, as if the information he related was contained therein.

Stella ignored his digression. She said to Georgina, "And this whole race article is about how race is just an illusion, anyway. And of course it is! Right? That's why my ancestors in Scotland and Ireland look *just* like Edward and Joseph." She said these names in a whisper, and motioned her head toward their Ghanaian coworkers. "That's why blue-eyed redheads are born in China every day, right?"

"It's all this PC," said Lonnie sagely, nodding at his paper. "PC, and Me Too, and LGTV...all that."

"Oh but it isn't LGBT anymore, Lonnie!" Stella said, bugging her eyes. "It's –" she paused to get it right in her head "– LGBTTQQIAAP."

"*What?* What's that stand for?"

"All kinds of nonsense," Georgina said. "All this made-up stuff about what sex you want to be on Tuesday."

"Right," said Lonnie. "Nowadays you can say, 'I don't care that I was born with two arms and two legs...I see myself as having four arms and six legs, and if you don't see it my way you're just frigging evil.'"

Georgina said, "Some people say you can't call someone *He* or *She* anymore. They have to be...I don't know... *They* or *It* or *E*."

Stella glanced up at a large flat screen TV affixed to the wall behind Georgina and Lonnie. Some strange news story, apparently shot from a helicopter, was running live...distracting her. She flicked her eyes back to her coworkers, however, and went on, "There's no such thing as gender and race! But, if there isn't such a thing as race, why do they keep telling white people we have to be careful not to do *anything* to hurt the feelings of 'people of color'?" She hooked her fingers in quotation marks. "We're all the same, right, so why worry about something like that? Our physical differences are *allll* just an invention!"

Georgina, overhearing some of their other coworkers chattering more loudly and calling attention to the TV, twisted her body around in her seat and grimaced at the screen. "What's up?"

Lonnie lay his paper down and said to Stella, "You ever see how they picture the average person in the future will look? You know, the wonderful people who are going to replace us terrible people? Oh, you can bet it always looks like a light-skinned black woman – and it *haaas* to be a woman. Maybe she looks a little Hispanic, too, of course, but they give her blue eyes and maybe blondish hair just to make us shut our mouths. They don't add Orientals in the mix, though, because Oriental people don't complain as much."

"You can't say 'Oriental' anymore, either," Stella told him. "Though somebody ought to tell it to that gift store *Oriental World*, in the Clearwater Mall...*which is run by Asian people*."

"Guess they didn't get the memo," said Lonnie. "You know, it's always the white people who get worked up about this stuff the most. Going for those, what is it? Virtue points?"

"Ex-*act*-ly," Stella hissed. "Look, I'm not a racist, but –"

"What the hell is going on?" Lonnie asked, at last registering the rising commotion and shifting around in his chair, too.

Stella huffed – exasperated at having to let go of her exasperation prematurely – returned her gaze to the TV screen herself, and in a moment her mouth was dropping open.

😀😀😀

When Stella got back to her home late that afternoon the news story was still running live, now on a number of channels, but with frequent clips filling in new viewers – who hadn't yet caught the story in full – on what had transpired earlier that day.

The earliest footage – queasily jittery, apparently taken by a cell phone's camera – showed a naked (and hence partly pixilated) individual climbing up a metal staircase that curved along the side of a large, outdoors storage tank, one of several on the grounds of an company called Adventum Bioamalgamates. Stella would have recognized the sprawling complex even if the title hadn't been superimposed across the bottom of the screen; the place was right here in the town where she lived, thankfully near its border, about a ten minute drive from her house.

Her house was in a pretty, quiet little neighborhood that felt to her, cozily, like a nest of robin's eggs that had mostly been missed by the tramping boots of time. The houses here were small, modest, white or pastel colored. A lot of the owners, like Stella and her husband Wayne, had been here for decades. Stella fondly recalled trick-or-treating on the doorsteps of these houses as a child...and with her son Tyler, now a married adult, when he had been a child. It saddened her that in recent years a few of those old townies had passed away, like Mrs. Parker who had lived directly across the street and been a friend of Stella's mother. This year a Brazilian family had bought Mrs. Parker's home. They seemed nice enough, but Wayne would try showing Stella videos he found online of youths in favelas getting their hands shot through for minor thievery, or gang members beheading or dismembering rival drug dealers alive. "See what these people are like?" Wayne would snarl, but of course Stella wouldn't watch the videos.

As she waited for Wayne to get home, and started on dinner for them – which would be chicken and dumplings – Stella watched the small kitchen TV. She saw how that nude figure with its wild dark hair had reached the top of the huge tank, and was struggling to pull open a hatch of some kind up there. Two out-of-shape looking men in gray security uniforms scampered up the staircase in pursuit of the person, who was indistinct even when the cell phone user awkwardly tried to zoom in on them. The security guards approached cautiously, reaching out, motioning for the figure to come to them.

The nude person did. It rushed the closest of the two men, partly lifted him off his feet as it drove him to the edge of the storage tank's upper surface.

"Oh my God!" Stella cried out loud. She hadn't seen this footage before. But thankfully the video had been edited, the guard's plummet removed. When the footage resumed, in fact, both of the guards were gone and the naked person had resumed prying at that cap up top the huge white tank.

More people, mostly in white lab coats, had gathered around the foot of the tank by then. Some crouched low, apparently clustered around the bodies of the two guards. Others looked up, shielding their eyes against the early morning sun...but none of these people braved that metal staircase as the guards had done.

The next footage, sequentially, was a bird's eye view, this time obviously taken from that helicopter. This was what Stella and the others had seen during nine o'clock break. Apparently this person – mentally disturbed? drug-addled? – felt trapped up there, cornered, and considered that hatch it fought to open a means of escaping its pursuers. Or, Stella found herself wondering with a disquieting tickle of intuition, did it sense inside that tank something of importance? Something vital to it, in some way?

Stella didn't know quite what they did at Adventum Bioamalgamates, though her cousin Florence's husband Earl had worked there for a time. A biotech place, apparently engaged in a great deal of research. Earl had been evasive about it...when pressed at a family Fourth of July gathering had only mumbled something about "chemical genetics" and "DNA synthesis." He hadn't liked the job; Stella remembered that much. He hadn't explained why.

The next bit of helicopter footage, still dating from that morning, showed police cars and emergency vehicles pulling up around the base of the tank, white-frocked Adventum staff rushing to meet the emerging officers, pointing down at the fallen guards (their bodies pixilated), pointing up toward the summit of the tank.

Stella gaped, a knife suspended in her hand, having forgotten about making sure dinner was ready for Wayne when he got home. Luckily, he was apparently running late anyway, as normally he'd be home by now.

It was as the first policemen started rushing up that spiraling staircase, armed with tasers and handguns and a shotgun or two, that the naked person – and Stella still couldn't tell if it was a man or a woman – tore the hatch open at last with a final superhuman wrench, and without hesitation dropped down into the tank feet first, disappearing completely from view in the blink of an eye.

"Oh Jee-sus," Stella said, wagging her head.

Stella didn't know if that vast drum was like those "continuous stirred-tank reactors" that were used in waste water treatment, that had an agitator spinning inside, but she figured if it was, that crazy naked person might have been torn into pieces before they even had the chance to drown. If there was a fan-like agitator in there, though, it had probably been turned off by the time an Adventum worker up top inserted a long rod with a hook at the end, and started probing, poking around, as if he meant to stir by hand whatever concoction was in the tank.

It was five past noon when the metal pole was suddenly seized, jerked downwards. So the fan was still rotating after all, and the pike had snagged it? The whole rod disappeared in a flash, which threw the white-smocked worker forward. It looked like he might pitch head-first into the uncapped opening, but before that could even happen a hand rocketed up from the hole, sending sprays of some type of fluid flying, and it caught the man around the throat.

"What the risen Christ?" Stella screeched.

The hand was large. Much too large. It didn't just grab the worker by the neck, really, but in closing into a fist engulfed his entire head. And then, the hand was sucked back down into the tank...and the worker with it.

Policemen closed in, pointing guns at the hole, but they didn't fire for fear of hitting the worker, obviously, and because they couldn't see what was in there to fire at.

Also, one of the Adventum people, wearing an open smock over a business suit, grabbed at one of the officers who pointed a shotgun. Though she could make out no voices but for that of the commentator, Stella could tell this Adventum man was afraid for the policemen to harm the thing in the tank.

Stella was tempted to flick to a different channel, to see where things stood *now*, at six PM, but she was too caught up in this station's edited-together recap that detailed how events had unfolded while she was still finishing up her work day. And so, she set her knife down on the cutting board and continued to watch, mesmerized and appalled, just like when she watched the TV news or read it on her phone on any other day...only more so.

Stella had to sit down, clawing over to her one of the breakfast counter's stools and almost toppling it in the process, when she saw the thing tear its way up through the top of the storage tank, like a stripper bursting from a pop out cake.

It was like...well, what was it like, this being, this titan, its gracefully muscled body running with rivulets of that unknown amniotic fluid? Nude as it was, with its long, thick dark hair plastered to its head and back, it somehow looked to Stella both a throwback and a throwforward – its oddly sculpted face, with its prominent cheekbones, like that of some alien being. Its skin had an earthy golden tone, its face spattered heavily with dark freckles. Its too-large eyes – wide-spaced, almond-shaped – were as dead black as those of a shark, and at the same time piercingly intelligent. It pulled itself up and out, unmindful of the metal's jagged edges, as if it possessed advanced healing abilities that made it unafraid of mere lacerations.

Those policemen and Adventum people who had still been perched atop the tank at this point tried to flee down the staircase that wound around it. Most of them made it, too. The last individual, though, was a slow-moving pot-bellied policeman who got swept up like Fay Wray. Instead of pinching his clothing away, however, the glistening giant pinched his screaming face between its fingers, pulled the flesh from his skull (this pixilated, but unmistakable), then cocked its arm back and threw him as far as it could. Stella, horrified, figured the cop ended up in the middle of Adventum's parking lot.

It stood up, atop the storage tank, to its full height, and Stella felt faint. She had to look away. She snatched up the remote.

She switched to another channel, maybe accidentally, and now the footage was *live*.

The giant had left the grounds of Adventum Bioamalgamates, but hadn't got so very far considering the hours that had passed. Stella supposed there had been a lot of opposition from the town's police force, maybe too the state police and National Guard by now, plus obstacles in its way. When the camera (this time on the ground) zoomed in on its towering body – and was it even larger now, maybe 25 feet? – she saw blood trickling from pinholes peppered across its flesh. There was a lot more blood than that, though, slathered on its bare feet, its ankles, and on its hands, but she suspected this wasn't the titan's blood.

Its lower body was no longer blocked out by pixilation; it had never really been necessary. Stella saw that the giant possessed no genitalia. No elephant's trunk of a hanging penis. No hillock of split vulva. Its crotch was as smooth as that of the Barbie dolls she had played with as a child. In fact, she realized, the being didn't even have a navel.

Stella could see these details all the more clearly when the titan – in a wide stance and shot from below – looked down and noticed the insect who was filming it. Its thick lips curved in a sneer of contempt, its eyes blazing with black fire.

The obstacles in its path that had slowed its progress (and did it have any conscious sense of direction or destination?) had been trees and houses, and cars, and now the buildings at the heart of this town. There behind the titan Stella saw St. Luke the Evangelist Church, all red brick, and directly across the street – like a Burger King competing with a McDonalds for one street corner – the white-steepled Congregational Church. Next to that was the school library, where Stella had worked a part-time job while in high school. Her pretty, beloved town...with this naked, bloody *thing* tramping through it.

The being reached out beside it, took hold of the steeple of the Congregational Church, wrenched at it with violent jerks. The steeple broke off in its hands like a club. Then the titan turned its attention back to whoever was making this video. The person whirled away; the footage went wild, ricocheting off the pavement. Then the video was cut off, and a different angle, shot by someone else's phone or camera, took its place.

The Congregational Church? If the monster was there, it finally came home to Stella with a jolt, then it wasn't all that far from her neighborhood, on the other side of the town center.

She finally became aware that she had been hearing distant cracks of gunfire. Cars honking. Police or emergency vehicle sirens. It all swam up into her consciousness at once, like a wave of blackness preceding unconsciousness. Or death.

Her cell phone rang, causing her to start again. She slid off her stool, snatched the phone from the breakfast counter, saw it was her son Tyler. She took the call. "Honey!" she cried, before he could say anything.

"Mom, what the *hell* is going on over there? Are you okay?"

"I don't know, honey, I don't know," she sobbed, leaning against the counter lest she crumple to the floor tiles. She kept her gaze on the TV screen. She flinched when she saw the titan kick aside a car that its owner had abandoned in the middle of West Main Street. The car flipped over onto its back.

"Is Dad with you?"

"No, he...oh my God, he hasn't come home yet! He hasn't come home yet, Tyler! Do you think he's okay?"

"Listen, don't panic...I heard they have roadblocks all around town...he probably can't get through."

"But why hasn't he called me? Oh God, I've got to call him...I've got to call him right now!"

"Okay, Mom, call him...let me know what happens. But please, before you do that, go down in the basement, okay?"

"Oh dear Lord..."

"Mom, listen to me: *go down in the basement!*"

"I will, I will!"

Stella disconnected, and poised her thumb to begin entering Wayne's number, but at that very second she heard an explosion – a *whump* that went deep into her ears like cotton balls jabbed in with chopsticks. A car exploding? A missile fired at the titan?

Stella was tempted to go to her windows and look out, to see if she could spot a plume of black smoke unfurling above the trees of her neighborhood. To see if a monstrous naked being towered above the trees of her neighborhood. But her terror outweighed her curiosity, and she dove to lock the back door. That thing might not be able to fit its body in here...but it might try reaching its *arm* inside.

She ran to the front hall, locked that door too, then fled back to the kitchen, where the door to the cellar was.

😬💀😬

Standing in the bald glare of the light above her husband's tool-strewn workbench, Stella tapped out his cell phone's number. His phone rang...rang...rang...finally went to voicemail. Stella tried again, only to achieve the same result. She barked a single harsh sob of frustration. Before attempting to reach Wayne again, she decided to look at her phone's news feed, to see what people might be reporting. To see if they had any answers about what was happening. About what Adventum Bioamalgamates had been *doing*...

She poked the icon for the news, the stories scrolled into place, and right off she saw a number of pieces from various sources on the events unfolding in her little, hitherto under-the-radar hometown. (Who would have ever thought? Not the Stella of up-to-today.) Just then, though, two things happened in rapid succession to divert her before she could open one of the stories. She heard a burst of fully automatic gunfire, much closer than the gunfire she'd heard up to that point, closely followed by a man's shrill scream. (*Abruptly cut off.*) Almost overlapping this was the jarring ringtone that told her a video call was coming in. The gunfire/ringtone combination caused Stella to flinch, but her heart gave a kind of *glub* of excitement when she saw the name on the screen: WAYNE.

She accepted the video call, and saw her husband's face on the screen...though she might not have recognized him if she hadn't known in advance who was calling.

Wayne lay slumped to one side in his car, his hair gooey with the blood that had flowed across his face from a deep gash that started at his hairline and ran down to the corner of his left eye, which was swollen shut, and on to the side of his nose.

Stella shrieked. Babbled, "No! No! No! *Wayne!*"

"I told you," her husband croaked, his voice almost inaudible. His good right eye, blue in all the red, gave a dreamy kind of slow-motion blink.

"Oh God, honey!" Stella wept.

"Told you..."

"Told me what, honey?" she wailed. "Oh God, where *are* you?" She could see his car's rear passenger's side window at this angle. It was smashed. She saw only trees on the side of the road through the gap, in the golden light of dusk. He could be anywhere.

"Told you...it would be like this," he rasped. Another dazed blink. She could actually see the blood pulsing from his wound. Blood upon blood. He looked like someone in a video on one of those true-life gore sites he would look at, that worked him up so much.

"Wayne! Tell me where you *are!* Call 911, honey! *Call 911!*"

Her husband, *her man*, the father of her son. She remembered how handsome he had been on their wedding day, in his steel gray tuxedo, when they'd been married in this town's Methodist church. Now, he was like *this*...smashed...disfigured...nearly unrecognizable. Just like her town.

And that *thing* out there. So gigantic, so powerful, so potent. Intact, impervious to harm. So weirdly, horribly beautiful. (Yes, she would admit to that.) Like those weird models you saw in fashion magazines...chosen for their unusualness, chosen for their diversity. She hated those kinds of models...*hated* them...

"Wayne, stay with me, honey!"

Thump. A vibration rattled the small basement windows that ringed her house. *Thump.*

Stella jerked her head, looked toward one of them. Through its foggy-looking dirty glass she saw only the green suggestion of the hedges Wayne always clipped *just so*. She'd teased him that he had OCD. She knew now, after having forgotten for so long, how much she loved him.

Thump. Thump. Thump. Like the throbbing of a gargantuan heart, drowning out her own.

"Oh God, oh God, oh God," Stella chanted.

"It's coming," Wayne muttered, and then he dropped his phone. The picture somersaulted crazily. The phone ended up on the floor of Wayne's car. Stella saw only a confusion of dark shapes now.

THUMP. THUMP. THUMP.

The basement windows rattled more dramatically, with each encroaching footstep.

A shadow fell over the windows, then, as if an eclipse were occurring, blotting out the mellow evening sun. A shadow that insinuated itself into this basement shelter. Stella's final refuge.

THUMP.

"Wayne!" she moaned, but not too loudly. It would hear her. But of course, the titan already knew where she was. Where she cowered, waiting to be stomped out of existence. Eradicated. Made extinct.

THUMP.

The small panes of the cellar windows vibrated. The plates of Stella's skull, grating against each other as if in an opposition they had never known before, vibrated.

THHHUUUMP.

FADE OUT
Duane Pesice

The monsters, they're fading into the background as day turns into night and night wears on, and a new set of creatures prepare for their fifteen minutes of infamy, posing coyly for their individual portraits, for their star turns.

The Test Patterns begin immediately after the anthem plays, and the neon colors of insomnia mesmerize you, hypnotize you, transfix you, and the show that never ends begins anew...and there, behind the glass, the new reality lies.

Or does it? Perhaps the mundane existence wasn't the reality the whole time, merely a simulacrum. Perhaps if we scar it often enough with Occam's razor, the truth will emerge.

Perhaps.

Special Thanks to the creators of the unique fonts used in this volume:

CREATURE! 😱😵😨
by Patrick Broderick / rotodesign
pat@rotodesign.com
(http://www.rotodesign.com)

CREEPSTER
by Font Diner, Inc
diner@fontdiner.com
https://www.fontdiner.com

CHANNEL TUNING
by Brad O. Nelson/ Brain Eaters Font Co. & Jeff Levine
BrainEat@aol.com
(http://www.BrainEaters.com)

Made in the USA
San Bernardino, CA
07 February 2020